GOD OF ASH

SPARK OF CHAOS
BOOK THREE

SABRINA FLYNN

GOD OF ASH

SPARK OF CHAOS

BOOK THREE

SABRINA FLYNN

GOD OF ASH is a work of fiction. Names, characters, places, and incidents are either the product of the author's overactive imagination or are chimerical delusions of a tired mind. Any resemblance to actual persons, living or dead, events, or locales is entirely due to the reader's wild imagination (that's you).

Published by Ink & Sea Publishing
www.sabrinaflynn.com

ISBN 978-1-955207-24-9
ebook ISBN 978-1-955207-25-6

Book 3 of Spark of Chaos
Book cover by Miblart

ALSO BY SABRINA FLYNN

Ravenwood Mysteries

From the Ashes

A Bitter Draught

Record of Blood

Conspiracy of Silence

The Devil's Teeth

Uncharted Waters

Where Cowards Tread

Beyond the Pale

A Grim Telling

Spark of Chaos

Flame of Ruin

God of Ash

Untold Tales: Prequel

Bedlam

Windwalker

www.sabrinaflynn.com

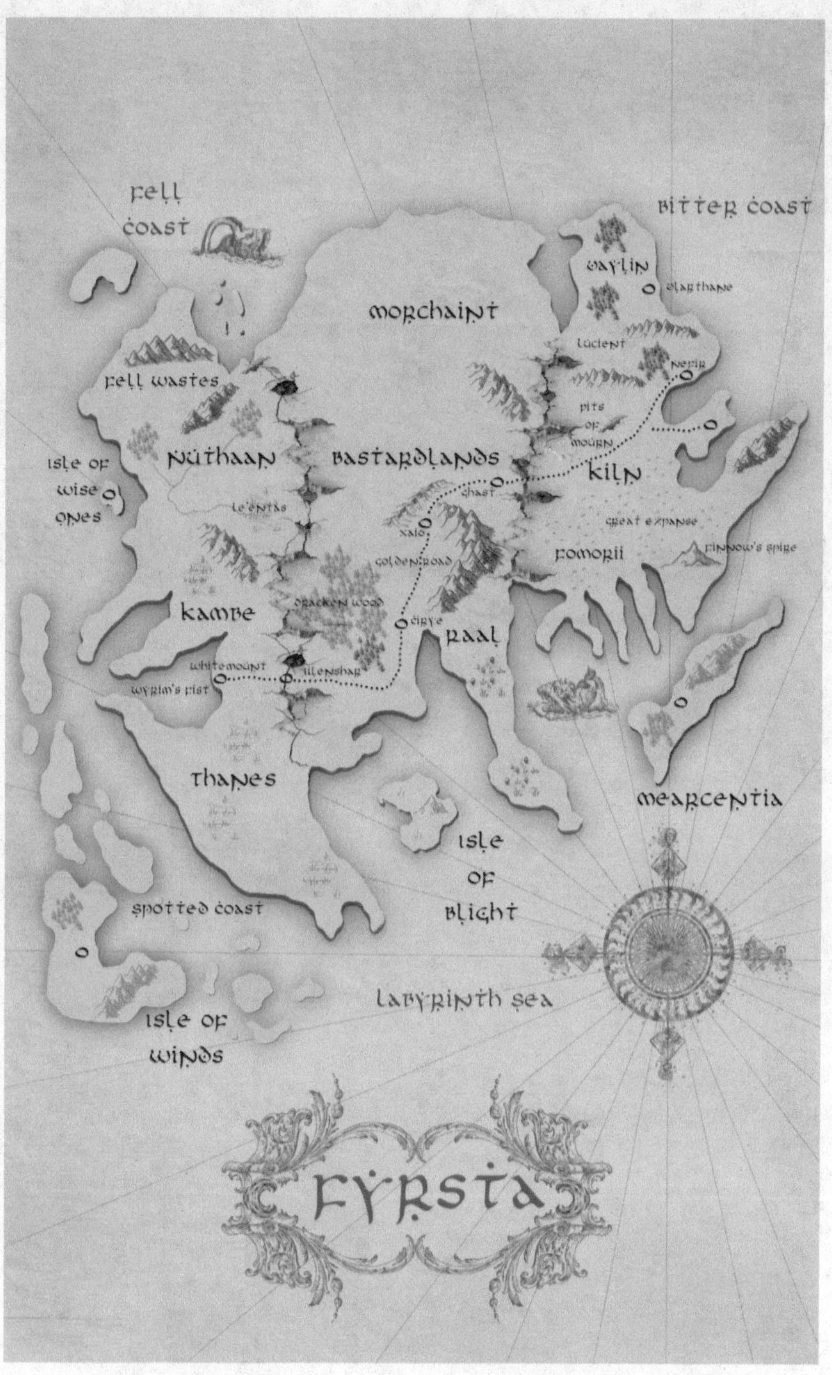

fell coast
BITTER COAST
MORCHAINT
waylin
olagthane
lucient
fell wastes
nepin
pits
of
mourn
NÜTHAAN
BASTARDLANDS
KILN
isle of
wise
ones
le'entås
ghast
great expanse
xalo
FOMORII
FINNOW's spire
golden road
KAMBE
bracken wood
eirye
whitemount
RAAL
wyrim's fist
lilenshar
THANES
MEARCENTIA
spotted coast
isle
of
BLIGHT
isle of
winds
LABYRINTH SEA
FYRSTA

"It is not so easy a thing to match a legend with truth."
—*Minnow, Sage of Mearcentia*

CHAPTER I

A BOY STARED up at a mythical tower. He felt like he was falling, and it hurt his head. It felt wrong, too. As vile as the pit where his brothers were slaughtered. Zoshi tried not to think of that day.

Four statues flanked the Storm Gate, and Everlight flickered in sconces, casting an eerie glow over the stone. He did not like those armored things.

Zoshi wiped snow from his face, and looked at his guards. They were all dapper and straight in the Wise Ones' colors: crimson and black with an eye emblazoned on their breastplates. One of them gripped his shoulder, keeping him in place. He wondered if he was a prisoner again—escaped from one dungeon to be put into the next. That was a street rat's luck.

A lone black crow gave a rattling caw as it perched on one of the guardian statues. The thin old Wise One called him Crumpet. When Zoshi had first met the animal, Crumpet had been a mammoth; now he was a crow.

He tried not to think about that.

Someone had etched strange symbols on the Storm Gate. Not the idle markings he carved into posts, but cruel looking ones done for a purpose. They looked dangerous.

The crow hopped in front of the gates. Crumpet tapped his beak on the strange wood, then looked right at the boy and croaked. Those beady black eyes shone with more wit than Zoshi had seen in most men.

Animals know more than we do most times. That's what his mum would say. He tried not to think of his mum. Thoughts like that made his stomach twist with worry. He'd have to tell her Pip and Tuck were dead. He'd failed his family.

The bird cawed in question. Zoshi did not speak Crow, but he understood *this* bird. *Will you open the gates for me?*

Zoshi pulled down the hood of his fur coat. Morigan had stolen it from the manor for him, along with food, a waterskin, and a large pouch of coins. It was a fortune to a street rat like him. When they'd been in the dungeon, Morigan had taken care of him, and now he worried about her.

The boy looked up at the forbidding gates. This time the crow's caw held a strong demand. Crumpet wanted to find his mistress: the thin old woman, Thira. She was terrifying. But he understood the bird's concern —if things went badly, who would watch out for Morigan? It was left to him. He wouldn't fail again.

Zoshi nodded to the crow. It took flight with a terrible screeching that drowned the sound of its flapping wings. The crow circled once, then drove at the guard who held the boy's shoulder. While the guard was fending off the crow, Zoshi ran straight for the Storm Gate. He tugged with all his might, but it did not budge.

There was a smaller door hidden in the larger: a wicket gate. He cursed his slow wits and wrenched open the smaller door. He held it open long enough for the bird to fly through, then darted in after.

Zoshi slammed the wicket door, and slid a heavy bar into the brackets. He turned and tripped over his feet in shock. The hall was massive. Larger than most buildings in Drivel. Stars shone and twinkled in a clear night. He thought it was a window to the sky, but it was solid stone—a shifting enchantment. This was no place for a street rat.

He bolted after the crow as it flew through a long row of columns into a side hall. More sleek marble, open space, and doors. But stars didn't sparkle from the ceiling; instead, a storm of energy churned overhead. Zoshi followed the bird's lead and skirted the unstable weave.

Crumpet landed in front of another enormous set of doors. The crow croaked, and waited. Zoshi tiptoed towards the door. He felt exposed in the open, and when he got to the wall, he put his back against the stone. The emptiness of the grand hall made his head swim.

Crumpet tapped an impatient talon.

Swallowing his unease, Zoshi grabbed the handle, but before he could yank on it, the doors flew open, knocking him flat. A blizzard howled into the hall. Soldiers and robed ones charged from the door-way, tripping over each other as they tried to flee. Ice spread over the marble.

Zoshi's breath froze. He couldn't breathe. With ice pelting their backs, soldiers turned on each other, and so did the Wise Ones. Energy lashed, and clashing blades burst into the great hall. He scrambled backwards, trying to escape the chaos. It was worse than a tavern brawl.

A fluff of black in the whiteness caught his eye. Zoshi slipped and crawled towards the crow. Crumpet flapped uselessly on the floor. One of his wings was bent at an odd angle.

Zoshi picked up the crow, and ran. He wove through the fighters, sliding under legs, ducking and dodging furious men. Energy crackled over his head, and steel rang in his ears. In the chaos, he spotted a pair of open doors, and without a backwards glance, raced for the exit.

A great rasp and creak drowned out the screams. He quickened his pace, flying past a pair of mongrel statues. The chamber beyond was all black. Terror scratched at the inside of his skull.

The boy kept running.

With ice and wind blowing hard at his back, he darted through another gate and hid behind a pillar. This new hall was even bigger than the first. He felt like he'd wandered into a forest of stone pillars.

Crumpet twitched in his arms.

"Shh," he told the bird.

A decisive bang silenced the raging battle in the main hall. Had the gates between the mongrel statues been closed?

Zoshi squeezed his eyes shut. He did not want to be trapped in here. Mutilated stone faces ringed each pillar. Every face was caught in a scream, but eyes had been gouged, noses broken, and tongues crushed. Zoshi rubbed his throat. He knew what it was like to be Silenced.

He could not stay here.

Zoshi stuffed the wounded crow under his coat to free up his hands, and edged around the pillar. An obsidian throne sat at the far end of the great hall. It was empty. He kept edging around until he could see the gate. It was closed now, but he could see through the metal vines. A man stood alone in the room of black. He was sleek and wore crimson robes.

Zoshi's breath caught. It was the man from the ritual circle—the man who gave the order to kill his brothers.

Zoshi reached for a dagger, but Crumpet poked his head up from the coat, and bit his cheek. He choked back a cry.

The man extended an arm, and turned his hand. The stone rippled like water. And even the air. Zoshi could feel it in his mind, too. He backed up a step, then froze. A dark mist seeped from the obsidian room. And a multitude of voices whispered in his ears—all hushed and sinister, speaking of wicked things.

A blue light flared in the darkness, streaming through the stained glass windows high overhead. As the light hit the sickly fog, it fractured, illuminating the mist with an eerie glow.

The crow cawed in warning. Zoshi shushed the dumb bird, but it was too late. The whispering voices filled his mind, then took shape. Figures materialized in the fog. They were thin and fragile, like shadows at the edge of his mind, fleeting and indistinct. Their long arms reached for him.

Zoshi ran through the gloom. The floor lurched, and he was knocked off his feet. He slipped, skidded, and hit a pillar. Spots danced at the edge of his vision. He blinked them away, trying to move his arms and legs, but nothing seemed to work.

A burst of brightness blinded him. It chased away the shadowy figures, and slammed into his chest—right into the crow. Something cracked. And the boy remembered nothing more.

CHAPTER 2

A SINGLE DROP formed between a crack in the wood. It shimmered in darkness for a breath, clinging to its perch. Time stopped to study the perfect drop.

Marsais zar'Vaylin peered into the shimmer. A roguish man stared back. He was tall and lean, and he sprawled in a hammock. His snow-white hair was unkempt and a scruffy goatee jutted from his chin. Three small coins were woven into his hair—all that was left of a shattered realm. Along with a broken god.

Time blinked, and began again.

Drip.

The drop rolled down his unshaven cheek like a tear. Back and forth he swung as saltwater pelted his skin. But there was no pitter-pattering of water—only a constant roar.

Time was lost in a storm's fury. It was exhausting.

A sailor rushed by, bumping his hammock, knocking it to the side with a wild swing. The howling sea drowned the sailor's frantic shouts, and Marsais closed his eyes, listening to a plea that haunted the storm.

'*Grant me peace,*' the voice whispered.

In the endless hallways of memory, Marsais stared into the pleading eyes of a girl, the chained Scryer in the Ardmoor's fortress. He felt leather in his palm and the drag of the blade across her throat. In that moment, peace entered her eyes.

"Grant me peace," he begged. But there was no one standing over him with a blade. No matter how much he dreamed.

Something tapped his forehead.

Marsais opened his eyes to find a parrot perched on his head. Its emerald eyes stared into his own. Marsais blinked, and in the flutter of lash, the bird vanished.

"Madness dreaming," he said, wryly.

He roused himself to look over the edge of the hammock. A swirl of seawater churned on the deck. Unfortunately, he was not dreaming. He collapsed back into the hammock and brought a flask to his cracked lips. It was empty.

With a muttered oath, he tossed it away. Inevitably, his hand strayed to his bare chest, scratching at the burning scar that slashed from shoulder to hip, always healing and yet never healed.

The coins woven into his goatee chimed a warning. Angry men descended on his hammock, but Marsais didn't fight them. Instead, he lay in his hammock, cackling at the vision of his near future.

He was still wheezing when time caught up with him. Desperate sailors surrounded his bed. They turned his hammock, rolling him inside, then bound him with ropes. He was hoisted like a spare sail.

Grant me peace.

Why fight his Fate?

The deck lurched, throwing the sailors off their feet. They dropped their load and Marsais bumped down the companionway ladder. Wrapped in a cocoon of canvas and rum, the fall felt more like a caress. His abductors rallied, hoisting him off the deck to make another dash at the companionway.

A wave of water hit his body and knocked loose a thought: there was something he had left to do. One final task. But a dense fog clouded his mind as his body was carried towards a watery grave.

Marsais cursed his memory. He needed a higher perch. *Wings.* A door opened in the maze of his mind. Water turned to fire, the realm burned, and the Void swallowed the ruins.

The vision crumbled to ash.

He needed to stop it. Marsais fought against the canvas prison. The sudden burst of movement surprised the men, and they dropped him on deck again.

Another wave crashed into him. The force of it propelled Marsais across the deck. He slammed into the bulwark with enough force to knock the air from his lungs. Water swirled all around. The cutter tilted with a wave, climbing, and the water carried him aft.

Marsais twisted and strained, clawing at the hammock from the inside, until his head was free from the canvas cocoon. He sucked in a breath. And spotted his determined abductors in a flash of lightning. They were scrambling towards him, reaching from one line to the next as waves crashed on deck.

Marsais freed his arms.

A hulking shadow emerged from the storm. He punched a sailor, dropping the man with one blow. But another wave washed over Marsais, stealing his sight. The sea sought to swallow him and the sailors were keen on chucking him down its gullet.

Marsais snatched at a coil of rope. When the wave subsided, the hulking shadow took shape. Over seven feet of Nuthaanian muscle stood on deck, one hand on the rigging and the other latched onto a sailor's ankle. Oenghus squinted at the leg, then his gaze traveled to the face. It wasn't the person he wanted. He let the man go.

Marsais wiggled out of the hammock. A wave hit him again, and the rope slipped through his fingers. He floundered in the swirling cold until a steel-like grip latched around his wrist, holding him fast.

"Get on your feet, you drunk bastard!" Oenghus bellowed.

Marsais spluttered and coughed, slipping on deck before Oenghus yanked him towards the poop deck.

Captain Carvil stood at the helm, wrestling with the wheel. A knot of Windtalkers stood close by. The sea-shamans had abandoned their drums, and their voices rose in a beseeching chant as they tried to calm the sea god. But Nereus would not be calmed.

"Did you order your men to throw him overboard?" Oenghus yelled at the captain.

Captain Carvil thrust his chin forward. "Look!"

Marsais squinted into the storm. The sea was black, slashed with towering white crests. Beyond the waves, beyond the black sky, there was a horizon. A clear, starlit night with a silver moon.

This storm was not natural.

With a groan of wood, the fore of the ship disappeared beneath a wave before bursting through the other side. Water swelled on deck. The sea tugged at Marsais, but Oenghus refused to give him up.

Marsais shook off his grip and slipped towards the bulwark, catching the rail to look overboard. The sea around the ship churned with whirlpools.

Oenghus grabbed his waistband. "You're mad!"

Marsais ignored the obvious. His fingers flashed, layering one rune over another, drawing the moon's silver light to his fingertips. With a final sweep of his hand, he Bound a message to the water, and hurled it down like a spear. The weave hit the sea and rippled outward with a boom.

In answer, lightning struck the foremast. Timber cracked, and rigging snapped, flapping in the storm. And then the sea went still. The storm clouds dispersed, and moon and stars appeared, reflecting in the water's surface.

The clipper bobbed like a cork in the silence. And slowly, the crew stirred from their terror, gazing at the wreckage in a daze.

Knight Captain Acacia Mael emerged from below deck, staring at the sky in wonder. "What did you do?" she asked Marsais.

"I sent a message."

"What kind of message?" Captain Carvil demanded.

Marsais waved a distracted hand. "The reasonable kind." His coins chimed, his features sagged, and he threw himself forward. But rum was running through his veins, and it slowed his reaction. A tentacle whipped over the rail and yanked him backwards.

The seer disappeared overboard.

CHAPTER 3

"Bloody Void," Oenghus growled.

A split second later, he unsheathed his knife and dove overboard, plunging into a writhing mass of tentacles. It was like diving into a briar bush. Small barbs caught and tore at his skin.

A coil of muscle wrapped around his body. He was dragged down into the deep. A strange clacking noise rose over the rush of water. It came from a razor-sharp beak buried in the mass of appendages. The creature was pulling him towards its beak.

Oenghus stabbed at a tentacle. It released its hold.

A shock wave hit the creature. It stopped moving, but the pulse of energy slammed into Oenghus, too. His arms and legs went numb. For a moment, he was paralyzed in a tangle of floating tentacles as air bubbles spewed from his mouth.

Oenghus shook off the charge with a growl. He jerked once, then rallied, kicking towards the bulbous head. A massive eye watched his approach. Oenghus bared his teeth at the eye, then stabbed it. The creature thrashed in pain. And quick as a retreating spider, the tentacles spread, propelling it into safer depths.

Swallowing the urge to breathe, Oenghus swam upwards, catching up to another swimmer. Both men broke the surface with a gulp of air.

Marsais choked and went back under, but Oenghus wrenched him to the surface. Small red circles from a tentacle ringed his neck.

"How rude," Marsais coughed.

"Did you expect something else?" Oenghus growled.

"Some level of civility?"

"You bedded his daughter!"

"You two have a lot in common."

Oenghus clenched his teeth. "I'm tempted to kill you myself."

Marsais frowned at the distant clipper ship. It had drifted away. "You might not get the chance."

"Nereus will have to get in line."

But it was an empty threat. They were vulnerable to an attack from below. With knife in hand, Oenghus dipped underwater, searching for another assassin. When he surfaced, he noticed a smaller blot on the moonlit horizon.

A rowboat.

Oenghus pushed at Marsais to swim, bracing for an attack: a fin piercing the surface, the scrape of teeth, or a grip of tentacles. But none of it came. Nereus, the God of the Seas, had sent a message. That was all.

As the rowboat neared, Oenghus spotted Rivan at the oars. The young man set his oars in the locks, and reached for Marsais, pulling him into the boat with a stream of saltwater. Marsais slumped against the bow.

The boat tipped dangerously as Oenghus climbed in after. He sat down with a thud and peeled a tentacle from his leg. "I hate the ocean," he growled, chucking it into the water.

Rivan was gaping at Marsais in shock. "So it's true what the sailors are saying... You're *the* Trickster of legend?"

Marsais let his head fall back against the wood. "One of my many names," he confirmed with a sigh.

THE CREW GAPED at Oenghus as he climbed aboard. He planted his feet, looked at the sailors and soldiers, and cracked his knuckles. No one had expected to see him again. But the crew's shock turned to fear when Marsais hopped aboard.

The Trickster had defied the sea god. Again.

Marsais turned his back on the crew that had tried to toss him overboard. "Are you through with me, Nereus?" he demanded, his voice booming over the water like a thunderclap. "Because I'm the least of your worries. Your realm will burn with this one!"

Arms spread in surrender, Marsais slowly turned, making a single revolution. A streak of red flew at him, squawking. It was a parrot. The bird soared past, landing on the rail.

Marsais tilted his head. "Blood and ashes," he whispered. Quick as a viper, he lunged at the parrot. It surged with a cloud of feathers, soaring towards the mainmast. "Blast it! The Void sodding—" Rage overwhelmed him, and he turned back to the sea. "On second thought, Nereus—go plow yourself!"

The crew paled as one.

Ship Captain Carvil stepped forward. "How dare you!"

"How dare I?" Marsais snapped. "I'm done with all of this... I'm tired of playing nursemaid to this realm—tired of petty gods and their childish grudges." He turned back to the sea. "Go ahead, Nereus, kill me and stop Karbonek yourself!" he howled into the night, then thrust a finger at the moon. "And that goes for you, too."

Marsais spun on Oenghus. "What's her plan? Is she tormenting me for amusement?" he demanded.

Oenghus cleared his throat. "You're soused to the bone. Now's not the time for this conversation."

"Not the time?" Marsais asked, taking a step forward. "The time would have been from the very beginning. She should have consulted with me. What's her scheme, Oen? Tell me!"

The last was said with a crack, an explosion of command that made the water surge, tossing the clipper down a swell. Everyone lurched forward with surprise, but Marsais remained planted to the deck, eyes glowing silver in the night. His fingers twitched.

"Tell me."

Oenghus shifted under that burning gaze. "When you're sober," he said, hoarsely.

"That parrot has ruined *everything*," Marsais hissed.

"The parrot?"

"The parrot," he repeated. "*Tell me*, Oen."

"I swore an oath."

"Curse you!"

Marsais' fingers flashed, and his coins chimed in warning as Oenghus threw a punch. Marsais ducked easily under the blow. His weave churned in the air, but it never hit its target. Acacia cracked a belay pin over his skull.

Marsais crumpled to the ground.

"He's utterly mad," Acacia said, crouching to check his pulse.

Oenghus blew out a breath. "No more than usual—drunk, more like." With those words, he hoisted Marsais over his shoulder. He straightened and slowly looked around the ship, putting all his threat into the task. "If anyone tries to toss my friend overboard again, they'll answer to her." He pointed at Acacia, and stomped below deck.

CHAPTER 4

Oenghus Saevaldr glared at the Windtalkers. Men and women alike were bare-chested, beating sticks against drums like footsteps striding across the sea. Only the ship wasn't moving. There was no wind. The shamans' efforts to summon even a breeze had failed. The white sails hung limp.

He wanted to bellow at the sailors, snatch a stick of his own and beat the drum senseless. But the Isle would be no closer.

Oenghus ran a thumb over the pipe nestled in his hand. The embers still glowed, protected in the cradle of his fingers from the wind. He wished he could shelter those he loved in the same way.

With a sigh, he looked to the horizon, as if he could see over the wild Bastardlands, the Gates of Iilenshar, pass over Whitemount and its cursed Emperor, and travel all the way across the treacherous channel to that little speck in the vast ocean: the Isle of Wise Ones. But no matter how his heart ached with worry, he could not fly there.

"The waiting is always the worst," a voice said at his side. He started in surprise. He had not heard her approach. Knight Captain Acacia Mael studied him with calm, knowing eyes.

"Never been at my best during it," he admitted. "I usually find a well-stocked tavern and a few frisky women. You?"

"Meditation and prayer."

Oenghus snorted. "Sounds like an orgy of excitement."

"It passes the time. How's Marsais?"

He shrugged. "The Scarecrow is having a bit of a rough time, is all." That was an understatement, and they both knew it. Marsais had not been sober since Mearcentia.

"Would it help if I spoke with him?" Acacia asked. There was surprising compassion in her voice.

"I'd keep clear. His fuse is long, but powerful. And right now he's at the end of it."

"If Marsais is unstable..." She let the thought flutter in the air. "It's not too late to turn west and sail for the Spotted Coast."

"He'll come through," Oenghus said.

"Are you sure?"

"Right now, I'm not even sure if we have the option of sailing west." He jerked his chin towards the flat sea.

"Telling Nereus," she lowered her voice to a whisper, "to go plow himself likely didn't help our mission."

Oenghus grunted.

"That old sailor accused him of being the Trickster when we first set sail, but I thought the man was mad. Is it true, then? He's the infamous Trickster of Mearcentian legend?"

"What do you think?"

Acacia blew out a breath. "Well, that complicates matters."

"Nothing is ever easy with him," Oenghus said, leaning against the rail.

"I'll put Rivan and Lucas on guard duty. Between the pair of them, they can keep him away from the rum."

Oenghus eyed her sideways. "They're your men, but fair warning... Knowing the ol'bastard, you'll end up with a pair of rats. Like I said, his fuse is powerful."

"If he transforms my men again, I'll toss him overboard."

"I'm sure Nereus would be happy," he grunted. "That would likely take care of our wind problem. And then we could sail west."

The mutinous idea was attractive. Over the years, Oenghus had threatened to abandon Marsais in just about every corner of the realm.

"But you couldn't do it," he said, more to himself than her.

Acacia sighed. "No, I'm far too..." She searched for a word.

"Caring?" he offered.

"I was going to say foolish."

He chuckled. "I'm right there with you, then."

"I certainly feel the fool," she said, tightly. "I'm following a madman into Fomorri. He's given us no information other than we're to find a mythical ruin in the middle of an endless desert. *I'd appreciate some* explanation. Has he said anything about Finnow's Spire? Or even how the Isle of Wise Ones is faring?"

Oenghus felt like she'd punched his gut. The Isle. *Morigan.*

"You know all I do about his plans." His voice came rough. He spun away, towards the horizon, puffing furiously on his pipe. But the calming weed didn't soothe his worry. He itched to guzzle his Brimgrog and let the sacred brew burn away his heartache. "Even if the Scarecrow told us that the Isle was going to sink into the ocean, there's nothing in the Nine Halls we can do about it from here."

Helplessness was an enemy, and he hated it with a passion.

Most men flinched when he growled, but Acacia only smiled, sadly. "Doesn't stop us from worrying, does it?"

That smile deflated him. Oenghus wasn't the only one frustrated. "Do you have friends on the Isle—besides those under your command? A lover maybe?"

This was asked with a glint in his eye.

"A harem full," Acacia said.

Oenghus choked on his pipe smoke. After the smoke cleared, he wheezed with laughter. The edge of Acacia's lip quirked, but the moment of whimsy was fleeting. She leaned on the rail and stared into the sea.

"I loved my Oathbound. I still do." Her voice was soft, and full of ache. He had to lean close to catch the words. "When I saw his body—it was emptiness. Duty keeps my heart beating, but it's those we love that we ache for. If I could spend one more day with him..." She ran her fingers through her short hair.

"Aye." He knew that ache well.

Acacia cleared the grief from her throat. "What of you?" she asked. "Do you have children on the Isle?"

He looked into the smoldering bowl of his pipe. "No children there, but the mother of a good number." In the silence and stillness, the lull between battles, his worry had grown. And now it bubbled over, filling his heart with dread. "Morigan wouldn't even be on the Isle if it wasn't for me—she'd have gone home to Nuthaan years ago."

Acacia raised her brows in surprise. "*Morigan Freyr* was your Oathbound?"

"You don't have to sound so surprised," he grumbled. "We've taken a lot of Oaths over the years."

"You said your daughter is Clans Head of Nuthaan..."

"Aye, Morigan is her mother."

"And she's the *matriarch* of the ruling clan? The one who—"

Oenghus bared his teeth in a grin. It seemed Acacia was familiar with Nuthaanian history and culture. Morigan was a legend in Nuthaan. She united the clans and saved them all.

"She sounds like she can take care of herself," Acacia muttered.

"Doesn't stop me from worrying about her."

Acacia was quiet for a time. The two watched the sea bump lazily around the hull, both lost in their own worries. Eventually, she broke the amiable silence. "My Oathbound, Henri, always worried about me. When I was presumed dead in the Fell Wastes, it broke him. There's nothing worse than losing hope, Oen."

"That's the kick right to the bollocks," he grunted. "When you lose something, it's never by choice."

"Never," she agreed, faintly.

Oenghus cleared his throat and pushed off the rail, thumping it with a hand. "I'm sure Mori is tossing those bastards to the Nine Halls."

"She's a warrior, too? I thought she was mainly a tactician and diplomat."

"Morigan is a healer," he said. And all those other things. Including a woman he loved with all his heart.

"If she's anything like you, I'd wager on her in a fight."

Oenghus feigned shock. "I'm corrupting you."

"Terribly."

He offered her his pipe.

Acacia held up a hand. "I prefer the sea air, but thank you."

Oenghus mulled over her words. "Mori is tougher than I'll ever be."

"Is that because she's had to put up with your 'hairy hide' during your Oaths?"

"There is that," he admitted. "But no... she's a mother." With that thought, some of the dread left his heart. "The Sylph will keep an eye on her, too."

Acacia narrowed her eyes. "I thought Nuthaanians didn't worship gods?"

He tugged on his braided beard. "We don't. But we do count on friends to watch our backs."

"You and the Sylph are friends?"

"Aye, me and her go way back."

Her pale eyes flashed with righteous outrage, but as quick as it came, the reaction faded, turning into a laugh. "I think Marsais is rubbing off on you. The only thing I wonder now is, who was mad first?"

"A drunk will find another drunk as fast as a fly to dung."

"Spoken like a poet."

"Just so I'm the fly," he said.

"I don't see wings on you."

Oenghus laughed, eyeing her pointed ears. "You sure you're not Nuthaanian?"

"I'd be the shortest of your kin ever to walk the realms."

"If we survive this, I'll make you an honorary clanswoman."

"I'm afraid to ask what that would involve."

"A sea full of ale, rousing tales, and the right to ask any woman to borrow her Oathbound for the night—with the man's permission, of course."

Acacia clucked her tongue and gave a quick shake of her head. "And you wonder why the rest of the realms think you're a horde of barbarians."

Nuthaanians were notoriously free with their love. At least it seemed that way to outsiders. But there were lines one did not cross.

"With as hot as our blood runs, the last thing we need is to add jealously to the mix. As long as a man leaves his boots at the door, and not on the hearth, what's a good tumble between friends?"

"I'll keep that in mind." She sounded dubious.

"We could put it to practice."

"I'll pass."

"No harm in asking." He knocked his pipe against the rail, clearing the ash before tucking it through his belt. "I'll leave you to your prayer and meditation."

"Good luck with your own."

Oenghus bared his teeth. "I'm sure there's at least one woman on board who'd like a good, hard plow to pass the time."

"And if that fails?"

"I'll pick a fight with the crew."

"I'll chain you to the oars myself," she warned.

"Anything to get your hands on me."

As he swaggered away, her laugh touched his ears.

CHAPTER 5

Morigan Freyr walked over a red field. The once virgin snow was trampled and stained with blood. Screams filled her ears. She bent over a dying warrior. He clutched a hand to his gut, holding the slick, ropey cords of his insides. His eyes were full of fear. And a plea.

There was no way to know who he was loyal to. Did he serve Tharios or the Order? It didn't matter. Morigan couldn't leave him in agony. She laid her hands on his ravaged gut. Closing her eyes, she summoned the Lore, and her awareness plunged into his broken body. With a skilled touch, she directed the Gift, but he was too far gone.

Morigan looked into the eyes of the soldier. "May you piss in the ol'River," she said.

The soldier laughed, or tried to; instead, blood bubbled from his lips. He shuddered, and went still.

Morigan wiped her hands on her apron. It looked more like a butcher's apron than a healer's. She moved on to the next warrior. A mere lad. Tears leaked from the corners of his eyes, sliding into a gruesome mess. There wasn't much left of his face. He died before she could even summon the Lore.

She hurried to the next. The dying came in all sorts. Some lay quiet, waiting patiently for their death. Others struggled and fought Death's touch. This soldier thrashed. Her leg had been cleaved off at the hip.

Healing a dying patient was risky. Some healers lost all sense of direction and became trapped if their patient died. The sensible healers avoided it.

Morigan was not one of those healers.

She pressed her hands to the ghastly shreds. But as she fought to save the woman, the soldier's spirit bled from her body. It left behind a cold, empty shell.

Morigan felt like her head was submerged in ice. Gathering her inner sight, she scrambled back along the fading tether to her own body. She opened her eyes, and retched into the snow.

It took everything she had to climb to her feet. Morigan shivered violently as she gazed over the battlefield. Fallen soldiers cried for help —all on the verge of death. She could never hope to save them all. But she would try, because that was her way.

Blood trickled from her ears and nose. The blood was hot against her skin, but other than that line of heat, Morigan was numb. She looked down at her frozen hands. They were covered in blood. She focused on curling her fingers. It felt like her bones were cracking.

Her left arm throbbed with pain. She pitched forward, catching herself on a dying man. She blinked down at his face. He looked familiar. She searched her memory for an answer, but when one came, it made no sense. It was the guard she had broken during the battle outside the council chamber. And now she watched him die—not of broken bones, but from a severed artery.

She rubbed a hand over her eyes in confusion. But instead of clearing her mind, the gesture smeared blood on her face—the blood of those she'd failed.

Every single patient had died today.

More warriors screamed for her attention. But she was only one woman—the sole healer on a battlefield of dying.

The only one left standing.

That thought pricked Morigan's instincts. She looked past the dying, to the grey horizon, to the fog that washed over the snow and corpses. Every warrior was near death, begging for help.

"Impossible," she breathed.

No battlefield had ever looked like this. Instead of racing to the next patient, Morigan eyed the fog. It felt like a breathing, irritated thing. More alive than the soldiers writhing on the battlefield.

A weak hand tugged at the hem of her skirt. She looked down at the half-dead man. Oenghus. His black beard was frozen with ice, and his lips were blue. Each breath gurgled and bubbled out blood. He had a hole in his lungs.

She tensed to help him, but caught herself. None of this made sense. Something was wrong.

His final breath rattled past his lips.

Morigan frowned at the father of her children. He was as vexing in death as he had been in life. She loved him with every bone in her body. So why was she staring down at him in puzzlement rather than grief?

Dead berserkers were a common enough sight. How many times had she expected him to come home on his shield rather than his feet?

Why wasn't she weeping? Better for him to die on a battlefield than wasting away in a bed. It was a strangely comforting sight. But that was just it... Oenghus was not on the island.

With that realization, a veil was ripped from her mind. The dead turned to flurries and deep snowdrifts, and the cries of the dying turned to howls of terror.

Morigan blinked. She was lying in the snow. Being smothered by a dense fog. She could barely breathe. Thin, ethereal shadows with burning eyes swarmed around her. They caressed her skin with a whisper of a touch.

A spasm of terror clutched her throat, but she swallowed it down, forcing herself to think. How long had she been here? The shadows had ample time to kill her. So what was their aim?

Morigan Freyr was no timid healer. She had stood against hordes of Wedamen, Forsaken, and Voidspawn, and pushed her way through battlefields to reach the dying. Through it all, she had kept a clear head—she had remained calm.

The endless battlefield had been an illusion—feeding off her own experiences, her failings, and the suffering of others. Morigan calmly studied the Shadows. They hissed vile things in her ears, but she ignored pushed the voices away, wrapping peace around her like a cloak.

Her heart slowed to an even pace, but she still shivered, her teeth knocking together with a chatter. The cold was no illusion. It was strangely reassuring. She tried to sit up, but a searing pain sliced down her arm, and she fell back to the snow, landing beside a frozen corpse.

Snow. Why was she lying in the snow? A wave of disorientation rocked her. She had been in the castle, fighting in the corridors, and now memory rushed in with beating wings. An ice elemental and a battle of steel and runes. Yasimina and Sidonie had attacked her. Sidonie was dead, or at least close to it, but not Yasimina. That memory twisted her heart.

Yasimina was a friend, and now, the woman was an enemy of the worst sort—a Bloodmagi. She could thank Yasimina for the pain in her arm.

Another flash of memory returned. Taal Greysparrow fell to a blade. Someone had impaled Shimei Aleeth with a spear, and Eldred had been caught in a backlash. But none of it mattered at the moment. She had to find shelter.

Screams echoed in the fog. These, she thought, were real, coming and going, fading and nearing. The phantoms lingered, but she ignored their burning eyes and hissing words.

Morigan tucked her injured arm close and climbed slowly to her feet. She summoned the Lore with chattering teeth, and traced a crude but adequate air rune, binding it to spirit. A light breeze swirled around her body, and the weave pushed back the fog. The phantoms retreated.

They weren't Voidspawn. She was sure of it. But they didn't feel like Forsaken, either. The things were partly there, able to brush and touch, but only with a whisper of corporeality. Morigan wasn't sure what the things were—an enchantment gone wrong? She put the question aside.

Her memories were as hazy as the gloom. The last she remembered was fighting inside the castle. She kicked at the snow, searching for the stone that must be underneath, but the crunch of her boots gave way to earth.

A scream bounced in the fog, and a man dressed in black-and-crimson livery emerged from the swirl. His eyes were wide with terror. A knot of phantoms clutched at his back, following on his heels. She recognized him from the stables. Morigan shouted his name, but he kept running.

An ache twisted her heart. She had left the boy Zoshi outside with the guards. Children were often more resourceful than most adults, but every motherly instinct she possessed urged her to shout his name.

That instinct clawed at her. And she knew immediately that the phantoms would converge—to feed off her fear. Morigan tucked her worry away.

Sobs reached her ears, and she paused, searching the fog, wondering if it was illusion or real. Morigan edged forward until she found the source. Phantoms gathered over a trembling man like flies on rotten flesh.

At her approach, the phantoms turned on her with hungry eyes. She strode forward without hesitation, and slowly they parted, oozing to the side to reveal their victim. A guard wept into his hands like a child.

Morigan placed a hand on his shoulder. At her touch, he flinched, but her weave was still active, and the breeze dispersed the fog. As the air cleared, she caught his eyes. "It's not real. Timothy, isn't it?"

"Morigan?" He sounded unsure.

"Who else would it be? On your feet," she ordered.

Timothy obeyed, but when he raised his sword, she pushed it back down. If the phantoms fed off fear, then they would surely feed off anger.

"You must remain calm. Whatever happens—*do not attack*. Do you understand, soldier?"

The command in her voice took him by surprise. He straightened to attention with a crisp, "Yes, sir."

As they traveled through the murk, she gathered more of the lost to her, but the survivors were few. The dead littered the snow. Some had been wounded, but most appeared physically fine. The damage inflicted was done to their minds—their faces frozen with terror.

Reapers fed off blood, and when the Voidspawn feasted, they grew in strength. Were these phantoms similar? Would fear and hate give these phantoms substance? With that thought, she began studying the fog and phantoms more closely. Some shadows were more distinct than others. They bore a corporeality that the others lacked. The possibility that these creatures might take shape disturbed her.

A stone wall rose out of the fog, and Morigan stopped, placing a steadying hand against its surface. She was cold and hurt, and for every soldier she added to her group, it took more of her concentration to hold the weave.

Timothy hastened to her side. "Are you all right, sir?"

"No, likely not," she said.

There could be others in the mist. Brinehilde and Zoshi might be weeping in the cold, but she had a responsibility to these survivors. And she was in no condition to keep searching.

"Stay close to the wall," she whispered. Keeping her good hand on the stone, she let it guide her until she came to a door.

Morigan muttered an oath. The fog filled the hallway, too.

She focused on her weave and drew more of the Gift, strengthening the breeze. A strong wind whipped past her hair, pushed into the hallways, and parted the mist. She recognized this passage; it led to one of the kitchens.

"These phantoms are Tharios' doing," she stated to the group of survivors. "I don't care whose side you think you're on—I won't ask. Only a fool would believe there's any kind of future as long as this fog is here."

Morigan looked at each in turn. After everyone gave her a nod, she set off through the fog. The kitchen doors were barred, a standard protocol when the castle was under attack. Morigan knocked—a rhythmic rap that only castle residents knew. But now the precaution seemed foolish: the castle was under attack by its own guards.

As the bar scraped on the other side, she braced herself for a fight, not knowing what she would find. The door cracked, and a beefy cook with a butcher's knife stared through the opening. Relief shone in the man's eye. He was called the Ogre by his staff, but Morigan knew his real name. "Thank the gods, Noa."

At her words, he ushered the survivors inside, and the door slammed shut on their heels. The cooks and bakers rushed forward to help, and Morigan sank onto a bench.

The kitchen staff were all accounted for, but her dim hope that Zoshi and Brinehilde had found refuge in the kitchens was crushed—neither one was present, nor were any of her fellow Wise Ones.

"What is going on?" Noa demanded, draping a heavy cloak over her shoulders.

That, she thought, was an excellent question. She had no answer for him.

"What do we do?" another cook asked.

The kitchens were the Ogre's domain—his power and confidence did not extend beyond its walls. Everyone in the kitchens, from scullery maid to soldier, looked to Morigan for direction. But she could barely think. Exhaustion had left her with a sense of floating while being heavy all at once. Unfortunately, there was no time to rest.

Morigan closed her eyes as she probed her arm. Pain shot along the nerve and took root in her head. "I need bandage—something to splint this arm. Two wooden spoons will do and a good tug." As she issued orders, Morigan unbuttoned her sleeve and carefully rolled it back over the broken bone. She froze.

Inky tendrils blossomed on her flesh like a spider's web. The taint followed the path of her veins. "Never mind." There was no time. Yasimina had left her mark. The cold had slowed its taint, but now it seeped towards her heart.

"What is that?" asked Timothy.

"Poison." Morigan struggled to her feet. "I need to get to my infirmary."

THE POISON SPREAD through her body like oil. It was the source of her exhaustion and her muddled mind. Morigan gathered her wavering strength, and traced a crude air rune. A breeze swirled to life around her body. She cracked opened the door.

The hallway was not precisely empty. The fog was there. It was like a living, hunting thing, and seemed to sniff the air. It waited for her, but when she stepped out of the kitchen, her weave of air pushed it away.

Morigan stood waiting with her hand on the doorknob. When no phantoms appeared, she nodded to her waiting escort. Timothy stepped into the hallway.

The air was frigid. But didn't know whether the chill was from the fog or the elemental. She did not care. Morigan couldn't afford the luxury of thought. It taking all her concentration to hold the air weave and place one foot in front of the other.

Their footsteps echoed strangely in the gloom, amplified and muffled, thrown around the stone like a child's toy marble. It was likely an effect of the poison.

Her boot hit a lump on the ground. A body. Morigan bent to check the woman's pulse. Dead. Drained of spirit like the others.

"You'll never make it if you stop for everyone." Timothy's voice drifted from far away.

"I stopped for you."

"And I'm glad for it," he said, helping her stand. "But you need a healer now." He was right. She'd do no one any good if she fell over dead.

Morigan could find her infirmary blindfolded, but they still moved cautiously through the fog. She was not the only Wise One who could weave a simple air rune. The Unspoken might be lurking in the castle.

Footsteps echoed in the hallway—her own, Timothy's, and another's. Morigan tugged Timothy to a quick halt. The footsteps stopped. She edged forward, in front of the soldier, listening for that whisper over stone.

Another corridor, another corner, and she heard it again. Morigan glanced over her shoulder. "Do you hear that?" she whispered.

Timothy jerked his head. He heard it, too. And he was afraid.

Void.

A shadow stepped out of the fog behind him. It had the impression of a face: sharp ears and slanted eyes that burned with cold.

Timothy spun, swinging at the phantom. His blade cut through the fog with a fitful swirl. Morigan stepped out of his reach. The soldier was spooked. He struck and sliced at shadows. More emerged, gathering like crows over the dead. She focused, strengthening her weave.

A strong wind swept from her hand, creating an orb of clarity around them. The phantoms retreated to the edges of her weave. But Timothy had lost control, and his fear gave him foolish courage. He charged the nearest phantom, bringing up his sword. Steel clashed in the hallway like a gong.

The phantom was a man with wild eyes and a real blade. The man stabbed upwards with a skilled half-sword thrust, catching Timothy under the arm.

Timothy stiffened. His wild-eyed attacker wrenched the blade free and charged Morigan. In that mad rush, Morigan recognized the man. A scribe she'd once treated for neck pain. He was lost in his own mind, and now she split his skull with her axe. He crumpled at her feet and a phantom rose from the body.

Morigan took a calm step towards the phantom, whose face was more impression than substance. It flashed a maniacal grin, gave her a mocking salute, and faded back into the mist.

She bent to check on Timothy. He had a hand pressed to his side. With every wheezing breath, pink blood seeped between his fingers. His lung was pierced.

The phantom's parting smile had been like a cat preening over a twitching mouse, and now Morigan was left with its half-dead offering. On the brink of death, she faced a choice: leave him and save herself, or save him and die.

Morigan grabbed Timothy's jerkin, and tugged. Pain rattled her bones. She gritted her teeth and dragged the whimpering man over the stone, leaving a long trail of blood to mark their path.

The walls swayed, the world flickered, and Morigan fought to stay on her feet. Her weave unraveled, and the phantoms closed in. Their hungry eyes leered from the gloom, and their whispers filled her mind.

Leave him healer. Save yourself. Leave the foolish human.

Morigan ignored the cowards. She'd never left anyone on a battle-field, and she would die before that day came.

CHAPTER 6

A COMMOTION JERKED BRINEHILDE AWAKE. Healers and recovering guards rushed to the door, ushering in Morigan, who was dragging a dying soldier.

"Heal him," she ordered.

Leiman knelt to obey. A flurry of questions were thrown at Morigan, but she didn't answer. She was pale and stretched, and swayed on her feet. And no one but Brinehilde noticed.

Morigan took a step, and collapsed. Brinehilde lunged forward to catch her. The barrage of questions cut off in shocked silence. Morigan Freyr was indomitable. She did not collapse. Until now. A fit of bloody coughing wracked her body.

Brinehilde looked to the others. "Don't bloody stand there—heal her." But as a healer snapped to obey, Morigan pushed herself away and staggered towards a cabinet, catching herself on a table of supplies and scattering vials across the floor.

Brinehilde hurried to help. "What do you need?"

"The lock," Morigan croaked. Black lines traced her veins, reaching up her neck like claws as she tugged at a cord around her neck. It was a key.

A nearby novice gaped at the dying healer.

Brinehilde sliced the cord, and jammed the key into the locked cabinet door. "What's wrong?" she asked the novice.

"The potions in there are more likely to kill than cure."

Brinehilde threw the doors open. "She's already at Death's door. It can't bloody well hurt, can it?"

Morigan selected a vial with a rune stamped on the clay. Brinehilde had no idea what the rune meant, but she had to trust that the healer knew best. She took the vial from Morigan's clumsy fingers, pulled out the cork, and passed it back to her.

Morigan raised it in a weak salute, then drank. The vial slipped from her fingers, shattered, and her knees gave out. Brinehilde lowered her slowly to the floor.

Death was never pleasant. The lucky few went quietly, but most took their time reaching the end. Brinehilde knew the look of death. She knew its smell, the small twitches and convulsions, and she knew that glassy-eyed stare.

Brinehilde would have none of it. And neither would the Sylph. Her voice whispered in the back of Brinehilde's mind like a gentle breeze. She'd learned to listen to that voice. Brinehilde slung Morigan over a shoulder.

"What are you doing?" Leiman asked, rushing towards them. "Let me try."

Brinehilde grabbed her quarterstaff. "No time." She barreled over the thin man, and walked to a side door, yanking it open. Outside, the mist swirled, and Brinehilde plunged into its depths.

The phantoms converged.

Brinehilde had learned one thing about the phantoms: they couldn't hurt her. And that was all she needed to know.

The voice guided her through the fog, around a corner, and to another door. She kicked it open. The air was clean, and smelled of pine trees. Flurries tumbled from a winter sky, blanketing the castle garden, and small dots of light zipped from the trees.

With a flutter of wings, Wisps landed on Morigan, buzzing frantically. Brinehilde followed the voice to an ancient oak. Beneath its broad branches, she set her shield-sister down, where the earth was warm and the roots twisted from the ground.

Morigan's breath rattled from her lips. There wasn't much time left.

Brinehilde placed a hand on the gnarled trunk, and closed her eyes, surrendering to the voice in the back of her mind. The blood in her body warmed, and a spark traveled from her heart to her fingertips.

The roots came alive. They grew and stretched, wrapping Morigan in a woody cocoon. The earth opened, and she was gently pulled into its embrace.

CHAPTER 7

Zoshi slowly opened his eyes. His skull throbbed with pain and a blurry dark spot filled his vision. It screeched at him. The crow. His skull felt like a cracked melon. He was sure his brains were leaking from his ears with every pulsing stab.

Get up, the crow squawked.

Zoshi cautiously probed his head. There was a large bump, but no cracked skull. That was good. Heartened, he gingerly sat up, but with every movement, ice cracked off his coat. He was freezing.

A layer of ice coated the stone floor. He slipped over to a pillar to lean against it for support. A fitful mist swirled in the air. Wasn't it too cold for fog? Shadows moved in the gloom. Zoshi didn't know who or what the shadows were, so he kept quiet.

Crumpet stretched his wings. Odd that the crow was no longer wounded. It hopped from the ground to his shoulder, and Zoshi winced, waiting for the prick of talons. But they never came. The bird gently gripped his perch.

"I can't see anything," he whispered to his companion. As if in answer, the fog parted, opening a pathway.

Crumpet made a clicking noise in his ear. Zoshi hushed the crow—there were things in this fog. But where was he? His last memory was fuzzy. The evil man in crimson had stood in the black room. Then the stone had rippled.

None of it made any sense. Neither did a crow that used to be a mammoth perching on his shoulder.

His fingers brushed a face. He reared back with a jerk. But it was only one of the stone faces on a pillar—not a not a dead man's frozen skull.

Zoshi had daydreamed about life in the castle. He imagined mountains of sweets, flying carpets, and all the food he could eat. But this wasn't anything like his dreams. It was like the pit where his brothers were slaughtered.

He shuffled along the pathway through the fog. A twining shape materialized. The gate. He touched the iced-over metal and quickly snatched back his hand. It nearly burned.

The ice monster. How could he forget? He'd heard the thin old woman chanting beneath the ground. Morigan told him Thira was binding the monster to a jar. The monster must have gotten loose again.

Zoshi eyed the gate. He didn't want to meet the monster, so he turned away to look for another exit. The crow cawed right in his ear.

"Shush!" he hissed.

The crow cocked his head. *Daft fool*, he said, and flapped to the floor, tapping his beak on the gate.

"Are you sure?" Zoshi whispered.

In answer, the crow hopped between the twining metal vines. Maybe the crow knew something he didn't. Crumpet's mistress *was* a Wise One. His only other choice was to wander around a creepy throne room. That thought made him uneasy.

Zoshi pushed at the gate, but it didn't move. No matter, he was small, and no one made gates with children in mind. He unslung his sack of loot, and squeezed through between the vines.

It was freezing in the black room. Someone had closed the large solid gates, then something else had destroyed them. One half remained. The rest of the giant doorway was covered with a web of runes.

Zoshi kept well away from the shimmering blue lines. He peeked through the hanging gate of icicles. A slab of metal lay on the ground with a lot of ice-coated rubble. It hurt to breathe. He pulled up his collar, breathing into the fur.

The guardian statues beside the gates were gone. How did four giant stone statues disappear? Zoshi searched the great hall from his vantage point. His breath caught. A hound-statue was frozen in mid-stride. He looked more closely at the rubble and spotted a stone eye coated with ice. At least one statue had been cracked into bits.

As he studied the frozen palace, something creaked and rasped, like a great, slow breath. Zoshi ducked back away from his icy window. If it was cold enough to crack a metal gate, cold enough to freeze stone statues, then the boy didn't stand a chance.

Crumpet seemed to sense his thoughts. The crow flapped over to a wall to wait. Zoshi frowned at the wall. It looked like the others, but what did he know? He shivered his way over to the bird.

Zoshi was sure he was no hero. Not like in the legends. A hero did not fail, and he had done that plenty. He had not saved his brothers; he had not saved Morigan; and all he wanted to do was run away.

He scrubbed at the tears brimming in his eyes. They would have frozen on his cheeks.

Crumpet tapped his beak on the ice.

"Is there another way out?" Zoshi asked.

Yes.

Crumpet knocked on the ice again, insistent. Zoshi tapped his own knuckles against the cold surface. It split his skin and a few drops of bright blood spattered on his boot.

The crow glared.

Maybe there was a secret door? A castle like this must have secrets. Zoshi rummaged through his sack. When his knife didn't turn up, he remembered he had thrust it in a pocket. There were lots of pockets in the fur coat.

Zoshi drove the tip against the ice. It chipped. Encouraged, he kept at it, and the bird gave a trill of approval. The work was noisy and rhythmic and sure to draw attention, so he worked quickly.

The ground began to quake, and the air turned so cold it burned. Crumpet clawed his way up Zoshi's clothes, wings stiff with frost. Soon, the boy couldn't feel his fingers or toes, but he didn't dare turn; the ice monster was coming. *Chip, chip, chip*, and finally a *smack*. The blade hit solid stone, black and harder than any sheet of ice. There was no door.

A giant icicle shook loose, shattering on the floor. Bits of ice swirled in the frigid air, making it too painful to breathe. Desperate, Zoshi pushed at the obsidian stone.

It swallowed him whole.

He fell right through, tumbling into a void. A hiss and a flap of wings fluttered at his ears. The crow flew off his shoulder, and as Zoshi bounced and tumbled in darkness, he envied that bird. Crumpet had wings; he did not.

CHAPTER 8

Sweat trickled down the back of Rivan's neck. The small cabin was stuffy and guard duty was boring. Even if he was guarding a legend—an elf who had lived through the Shattering, some two thousand years ago.

The thought hurt Rivan's head.

In the creaking quiet, Rivan studied the immortal. Marsais was sleeping off a bottle (or three) of rum, but even intoxicated, looking more like a pirate than the former Archlord, he was striking in appearance. A mixture of power and grace; of nobility and beauty. He was tall and lean, and perfectly sculpted for speed.

He looked unreal.

Rivan resisted the urge to touch the elf—to trace the hard lines of muscle, to feel the sweat on his skin. He cleared his throat, and looked elsewhere, tugging on his collar.

Marsais possessed an alluring combination of roguish charm, confidence, and masculine beauty. Rivan found him intoxicating. He was also infuriating.

And he's taking you to Fomorri.

The thought was sobering.

Memories of the Fomorri filled his dreams: howls, claws, and grotesque forms charging from the night to slaughter his family.

Despite the heat, Rivan shivered. A part of him hoped the ship would sink before they reached Fomorri. Better to drown than be tortured to death.

Marsais groaned, rolling to the side. Rivan thrust a bucket under the man's mouth and held his hair out of the way as he retched. Bruises from the sea-creature's attack mingled with a puckered maze of old whip scars on his back. The injuries looked out of place on the immortal.

Marsais dragged a hand across his lips. "By the gods," he groaned, falling back onto the berth. "You'd think I'd be used to this by now." He rubbed at a lump on his head in confusion. "Did I fall?"

"A belay pin, sir."

"Oenghus?"

"Captain Mael."

"Probably for the best."

"You're still alive," Rivan agreed.

Marsais pushed the hair away from his face. And Rivan found himself transfixed by the casual elegance in such a simple gesture. He looked up from those long, clever fingers to find Marsais watching him. His eyes were like steel, piercing flesh and bone.

Rivan felt his cheeks warm. "Erm... can I get you anything, sir?"

"Where am I?"

"The Mearcentian cutter—the *Squall*. We're sailing to Fomorri."

"Is Oen all right?"

"Yes."

Marsais sighed with relief. "When Oen drinks too much, he destroys a tavern. When I drink, I..." He waved a hand, a careless gesture that brought to mind the wind.

It seemed like the sentence wanted finishing so Rivan filled the lapse in memory. "You told the sea god to go plow himself."

"Did I say that?"

"Yes, sir."

Marsais began to convulse with wheezing laughter. But the humor turned to tears, then to a fit of coughing that had him reaching for a waterskin. He drank long and deep, his Adam's apple bobbing with every gulp. When he was through, he wiped the tears from his eyes, and let his head fall back against the bulkhead.

Rivan shifted on his seat. He reached out to offer comfort, but hesitated. Marsais was a legend who defied the gods themselves. A former king and Archlord. And yet, he was also a man—hungover and stretched on a dingy berth with tear tracks on his cheeks.

Rivan touched his shoulder in comfort. The gesture surprised Marsais, and he opened his eyes to study the young man. His eyes softened a fraction.

Rivan removed his hand. "Do you need anything, sir?"

"Can you fetch that parrot of yours?"

"The parrot?"

"The brilliant red bird that lives on this ship."

"There's fruit and bread and cheese..."

Marsais arched an amused brow. "I don't intend to roast the bird."

"Oenghus threatened to eat it," Rivan explained.

Marsais looked at the overhead and muttered something rude. In a clearer voice, he repeated, "I'm not going to eat the parrot."

"What do you want with it?" Rivan asked, slowly.

"It's none of your concern." Marsais swung his feet off the berth and sat up straight.

The room seemed suddenly smaller, and Rivan wanted to melt into the wood, but he wouldn't let anyone hurt his parrot. Steeling himself, he looked Marsais in the eye. "I beg your pardon, but it *is* my concern. I've been looking after the bird—during the storm and such."

"Does this 'pet' of yours have any trinkets on a cord around its neck or leg? Something like these?" Marsais tapped a coin that was woven into his goatee. It chimed like a soft bell.

Rivan shook his head.

"When did you find the bird?"

"Why does that matter?"

"It matters," Marsais snapped.

"After we set sail, it landed on the mainmast yard."

When Marsais stood to leave, Rivan hopped to his feet and blocked the door. "Captain Mael ordered you to remain in your cabin."

Marsais stared imperiously down his nose at the young man. Rivan swallowed under that glare, but held his ground. He had his orders. And he wasn't sure whose ire he feared more: Captain Mael or Marsais.

The standoff was cut short when Marsais swayed on his feet. He winced with pain, and quickly sat back down to rub at his temple. "If you fetch me the bird, then I'll remain in my cabin," Marsais murmured.

"I was ordered not to leave your side."

Marsais cast around the cabin with a sigh. He stretched towards a piece of leather that had fallen on the floor, then swept back his hair, cinching it with the cord.

"Rivan." Marsais smiled like a shark. "Fetch me the parrot, or I'll turn you into a rat."

"I have my orders," he said.

Marsais frowned at his refusal.

"I'm more afraid of my captain than you." And he liked rats.

"You're a terrible liar."

"Thank you, sir."

Marsais gave him a lopsided grin, then lay back on the berth. "Why do you keep calling me sir?"

"Out of respect."

"If you respected me, then you would follow my orders," he said to the overhead.

Rivan cleared his throat. "I don't want to sound disrespectful."

"How is using my name disrespectful? Calling me sir makes me feel old."

"You are."

Marsais barked a laugh, then winced in pain. Rivan sat back down, watching him as he settled on his berth. After a minute, Marsais' voice rose casually in the cabin. "It will be on your head when she dies."

"Excuse me?"

"Her blood will be on your hands."

"Who?"

Marsais told him. And Rivan shot out of the cabin.

THE SEA WAS EERILY QUIET. It was hot, too, even for Rivan, a native Mearcentian. The flags hung limp and the swells rippled lazily. Sweat glistened on the backs of sailors as they made repairs, and although the Windtalkers drummed a steady beat, the air was still.

The *Squall* was dead in the water.

Rivan searched the ship's rigging for the bird. A slash of crimson on the topmast caught his eye. He backed up and craned his neck. The parrot was basking in the sun.

He put his two fingers in his mouth, and whistled. The crew looked up from their various tasks in question, but Rivan ignored the others. He'd caught the bird's attention. But it seemed the sun was more alluring than a man with a hard biscuit. The parrot didn't move.

Rivan reached for a ratline, but a voice brought him up short.

"Why are you on deck, soldier?"

"I have to get the parrot, sir."

"I gave you an order," Acacia said.

"It's import—" He never had the chance to finish. A commotion exploded from the depths of the hold. A feral hiss mingled with shouting men and rough voices.

Rivan and Acacia raced to the hatch, shouldering past the Elite warriors to look down into the cargo hold. A scuffle of shadows lurched far below. One combatant moved with hissing, claw-like swipes.

Reapers.

The thought had him reaching for his sword, but a child's voice yelled from the shadows and brought him up short. "Kiss my arse!"

"Elam," Rivan realized.

"Let them go!" Acacia shouted into the hold. Kasja and Elam, the Lome natives, thrashed like wild animals in the soldiers' hands. The men looked up at their own captain in question.

"They're stowaways, Captain," a sailor called from the depths.

"The boy and his sister are our companions," Acacia said to Carvil.

"They are still stowaways," Carvil replied. "Bring them up."

Rivan's heart sped. He knew the fate of stowaways on a Mearcentian ship. "Please, Captain Carvil. They are foreigners—savages. They don't know our ways."

Carvil regarded him with the impassiveness of a cliff. "The Trickster has already put the *Squall* at risk. I will not risk further insult to Nereus."

Rivan looked at his own captain. "Go get Oenghus," she ordered.

RIVAN SHOULDERED his way past the crew. The sailors had taken control of Kasja and Elam. The Lome woman had returned to her feral glory, scavenging a costume that blended with her hiding place in the hold: netting, driftwood, bits of sail and canvas. She looked like something from a shipwreck that had washed up on shore.

When Elam caught sight of Rivan, he yelled one of the few common phrases he knew. "Kiss my arse!"

"I'm getting Oenghus," Rivan said.

The boy bared his teeth in a fair imitation of his hero. "Bastard!" His tone was triumphant.

Marsais emerged from his cabin. He looked lost, scratching at the terrible scar that slashed across his bare chest. Whatever had caused the wound had nearly cut him in half.

"Marsais, sir—"

Marsais wandered away, muttering under his breath, oblivious to the world. There was no time to escort him back to his cabin. Rivan decided his captain's last order trumped the previous ones. Kasja and Elam had little time.

Mearcentians worshipped the sea. Sailing was a spiritual awakening, akin to prayer. Stowing away on a Mearcentian ship was comparative to breaking into a temple and stealing its most holy symbol. While the crime warranted a death sentence in the Blessed Order, here, thieves were flogged without a care if they survived.

Why Marsais had not been dumped in a dinghy and sent adrift, he did not know. But he suspected no one was keen to get between a mythic legend and a god.

Rivan flung the door open to Oenghus' cabin. And froze. Heat spread over his body.

Oenghus was not alone. Armor and clothing littered the floor, and there was a half-naked woman in his arms. She glanced at Rivan, and gave a breathless laugh.

Rivan shut the door, and tried to ignore the sounds coming from the cabin as the pair finished. A few minutes later, Oenghus emerged, lacing up his trousers. "I'll toss you in the Pits o'Mourn," he growled.

"Kasja and Elam are aboard. Captain Carvil issued orders to flog them," Rivan blurted out before the man could carry out his threat.

"They snuck aboard?"

"Stowaways."

"Daft, crazed, fools," Oenghus bit out each word, then opened the door. "Trouble up top," he explained.

The woman started grabbing her own things. Rivan recognized her as Cas, one of the Elite soldiers. As Oenghus strapped on his belt, he paused to give her a kiss, and in return, she bit his lip. He growled low in his throat, looking as if he'd take her right there and then, all over again.

"Kasja and Elam," Rivan reminded.

Oenghus grunted, slung his targe on his back and snatched up his war hammer, making for the companionway ladder.

"Captain, with all due respect, they don't know your laws. Surely you could allow someone to stand in their place?" Acacia asked. She was calm and collected, but Rivan knew his captain was prepared for a fight. And he'd stand with her. A flogging would kill the boy.

Carvil shook his head. "It's out of my hands. They did not beseech Nereus to board."

Oenghus crossed his massive arms. "But I helped them sneak aboard. How else did they get past your crew?"

"Why didn't you tell us?" Carvil demanded. "Why the deception?"

Oenghus pointed at Acacia. "She's jealous of the woman there."

"Terribly jealous," she agreed dryly.

Carvil glanced doubtfully at the feral woman, who hissed and spit back at him.

"She's, erm…" Oenghus tugged on his beard, searching for an adequate word.

"These two owe him a Blood Debt," Rivan cut in, stepping forward. "Oenghus holds their life in his hands. He's responsible for their actions."

All eyes settled on the young paladin. Rivan was a student of the Law, of all cultures, especially his own. Acacia had always valued his bookish ways. She gave him a slight nod of approval.

"Aye, that's right." Oenghus agreed. "What he said."

"Do you accept responsibility?" Carvil asked.

"I told them to come aboard."

"Both of their punishments?"

Oenghus grunted.

"Eighty lashes, then. All hands to deck!" At his order, the crew gathered around, but Sergeant Nimlesh and his Elite stood off to the side. The warriors had no say in matters at sea.

Oenghus handed Acacia his war hammer, let his belt and cuirass drop, and stripped down to his waist. He waggled both eyebrows, and flexed his muscles for her benefit.

"Only you would flirt before a flogging."

"I'm looking forward to your hands on me again."

"I don't think eighty lashes is worth that."

"It is," he purred.

"She looks far more appreciative than me." Acacia nodded towards the dark-haired warrior whose gaze lingered on his physique, the same woman who'd had her legs wrapped around the berserker only minutes before.

"She's already appreciated it."

Oenghus flashed a grin at both women, and turned away. The master-at-arms was waiting with a length of rope. Oenghus ruffled Elam's hair before submitting to the binds, allowing the man to tie his wrists. His arms were hoisted upwards and secured to the shrouds.

Rivan shifted on his feet. He hated whippings. They were barbaric and hardly worthy of his people.

Marsais climbed on deck, looking lost. He cast about, searching for the gods knew what. After a moment, his grey eyes narrowed on

Oenghus, and he stopped, cocking his head. "Are you about to be flogged?"

"Aye."

Marsais arched a brow at Carvil. "You're going to flog a *berserker* on a floating island?"

"I will not risk further offense to the sacred sea." Carvil leveled a disapproving glare at the larger offense—the seer.

"Ah," Marsais said, slowly. "Well, by all means, carry on. I'm sure Nereus will be pleased." Rivan caught a quick flash of fingers before Marsais patted his friend on the back for good luck. "Try not to slaughter everyone, Oen."

Marsais wandered away, looking under sails, inside barrels, and searching the rigging before he spotted Kasja. His eyes widened, and a series of emotions fluttered over his features: recognition, sadness, and finally relief. He hurried over, and bent close to the wild woman, whispering in her strange, lilting tongue.

"Captain," Acacia whispered. "The seer is right. A berserker feeds off pain. A flogging could very well send him into a frenzy."

Carvil gave a grim nod. "I do not wish to flog a crazed woman and child any more than you, but I cannot break tradition—not in front of my men. This man will have to do."

Elam's smile faltered when he saw the master-at-arms uncoil the whip. Realization dawned. The boy threw himself at the whip-wielding man, but Acacia caught Elam's arm and pulled him back. His sister was oblivious to the commotion. She held a red feather, mesmerized by its details, untroubled by her little brother's screaming.

"Calm down, boy. It's only eighty lashes." At Oenghus' reassuring growl, Elam stopped struggling, but kept glaring at the man with the whip.

A Windtalker began to speak in the flowing tongue of the seafarers. Rivan translated for the benefit of the others. "We humbly beg forgiveness of the Sea. Grant these land dwellers passage over your waters. We ask with blood and sweat and pain for the privilege of touching the wind."

As the Windtalker spoke, she splashed saltwater on Elam and Kasja, just as she had done when the rest of the group had boarded the ship. Kasja did not notice. The wild woman seemed to be in a trance.

When the ceremony was complete, the Windtalker nodded, and a single note on a drum propelled the whip. Leather struck skin. Rivan flinched. And Oenghus snorted. "What was that—a tickle?"

Battle scars marred his back and shoulders, but the only recent mark was a series of fingernail scratches trailing over muscle. The master-at-arms frowned, brought back his whip, and struck again. Nothing. Oenghus laughed. And the whipping continued.

When the master-at-arms grew fatigued, he surrendered his whip to a fresh arm who took up the count. The larger man threw his entire body into the strike. A slight, red weal appeared, more like a slap than a whip slash.

Rivan gawked. Then reason returned. The slap. Marsais had patted his friend on the back. The Wise One's stone-skin weave was powerful. It had saved Rivan's life more than once in the past month. But if no blood were drawn by the end of the flogging—the ship would be cursed.

Pushing his way through the grim crew, Rivan searched for Marsais on deck. All the while, the berserker's laughter rumbled over the ship. But there was nothing amusing about the situation, not to the Mearcentians—no more than if the pair had pissed on Zahra's Sacred Sun.

Rivan pushed that thought out of his head. Marsais and Oenghus had probably desecrated every holy symbol in the realm. He found Marsais and Kasja midship. The seer had his head under a tarp, rummaging through a longboat.

"Marsais," Rivan hissed. "Blood must be drawn or the ship will be cursed. You *must* remove the armor weave."

"I'm familiar with Mearcentian customs," Marsais said, his voice muffled. "Aha!" He tried to straighten, hit the tarp, and wrestled with it until he fought his way free to hold up his prize: a small leather pouch dangling on a leather thong.

Marsais beamed at Kasja. It was the first hint of joy Rivan had seen since the Ardmoor attacked the Lome city.

Marsais reached for the shrouds, swung easily onto the rail and around, and began to climb the ratlines as swift and sure as an experienced sailor. As Marsais climbed towards the tops, Rivan hurried back to his captain's side. There was nothing to do but pray that the leather cut the berserker's flesh.

"Seventy-eight!" The whip cracked. "Seventy-nine!" Oenghus' back was a maze of fine red welts, but none of them bled. He flexed his arms, leaning his weight against the shrouds as if he planned to tear the rigging from the pins out of sheer boredom. "Eighty!" The whip tore flesh.

"Finally," Oenghus grunted. "You nipped me." He flexed, breaking the rope binds around his wrists.

Rivan blinked in shock. Marsais had either timed his armor weave to perfection, or luck had played a heavy hand. He wouldn't wager on luck.

CHAPTER 9

THE PARROT PERCHED on the topsail yardarm. Her beak was turned towards the sun, feathers smooth as she basked in the heat. Marsais climbed out and swung himself onto the maintop. He whistled at the bird. She cocked her head, but did not look his way. He tried again, a more complex call. This time, the parrot pinned him with an emerald eye.

Five days without her token. Would there be anything left of her?

Marsais shoved the thought aside. A life as a parrot would be far preferable to the fate that he had worked and maneuvered so delicately to avoid. Despite his every effort—his sacrifices—here she was. His schemes had failed.

Marsais held out her token pouch, letting it sway like a pendulum. The parrot tensed.

"Yes," he whispered. "You recognize this, don't you?"

As if his words were carried by a weave, the bird sidestepped her way along the yard. But a shout bellowed from the deck, sending the bird flapping with irritation and sauntering back to the yardarm.

Marsais started to search his pockets, but his hand stopped on his chest. It was bare. He looked down, cringing at what he feared he wouldn't find, but he had remembered to dress. Partially, at any rate. A pair of linen breeches sagged on his hips. Unfortunately, there were still no pockets.

His gaze flickered to the leather pouch. It was enchanted. He traced a spirit rune to inspect the ward. To say that it was complex would be an understatement.

A nasty little fire rune was hidden in the complex tangle. Instead of unraveling the ward, he wove water runes around the fire, and loosened the ties. Steam hissed from the opening. He dipped two fingers into the small pouch, and blinked. His blind search was met with air—not a small physical space with sides and a bottom, but with the feeling of emptiness.

Marsais squeezed his hand through the opening, and then his wrist, forearm, all the way to his shoulder. A jumble of items lay in the enchanted space. Working by touch, he rummaged around the cabinet-sized pouch until he found what he wanted. He held it, poised on his fingertips, and turned it this way and that, catching the sunlight: a perfect strawberry.

The parrot spread her wings and dove from the yardarm. With a flap of red feathers, she soared, and landed on his outstretched forearm. Talons dug gently into his skin as the bird attacked the berry.

"Now then," he murmured. "Let me see if I can find you."

Marsais stroked her feathers and calmed her with his voice. She watched as he retrieved another strawberry. His second offering won the parrot's trust, and she sidestepped her way to his shoulder.

Marsais peered over the edge of the platform. The ritual flogging was over, the crew had dispersed, and some were climbing the shrouds. "I'm going to climb down. I hope you'll join me."

He fed her another berry for good measure, but as he reached for the futtock shroud, he paused, watching the sailors climb upwards. If he brought her aboard—on deck—would the Mearcentians view her as a stowaway?

Probably.

Marsais sat down to lean against the ropes. And when a sailor reached the top, he smiled. The man started to climb back down, but his companion barked at him to get moving. The sailor scrambled up, and reached for the next shroud, climbing aloft to the topgallant. One by one, the action was repeated, until the sailors spread out over the yards, balancing on foot ropes.

A ripple of unease hung over the men, but it had nothing to do with their precarious positions.

Marsais focused on the bird. Another bribe lured the parrot onto his knee. "What have you done to yourself, Isiilde?"

At the sound of her name, the parrot cocked her head and squawked. Marsais set down the pouch, pinning the cord with a foot so the bird wouldn't fly away with it. Weaving a transformation on oneself required a tether to anchor the weaver to her original form. Either Isiilde had lost hers when she landed, or she had forgotten to hold on to it.

The latter seemed the likeliest.

"I should leave you like this. It would be safer," he said, tracing a runic eye over a spirit rune. The weave glowed in the air, and he let it fall over the parrot like a net. A complicated web of runes flared to life around the bird.

Marsais stroked his goatee. "You made a knot," he sighed.

The bird sidestepped, dipping her head.

Marsais was not the weaver. He could not simply reverse the transformation; instead, he would have to pluck the threads one at a time until it unraveled. Not unlike a ward.

True to her nature and blood, Isiilde had woven a brilliant transformation. The runes were like silk rather than coarse wool, nothing like the threadbare weaves that most Wise Ones managed. But if he pulled the wrong thread, her spirit might be lost, or the backlash would send him flying off the tops. Of course, there were safeguards that could be placed for when a transformation was shattered, but he could not be sure that Isiilde had added them to her weave.

Muttering the Lore under his breath, he traced a bind for Isiilde's spirit, and with care he began to pluck and nudge the strands, one by one. A gossamer thread loosened, waving in the air beneath his arcane sight.

The parrot squawked, shifting restlessly, and Marsais deftly plucked free another thread. Ethereal frayed edges opened like a cocoon.

"Do not burn the boat," he warned, then tugged on the last.

The parrot jerked. Feathers flew, and a shriek shattered the quiet. With a flapping, wounded thrashing, the bird writhed on his lap.

The feathers molted, bones cracked, and a light flared. When it faded, a lithe, shimmering nymph lay across his legs. Disoriented, she coughed and sneezed. Three bursts of flame erupted from her ears, sending heat sizzling across his stomach.

Marsais could not tear his eyes from the vision. Her hair was fire, and her skin wavered like a mirage. A dream, even here.

Isiilde blinked, and shifted on his lap. She looked into his eyes. There was no fury, no anger, only sadness.

"You're a fool," she said.

"Better fool than king," he whispered.

Isiilde arched a brow. "Why?"

"As a fool, my blunders are laughable." He dared not move lest he reach for her.

"I'm not laughing."

"Forgivable, then?"

"Are you apologizing?"

"For wanting you safe?" He shook his head. "Never." The word came out as a desperate rasp.

Isiilde frowned, and stood, swaying comfortably on the platform as she surveyed the surrounding ocean. Naked and gleaming beneath the sun, the nymph captivated every man on the yards. But she seemed to ignore their eyes, as unconcerned as if they were dogs.

If he had been able to form thought, he would have counted himself among the dogs. His gaze lingered on the soft curve of her hip. He wanted to kiss the exquisite hollow beside her hipbone and work his way from there.

"I see you missed me."

Marsais blinked at her words. She was eyeing his obvious arousal, and he gave himself a mental slap. Clearing his throat, he adjusted his breeches.

Isiilde turned back to the sea. She ran a hand through her hair, trying to tame the wild mass. The gesture drew his attention from her backside to her shoulder blades. Clarity came. And anger. A fiery

Ouroboros circled her back—a nymph's mark like no other. She had bonded with her fire.

Marsais pulled himself to his feet. "You should not be *here*."

At the sound of his voice, Isiilde turned. "Why? Because the road is dangerous? You said it yourself, Marsais—I am free to do as I please."

"You have no idea what awaits you!"

"I don't think you know either," she argued. "For all your plotting and scheming, I am here. You misplayed your turn. Now stop trying to steer my Fate. I do not want your help."

Marsais snorted, and bent closer; close enough to feel her breath. "Without *my* help, you would still be a parrot." His words were clipped.

Isiilde beamed. "You're angry with me."

"No, I'm furious with you. Your naiveté, your foolishness."

"Finally! You're treating me like an equal rather than a pet to be indulged. I will not become one of King Syre's pet nymphs, and I am no longer yours."

The words struck his heart. He opened his mouth to deny her accusation, but the words stuck in his throat. He shut his mouth with a click.

Isiilde snatched her enchanted pouch from the platform. She reached in and pulled out the garment that she had worn in Mearcentia. A silk wrap that was impossibly loose and clinging at the same time. She slipped it on, and somehow, it was even more alluring than her bare flesh.

Marsais took a breath, and closed his eyes, fighting conflicting urges of either dropping her off with the first passing ship they came across, or taking her in his arms and making love to her in the tops.

When he opened his eyes, all was calm. "Please, Isiilde," he said, kneeling on the platform. "I am begging you: do not set foot in Fomorri."

Isiilde studied him with surprising sympathy. "No," she said.

The nymph swung around and down, oblivious to the height, and climbed the ratlines to the deck, leaving Marsais on his knees.

Isiilde Jaal'Yasine touched the deck with a bare foot. She marched aft, past a sea of murmurs and wide eyes, heading straight for the helm.

Oenghus stepped in her path. "Blood and ashes, Sprite!" he bellowed. "What the Void are you doing here?"

"I'm coming with you." She squeezed past her furious father, and slipped up the companionway ladder, presenting herself to the Windtalker chieftess.

Isiilde crossed arms over her breasts and bowed deeply. "I came on the winds, and ask your blessing to sail over the seas."

While she had endeavored to teach Rivan the rudiments of King's Folly, he had been teaching her in turn, answering all her questions about his homeland and customs. Isiilde never forgot a thing. Unless it suited her.

The Windtalker simply nodded, as if nymphs made a habit of flying on the winds and landing on her ship. The wrinkled, nut-brown woman, sprinkled sea water on the nymph's head, and blew. Wind and sea, the eternal cycle of Mearcentian lore. Isiilde straightened.

"May the Sea God be pleased," the woman intoned.

Isiilde turned to the sea captain, denoted by the scrimshaw interwoven into his sash. "Princess Jaal'Yasine. Is there a cabin for me?"

Carvil blinked at the title, but recovered quickly. "We will make room, Your Highness."

It was apparent that no one on board, save for Kasja and Elam, was pleased to see her. But their opinions didn't matter. She wished to stay, and short of turning the ship around, there was absolutely nothing anyone could do about it.

CHAPTER 10

Oᴇɴɢʜᴜꜱ ʟᴇᴀɴᴇᴅ ᴀɢᴀɪɴꜱᴛ ᴛʜᴇ ʀᴀɪʟ, smoking a pipe. He ignored the man who stepped up beside him with a warning chime of coins.

Marsais took out his own pipe and tobacco pouch. "Any luck?"

Oenghus shook his head. "She won't leave her cabin. I even yelled."

"The entire ship heard."

"She stood her ground. I'll give her that."

"Did you expect any less?"

Oenghus grunted.

Marsais sprinkled tobacco into the bowl of his pipe, tapped the wood, and repeated. When he was satisfied with his efforts, he summoned a flame, puffing until the weed caught. He shook out the flame, and took a long draught, savoring the fragrant herb.

The Windtalkers' beat thrummed in the stillness, but no wind blew. The Sea God had abandoned the ship. It slugged through the water under the power of long oars and strain. During the days, Oenghus took out his frustration on the oars. It benefited everyone. Still, the ship's progress was slow.

The two men stared at the horizon. To the west, the sun kissed the water, sending flames rippling across the sky. And when the world closed its curtain on another performance, Marsais exhaled a long stream of smoke.

"I tire of breathing," he admitted. "But in all these years, I never tire of watching the sunset."

Oenghus didn't trust himself to speak. He refilled his pipe and the two smoked in comfortable silence until the Sylph's silver moon hung heavy in the stars.

"I need to know something," Marsais murmured.

"You can ask. It doesn't mean I'll answer."

Marsais wove an Orb of Silence. More for the gods and their keen ears than the sailors on deck. "You danced around my questions before, but I need to know—What does the Sylph plan for Isiilde?"

Oenghus studied the dark bowl of his pipe. "There are days when I can't stand your hide, Scarecrow. And still..." His voice choked.

Marsais waited.

"I... I mean to say that you are..." Oenghus blinked, rapidly.

"I love you, too," Marsais said, dryly.

Coins chimed, but he was too slow. A fist crashed into his shoulder, knocking him to the side. The blow jolted him off balance. He stumbled, caught himself on a rope, then straightened, returning to his friend's side.

"Bastard," Oenghus muttered. "But, aye, that's what I was trying to get at."

"Ever affectionate."

Oenghus glowered. "Shut it, or I'll chuck you overboard and leave you to Nereus."

Marsais patted the man's shoulder. Oenghus spun on him, and for a moment, he feared the berserker would make good on his threat; instead, Oenghus looked him straight in the eye. "I'd rather not repeat Yasine's words."

"You don't want to offend me?" he asked slowly.

"I don't want to hurt you." Oenghus turned away towards the moon. Its silver light seemed to drape over him like a cloak.

"A friend speaks the truth, whether or not it hurts."

Oenghus gave a slight nod. From the side, draped in moonlight, he looked like a cliff, all chiseled and strong, solid in the sea. "She begged me not to interfere with Isiilde's Fate. And I swore I wouldn't. I told you some of what she said—that this realm is lost. That it's broken, but she said something more... She said *you* are as broken and as fractured as this realm."

Marsais closed his eyes. The words stung because they were true.

"What was done, she said, is done. What is broken, cannot be mended. That Life only attracts the Void, and that something more was needed—a child between her and me."

Marsais ran a tired hand over his face. *Grant me peace.* The dead child's voice whispered through a maze of memory in his mind. "I know I'm broken," he admitted. "I've known for a very long time. But what I don't know—what no one knows—is what will happen to my spirit when I leave this realm?"

Oenghus narrowed his eyes. He knew where the conversation was going and he didn't like it. Talk of past lives gave him a headache.

Marsais ignored his glower. "The Sylph gathered the complexities of Life into the Orb to fight the Void. When the Orb shattered, it tore the realm apart. Unfortunately, I was here during the Shattering and the backlash tore my wards to shreds. It changed me. But I am still who I am. Otherwise, I would have given myself over to the Keening years ago." There was pain in his voice, and a longing that kept poets dreaming.

Marsais rested his elbows on the rail. His coins chimed softly, not in warning, but in comfort. The moonlight touched his shoulders, illuminating his long, white hair. The Sylph was listening. He should have known: the goddess slipped between wards like water through rocks. Not unlike her daughter.

"What happens when Time dies?" he whispered, more to himself than his companion.

Oenghus tugged on his beard. "If Time is a tapestry, then I'd wager everything unravels."

"Not bad for a mindless brute."

"I like tearing things apart. I understand that."

"Hmm."

There was truth in Oenghus' words, the plainest, simplest, and therefore, most powerful kind. Marsais chewed on the thought for a long while, watching the moonlight dance on the dark water. Flying fish played in the light, and other, more ominous shapes slithered in the dark, bumping against the hull. Finally, he stirred, dragging his thoughts back to his original purpose.

"The Sylph is right," Marsais admitted. "The Void is attracted to Life. But why a child sired by you? And *don't* say your cock."

"It's the truth."

"There are far larger gods than you in the realms."

Oenghus snorted.

Realization lit the hallways of Marsais' mind. "Death and Chaos," he whispered.

"Plenty of that already."

Marsais shook his head. "Yasine's sisters. Chaos and..." He choked over memory, of love and longing, and loss. "Death. The history I recited to the paladins in the ruined Lindale city. Chaos hid her children in the darkness, and they reached out, dragging her in. The Void was born. Death stood against it, or at least, she tried to."

Oenghus scratched his beard. "Could you make some bloody sense once in a while? All I care about right now is that my little Sprite is on a boat headed for Fomorri on some half-cocked suicide mission baked up by a madman."

"Ulfhidhin," Marsais said, slowly.

The name made Oenghus wince. He pressed a hand to his head, and growled at the seer to be quiet.

Marsais ignored the threat. "You're the epitome of Chaos. Born from a lightning strike against a crag."

"Bollocks."

"Blast it, Ulf, if you can't even bear to hear your old name said out loud, how in the Nine Halls are you going to face Karbonek again?"

Oenghus clenched his fists. "Not. Another. Word."

"At any rate, you're unpredictable. That's why the Sylph wanted your seed—so your chaotic nature would be passed on to her daughter."

"You bloody well know how to flatter a man. I hope you plan on cooking me dinner after."

Marsais was in no mood for banter. He looked at the silver moon and its faithful red companion. And in the distance, far into the night, was another, more ominous outline. A dark circle, growing closer, speeding the realm towards the Shadowed Dawn.

"The Sylph," he explained, "is trusting in Chaos. She's sailing us all into uncharted waters without a rudder. *That* is insanity."

Feeling the weight of the realm settle on his shoulders, Marsais walked away with only a vague plan that involved drinking himself senseless.

CHAPTER 11

Zoshi was blind. His melon had cracked open and his eyes had burst. Only when he carefully probed his head, there was no leak. Eyelids, eyeballs, all there. Plus a swollen knot under his tangled hair. But the real pain came from his ankle.

Feathers ruffled in the dark. The crow gave a demanding croak.

"I can't see," he whispered.

A swish of feathers and a distant flapping told the boy that the crow had abandoned him. Fear crept into his heart. He was alone in the pitch black unknown.

Think of what you have; not what you don't. That's what his mum always said. He'd told his little brothers the same, but he'd never get to tell them again.

Fighting back a wave of grief, Zoshi felt the ground, trying to make sense of the darkness. The stone wasn't frozen. That meant he was safe from the ice monster. He had that to be thankful for.

His blind exploration brought him to a wall. He put his back to it, and checked his ankle. It was swollen and thick in his boot. He quickly removed his boot, and his ankle gave an angry throb.

Zoshi used his scarf as a makeshift bandage, wrapping it tightly around his ankle. It would have to do. He tied his boot on to his belt, and began exploring this new world with questing fingers.

There were stairs going up, and stairs going down. Keeping one hand on the wall, he stretched out, but didn't feel another wall. Zoshi edged blindly along his stair with his hands. The stone dropped abruptly. He scrambled away from the edge. The stairwell wasn't very wide.

His breath echoed harshly in his ears as he fought for breath. It took a long while for his breathing to slow—even longer for him to work up the courage to move again. But eventually he did.

Zoshi found a pebble, then crawled cautiously towards the edge. He stretched out his arm, and dropped the stone, listening hard. More nothing; not even a faint *clack* of its landing.

A dim, bluish light zipped around the darkness. It was coming towards him, bobbing in the sea of black. Zoshi scrambled back to his wall, and quickly scooted up the steps. But the blue light kept coming.

A breath later, the crow landed in front of him, its feathered-face aglow. Zoshi squinted at the brightness. The light came from a tangle of glowing moss. Crumpet had brought him light.

Zoshi shuddered with relief. He picked up the plant and cupped it in his hands like a treasured jewel. It illuminated the stone stairs. He could see one step up and one step down, but not much else. A fine layer of dust covered the stone steps. No one had come here for a long time. Even the stone looked old.

Zoshi rooted around his sack, but he had nothing to hold the light except for his waterskin. Keeping the moss cupped in one hand, he started scooting up the stairs, one at a time, back the way he had fallen.

The crow rattled and clicked its disapproval.

"I'm not going down there," he said. But the stone said otherwise: the top of the stairs was blocked.

Zoshi shone his meager light over the obsidian wall. It sucked the light up and swallowed it whole. There was no sign of a door. How had he fallen through? He pushed against the stone, but nothing happened this time. When further attempts failed, he tried to slide it. Then he stood on his one good leg, on his toes, and felt as much as the slab as he could. Still nothing.

Desperate, Zoshi punched the wall. That was a mistake. He sucked in a breath, and clutched his hurting hand, melting to the ground in defeat.

Something tugged on his trouser leg. Zoshi raised his light. Crumpet was nipping at his clothes.

"Is there a way out, then?"

The crow's eyes glowed in the darkness. Zoshi shivered. *Yes,* said those eyes.

CHAPTER 12

A SINGLE DROP stained the stone. The copper-skinned Rahuatl crouched, running a claw through the mark. She brought it to her forked tongue. Blood. Rashk sneered at the fog. It had ruined her hunt. Phantoms drifted in the mist—lost spirits with no blood, no form.

Cowards.

Rashk turned back to that drop of life, listening to the songs of distant clashes, the screams and vague battle cries that were shouted from the stones.

The fog was mad. And poisonous.

Rashk ran her tongue over her teeth. Her tongue-piercing clicked along each tip, soothing her senses, and more—the rune-etched stud kept the poison at bay. With curved blade in hand, she rose with the smoothness of a cat, and padded silently through the gloom. Thira and Morigan had not returned her Whispers. Either the women were dead, or the fog was hampering weaves. Whatever the reason, she required a bird's-eye view.

When she put weight on the first stair leading up to her tower, the ward pulsed in warning. Someone was in her tower.

Rashk paused to listen and sniff the air. The mist smelled of frost on a grave. Halfway up the long climb, she broke through the fog. It lay at her feet like a filthy pond, lapping at the stone step. She'd placed a complicated spirit ward on that step: a weave of air and spirit and light. The ward repelled Reapers and Forsaken. And apparently this fog.

She rubbed two finger caps together, activating a dormant rune. When the enchantment hummed to life, she placed her palm flat against the stone, and listened. The stone vibrated like a wounded beast. The castle was unsettled.

Rashk snatched her hand away, shaking off the sensations. She did not pause at the next landing, or glance down the passage that veered off to another set of rooms. A dark spot caught her eyes, and another— the trail of a wounded predator.

On the third landing, there was no passage, but an alcove with a bench that faced a narrow window. Without warning, Rashk lunged into the alcove, bursting through a mirror weave. She brought herself up short, her blade whispering against a high collar.

Thira dropped her weave. "You're late."

Rashk withdrew her unbloodied blade. "Whispers do not travel in this muck." She looked at the man who shared the small space. Thedus faced the wall, his palms flat on the stone. He was still naked.

"I suspected as much," Thira said. "I knew you'd return to your tower, eventually." A deep cut ran down Thira's cheek, and a dark stain saturated the shoulder of her long coat.

Rashk looked at her in question.

"It took some effort to shake Eiji from our trail," Thira explained.

In silence, the group climbed the winding stairwell. When they reached the top, Rashk stepped forward, wrapping a hand around an innocent looking handle. Her tower had more wards and traps than a nobleman's vault. She clicked her claws against the metal in a precise pattern. It whispered like a chattering cricket. The wards unraveled and the door opened. Rashk motioned her companions inside.

Rashk reset the wards, then walked through her rooms, searching for lurkers. But no one had breached her tower. She heard a whistle.

Thira whistled from the main room, and Rashk hurried back. The woman stood by a window that faced the inner bailey. She repeated the call.

"Did you kill the cowardly Archlord?"

Thira cocked her head. "Marsais? No, he's likely still alive."

"I meant *Tharios*," she hissed.

"I did not," Thira sighed. "He ran into the Nameless and closed the Titan Gates."

Rashk stepped into the shadows by the window. "Isek Beirnuckle lives. He is a slippery foe." She had lost Isek during a skirmish with guards. The traitor had disappeared—to her eyes, to her nose, to her instincts.

Spymaster or no, how did a man disappear so completely?

She searched the fog-covered grounds. Her tower, the Spine, and the guardian statues at the Storm Gates poked out of the murk. Everything else was lost. She eyed the shield of wards that covered the Spine like a net.

"Thedus activated the castle wards," Thira said.

Thedus stood in the middle of the workshop, gazing at the rafters. The pattern always seemed to captivate the lost man.

"How?" Rashk asked.

"He placed his palm on the Titan Gates."

It explained nothing, but then Thedus was a mystery. No one seemed to know when he had come to the Isle, or even if he was a Wise One at all. Like the stones underfoot, he had always been. Rashk glared at his tangled hair, wishing she could pierce his skull. If she ever discovered a way to dissect thoughts, she would. Bloodmagi could, and did, by scooping out brains. But even Rashk had her limits; she had no wish to kill the man.

"Do you have anything that might pass as tea?"

Rashk pointed a claw at a shelf. "Bandages and salve." It was an order.

Without argument, Thira shrugged off her coat and set about cleaning her wounds.

Rashk sniffed at a pot, trying to recall what she had last used it for. A poultice of entrails. It would do. She cleaned the pot with sand, rinsed it, and dropped a water rune in the bowl. When it filled, she set the pot on a heating stone. In minutes, the water began to spit, and Rashk added a pale root to the boiling water.

Thira sat by the window, tending her shoulder. Every so often, she paused to whistle. When nothing answered, she returned to her wounds.

Rashk poured three cups of milky liquid, handed one to Thira, and set another beside Thedus. He was sitting on the stone floor, gazing at his hand as if only just noticing it was attached to his body.

"Is this poison fog part of the castle Wards?" Rashk asked.

"Thedus said it was the Fey."

Rashk met the woman's dark gaze. Strain etched the corner of Thira's eyes and that ram-rod spine was slightly bent. The Mistress of Novices smelled of defeat.

"The *Fey?*" Rashk hissed. "But—"

"They are bedtime stories used to frighten brats."

"Yes."

Thira took a thoughtful sip of her tea. "However muddy the water, it's still water. Truth can be buried in myth. Sifting through the lies simply requires finesse." She gave another whistle, and waited, searching the mists. When nothing stirred in the dim light, she set her cup on the ledge, nearly shattering it. "I shouldn't have left him outside," she murmured.

Rashk did not ask whom she meant. It was certainly not the small man-child Zoshi, but her shape-shifting familiar. She'd left him outside of the Storm Gates as a crow.

Thira looked lost without the familiar by her side.

"*Is* it the Fey?" asked Rashk.

"The one man who may know is not here. And the man who surely knows is madder than the first." Thira pinched her nose and closed her eyes. "I'm open to suggestions, but those... *phantoms* are not Forsaken, and they are not Voidspawn. So let us work off the assumption that those things are Fey, of which we know very little." She opened her eyes. "With that in mind—what *do* we know?"

"That Tharios needs his throat slit."

"Practical as always." The thought seemed to bolster the woman. "I think it's safe to conclude that Tharios has been scheming for some time. He already possessed forbidden power. And yet... he had his eye on the Archlord's throne. Why?"

"The Fire Imp talked of libraries in the upper levels," Rashk confided. "Could he have wanted knowledge?"

"Perhaps." Thira plucked up her tea. "You said Tharios showed you a sketch of Soisskeli's Stave."

"He did," Rashk said. "And the man-child, Zoshi, described it from the ritual chamber."

"The stave that Tharios used to open the portal?"

"Yes."

"But Soisskeli's Stave binds; it does not open portals."

"A staff has two ends. What good is the power to bind if you have nothing to bind?"

Thira frowned, considering the possibility. "As common as portals were before the Shattering, legend may not have even thought to mention the portal enchantment. But that..." she hesitated.

"Would be formidable," Rashk finished. "Most artifacts are. I've long suspected as much. Legend never explained where Soisskeli found the dragons he used in the war."

"If it is the same stave that Zoshi described, then that means Tharios had the stave before he was named Archlord," Thira pointed out.

"Yes, but Isek could have escorted him to the Archlord's chambers after Marsais fled... or maybe he only had a part of the stave. A segment could have been in the vault."

"Perhaps." Thira took another thoughtful sip of her tea. "Tharios didn't have the stave when I chased him into the Nameless. That means he didn't use it to open a portal to the Fey. There's something more that we're missing—some greater plan. And I wonder...were the Fey even part of his schemes? What if we forced his hand when we barged into the council chamber?"

"The hawk was waiting and we startled it."

Thira stood and leaned on the windowsill, gazing down at the mist. "I have often wondered what curse lay on that Nameless chamber. The wards, the guardian statues, all of it centered on the Spine; not the castle. What if the wards were designed to keep something *in* and not out?"

"A prison."

"Exactly."

"You think the Fey were trapped in the Nameless chamber?"

"Considering that he locked himself in that room, and the mist appeared shortly after, I would say it's a plausible theory."

"If the mist is really the Fey, and we startled the hawk, then what is his real prey?"

"Likely something far worse," Thira breathed. "I think Tharios simply needed a diversion."

Rashk followed that line of thought. "Most of the Isle still believes he is Archlord. He is using the mist to hide in confusion—to scatter and divide and kill us one at a time." Rashk had used the tactic herself; it was effective. "And as long as the poison remains, we can't even send a Whisper."

A tight smile cracked Thira's lips. "We need to find Tulipin."

SILENCE HAD MANY FORMS: the warm cloud that filled a mind; a chill of clarity; the emptiness of an abandoned home; the charged air of a hunt. These empty passages should have been silent. But the castle was not quiet. Voices whispered in the mist.

Those voices drowned out the hunt. Words buzzed in her ear and busy thoughts clouded her mind. Soundless, and yet, not. The whispers pushed at the boundary between silence and a scream. With the Fey, that distinction was impossibly thin.

Thira followed on her heels. The air was fitful, and the mist angry. And the woman was encased in a Barrier of runes that she could keep cycling in her sleep.

Rashk stopped at a corner to listen. A needle pricked her instincts. Rashk moved without thought, pulling Thira into a side passage. She threw up a mirror weave, and waited.

Boots thudded, the mist parted, and a group of guards marched past. The Quartermaster, Kreem Wyrmbane, led the squad. He was a hulking southerner from the Thanes who rivaled a Nuthaanian berserker. A dangerous warrior.

Rashk eyed the crimson bands around the guards' arms. That was not part of the Isle uniform. The bands likely distinguished men loyal to Tharios from those who were not.

Two Wise Ones, one at the front, and one at the back, marched with the troop, their weaves parting the mist. After the mist had swallowed the group, Rashk whispered in her companion's ear. "The infirmary is that way. They smelled of the hunt."

Thira hesitated.

"Tulipin may be there," Rashk pressed.

But Thira shook her head. "With Bloodmagi and foul fog invading the castle? There's only one place Tulipin Tuddleberry will be."

Rashk cracked open an ornate door, and eyed the chamber. The blinding light of golden sconces, braziers, and tiles burst through the crack. She sneered as she stepped into the temple of Zahra. The great hypostyle hall appeared empty. She sniffed the air, but the powerful fumes of incense masked any would be assassins.

Mist clung to the floors, but stopped at the far end, curling back, away from the feet of a towering statue. Zahra, The Radiant One, stared from beneath her golden cowl. She held scales in one outstretched hand and a sword in the other.

Rashk did not like Zahra—her breasts were covered, proclaiming her mother to no one. But the Rahuatl had learned to keep such thoughts to herself. The Blessed Order had burnt people for less.

Thira strode down the center of the chamber. Rashk kept to the darker areas, slinking alongside, searching for lurkers. While Thira was looking up into the face of Zahra, Rashk cracked the acolytes' door and slipped through. The rooms were empty of life, but a few acolytes lay curled on the floor. Their god had not saved them from the Fog.

Satisfied, Rashk walked back to the main chamber. "Tulipin is not here. Maybe he ran to another shrine."

With a snort, Thira walked around the massive statue, and Rashk followed her to the back. The woman touched each point of a Sacred

Sun carved into the base. "Praised be Zahra," Thira murmured under her breath. The sun symbol cracked, and a panel opened.

Rashk narrowed her eyes. The Wise Ones' castle did not give up its secrets easily, and although she had teased many from its stone, it was as twisting as a Reaper's lair.

Thira disappeared inside, and Rashk stepped in after, sniffing the air. Zahra's innards smelled of fear.

A tight spiral staircase climbed the statue, ending in its head. Tulipin was there, but the red-haired gnome was not levitating. He was sitting with his back against the statue's skull. The hollow eyes looked down at the temple proper. A perfect vantage point for a spy.

"Thira," the gnome breathed. Huddled as he was, he looked tiny—like a frightened child cowering from shadows. Only he was wizened and hunched, and his quick eyes darted to Rashk. "*She* cannot be here—she's with *them*."

Thira ignored the accusation. "Get off the floor and stop sniveling. You were in the council, too. I could say the same of you."

The gnome climbed to his feet. "I didn't know Tharios was a—" his voice dropped to a quivering whisper. "A Bloodmagi."

"Tharios is one. Rashk is not."

"She's a Rahuatl."

For effect, Rashk flashed her teeth. "I've come to drink your blood and suck the marrow from your bones, Gnome."

He paled and backed against the wall.

Thira made an impatient noise. "Where are all the clerics and acolytes?"

"Yasimina came and rounded them all up."

"And you *hid*," Rashk accused.

"I was protecting the sacredness of the inner sanctum—"

Thira held up a hand. "We made a grave mistake, Tulipin. You and I plotted with a Bloodmagi."

"I had no idea!" he shouted.

"Nor did I. We traded one fool madman for someone far more sinister. Thedus claims this fog is the Fey. I have no reason to doubt him."

Tulipin spluttered. Words like legends, stories, and nonsense flew from his lips. Thira cut him off with a reasonable question. "Do you have a better explanation?"

"Bloodmagic filth."

"That doesn't change the fact that you had a part in this. As did I. Now it's time, in Zahra's name, for you to make amends."

"What can I do? I'm not a warrior."

"True," Thira admitted. "But you are a Wise One who can manipulate air in his sleep."

"What of it? I can't *blow* Tharios away." The gnome fluttered his fingers.

Rashk looked from one to the other, and when the words clicked, she smiled, a slow, feral grin.

CHAPTER 13

BRINEHILDE, priestess of the Sylph, stood alert. Questions swirled in her mind like the falling snow. The day was cold and sharp, and she watched her breath puff into the air. At least it was a natural grey, and not the cursed fog. Under the oak's sprawling branches, there was peace —for now.

Brinehilde glanced at the roots that cradled her shield-sister. If anything happened to Morigan—she could not finish the thought. That path led directly to Oenghus, and the priestess didn't want to be the one to tear that chunk out of the brute's heart. Her thoughts drifted to another, to the boy Zoshi. Was he lost and wandering through the fog? She hoped not.

The Sylph no longer whispered to her. The goddess had fallen silent. With nothing else to do but worry, Brinehilde became restless. Wisps fluttered around Morigan's earthy cradle, but aside from the tiny faeries, the healer was better hidden than herself. As tall as Brinehilde was, and with her distinctive red hair, hiding didn't come easily. But then Nuthaanians weren't known for their stealth, and certainly not for their patience.

She snatched up her quarterstaff and stalked back towards the castle. The moment she walked into the hallway, she heard a distant thud. A knock on wood.

Brinehilde hurried towards the infirmary and stopped before the last hallway. She peeked around the corner. Vague shapes moved in the mist. The shift of chain announced them as soldiers, and one man stood a head taller than the rest. Another knock echoed in the gloom.

The dwarf, Eldred, was in there, injured and helpless, and she did not know if these guards were friend or foe.

The door opened and the guards filed inside. She edged closer, following in on their heels. Immediately, she noticed the crimson bands around their arms—a recent addition to their uniforms.

Brinehilde used the commotion to disappear down a hallway. Keeping an ear to the conversation in the main room, she set her staff against a corner, snatched a blue robe from a hook, and quickly wound up her hair and hid it under a scarf. Only a few stray wisps of red stuck out. It would have to do.

With shoulders slouched, she walked back into the main ward. Leiman was talking with a soldier who rivaled her in height.

"There are traitors in the castle who served Marsais," the large man was saying. "Some guards remain loyal to the Bloodmagi."

What the Void? Brinehilde wanted to shout, but she stilled her tongue and walked towards the room where Eldred had been healed.

"Are you sure, sir?" Leiman asked.

The large man listed the names of traitors: hers and Morigan included.

One word from Leiman, and the troop of guard would turn on her. But the young healer did not so much as glance at her.

She was not well known, but Eldred was, and it was much harder disguising a dwarf. She hurried to his room. A thick bandage wrapped around his skull and his one good eye was closed.

Taal Greysparrow and Shimei Al'eeth had nearly killed the man in the chaotic battle that followed the elemental's release. But thanks to Morigan and Ielequithe, the two men were the ones who were dead. Currently, Eldred slept soundly and quietly—a side-effect of an intensive Healing. There'd be no waking him from that deep sleep.

Brinehilde opened the shutters and looked out. The garden was too far down. She stepped back, surveying the small room. The bed was too low, the cupboard too small. She fixed on the chest at the end of the bed.

Moving quickly, she opened it, eyed the dimensions and began taking out armloads of linens and stuffing them under the bed. When it was empty, she bundled the dwarf in his blanket and wrestled him into the chest. She shut the lid, and quickly stripped the bedding, dumping the linens in a heap on the floor.

A guard stopped at the doorway. He eyed the empty bed, the soiled bedding, then looked at her. Brinehilde arranged a look of solemn duty. "I'm making room for the next unfortunate."

The guard's eyes narrowed. He ordered her to stand back as he moved to the window. He looked over the sill, at the garden beneath, and then his eyes traveled to the chest.

With a muttered oath, Brinehilde grabbed the man's cuirass, clamped a hand over his mouth, and snapped his neck with a clean jerk. He crumpled as she helped him into the bed. Off came his helm, which she chucked out the window before tossing a blanket over him. As soon as the blanket had settled, another guard came to inspect the noise. The woman found Brinehilde solemnly changing the bedding of a patient.

The guard looked at the recently dead. Brinehilde held her breath, then released it when the guard kept walking. Brinehilde edged out into the hallway.

"We *can't* abandon the infirmary," Leiman's voice came firmly down the hallway.

"We need to move you somewhere safe," a deep voice answered. "You can leave two healers here. I'll place a guard. I won't risk the rest of you."

"A pair of healers aren't enough to tend to the patients."

"Three at most," the large man growled. "Unless you want to defy the Archlord, too?"

Brinehilde joined a knot of healers who stood watching. She kept her knees bent and her back slouched. No one betrayed her presence, but Leiman glanced at her.

She gave him a slight nod. Morigan and Eldred were safe. The message seemed to get through to him. He argued for four healers, and once the large man grudgingly agreed, he began issuing orders. The staff hopped to action, emptying shelves and gathering supplies.

When Leiman picked two healers and himself to remain behind, the large man shook his head. "We need skilled healers."

"What of the sick here, sir?"

"You're not staying."

Leiman pressed his lips together, then selected the four who would remain. Brinehilde was the fourth.

The guards and healers filed out, leaving a traitorous Wise One, four guards, three healers, and a suspicious Nuthaanian.

Brinehilde bent over a wounded soldier with a gash on his shoulder. She felt his brow, poked at his bandages, and watched the guards out of the corner of her eye. They were far from relaxed, and rather than taking up positions by the doors, they spread out, watching the healers work. She covertly eyed the remaining Wise One. His robes stretched over his gut, and as he toyed with a medallion around his neck, he stared down his nose at the room.

The Wise One dropped his medallion and nodded to a guard. Tension bled into the air. There was death in the guards' eyes. She needed a distraction. Either the Sylph answered, or it was pure luck. A loud noise, like splintering wood, crashed down the hallway. The Wise One motioned the guards towards the sound, and the two men abandoned their targets, reaching for swords.

As a guard passed, Brinehilde grabbed the man's arm, halting the blade in its sheath. She straightened, yanked him forward, and drove her fist into his jaw. It cracked. Brinehilde lifted the stunned man off his feet and chucked him at his fellow guard. The two went down in a tangle of armor and limbs.

A healer threw himself at the third guard, but the young man was no fighter. The guard drew his sword, and rammed the hilt into the youth's gut. He doubled over, dropping to his knees.

Brinehilde charged at the closest soldier. Beneath her powerful hands, an arm cracked and ribs broke. She swung the reeling guard around and used him as a shield, blocking a sword strike from his fellow guard. Metal scraped against metal.

The sword-wielding guard recovered. He skipped to the side, reaching around her human shield. A blade sliced across her ribs.

An older healer stepped behind Brinehilde's attacker and stabbed up, under his helm. Blood gushed, the man reeled. Brinehilde snatched up a pestle and drove it into his face. As the guard staggered backwards, chanting filled the air.

Brinehilde spun, hurling the pestle at the weaving Wise One. He ducked under the stone missile and dropped his weave. A force slammed into her like a charging bull, and she was blown off her feet. Broken vials and scattered supplies tumbled around her as she hit the ground.

A deep voice burst into the infirmary. A crack split the air. And then, silence. It rang in her ears like a gong. Brinehilde tried to lift her head, but the room was spinning. Knowing death lurked nearby, she struggled to stand, but found her legs useless.

A grizzled, bandaged face came into view. "Who the Void took my armor and stuffed me into a trunk?" Eldred asked.

Brinehilde chuckled, and let her head fall back to the stone.

CHAPTER 14

THE EARTH WAS WARM. It cradled her, and she was loath to wake. Morigan Freyr could not remember the last time she'd slept so soundly.

Before the Wedamen invasion, she thought, *long* before that. But in this cocoon, so like a womb, even thoughts of those terrible years could not shatter the peace.

Morigan had felt this calm before, with Isiilde's mother, Yasine, the Sylph.

A whisper brushed her ear along with a dream-like caress. Mother, sister, daughter, friend, lover, goddess—that brush was everything.

Have courage, Morigan. He lives. And so does my daughter.

The voice washed over her like a cool spring.

A knot untwisted in her heart. *What of the boy?*

The boy is in darkness.

There was sadness there, and regret. But whether that meant the boy was in actual darkness, or caught in the mist, Morigan did not know. The Sylph had little power in this realm.

This darkness must not spread.

With those parting words, Morigan opened her eyes to damp earth and a sliver of light. The roots released their hold, slowly unraveling like snakes, nudging her into a winter's day.

Disoriented, she sat up and put her back to a tree, blinking against the brightness. The world was grey. It usually was on the Isle. Her heart yearned for the starkness of Nuthaan: the endless sky, white-capped crags, and emerald valleys.

Morigan studied her hands. They were stained with blood and earth. As were her clothes. She was a mess.

Footsteps crunched in the snow.

Morigan palmed a knife before playing dead. It didn't take much acting. A tall, broad-shouldered redhead limped into view. Brinehilde's breath caught.

"I'm not dead. I only look it," Morigan croaked.

"Thank the Sylph."

"Beyond a doubt."

Brinehilde sank down beside her. A flask was pressed into her hand, and she drank deeply. The water soothed her throat. Morigan felt like her veins had been drained of blood and refilled with sand. "Oen is alive."

"I'd have to give his body a few good kicks before I believed otherwise. Takes a bit to kill that brute."

"Aye."

"What about Zoshi?"

"He's in darkness."

Brinehilde narrowed her eyes. "That's all she said?"

Morigan nodded, and finished the water.

"The stars never explain themselves," Brinehilde sighed. "They just think the earth will know."

Morigan searched the ground for a clean spot of fresh snow. When she found one, she scooped it up and stuffed it into the flask. Wisps swarmed, heating the flask. She murmured her thanks and drank the melted snow.

"The Quartermaster came by your infirmary with a squad of guards. They were looking for traitors."

"Eldred?"

"Still alive." Brinehilde told her what had happened, and as her words painted the scene, a rage overcame Morigan that made the winter day seem hot.

"Are any of them still alive?"

"Aye, the simpering Wise One. He pissed his pants."

"And?"

"You best hear it for yourself."

Morigan roused herself to stand, but Brinehilde shoved her back to the ground. "Piss Pants isn't going anywhere. If you love your shield-sister, sit and be."

Morigan subsided. Mostly because Brinehilde's grip was like iron, and she was too weak to fight it. She let her head fall back against the tree. Snowflakes fell from the grey sky onto her face. Their touch cooled her skin.

"Besides," Brinehilde said, "If anything happens to you, I'm not keen on dealing with that oaf."

Morigan snorted. "Oen's not going to blame you for my death."

"I don't fancy telling him all the same," Brinehilde insisted. "It'd send him straight into the Keening."

She'd witnessed his grief when Yasine died. She had worried for him then, and she'd worried every day since. A foolish habit she found difficult to break.

Berserkers were dead men walking.

"I'm sure he's headed back. His heart is here," Brinehilde said with certainty.

Morigan chuckled. "His heart belongs to another."

Brinehilde fixed her with a hard eye. "Is that what you think?"

"I've known for some time, Hilde."

"Do you know why I never asked him to take an Oath with me?"

"Because you had more sense than me?"

Brinehilde smirked, and withdrew a second flask, her usual one that was filled with brandy. She took a long swig before continuing. "I won't settle for half a heart. As you well know, that brute talks something awful in his sleep. He's favored by the Sylph, to be sure, but so are you. A stone can gaze at the stars, and the stars gaze back, but neither really understands the other. You're his earth, Morigan."

Morigan looked at her like she'd gone mad. "I think the guards hit your head too hard."

Brinehilde smiled, glancing towards the sky. "I'm only passing on what I'm told." She climbed to her feet. "As long as you let me borrow him. He's always good for a rough tumble."

"As sturdy as they come," Morigan agreed. She gripped Brinehilde's offered hand, and the woman pulled her to her feet.

Brinehilde kept her hand. "Oenghus will find his way back."

"Bloodied or on his shield."

Both women spat.

CHAPTER 15

"Is the Labyrinth Sea usually this calm?" The only sea Isiilde had ever glimpsed was the Fell Sea. It was nearly always windy. And yet here, the sails and flags hung limp.

Rivan shook his head. "Not like this. Not this still. We're dead in the water," he admitted, then lowered his voice. "There's talk of a curse, on account of Marsais."

"What has he done now?"

Rivan gave her a lopsided grin. "Nothing recent. I mean, he hasn't helped himself much." He cleared his throat, and glanced over his shoulder, expecting the immortal to materialize. "It's what he did in the past. Every Mearcentian child is told about the Trickster. I didn't realize *He* was the man himself."

"The Trickster?"

"You haven't heard the legend?"

"No."

"The Trickster abducted the Sea God's own daughter: Faamu-sami. Her name means to 'make the sea burn'."

Isiilde frowned. "Oh. That. How could you have not known? He started telling you the story while we were walking through Vaylin on the ridge."

"The fish woman?"

"Yes."

"But he didn't abduct that, er… woman."

"Maybe the legend is wrong."

Rivan began worrying a splinter in the railing. "Or maybe Marsais lied," he murmured.

There was that. Isiilde could not deny it. With a sigh, she turned towards the ship, leaning back against the rail. Since her transformation, she felt the touch of eyes constantly, from the soldiers and sailors, from men and women alike. When she looked the humans in the eye, they glanced away.

What were they afraid of? Isiilde didn't know. She no longer cared what humans thought of her.

A sailor scraped flint against stone, and a spark leapt to a pile of wood shavings. He picked up a tinder and touched it to the bowl of his pipe. Before the man shook out the flame, Isiilde called to the spark with a gentle whisper.

The flame leapt from the tinder to her finger, and the sailor blinked, glancing in her direction. He dropped his pipe, and hurried away.

But Isiilde only had eyes for the flameling on her fingertip. It flickered around her skin. She could feel its heat, its rage, and the desire to consume. But for now, the flameling was content, and so was she.

Isiilde hummed a soft tune, and the flame flickered in the vibration. It grew, and she shaped it into a roiling ball that sat in her palm. She tossed the tiny fireball to her other hand, casually moving it back and forth.

The crew was watching her again. This time, they did not look away. There was fear in their eyes. It made her hum with pleasure.

"Please don't start the boat on fire," Rivan muttered. He wasn't afraid of her.

"As long as everyone behaves, I won't," she promised.

"Have you mastered your fire, then?"

Isiilde lifted a slim shoulder. "Can you master the sea?"

"Of course not. Only a fool would try."

"And yet, humans have been ordering me to control it my entire life," she said with feeling. "No one ever thinks to blame a ship captain for a storm at sea. Fire is like the wind and sea; no one can master it."

His eyes softened with sympathy. "I see." And she believed him.

Isiilde stared into the hypnotizing flicker. "Isn't it odd? Fire warms, fire cooks, fire comforts, and yet, it kills. Humans both love and fear it."

"I suppose," he finally said. "But maybe that's part of its wonder."

Rivan stuck a quick finger into her ball of fire and withdrew it before the flame latched onto his flesh. The tendrils flickered and danced merrily, and she grinned. It had liked his playful touch.

"Tell me the Mearcentian legend about the Trickster."

"It's been a long while since I've heard it, and I'm no bard, but the gist of it is that the Trickster abducted Nereus' daughter on the eve of her wedding to Aesir's son, the god of the winds. The union was supposed to unite the sea and wind. That way, the winds would no longer fight the currents, pushing ships backwards.

"After the Trickster abducted Faamu-Sami, he seduced her, and tricked her into giving herself to him—forgetting her promise to the wind. It sparked a war. Many ships were lost. The seas became too dangerous to sail. The armies of wind and sea searched for Faamu-Sami, but the Trickster hid her in plain sight and threatened the gods with her life. But Malietoa, Aesir's son, unraveled the Trickster's puzzle and took back his bride, uniting wind and sea. That's why the Windtalkers can beseech the wind for safe passage."

"Are Aesir and Nereus really gods, or are they simply kings?"

Rivan turned dark with anger. "Of course they're gods. Our prayers reach their ears."

She looked towards the drumming priests. Their prayers were not working now. Coincidence or curse? Isiilde tossed the ball of fire from hand to hand, watching it twirl in the air. "The only thing that separates a man from a god is knowledge," she said.

Marsais had confided that to her. He'd also warned her not to repeat it. Isiilde was intrigued by Rivan's reaction—the scar on his cheek went taut.

"Those are words of heretics and fiends."

"By your Order's decree, I'm only an animal. It shouldn't matter what I say."

He deflated. "You're not an animal, Isiilde."

"Are you a heretic, then?"

"I don't know," he admitted. "But I know you're no animal."

"Except when I was a parrot."

Rivan blushed. "If I had known—"

"You did not." She closed her hand, and the fire melded with her skin, trailing into a wisp of smoke. She could feel the flameling, sense the echo of joy that it had burnt—if only briefly. But that spark wasn't far. Flame roared, as constant as a bonfire, deep in her marrow.

"Your version of events is nothing like the one Marsais told me. But I suppose both could be true," she said.

Rivan frowned in thought. "I don't think so. There is only one truth."

"I think it depends on who's telling the tale. Just like my fire, it can be many things."

"If Marsais didn't abduct the sea god's daughter, then why would she go to him for help?" Rivan asked.

The question gave her pause. And it lingered with her through the night. King, madman, seer, Archlord, friend, lover, master, heretic— who really was Marsais zar'Vaylin?

THE WINDTALKERS CONTINUED their steady drumming, but the wind refused to stir. The sailors were restless, and that put the Elite on edge. They no longer appeared on deck without their weapons.

Whether it was the calm seas, or Marsais, or her own presence, she did not know. But something was brewing, and as she lounged on a longboat, every single Mearcentian gave her a wide berth.

A shadow blotted her sunlight. Isiilde cracked an eye at the intruder. Acacia stood beside her perch. She had traded her own armor for the Elite's desert gear. Otherwise, the paladins would be cooked in their steel.

"Oenghus wants to send you back on the first friendly ship we encounter," Acacia confided.

"Why are you telling me?"

Acacia settled herself on the edge of the boat, and Isiilde sat up, watching the woman's every move. "I agree with Oenghus. But I think you have a right to make that decision."

"At least someone agrees."

"You're a liability, Isiilde," Acacia said bluntly. "I wouldn't let any of these sailors join us. Not where we're going."

"Rivan is coming."

"Rivan may be young, but he's a soldier trained for war. You are not —you don't even have proper clothes. And what will you eat? We have provisions: bread, nuts, rice and dried fruits, but that won't last. Salted meat and whatever we can hunt in the wasteland will be all that's left."

Isiilde showed her pouch to the captain. "My clothes and provisions are in here."

"In there?"

"Yes."

"How much?"

"Plenty," she said vaguely, wondering if it was true. "And as for clothes, I'd be just as happy to walk over the hot sand in full daylight without a scrap on my skin."

"You'd stand out like a beacon, to friend and foe alike."

"I stand out wherever I go, Acacia."

The barest of smiles lifted the woman's lips. "I'll try to talk him out of it."

"Are you angry with Oen? Is that why you're so keen to help me? Rivan said he caught him with a woman—one of the Elite."

Acacia hesitated, weighing her next words. "The wait before a battle is the hardest part of all. Some warriors, men and women alike, need a release—some way to ease the wait. I was never one of those warriors, but I'm happy for those who find a moment's peace. There's little chance we'll return."

Isiilde narrowed her eyes. "Then why are you warning me of his plans? Why do you want me to come?"

"Because the only man who has an inkling of where to find Finnow's Spire is currently drunk and senseless, and steadily losing what is left of his mind."

"What else can Marsais do?" she defended. "There isn't any wind."

"I don't know, but the rum certainly isn't helping."

"What do you want me to do? We're no longer bonded."

"I see the worry in your eyes, Isiilde. You still love him.You're still friends."

It was true. Despite her anger over his scheming, Marsais had hooks in her heart. His slightest move tugged on the barbs. Love, she decided, was a decidedly painful thing.

"Oen is still his friend, too," she pointed out. It was the simple truth. The two men shared a bond far deeper than hers—one of tested time and long hardship.

Acacia nodded towards the hatch. "Oenghus isn't having much luck with him."

Isiilde followed her gaze aft to where Marsais stood on deck. His eyes were vacant, and he wore the same loose breeches that barely clung to his narrow hips. She reminded him of Thedus.

Oenghus stood by his side looking worried and helpless.

"There are some things only a woman can mend," Acacia confided.

Isiilde sighed, and after a moment's hesitation, walked over to the men. Marsais stared, unseeing, and seeing all of time. His eyes were wide and white.

"Don't touch him," Oenghus warned.

Isiilde chewed on her lower lip in thought, watching Marsais shuffle towards the fore. A ripple of movement swelled over the boat. Sailors scrambled to get out of his way—or maybe Oenghus' glare. She didn't like the look in the crew's eyes: dark, calculating, and full of fear.

The paladins formed a casual semi-circle around Marsais—even Lucas, whose stomach had calmed with the sea.

"Can't we just toss him overboard ourselves?" Lucas growled at his captain. The veteran paladin was scarred from his bald head to his missing toes, and his temperament was no less coarse.

"You have my permission—after the Isle is safe," Acacia replied dryly.

The man smirked.

Oenghus cracked his knuckles. The air was heavy with threat. Isiilde could taste it. She frowned at Marsais, then placed a hand on his chest, over his heart.

"No!" Oenghus hissed.

Marsais stiffened. His back arched as he rose to his toes, dragged upwards by some unseen force. His head fell back, mouth stretched wide towards the sky. Drops of bloody sweat rolled down his forehead while his fingers were pulled towards the deck. A scream tore from his throat.

"Marsais!" she gasped.

Something cut his strings, and he fell forward into her arms.

CHAPTER 16

Isiilde sat in the dark cabin, watching Marsais. Wood creaked, and a single candle flickered, casting shadows across his sharp features. From dark to light, and back again—not unlike the man himself. As she studied his face, she wondered what she really knew about her former master and bonded.

Lover of fiends. The thought of Saavedra set her on edge. But another unlooked-for memory drowned out the smirking fiend and her upswept ears: he had also set her blood on fire with his touch. *Lover of nymphs.*

The mere memory made her flush with heat. She let out a slow breath, and tried to focus on the days leading up to their fateful meeting with the fiend. Of the attack on the Lome, her capture, and the Ardmoor fortress. Memory played like a child's top in her mind's eye—spinning constantly, round and round, until she thought she would go mad.

In the cave with the chained girl, when the water had churned, she saw a vision in the pool: Marsais bent over the girl, his blade sliding into her throat. But his hands were gentle, and his eyes so full of love that one might think he'd simply lulled the girl to sleep.

Light and dark; a constant conundrum.

Marsais awoke with a gasp. He pawed at his chest in terror, then lifted the blanket to check the rest of his body.

"I'm sure it's still there," Isiilde said dryly. Her concern for him had not dampened her anger.

Marsais looked at the nymph. There was steel in his eyes, the kind that reminded her of daggers. A moment later, recognition softened his gaze and he let his head fall back on the pillow.

"Isiilde."

"We're not bonded," she explained, sensing his confusion. "We're on a ship bound for Fomorri that's dead in the water. The crew is scared of you, and likely mutinous. Oenghus is distracting them with ale and stories of valor."

Stomping feet and rowdy voices thrummed through the ship. The night, along with her father's boisterous presence, had cooled tempers.

"You're not supposed to be here," he whispered.

There was pain in his eyes, but whether it was genuine or affected, she no longer knew. "I barely know you," she said.

Marsais shifted on the pillow to study her. "Do you need to?" His voice was rough, like nails scraping against her ears. To give herself time to answer, she reached for a waterskin. With a sigh, he scooted up, slumping wearily against the bulkhead. She helped him drink.

"What is real and what is an act?"

Marsais laughed bitterly. "My existence in this realm is one large and ugly act. I tire of it."

"Of living?"

"By the gods, yes."

His fervor pricked her eyes. She could not imagine a life without Marsais. Faced with that grim vision, anger seemed a silly thing. She tossed it aside.

"I think you knew what Saavedra would ask of you. You knew bedding a fiend would destroy our bond. You wanted to protect me— even at the cost of pushing me away."

He did not reply, so she continued.

"You stole my blood for the very same reason. To protect this realm at any cost, even to yourself."

Still nothing. His lips were sealed, but there was a tremble, so very faint, and yet so deep.

"I love you, Marsais, whether or not you let me—I always will," she whispered. "But you're not the only one who wants to protect this realm. I bear responsibility for this mess."

The mask cracked. "You bear none."

"Regardless of what you believe, I do. Even unknowingly, I played a part."

"You're but a single thread in a tapestry of disaster."

"However small, I was still present. Stop shielding me. I won't run away—no more than you or Oen will."

He waved a tired hand. "You're here. There is no changing that."

Silence wrapped around the two, heavy with things not said and everything that could not be taken back. Isiilde looked down at her hands—the same that had struck him with anger.

"I'm sorry I slapped you in the garden."

"You had every right to."

She shook her head. "It was childish. You're trying to stop a madman on the other side of the realm. You sacrificed far more of yourself than a vial of blood. Despite what you said in the garden, your heart was not in it."

Marsais snorted, a derisive, bitter sound. "A whore sells her body for a crust of bread to feed children she never asked for. It's merely a sacrifice for survival. There's little difference. I simply whored myself out for a realm."

"Both are born of desperation. Not by choice."

"I have no pride left to lose," he said bluntly. "I've endured far worse. And I would suffer a thousand such nights to see you safe. Do you understand? The only thing that concerns me is your safety."

"I won't be put into a box."

"I offered you a luxurious island!" he snapped.

"It's still a cage," she bit out.

"If Mearcentia is a cage than Fomorri is the Nine Halls." There was anger in his voice, but pain in his eyes. His breath was shallow with near panic.

Isiilde laid a hand on his chest—over his scar. The tension in his brow eased, and quiet tears rolled down his cheeks; tears that he did not notice.

Isiilde stared into his eyes. "You told me once that there are a thousand terrible deaths; a myriad of unbearable Fates—all suffered before by others. You're afraid for me. But I am sick of being afraid."

"Fear makes us human."

She ran her fingers over his cheek, catching his tears. "I'm not human. I'm a nymph. And I won't be collared or locked away like a fragile vase. Until you understand that—I will not share my bond with you. I can't."

"I'm not asking you to give yourself to me again. I do not want it. I severed our bond for a reason." The moment he said it, he clenched his teeth, lips forming a thin, hard line.

Isiilde narrowed her eyes. "Why?" She waited, hand on his warm skin, feeling the rapid gallop of his heart. But he remained tight-lipped and silent.

"Answer me, Marsais," she demanded.

"There is nothing but death down this path," he finally whispered.

The words triggered a cascade of thought. Pieces connected like a pattern of runes on a board. In that instant, she saw his strategy, as she so often did when they played King's Folly.

"Two spirits intertwined," she mused aloud. "What would happen if one half died? The surviving half would never be whole..."

"It could kill you," he rasped.

Isiilde imagined the cold touch of death wrapping around her spirit and snuffing out her fire. She shivered. But a life without Marsais was a far worse thought. She pushed it aside and focused on the present.

"When we arrived in Mearcentia, you said that visions of death are never set in stone."

Marsais sighed in defeat. "The heart does not always listen to reason. When it comes to you, I'm a sentimental old fool."

"I've told you before, you're not old," she whispered.

"Then a fool, at the very least."

"I've said as much," she agreed.

A pained laugh escaped his lips. He choked on it, and took a shaky breath. "I'm sorry," he said.

"For what?"

He scraped a palm across his eyes. "For not asking to use your blood."

"I wouldn't have given it to you—not for a Blood Portal."

"I know."

"Then don't be sorry. It had to be done. Isn't that why you killed that girl, the scryer? So she wouldn't slow us down?"

The chill in her voice gave him pause. It was like the first crack in a pane of glass. Marsais looked away. "A Blood Ritual dragged a fiendish spirit into this realm and bound it to her pliable mind. She could not have survived outside of that pool," he murmured. "But yes, I did what needed doing."

Isiilde paled. She had no idea such a thing was possible. The thought of her spirit bound to a fiend made her sick.

It is a mercy, Marsais had said before killing the girl. But she had thought it was an excuse—an easy way out. How could she have thought so ill of him? He had not murdered the girl for convenience, but rescued her from torment in the only way he could.

A jumble of words rose in her throat, but in the end, they all fell short. Isiilde sat speechless, silently berating her own foolishness. But then, had that been part of his plan? Did he *want* her to believe him capable of such a selfish act to push her away? Her mind spun with possibilities.

"Do as you will, Isiilde. I will play my part." He struggled to rise, waving her off when she moved to help.

"Marsais," she finally managed. Her voice only a whisper.

"Hmm?" he asked, reaching for a shirt.

"You can't do your part if you starve yourself to death. You need to eat."

Isiilde plucked a strawberry from her pouch, and his gaze fell on the fruit poised between her fingertips. His eyes misted with emotion—a look of pure agony. She nearly pulled him into an embrace, but resisted the impulse. They could not be. He would not risk her.

"That is an exquisite weave," he said, hoarsely. Then plucked the berry from her hand and tossed it into his mouth, stem and all.

"Did you expect any less?" she asked, pushing a plate of food towards him.

"Never."

Marsais sat down to eat.

"What did you see earlier?" she asked after a time.

"What don't I see?"

"On deck... when you screamed."

"Ah, that..." His lips twitched. "I saw the end."

CHAPTER 17

Acacia Mael knelt on deck. Her forehead rested on the hilt of her sword, knuckles white around the leather. She clutched the Sacred Sun, pressing it between flesh and hilt. The echoes of singing bellowed from the depths of the hold, but she ignored the festivities.

When she opened her eyes, there was no flare of light, no warmth between her fingers. Her prayers had gone unanswered.

She heard the approach of a familiar gait. Moments later, Lucas Cutter stopped at her side to stretch his broad shoulders. A few beads of sweat glistened on his dark brown skin. He'd lent his back to the oars.

"Rivan looked about to try his hand at drinking, so I had him take my place on the bench."

Acacia climbed to her feet with a creak of leather. She glanced at the holy symbol in her palm. Still cold. Despair threatened as she looked to the Sylph's moon for answers. Its red companion trailed in its light, while the Dark One's moon was a vague, swiftly approaching silhouette.

If only they had more time.

"It's not too late, Captain. We could turn southwest and sail for the Fell Sea like normal men."

"Has anything about this past month been ordinary?"

"Not a thing," he admitted. "I want to heave that seer into the sea."

"The crew already tried."

Lucas rasped out a laugh. It was a rare sound these days. After what he'd lived through, humor was buried deep. It had a long way to travel, giving his laugh a frigid edge.

"There is that," he said. "It helps to have a berserker as a friend."

"Of the two, the seer is far more dangerous. Have you heard the legend of the Trickster?"

Lucas shook his head.

"The Trickster challenged Nereus, the God of the Sea, and lived."

"Nothing but fear and superstitious myth."

"Maybe so," Acacia admitted. "But you were there when Marsais fought the Hound."

A muscle in his cheek spasmed. He could not deny that duel.

"I don't know what we'll find on the Isle of Wise Ones, but I do know we'll need him."

"*If* we return."

She searched the sky. Not a cloud, not a breeze. Even the water looked lazy, like a slow rolling pond of silver. The Windtalkers continued their steady beat, but their drums had taken on a note of panic. Their god had likely abandoned them.

Acacia knew that feeling. That same fear clutched at her own heart. The cool metal in her palm felt unbearably heavy.

"Do you want to reach Fomorri?" she asked her lieutenant.

He looked her in the eye; a long history lay between the two warriors. Shared horrors and agony, and sights that could never be forgotten.

"I'd rather go down with this ship than return."

Acacia felt the same way. "Oenghus wants to leave Isiilde on the ship or send her away with a passing merchant. Either way, she'll need an escort. There are the Lome strays to worry about, too. Aside from Marsais, myself, and Oenghus, you and Rivan are the only ones I'd trust to guard her. You don't have to come."

The paladin stiffened to attention. "I would follow you into the Nine Halls and beyond, sir."

"You already have. You don't need to again."

"Always the jokester."

She smirked, extending her arm. "To the Nine Halls, then."

"And beyond." He gripped her forearm. "My blade has been itching to repay Fomorri hospitality."

Acacia eyed the scars covering his body. Fomorri relished torture. They were masters of the craft. And years ago, Acacia had rescued what they'd left of her lieutenant. On most days, he resented her for it.

"There's no place for vengeance on a battlefield."

"You know me better than that, Captain. If I promise to keep a clear head, will you swear you won't let them take me alive again?"

"I swear."

"Good." Lucas ran a finger along a patch of mottled scarring. "I have to admit to being curious—I'd like to see what the *ol'bastard* does next."

"You've been in Oenghus' company for far too long."

"Without a doubt." His lips curled upwards with a twist of scars. "Long enough to go join the festivities."

In the past month, she'd seen more life in him than she'd seen in years. "Have at it, Lieutenant."

"You?"

Acacia shook her head. "I'll keep praying. Perhaps Zahra will answer."

He touched his fingers to the Sacred Sun around his own neck, and bowed, leaving his captain alone beneath the moons.

Acacia returned to her supplication, resting her forehead against the pommel of her sword and clutching the Sacred Sun. She needed an answer to her prayers. Or even a rebuke. Anything would be welcome, but the Guardians felt distant.

Marsais' words had wormed under her skin. Doubt, confusion, and now heresy. The Knight Captain of the Blessed Order had conspired with a fiend. The gods, she feared, had abandoned her. And rightly so. She had broken the Laws of her Order.

"The gods have abandoned you, Captain!" a voice cut through her prayers with enough strength to thunder over a battlefield.

Acacia jerked to her feet.

"But I have not."

Marsais stood on deck with Isiilde at his shoulder. He was dressed in a clinging robe and trousers, and his hair gleamed white in the moon-light. For a second, his eyes flashed silver, or so she imagined.

His words were for Captain Carvil, not for her. Still, Acacia found his word choice unnerving. She always had the impression he was reading her mind.

Was Marsais trying to incite a murderous mob? If so, the Windtalkers looked as though they were planning on throwing the first stone.

Acacia sheathed her sword as she hurried to his side. The Windtalker chieftess was fuming at the seer. "You have cursed us! The wind no longer sings to my ears."

"My dear woman," Marsais said softly. "Once the blight is gone from your ship—namely me—you will hear the wind again. But not in the way the captain had planned." He gave Carvil a pointed look. "I'll be gone from your sight soon enough. Is she ready to sail?"

"She has been ready to sail for days," Carvil growled.

Marsais looked at the limp sails. Not even a flutter. "Quiet your drums, if you please, clear the poop deck, save for the helmsman. The wind is about to pick up."

Carvil didn't question his claim. "All hands on deck!" he bellowed.

The call was taken up by others, traveling below deck as sailors raced to their positions. Marsais stepped in front of the helm.

"Do you know what he's doing?" Acacia asked under her breath.

Isiilde raised a shoulder in a casual shrug. "You'll get used to it."

"What did you say to him?"

"I gave him a strawberry."

Oenghus stomped up the companionway ladder, took in the scene, then glared at the two women. "What's he up to now?"

Isiilde spread her hands. "Why is everyone asking me? He never tells me a thing."

Acacia doubted Marsais confided in anyone. Spending any amount of time in his company felt like playing a game of King's Folly. She wondered if he was cryptic by nature or was it a cultivated habit?

"Well," Oenghus rumbled. "You won't have to worry about him much longer. You're going back with the ship."

Isiilde turned on her father. "I will burn this ship into the water before that happens. Do you understand?"

Oenghus bared his teeth. "I'll have Acacia truss you up and dunk you in the sea."

"Don't bring me into this," Acacia warned.

The rail creaked in protest as Oenghus leaned against it. "I was hoping you'd join the festivities."

"I'm told you found another woman with calloused hands to distract you."

"I didn't have a kilt handy, so I figured I didn't stand a chance with you."

"You don't. And won't."

"You're still talking to me."

"Would it help if I ran a blade through you?"

"That's how I met Morigan. She ran me through, then afterwards we took an Oath."

Before Acacia could ask for the rest of the story, Marsais dragged his toe across the deck, tracing a perfect semi-circle. An expectant hush fell over the ship.

"Whatever happens... Do not disturb me." Marsais looked from the ship captain to Oenghus, issuing the same order with his eyes.

He stood for a moment, body tense, face raised towards the stars, bathed in the moon's light. Acacia had seen that stance before—in the wilderness of Vaylin, when he stood on a rock in a river.

With a breath, he began to move, as fluid as a dancer. Ethereal runes flared to life as his fingers weaved. The Lore sped from his lips, a murmur that gained strength with every added rune.

Isiilde watched with wide, captivated eyes. Her lips parted, and Acacia edged away from the combustible nymph.

"Do you see what he's weaving?" she asked Oenghus.

"Void if I know."

"He's weaving wind."

"Bollocks." Oenghus spat.

And then Acacia saw the wind. The ethereal runes took shape, rising into the sky over the ship. Marsais' voice boomed like thunder, the coins woven into his goatee chimed wildly, and he thrust out his arms, fingers splayed. A spidery tendril of mist wavered from each fingertip, shooting towards the sails.

A squall slammed into their backs. The entire ship groaned, and Isiilde lurched, catching herself on the rail.

The wheel spun wildly as Carvil and the helmsman tried to wrestle it back under control. Waves rose over the rail to crash on deck, and Acacia pulled Isiilde down beside the bulwark.

One man faced the wind—Marsais was floating over the deck. With a powerful chant that thrummed in the air, he spread his arms and brought his hands together with a slap.

The whirlwind calmed to a steady breeze. It pushed at the sails, filling them to bursting. The *Squall* leapt forward. The captain bellowed out orders. Men raced up ratlines, climbing aloft, while others secured lines on deck. The clipper heeled so far that its lee rail touched the water.

"Twenty knots!" a man yelled.

"Let's hope he doesn't summon more wind," Carvil shouted to his second.

Oenghus held Isiilde firmly by the arm, keeping her upright. But the nymph barely seemed to notice. Her gaze was fixed on the swirl of runes that pushed at the sails.

"Is this normal for a Wise One?" Acacia yelled at Oenghus.

"Not one bit. Are you surprised?"

"No."

"Sprite, can you tell what the ol'bastard did?"

"He bound the wind to each sail," she answered without hesitation. There was wonder and fear in her eyes. "But that's not all…"

"What more is there?" Acacia pressed.

"Do you remember when he taught me to weave a Barrier?"

Acacia nodded.

"There's a Barrier over his air weave. I don't know how he's juggling all of those runes. It should be impossible."

"Why would he need a Barrier for the wind?" Acacia asked.

"The same reason he needed a Barrier for his water rune against my fire—he's pushing against another weave."

"What other weave?" Acacia asked, searching the seas.

"Nereus," Oenghus growled.

Acacia blinked. "That's impossible."

"It explains why there hasn't been any wind," Isiilde answered.

"Blood and ashes," Oenghus cursed.

Acacia followed his gaze. Blood trickled from Marsais' nose. When a Wise One drew too much power, they cracked like a dried out waterskin. She wondered how long he could keep channeling before he burst.

CHAPTER 18

Marsais juggled for a night and a day. When the sun set on the second day, mist rose from the sea, spreading a chill over the deck. Marsais collapsed and curled into a long-limbed ball, trembling with exhaustion.

Isiilde draped a cloak over him and Oenghus pressed a waterskin to his lips. Marsais gulped down the water like a parched man.

Some Wise Ones were swept away by the Gift's powerful currents, but Marsais had thrown himself into the river long ago. That didn't mean it was always gentle.

With the weave gone, the wind lost some of its power, but a soft breeze still stirred against the sails. Either Nereus had lost interest, or his domain did not stretch to Fomorri. Carvil shouted a string of orders at his crew. For sails to be trimmed, and others furled.

Marsais sat up, only to slump forward. Despite his exhaustion, he focused on the grey horizon. The *Squall* drifted in a murky realm of fog. And the silence soon gave way to something else—a distant wailing. Isiilde froze. The sound was inhuman, torn from some unholy pit. Every fiber in her body recoiled.

Oenghus slowly rose, stepping in front of the two like a protective bear, his gaze fixed on an unseen point. Every muscle in his body quivered with tension.

"What's making that sound?" Isiilde asked Acacia.

"The Wailing Wall," she whispered. "It is the screaming of Fomorri captives."

Isiilde felt sick.

Oenghus glanced at his daughter. "It gets worse. Much worse."

"I'm not leaving."

Oenghus looked as though he wanted to hit her over the head and send her back in chains. With a grunt, he unslung his targe and walked towards the fore, disappearing into the fog.

The leadsman dropped a knotted rope over the rail. The weight hit the water with a splash. It sank, and then the sailor hoisted it back up, whispering out the depth. As the *Squall* drifted through the murk, he repeated the process as fast as he could read the line.

The creak of the hull, the shift of rigging, and the splash of the lead line bounced over the water with alarming sharpness. Isiilde feared the ship was about to sail over the edge of the world.

She turned to Rivan. "Can you help me get him below deck?"

Between the two of them, they hoisted his arms over their shoulders and half-dragged him below deck. Kasja and Elam followed, eager to be away from the constant wailing.

Together, the four wrestled Marsais into his cabin. He collapsed onto the berth. Kasja pressed bread into his shaking hands while Isiilde tucked a blanket around his body. He caught Isiilde's eyes briefly.

"I need to rest." His voice was raw from chanting.

Hesitation reared its head. But only for a moment. Isiilde ushered the others out, then sat by his side on the berth. She brushed the hair from his eyes, and bent over him, touching her lips softly to his own. A part of her feared to find the fiend on his lips, but it was only Marsais; he tasted like the sea, only this time, she was the sun.

"You're not playing fairly. You waited until I was vulnerable," he murmured against her lips.

"I always cheat. Are you still angry with me?"

"Terribly."

"Good."

He buried his fingers in her hair, and drew her near, kissing her deeply. For a moment, she was lost. But she was not the only one who cheated at King's Folly. Isiilde pulled away. This, it seemed, would be their dance—two cheaters conning each other through life.

"You could bring a man back from the grave."

"That was my hope."

"I'll try my best," he promised, caressing her cheek.

Isiilde caught his hand, and kissed it before tucking it under the blanket. "You had better."

Fearing that her resolve would falter, she left. But once she stepped outside, she slumped against the bulkhead, closing her eyes with a shaky breath. Her blood burned hot with desire. But if she rekindled their bond, would he order her back to Mearcentia? She could not risk her freedom again. She would not.

Isiilde opened her eyes. Rivan was standing off to the side, waiting, while Kasja was pacing like an anxious dog.

"Isiilde," Rivan whispered, leaning in close. He stopped short of grabbing her arm. "We can't let Kasja and Elam go to Fomorri. You *must* take them back to Mearcentia."

"Only if you come, too," she said.

"If that's what it takes to see them safe, then so be it."

She studied him for a moment. "I always know when you're plotting during King's Folly—you get an overly noble look about you."

Rivan opened his mouth to deny it, but lying was frowned upon in the Blessed Order, so he closed it.

"Marsais needs me. I can't leave."

"I feel the same about my captain and lieutenant, but…" He glanced at the two Lome. "They don't *know* what is happening."

Isiilde frowned at the feral woman, an augur, dressed in a mangle of salvaged nets, canvas sacks, and bobbles in her hair. She was a matted mess. Elam could not be over ten. He worshipped Oenghus, even fancied himself a warrior.

Isiilde eyed the knife and sling hanging from the boy's belt. "I don't know," she said. "Kasja and Elam survived in Vaylin for years. Looks can be deceiving."

She was suddenly conscious of how close he stood. Rivan was tall and broad-chested. The tips of her ears barely reached his shoulders.

A month ago, she had been helpless and utterly clueless. Now she knew too much. The fire in her whispered of release. Of hunger and destruction. It no longer frightened her. It was beautiful and fearsome; light and dark, delivering both life and death.

Isiilde was no longer helpless.

"I'm sure Oenghus has the same plans for Kasja and Elam as he has for me. I wouldn't be surprised if he tried to drug us."

The thought alarmed Rivan. "Do you think my captain would do the same to me?"

Isiilde arched a brow, and Rivan sighed at her silent reply.

"I've brought plenty of food—an entire larder worth. I'll share."

"Where?" he asked.

She tapped the pouch that hung at her side. There was a question on the tip of his tongue, but before he could ask if Marsais had rubbed off on her mental state, she pulled a strawberry from the pouch and offered it to him.

"Is that one of those enchanted bags that's bigger on the inside?"

"Yes. I made a very large one."

"Are you sure I can have one of your berries?"

"Of course."

Rivan plucked the fruit from her fingers, and hesitated. "You wouldn't try to leave me behind, would you?"

Isiilde did not answer.

"I'm trusting you."

"I don't see why you shouldn't. If you don't come ashore, then I'll be surrounded by a squad of veteran soldiers who know exactly what they're doing. You make me look better."

Rivan gave her a lopsided grin. "I don't mind playing the fool." He carefully removed the stem and leaves before popping the berry in his mouth. His expression sobered. "Strawberries always taste like home to me." Joy and sadness mingled in his deep brown eyes. "I don't want to be that child cowering under a corpse again. I would never forgive myself if they left me behind."

"I feel the same."

THE SHIP CREPT through the fog. Voices were hushed, and the leadsman continued his rhythmic work—the plunk of water, the scrape of rope, and the dark water line that could signal danger at any moment.

Lucas Cutter stood like a statue at the rail. His face was turned towards the constant, skin-crawling wail. He did not stir when she approached.

"Are we near shore?"

"There is no such thing in Fomorri, Nymph."

Isiilde ignored his gruffness. For all the paladin's hostility, they shared the same goal, and out of everyone, Lucas did not seem to care if she set foot on Fomorri soil. She searched the mist, wishing for moon and stars—some beacon in the dreariness to anchor her in place.

"There are cliffs and narrow passages that cut into the land," he explained. "Nothing but rock and treacherous waves to tear ships apart. The few safe harbors are riddled with Fomorri war camps."

His willingness to volunteer information startled her. It was the longest speech she'd heard from the man.

"How will we land, then?"

"I don't know." He looked at her, his dark eyes flat. "The *seer*," he twisted the word as he always did, "has not told us."

For once, she understood his frustration. She looked towards the constant wailing, as if it were a thing that could be seen rather than heard. A distant flicker caught her attention.

"Fire," she blurted out.

"Where?"

Isiilde pointed. "Is it a lighthouse?"

Lucas squinted into the gloom, but whatever had mangled his body had left his eyes damaged, too. "Are you sure there's something there?"

"Yes. There are two pinpricks, like glowing eyes. I'm sure of it." She closed her own eyes, reaching out with her mind. Isiilde could feel the flames: hungry and gleeful. It was not a friendly fire. Not the kind she would curl up to on a chilly night.

Lucas hurried across the deck to the captain's cabin. He poked his head inside. Acacia and Oenghus emerged a moment later, and all three joined her at the rail.

"Where, Sprite?"

"Can't you see it? It's so bright, even through the fog."

All three shook their heads. Captain Carvil and the willowy Windtalker added their eyes to the search.

She reached out a hand. "I can *feel* the fire."

Oenghus pushed her arm back down. "Leave it where it is." He turned towards the captain. "I think Isiilde is sensing one of the brazen bulls."

She cocked her head, waiting for an explanation. But no one offered one.

"We can't be that close," Carvil said.

"Isiilde has a connection with fire and sharp eyes that far surpass our own," Acacia said. "But we may be closer than we like."

Carvil turned to issue orders to his crew.

"What's a brazen bull?" Isiilde asked Lucas.

"Your washroom," the paladin spat. He marched away, disappearing below deck.

A cold lump settled in her gut. It traveled down her legs, freezing her to the deck. Isiilde reached for her fire. It burned away feeling, leaving a smoldering rage that warmed her from the inside out. As long as she held onto that flame, nothing could touch her. Not even the past.

The fog swirled and sizzled around her. She focused on the distant fire, whispered its name, and called across the sea with a thrumming song, feeding all her rage into the slow burn. The eyes of flame surged with explosive power. A distant column of fire roared into the sky, then died.

Shouts of alarm rippled from the tops. "A burst of fire in the distance," a sailor reported.

Oenghus turned warily on his daughter. "What did you do, Isiilde?"

"What is a brazen bull?"

"The source of the wailing. It's a torture device that slowly cooks its victims."

Lucas had returned to deck. He stared towards the silence, and then looked at the nymph. She no longer wondered about his scars.

"I don't think it's still standing," she said without emotion.

"Would you have had anything to do with that?" Oenghus asked. "Because as hot as you are, I'm about to douse you with a bucket."

She glanced down at her hand. It glowed like a coal. Isiilde whispered its name, and a flame sprang to life in her palm—a small flicker of light. The sight of the flameling made her smile. "I'm perfectly fine, Oen." She closed her palm, and the flame dove back into her skin.

"Course you are, Sprite." Cautiously, he stepped forward to place a hand on her shoulder. He looked relieved to find her skin cool to the touch. "Why don't you come into the cabin to discuss our plans?"

When the commotion died down, Isiilde squeezed into the captain's cabin with the others. Nimlesh, the Elite Sergeant, was there, too. There wasn't much room, not with the expansive table of charts.

Isiilde wedged herself between Acacia and Oenghus, who had to slouch under the low ceiling. No one objected to her presence. But then their king had made a refuge for nymphs. Had her kind been elevated from animals to something more—not quite human—but sacred?

Isiilde studied the expansive sea charts. The details captivated her. There was hardly a blank area to be found. Lines intersected with dots, and a cryptic scrawl covered the map. Interwoven into the charting were notations of reefs, pirate activities, shoals, and sea-creatures. Off to the side, keeping a corner of the map pinned, a stone floated in a bowl of water. It reminded her of the purifying ritual that Rivan had performed in Vaylin. The slender stone pointed north.

It was said that Mearcentian sailors read the moon and stars, and even the clouds. That the seas spoke to them. Isiilde suspected detailed maps had a good deal to do with their success.

However, the humans were not studying the map. They were looking at a piece of parchment sitting in the middle of the table. She recognized Marsais' scrawl instantly.

It was a hasty sketch of the Fomorri coastline. Five peninsulas stretched into the sea like fingers—the Taloned Coast. An X marked a spot on the fourth peninsula. Another was drawn farther inland, to the northeast. Marsais' spidery handwriting named it Finnow's Spire: the mythical resting place of the Unicorn's Horn—a direct link to the ol'River. So the legend went.

At every festival, Hawkers waved scrolls at the crowd, proclaiming that their map would point the way to the legendary artifact. For a price, of course. Isiilde had never seen one of the maps—she wasn't *that* gullible—but she was sure the fakes would be more detailed than what Marsais had produced.

His map was far from reassuring. It lacked details of any kind, and Marsais' sense of direction was worrisome at best. On the Isle, she'd watched him scratch out directions for lost Wise Ones in the Spine. His directions usually caused even more confusion.

Oenghus glowered at the scrap of paper. It looked like a typical Marsais map.

"There are no known passages in the fifth talon," Nimlesh noted. "Only here: the bay, and the inlet between the first and second talon." He jabbed a finger at the two jutting peninsulas. "Both are riddled with Fomorri encampments. Heavily guarded bridges span talons two, three, and four, so the creatures can move quickly along the coast." He traced a dotted line that spanned the talons. "We've seen Fomorri raiders use pulleys to scale the cliffs from their boats on the outer coast along the Wailing Wall. But we've never chased raiders to the fifth talon. As far as we know, they don't sail between the fourth and fifth."

"They must be afraid of something there," Oenghus said.

The elite sergeant laughed, sharp and bitter. "Fomorri fear nothing."

"Only the dead have no fear."

Acacia frowned, absently tracing a scar on her arm. "Fomorri fear the Blight. It destroys their grafts."

"Some welcome it," Nimlesh countered.

Carvil frowned at the sketch in thought. "Could it be Forsaken?"

Isiilde shivered at the name. Her skin crawled at the thought of the drifting spirits. Neither living nor dead, their spirits were eternally cut off from the ol'River. Never to be reborn; never to find rest. She still felt the knife that N'Jalss had held to her throat in the Spine—a blade that separated spirit from flesh.

"I don't know," Nimlesh admitted. "But if they're afraid of that place, then we do not want to tread there. We'd have better luck capturing one of their raiding ships and using the pulley to climb the cliff."

"Why not sail to Kiln?" the Windtalker asked. "You could enter Fomorri from the north." Understandably, the chieftess did not want to risk her ship based on a madman's scrawled X.

"And cross the Great Expanse?" asked Acacia.

"There are ways," Nimlesh insisted. "Kilnish warriors train at outposts in the deep desert. And nomads traverse the border, even venturing farther inland. There's a rumor that they trade with the Fomorri."

Acacia shook her head. "A journey like that would take time."

"Aye," Oenghus agreed. "The Scarecrow drew us this map. We stick to it. Your task, Captain Carvil, is to find the mouth of the last inlet. Marsais will be up and moving soon enough. He can tell us more when he wakes."

"And what of this place that Fomorri fear? Does the Trickster expect us to sail the *Squall* into the inlet?" the Windtalker asked.

No one had an answer.

"I won't allow it," the woman said.

Carvil bowed his head in deference. "As you command, and with my agreement. This inlet is narrower than the others. The surrounding tides are treacherous. The longboats will have to do. May Nereus bless the backs of the rowers."

All eyes focused on the crooked little X that marked an unknown fear. But then, so much was unknown in Fyrsta. Isiilde had spent countless hours studying the maps in Marsais' study. There were stretches of uncharted terrain—penciled borders that faded to shadow and then tired out altogether, leaving bare parchment. The maps had always looked bashful, because really, a map ought to know. That was a map's job; unfortunately, explorers who tried to fill in the blanks were usually never seen again.

"Whatever the Void it is, we have one thing the Fomorri don't," Oenghus rumbled.

"What is that?" asked Nimlesh.

Oenghus cracked his knuckles. "Me."

Acacia snorted. "What could possibly go wrong?"

CHAPTER 19

Morigan frowned at the Wise One. He was gagged and tied, not with weaves but sturdy ropes and binds. She put a name to the face: Fallon Able. He had an ample gut, and a penchant for scullery maids and errand boys. At the moment, his eyes bulged like a toad's and his face was mottled with bruises and swelling. One finger had been bent at a painful angle.

"Never liked 'im anyway," Eldred said. The dwarf sat in a chair off to the side. He looked as pale and stretched as she felt. "The man has never done anything unless coin was involved."

Brinehilde gave a sharp laugh. "I could say the same of most Wise Ones."

"Aye, well, not all of us are greedy bastards."

"Only short," the priestess shot back.

"And you're too tall."

"The better to stuff your hide into a chest."

"I'd have had to toss your hide out the window."

"As if you could lift me," Brinehilde scoffed.

"Give me a bit to get my feet back under me, and I'll prove it."

Morigan interrupted the two. "If you're feeling up to lifting a Nuthaanian, then go help Greta and Simon."

Eldred grumbled at her.

Morigan tried to ignore the state of her infirmary. It was in shambles and short-staffed. And the care was left to Greta and Simon—far too many wounded for two healers to manage.

Morigan had other work to do. As long as Tharios lived, more would die. She needed to stop the disease at its root.

"Right, to work." Brinehilde looked at Fallon and cracked her knuckles. "Why don't you tell Morigan what you told me? I'm more than willing to have another go at your fingers." She waggled her own recently chopped off digits—courtesy of Tharios' lackeys.

Morigan removed Fallon's gag. She offered him water, and when he nodded, she tilted the flask to his lips.

"I heard you were planning to kill my patients and staff."

He licked his lips. "I wasn't."

"The guards were," she stated.

"I was ordered to escort them."

"By whom?"

"The Archlord."

"Where did he move my healers?"

"Somewhere safer—away from the traitors and this fog."

"Where?"

Fallon's eyes flickered to Brinehilde. "In the lower levels. The tunnel barracks."

"Why would Tharios move an entire infirmary down there? It's too far from the main gates to be of any use during an attack. Was he expecting visitors from the tunnels?"

"I don't know. Orders are orders."

Morigan knew the man's reputation well. Fallon had spent his life trying to wiggle out of responsibility. "I know you're one of his Unspoken."

"I am not."

"Do you know how I know?" She did not give him a chance to answer. "No Wise One, orders or no, would kill wounded in their beds."

"I'm not an Unspoken, Morigan. That's insanity."

"But likely profitable. Not only does a cabal of Bloodmagi put coin in your coffers, but they also create a city devoid of laws." She placed her hands on his armrests to look him straight in the eye. "An ideal place for someone like you."

"You're mad."

"Maybe so," she admitted. "But remember, I know every nerve and muscle—every bone and fiber in a body. I know what hurts, Fallon. The spots that stab your brain and set the world ablaze. And even better, I can heal you, and start all over again."

"You wouldn't."

"You were going to slaughter my patients." Morigan was calm. So frightfully so. "You and yours accused my kinsman, my once Oath-bound, of Bloodmagic, and you serve a man who slaughters women and children in pens like cattle. What do you think I'll do, Fallon?"

The man stared at her with growing realization. Morigan wasn't bluffing. "It doesn't matter if I tell you. The entire realm will know soon enough. It's not as if you can stop him."

"Probably not," she agreed. "So what would a few words from your tongue hurt? It might scare us into leaving."

Fallon swallowed. "Tharios has been searching the tunnels underneath the castle. It's been going on for a while. Only now he's found something. He's been making the captives dig."

"Why?"

"Karbonek. Tharios is going to bring Karbonek into the realm, and we will be his faithful few."

His words chilled her blood—not in fright, but rage. "And what of this fog?"

"A taste of *his* power."

"And what power is that?"

There was hesitation in his eyes. "Fear."

"You don't know, do you? But of course you don't. Tharios had to send his guards out with a Wise One as escort. He can't even make this fog friendly to his own allies."

"What does it matter?"

"It matters greatly, but not for you. Let me show you what control is."

Morigan pressed her hand on the man's chest. The Lore leapt to her lips, and she nudged that clog—that little gathering of fat in his heart.

The artery sucked up the clot, and he began to seize. She withdrew her focus, and watched as his own heart killed him. Fallon couldn't even scream. He frothed and choked and slumped back dead.

"Well..." Brinehilde blew out a breath. "I hope we didn't need him for anything."

Morigan turned away from the man and walked over to a mirror. She had glanced into that mirror many mornings, whether to tame a stray strand of hair or wipe blood from her cheek. Today, she plucked out what was left of her pins and watched her hair fall over her shoulders. It had been a long while since Morigan Freyr had plaited her hair into a warrior's braid. Years ago, her dark hair had been rich with threads of copper; now, it was streaked with grey. But her fingers had not forgotten the rhythm and weave.

"So who is this Karbonek?" Brinehilde asked.

"The god of the Fomorri and the Unspoken."

"Blood and ashes."

"This will never work."

Morigan glanced at her companion. They'd been hard-pressed to find armor that fit the priestess. The chain and tabard were stretched over her breasts. But at least the helm fit.

Morigan wore her own armor. A bearded axe hung from her belt loop. It was her own as well, its grip worn and familiar to her hand. But she'd had to leave her targe behind; it was too recognizable, so she held a shield of the Isle, and wore a tabard of the guard.

"Don't strut," she warned.

"I'm not strutting; I'm bloody limping."

Brinehilde attempted to shorten her steps. Instead of a limping strut, she took on a lop-sided swagger. It would have to do.

"Keep your eyes and ears open."

"These bloody phantoms can't hurt us."

Morigan gave the woman a stern look that deflated her bravado. The priestess had only experienced vague visions and laughable threats.

Either Brinehilde was protected in some way, or Morigan had been singled out. She shook the thought away to focus on the corridor.

A beat of footsteps warned of others. Brinehilde quickly draped a heavy arm around the shorter woman's shoulder, pressing a hand to the slice on her ribs. Morigan grunted at the weight, and dropped her weave. Mist rushed in. Whispers hissed of vile things, but mostly cackled with amusement.

The mist parted in the narrow corridors as a squad of soldiers rounded the corner. Swords bristled, and Morigan tilted her arm, displaying a crimson armband.

"We've lost our way," she explained.

There was little chance she'd be recognized. Tharios had brought in a fair amount of fresh faces over the past weeks. And no one expected to find the healer in armor.

The Wise One escorting the troop usually kept to Drivel. "You'll have to get there yourselves," the woman said, barely glancing at the pair.

"Which way?" Morigan called.

Before the mist swallowed the troop, one of the rear guards pointed down a corridor. As soon as their footsteps faded, she wove an air rune and chased the mist away. The whispers snickered.

"Do you hear all that, Hilde?" Morigan asked.

"Aye, the lot of these phantoms are a bunch of blowhards."

For now, thought Morigan. The dead did not always stay dead.

A chill pricked her senses, warning her of a ward. She pulled Brinehilde to the side, and traced a spirit eye. Runes pulsed like fireflies in the gloom, revealing a solid wall of air runes. Not strong, but enough. Morigan let her own weave drop and stepped through.

A breeze stirred her hair, and then it did not. The hallway beyond was clear, and the air stale. Four guards lined the corridor, horns ready at their sides.

Brinehilde staggered for effect, keeping up their ruse. Morigan caught her. "We need a healer," she said.

The guards glanced at their armbands, then motioned them past. The passages widened, becoming increasingly more populated, eventually opening to a great hall. In one corner, she spotted cots and injured, and her blue-robed healers. But the makeshift infirmary only filled up a small portion of the barracks. It possessed all the trappings of a war camp.

Morigan staggered into the infirmary, depositing the priestess onto an empty cot. She was happy to be rid of Brinehilde's weight. A healer rushed over—it was Leiman, her once apprentice and now friend. His eyes widened when he saw Brinehilde, and then he looked to her. Leiman hid his relief by bending over Brinehilde to unbuckle her armor.

"Is Tharios here?" Morigan whispered.

Leiman did not look at her, but focused on his patient. "Yes, down in the mines. He's brought peasants from Drivel and Coven and has them digging. I'm not sure all of them came willingly."

"Have you seen a boy by the name of Zoshi? From Drivel?" She described his appearance, but Leiman shook his head.

"Careful," Brinehilde hissed.

Leiman blinked in surprise. He had not realized she was actually wounded. He took more care, and finally examined the cut to her ribs. Greta had bandaged it but it needed changing.

"I need to have a look at those tunnels, and we need to get all of you out of here."

"And put a blade through the Archlord's heart," Brinehilde added.

"But the fog..." Leiman trailed off. His eyes were haunted. It was the nightmare under the bed; a person's worst fears brought to life. Few would willingly walk back into that.

"A simple air weave will keep it at bay."

"I can't weave that," he reminded.

Each Wise One had distinct talents and limitations. Leiman had very little skill with the Gift, but he knew his herbs, and his heart was in the healing arts. That's why Morigan valued the man.

"We'll worry about all that when the time comes," she soothed. "But I want a look."

"We're escorted into the tunnels when there's an injury. There's an awful lot—cave-ins and such. I don't think safety is of concern."

"Are you escorted by the same guards?"

Leiman nodded.

A plan started to form in her mind, but it was thrown to the winds when she spotted two women walking across the hall. The first was an elegant woman with a bandage around her neck. Yasimina. She had survived the fight, after all.

The second woman trailed on her heels. This one was horribly scarred and hairless. Zianna had not fared well after Isiilde's combustion in the library. And now, seeing her in the company of Bloodmagi, Morigan regretted saving her.

A spiky-haired gnome met the two halfway. Then Tharios himself appeared, garbed in a crimson half-robe that displayed a tattoo-covered torso. The tattoos never seemed to be in the same place twice.

The four bent their heads together. Abruptly, Tharios straightened, his face alight with excitement. He issued a sharp order to Kreem, and the Quartermaster immediately bellowed a call to arms.

"Void," Morigan spat.

CHAPTER 20

AIR SWIRLED AROUND THE TRIO, pushing back the murk. It felt like Rashk drifted in another realm. She touched a crenellation, reassuring herself that she stood on the rampart tower. There was no sign of the sea, no sight of Coven huddled in the bay, the looming Spine, or even night or day. All was sickly grey.

Rashk wondered if time moved differently in the fog. Without the sun or moon, she could not be sure of the day or hour. It skewed her hunter's instincts and played havoc with her mind. Shaking off unease, she focused on the task.

"This won't work," Tulipin stated.

"Coward," Rashk hissed at the little man. It made him bristle, but before he could explode, Thira interrupted.

"We've been over this from every angle. We must try."

They'd carefully scouted the castle, testing boundaries. In theory, the castle wards should have kept the fog inside the Spine, but they'd discovered holes in the shield—patchy, threadbare parts that had decayed over millennia.

"We need to leave," the gnome argued for the hundredth time. "We should go to the Chapterhouse in Drivel."

"We informed the Inquisitor before we confronted Tharios in the council chamber," Thira reminded him. Again.

"Then we should..." Tulipin faltered at her glare. "Check and see if they're waiting outside the gates."

"Tulipin, do it. *Now*."

At the click of teeth, Tulipin dropped a full inch, but he quickly restored his levitation weave.

"We will guard you," Rashk offered, spinning her blades for emphasis.

The trio left the tower top, and walked down the stairway, emerging on the lower rampart. Rashk could not see the steep drop-off that she knew was there, only a narrow, misty walkway.

A snatch of shadow moved ahead. Rashk rocked on the balls of her feet, ready to spring. Her black lip curled with distaste. These fleshless phantoms mocked and toyed, offering no challenge—only cowardly taunts.

"Here," Thira said.

Tulipin took a deep breath, then looked towards what Rashk hoped was the inner bailey and the Storm Gates. It was hard to tell. The fog swirled, throwing snatches of noise: errant screams, mad ramblings, and disconnected crashes. But mostly, whispers.

The gnome let his weave unravel, drifting down to the stone. He closed his eyes, and seemed to grow as he began to chant. At first, his voice quivered, then took flight.

Tulipin traced a weave of air runes. His feet left the ground, and he crossed his legs, levitating in the center of this new complexity. As the runes grew and swirled, his voice took on purpose. With each added rune, the air churned.

A mournful wail filled Rashk's ears. Wind snatched at her cloak, and she took a step back. There was silence for a heartbeat.

A blast of wind knocked her to the side. She nearly slipped off the narrow walkway, but threw herself towards the rampart wall and took cover as a fell wind rushed in from the sea. It plunged over the walls and into the courtyard, kicking up a whirlwind of ice. The fog was sucked into the cyclone, and for the first time in too many days, Rashk saw the sky: a dull, wintery grey.

She gawked at the gnome.

Tulipin hovered in midair, surrounded by a vortex of runes. Below, in the bailey, doors flew open, shutters were ripped from their hinges, and the summoned Fell Wind tore through castle corridors.

The roar battered her eardrums and stole her breath. A tornado screamed in the bailey, and she dug her claws into the stone as it threatened to rip her from the wall. And then all at once, the storm let go.

The Spine loomed overhead. It was bathed in bluish runes, with veins of power climbing its impossible height. But there was a crack in the Barrier—at the Storm Gates. The doors had not fully closed. Thick ice filled the gap, freezing them in a half-closed position.

Their hope lay in that crack between doors.

Encased in a Barrier of her own, Thira strode across the rampart until she had a better view of the Storm Gates. She uncorked a slim vial and tossed it off the rampart. The wind snatched it from the air. And the Lore came sharp and precise from her lips—not a word out of place, each one clipped with command.

The vial burst into flames. And the whirlwind sucked up the shock wave of heat. Tulipin thrust his hands towards the Storm Gates, and the fiery tornado moved between the guardian statues.

The ice began to melt. Tulipin pushed the storm through the gap, and wind and fire followed. But the howl of wind did not disappear, a remnant churned at the entrance.

A storm of ice burst from the gates. It snuffed the fire, shattered the weaves, and slammed into Tulipin. The gnome fell over the rampart wall. Rashk sprang up, grabbing for his ankle. She hauled him up and shielded him with her body. He was unconscious.

Eventually, the ice storm died. She nudged her hood back, dislodging snow, and squinted at the Storm Gates. The doors were nearly glazed over with a solid wall of ice. There was a crack, and out of that hole, the fog seeped back out into the open air. The elemental in the great hall was pushing the fog from its domain.

It didn't like the fog anymore than they did.

Another voice took up the chant. Thira did not possess Tulipin's skill with air, but the mist had already been gathered, and now she corralled it with a weave of her own. She kept her focus on the whirlwind even as she walked down the rampart steps. Thira hit the ground, and strode through the corpse-littered field, making for the gates that led to the outer bailey.

Rashk flung the gnome over a shoulder, and raced down the stairs. A missile shattered on the stone by her head. A group of guards with crossbows had emerged from a tower door. They fired another hail of bolts.

She snatched a shield from a fallen guard and deflected the bolts. The guards paused to reload.

Rashk cursed the aimless flurries and the wide open bailey. There was no cover—nowhere to lurk and strike from shadows—not with a tornado of runes lighting the sky ahead like a beacon.

She put her head down, and ran. Ahead, Thira and the imprisoned mist disappeared through the bailey gates.

Rashk could neither speed the woman up nor expect her to fight. The entirety of Thira's focus was on the cyclone. Rashk was alone, with a squad of soldiers on her heels, and a useless gnome bumping against her back.

"Close the gates!" she shouted.

A face peeked out of the gate tower, and she repeated the order.

It was a small chance, but she had to take it. Confusion was a double-edged sword. What Tharios used to his advantage, Rashk could also use to hers.

Rashk sprinted through the tunnel, and as soon as she sped out the other side, the portcullis slammed shut. But the gates were designed to defend—not keep soldiers from getting out. It would only slow the pursuing guards.

Rashk darted across the outer bailey as Thira manipulated her cage of air runes, squeezing the cyclone through the arena gates. When the air stilled, Rashk set Tulipin in a protected alcove, and then moved into a shadowed archway. She touched one piercing after another, activating Wards of Protection and Weaves of Speed. When all her enchantments flared to life, Rashk drew her kukris.

Across the bailey, the portcullis opened, and Isle guards poured through the gates. A buzz pricked Rashk's ears. She turned in time to see a dome of crackling green runes flare to life over the arena pit. Mist swirled under the Barrier. It did not seep out.

Thira stepped beside her. "Nothing ever goes according to plan, but it's done."

Across the field, soldiers advanced. Too many. "I would like your mammoth dog now," Rashk admitted.

"So would I."

CHAPTER 21

Brinehilde trotted beside Morigan as they followed a long line of soldiers. She was a head and shoulders taller than most men, and she could see over the silver helms. Through the bobbing heads, she caught glimpses of a tattooed back. Tharios. So close. Her hand gripped the hilt at her hip. She ached for her staff, but any weapon would do. If she could only get close enough.

They marched through the wide hallways, towards the King's Walk and the gap in the shield. Morigan had noticed the breach on their way inside. Right at the entrance of the King's Walk, the border of the Spine. Aside from the Titan Gates, it was the only other entrance to the tower.

Brinehilde passed through a hole in the shimmering ward. Its edges were frayed, like a tear in cloth, as if someone had picked those threads from the very weave.

They marched through the troop gate, and fresh air cooled Brinehilde's cheeks. She blinked at a grey sky—not the smothering blanket of mist, but a crisp winter day. Snow crunched under her boots, and frozen corpses. The dead were scattered across the bailey.

"The mist is gone," Morigan whispered. "Tharios is headed towards the bailey gates. Whatever he's planning—I need to alert the castle that he's a Bloodmagi."

"How?"

"I know everyone in this castle. I'll send a Whisper to them all."

That seemed like a lot of Whispers, but Brinehilde didn't waste breath on doubts. She knew little of Wise Ones and their runes. "I'll distract them."

"Careful, Hilde."

"Aren't I always?"

"As careful as Oen," Morigan muttered, and with a quick, parting squeeze, she slowed, falling back in the line.

Brinehilde tripped, crashing into the soldier in front of her and knocking another to the side. Her feigned stumble sent a ripple of disorder through the line, but the soldiers quickly fell back into order.

It was enough. Morigan had slipped away.

Brinehilde began working her way up the line, towards the crimson-robed Bloodmagi at the front. Sever the head and the body would follow.

The troop reached the bailey gates, and trotted into the tunnel. Everlight flickered in the dim murder holes glaring from above. In the middle of the tunnel, a Whisper slammed into her ears. It was not a soft touch, or a flutter of wings, but a roar.

Tharios is a traitor, a Bloodmagi, and the cause of this horror. Gather in the outer bailey. Either fight him or flee!

It was clear as day that it was Morigan's voice. And everyone knew and trusted her. Ahead, she heard a laugh. It was like cool silk brushing steel, and it grated on her ears. Tharios was highly amused by the Whisper.

The troop spilled from the tunnel. "Form up!" At the Quartermaster's order, the warriors formed a loose, three-rank formation. Brinehilde jostled her way into the second rank as the troop slowed to a march.

Rashk and Thira stood across the wide outer bailey, a runic shield shimmering behind them. The mist had been trapped in the arena shield—an intact Barrier, unlike the patchy, threadbare one that covered the Spine.

As the soldiers marched across the field, snatches of murmurs rippled through the lines. Morigan had planted a seed of doubt. And they were not the only ones to appear on the field. Isle Guards ventured onto the ramparts and castle residents drifted from their shops and homes.

Brinehilde barely noticed. Her eyes were fixed on the sleek, black head of Tharios. He was flanked by a gnome and the towering quartermaster. She'd have to take care, and be quick.

The troop advanced, stopping within shouting distance of the two women. There was nowhere to go. The arena was a dead end.

"Do you really think anyone will answer that pathetic plea?" Tharios asked. His voice carried, amplified by a weave.

"I expect them to run," Thira stated.

"Wise Ones are skilled at that," he acknowledged. "It's a pity. I should have liked you on my side. After all, you helped me gain the throne."

"I plan to make amends for my mistake."

"Morigan is mistaken," Tharios said to the assembled. His voice carried without effort to every corner. "Our kindly healer means well, but *this* woman is the real traitor."

Soldiers shifted uneasily, and blacksmiths and stablehands looked to each other.

"Come peacefully, Thira. And I will show you mercy."

"He lies!" Eldred's voice boomed across the field.

The dwarf stepped from the shadow of the bailey gate with Ielequithe at his side, and a mass of guards behind them. With a word, he activated his wards. His armor flared, pulsing with threat.

In the confusion, in the shifting front lines, Brinehilde struck. "For the Sylph!" she roared with a scrape of steel. The blade gleamed in the winter light. She slashed at Tharios' neck, but the Archlord was quick. He lurched forward. The tip of her blade sliced a fine red line across the back of his neck.

Something caught on her own body. But Brinehilde was intent on finishing what she'd started. Tharios swiveled with a weave on his lips, and she stabbed. The tip bit flesh, and something more. A tattoo on his bare-chest had come to life—a thick serpent that dripped inky blood.

The snake dropped to the snow. And Brinehilde followed, her body jerking with each stabbing sword. It was so very distant. And she felt nothing—no pain or fear, only peace.

Morigan had sown doubt and Brinehilde had sparked resistance. She bled into the snow, clutching that final thought to her heart as war swept over the bailey.

CHAPTER 22

The Squall creaked along at a snail's pace, groaning to the steady call of the lead line. Isiilde sat with her back against the shrouds. She was alone in the mist. It blanketed everything, but then that was its purpose—to conceal and soothe. She found it both ominous and comforting.

On this moody, fog shrouded sea, it was cold, and she had traded her silken wrap for warmer clothing days ago. But the chill barely touched her. In the tops, Isiilde was alone with her fire. A steady flame burned in her breast, as indifferent to the cold as a campfire.

As comforting as it was, she ached for conversation, for the cycle of King's Folly laid out before her and a worthy opponent plotting across from her. The thought twisted her heart.

The lump of flesh beating in her breast felt like a bird trying to fly—trapped in a cage of bones—heavy one moment, and airy the next.

"Sprite?"

Isiilde peered over the edge. Oenghus clung to the ratline, and the rope quivered with his grip. Her father was afraid of heights when he wasn't clinging to a rock.

"I have food for you."

She narrowed her eyes at him. "I have my own."

"Would you come down here?" he whispered, eyeing the tricky tangle of ropes that would force him to go up and around the platform.

"Are you going to bellow at me some more?"

"No," he spluttered. "I haven't bellowed at you for days." His entire body seemed to sigh. She ducked back from the edge to consider her options. After a minute, she heard the rigging creak.

She poked her head back over the edge. "I was going to come down."

"Well, you didn't," he huffed. Oenghus squeezed his bulk through the lubber's hole, and stood on the platform, gripping the ropes with an iron hand.

"Have you seen any more fires?"

"Only the lanterns on deck."

Oenghus handed her a linen handkerchief. She unwrapped the offering of bread and dried fruit, and stared at the food.

"Might as well save your own provisions." He sounded doubtful, but she had assured him that there was plenty of food in her pouch.

"Would you lie to me, Father?"

The use of father threw him off guard, and he blinked. Whenever she used the endearment, mist clouded his eyes. "What?"

"Would you lie to me?" she repeated.

"No."

"But you have withheld the truth."

"Not saying something is different from lying."

"That sounds a lot like something Marsais would say."

Oenghus tugged on his beard. "Maybe he's rubbed off on me... I've known the ol'bastard long enough."

"Is this food drugged?"

"What the Void, girl?"

"Answer me," she insisted.

"No."

"Do you plan on stopping me from coming with you?"

He looked into the bleakness. "No," he said faintly, and settled beside her. "In Nuthaan, we consider a man, woman, or child who's seen battle a warrior. Doesn't matter if it's a child who defended a sheep, or a farmer defending his land. Same goes for a woman who's given birth. Your life is your own now, Isiilde. What you do with it is up to you. I won't dishonor you by taking away that choice."

Isiilde searched his face for any deception, then took a bite of bread. "Acacia said you were threatening to leave me behind."

"I was planning to—that's all," he admitted. "I won't stop you, but that doesn't mean I want you to come."

"I know." She rested her head on his shoulder. "I don't want you to go."

"I have no choice."

"There's always a choice."

"I'm not one to turn away from what needs doing."

Isiilde looked him in the eye. "Why do you imagine your daughter would be any different?"

He swallowed down a lump. "I never have." On impulse, he draped an arm around her shoulders, drawing her close. "You keep your wits about you, Sprite."

"I'm not sure I've ever had any."

A laugh rumbled from his chest. "Neither have I." He took out his pipe and the little tool he used to clean the bowl. She found the gentle sounds of her father preparing his pipe soothing. "Do you, uhm…want to talk about the other day? With the fire?"

"Should I?"

"Yes."

Isiilde opened her hand, palm towards the grey sky, and with a soft whisper, she called to her fire. A flame sprang to life, dancing on her skin. Oenghus' hand stilled, his pipe forgotten.

"It burns inside of me now," she confided. "So brightly that it's more real than the wood beneath me now."

"And what about the fire on the cliffs?"

"I was angry."

Oenghus digested her words. When he spoke, it was with slow care. "A berserker feeds off rage and pain; he pours it into his blows. But he's limited by his own flesh and blood."

"Not you."

"No," he admitted. "I can feel the earth, the rocks, the storms in the sky. Most berserkers never learn to control the rage. It took centuries before I learned. And in that time, I killed far too many allies."

"You set them free," she said, her voice so cold and sure.

"No." He shook his head. "I killed friends, fellow warriors, men who did nothing but get in my way."

"Everyone dies."

"When it's their time."

"I'm not sure one less human matters in this realm."

Oenghus stared. His jaw nearly dropped. "*Everyone* matters."

"Even enemies?"

"Course not."

"I have very few friends."

Oenghus narrowed his eyes. "You need more than rage to live. Trust me, I know. Eventually, it will poison you."

"Right now, it keeps me warm."

Her father appeared at a loss. Whatever he might have eventually said was interrupted by a shout. "Land ho!"

Isiilde leaned over the side, watching the flurry of activity that followed. Sailors scurried up the shrouds and along the yards, furling the sails. Carvil called for the anchor to be dropped. A chain rattled, setting Isiilde's ears on edge. The anchor crashed into the water, and the ship groaned as the anchor dragged along the seabed.

"We're here." With a close of a hand, she extinguished her flame.

A crash of waves boomed in the fog. Land was close. Isiilde stood at the starboard rail with the rest of the crew. She could feel the sun trying to burn its way through the mist. It would not be long.

Marsais stood stiffly at her side, his hands clasped behind his back. It was disconcerting—to know him, to have felt his spirit burn in her breast, and now, to have him so distant, yet so close.

Out of habit, Isiilde reached for their bond. Her fire answered, burning love to a crisp.

The sun finally broke through the mist to touch the shore. Sheer black-and-red banded cliffs rose from the sea, shaped into columns of colossal heights. There was a gap in the cliffs—a dark mouth where the sea rushed in with foamy white waves. The fifth talon. Isiilde could see nothing of the land above the cliffs that dwarfed the ship.

"Are those carved pillars?" she asked.

Marsais' coins gave a soft chime as he shifted. "Cooling lava flow." He turned to Nimlesh. "Prepare the longboats."

"Before I send my men in there, I want information, Seer."

Marsais inclined his head. The others, Oenghus, the paladins, and Elite drifted closer. "That inlet is a graveyard," he said, gesturing towards the gap. "The water is deep, and the current is strong. Old, sick, and injured sea creatures get caught in the currents. They're too weak to swim out. I'm told that their carcasses litter the inlet."

Isiilde could see the current. A deep black gulf of water split the grey-blue sea. The *Squall* had anchored well away from it.

"Is there a landing?" Nimlesh asked.

Marsais roused himself. "There are sea caves, and a stairway."

"Are the Fomorri camped near these stairs?" Acacia asked.

"Not precisely."

Everyone waited. Marsais scratched his chest.

"A precise answer would be nice," Acacia pressed.

"The Fomorri avoid the inlet."

"And why is that?" Nimlesh asked.

It was like coaxing a confession from a criminal.

"A scavenger lives there. One that feeds on whale carcasses, and larger creatures. It's ancient."

Isiilde frowned. Marsais had said ancient as if it were older than he.

"And large," Oenghus guessed.

"Yes, but..." Marsais held up a finger. "I imagine lazy."

Acacia arched a brow. "You imagine?"

"I've never seen it."

"Why do you imagine it's lazy?" Rivan asked.

The edge of Marsais' lip quirked upwards. "I'm basing that presumption on my personal experience with being long-lived."

"How do you know this scavenger lives there?" Nimlesh asked.

"Saamu."

"The sea god's daughter?" the sergeant asked.

"Yes."

Murmurs rippled through the crew.

Acacia frowned. "How many years ago was that, Marsais?"

"Hmm." He rubbed a coin woven into his goatee, eyes growing distant with thought. "One thousand years ago... perhaps twelve hundred. I can't recall."

"You knew me when it happened," Oenghus grunted.

"Did I?"

"That's what you claimed."

Marsais glanced around the ship in confusion. His hand falling from the coin to his chest. He looked lost.

"It doesn't matter," Acacia soothed. "Give or take a few hundred years, it's still a long time. Things might have changed."

"Perhaps."

"And how do you know where Finnow's Spire is?" Nimlesh asked. The man might have had the face of a rock, but his voice betrayed doubt.

"You wouldn't believe me if I told you."

"I don't believe half of what you say, Seer," Lucas spoke up. "But you usually say it anyway."

"A Guardian told me."

Surprise rippled through the group. But they appeared to accept his claim. As the men dispersed to prepare the boats, Isiilde heard Oenghus mutter under his breath. "Who really told you?"

"A dragon."

CHAPTER 23

THREE LONGBOATS HIT THE WATER, and the Elite scrambled down rope ladders like a line of ants. The soldiers looked identical. Each wore a Kilnish turban wrapped loosely around head and throat, a leather breastplate, and sand-colored clothing ideal for the sun and its unrelenting touch.

At the moment, it was simply cold and dreary, but that would change soon enough. Isiilde could not wait.

"How long do you want us to remain here?" Carvil asked Marsais.

"Set sail as soon as we've cleared the cliffs. We will not be coming back by sea."

Isiilde eyed the man at her side. In turban, wide-sleeved robe, and a wider sash, he looked like a perfectly sane and noble desert nomad.

"You don't have camels, or enough supplies to traverse the whole desert. How will you return?"

Marsais thrust a curved dagger under his sash. "That's for me to worry over, Captain."

"May the gods..." Carvil faltered. The gods were not with the immortal elf. "Good luck."

Marsais slung an enchanted pack over his shoulder. He swept his gaze over the cliffs, the roaring waves, and the cold dark of waiting death, and finally, his eyes settled on Isiilde. She raised her chin. No one would stop her from coming.

A movement drew her attention. A small boy scurried over the rail. The deck shuddered, and her father rushed past, bending over the rail to haul not one, but two figures aboard. Kasja and Elam fell onto the deck.

"You're staying—the both of you," Oenghus growled. "There's no room in the boats." Since they didn't speak common, he used angry gestures to get his point across.

"Kiss my arse," Elam argued.

Marsais translated for the Lome, but that didn't seem to help either. Kasja hissed at the translator, too. Marsais shrugged, and pointed at Oenghus, blaming it all on him. With a parting word, he climbed down the ladder.

"Both of you are staying." Oenghus thrust a finger at the pair, then at the deck.

Elam sagged with despair while his sister paced the deck. Oenghus took pity on the boy. He leaned forward to place a kiss on the top of the boy's head.

Isiilde felt for the two, but she agreed. It was probably best if they stayed. She turned towards the rail. The longboat that Marsais sat in was full, so she went to the next, and climbed down the ladder.

The boat bobbed and bumped against the bigger ship. She balanced between rowers and sat on a bench at the fore. Oenghus climbed down after. When he sat down, Cas slapped his thigh.

The two had been making the most of the journey. Cabin walls were thin and privacy on a ship was scarce. But as far as Isiilde could tell, it seemed merely a way to pass the time.

Could Isiilde ever be so casual with men? The thought made her shudder. She quickly turned towards the cliffs.

The paladins settled in the second boat, and the third held Marsais. The Elite numbered thirty. Their own party added another six. It seemed a small number to infiltrate Fomorri, but then again, perhaps that was best.

"Cast off!" Nimlesh ordered.

Lines were untied and gathered, and the longboats broke free, drifting away from the anchored ship. At Nimlesh's signal, the oars were lowered with a splash that seemed too loud in the desolate sea. The Elite put their backs into rowing, and the boats glided forward.

As her longboat neared the channel of dark water, she half-stood, peering into that expanse. How deep was the abyss?

Two splashes whipped her head around.

"Man overboard!" a muted call came from the cutter, so distant now. Two flailing people splashed in the water, swimming towards the longboats.

"Void," Oenghus spat.

Isiilde looked at her father. "They're both warriors."

With a sigh, he ordered the men to reverse course. When the gap closed, Oenghus hauled Elam into the boat. The boy shivered, grinning from ear to ear as he climbed over the benches to sit next to Isiilde. Kasja avoided Oenghus, pulling herself into the boat. She stopped to run a hand over Isiilde's hair in greeting, then crouched on the bow like a figurehead.

The oars dipped back into the water. The other two boats had gained some distance, but Oenghus and Cas looked as though they meant to make it up.

As the boats passed into the shadows of the colossal cliffs, the crash of sea against rock drowned the scrape of oars. Isiilde eyed the massive waves, wondering if any of them would reach Fomorri soil alive.

Ahead, in the lead boat, she saw Marsais stiffen, his eyes on the water. A swell rose, and the longboat disappeared. When the lead boat bobbed over the next crest, its oars were raised and the crew were staring into the water.

Marsais gestured frantically. A ripple of alarm passed over the second boat. All eyes focused on the dark deep. No one moved.

The rowers in Isiilde's boat followed suit. For scant heartbeats they drifted, bobbing on swells, caught in a current that dragged them towards the cliffs. Strangely, the other two boats were moving *towards* them, opposing the current.

All at once, the water under Isiilde's boat shifted, pulling them back out to sea. Everyone in the boat froze.

The black sea had turned white—a great pale swath rippled underneath the longboat. Something was swimming under the water, a primal, ancient presence that wore terror like a cloak. It stretched in all directions, as far as she could see, and the sheer size of it was changing the direction of the current.

It flowed under them like a river, moving towards the distant ship. The anchor had been raised, and sailors were crawling over the yards, unfurling sails. But there was no hope of escape.

Between longboats, a long length of white scales breached the water. Barnacles clung to the creature's hide. And then it disappeared, diving back under.

A pale creature from the deepest dark broke the surface. It rose like a cobra, armored in barnacles with a head of reaching tentacles and a maw of pillar-sized swords.

A scream caught in her throat.

The creature dove at the *Squall*, splintering the tall ship like a child's toy. Screams were drowned in a roar of water that sent a wave raging towards the longboats.

"Row for your lives!" Nimlesh bellowed.

Oenghus reached over the woman who shared his bench, and gripped her oar. She scrambled aside as he moved to the center and braced his feet. "Row!" he ordered.

The Elite followed his lead. Oars dipped, and Oenghus heaved. The longboat leapt forward.

Isiilde was helpless. Her gaze was fixed on the rising wave, and the tail of the Leviathan plunging back beneath the sea.

The wave caught the longboat. They gained momentum, racing down its side towards the gap in the rocks. Cliffs rose on either side, the wave came crashing down, flooding their boat. The cold stole her breath, leaving her icy and drenched.

All was thunder and chaos, and wet doom. Another swell sped towards them. The Leviathan was coming.

Oenghus surged to his feet, and began chanting. His voice boomed in the narrow straight. The cliffs rumbled in answer. He wove a brutal weave, all quick and heavy, of air and fire and water. Lightning cracked the sky, hitting rock. A massive slag broke free, and the whole cliff face plunged into the narrow straight.

Oenghus sat back down with a thud. He was breathing hard and fumbling for his oars. The weave had exhausted him. But even as the others rowed, they looked to the spot where the cliff had fallen.

Had the landslide blocked the channel? The question was answered a moment later—the Leviathan surged from the sea, its head filling the sky. It plunged towards the boat, but fell short.

A wave of water slammed into their boat. Wood splintered, and a cold, gripping death embraced her. Isiilde spiraled in a watery grave, battered from all sides, caught in a current of confusion. Up, down, right, left; the words had lost all meaning.

Isiilde hit something solid, and pain sliced her back. She bounced, and came back down against something rough. Blind and spinning, Isiilde flung out a hand. She grabbed onto a wall of barnacles and was yanked through the water. Away from the whirlpool.

She clung to the leviathan's body as it surged through the water. Her lungs burned; she needed to breathe. Her throat convulsed with the urge. A single breath would stop the terror.

Isiilde pushed off the leviathan, shooting towards the surface. She clawed and fought, but for every stroke, the leviathan's wake sucked her back. She was light-headed, her throat constricting—she kicked harder. And with a last surge of strength, she broke the surface.

Isiilde gulped in air. And began to choke. The air smelled of rotting fish guts and bloated decay. She retched water and bile, and flailed on the surface, caught in the leviathan's powerful pull.

A rising swell gave her a fresh vantage point. The water churned with angry white water at the end of the inlet.

Struggling against the chop, she made for the cliff wall, swimming up, over, or through the waves. There was a dark cleft in the rock.

Bodies of soldiers and sailors, splintered masts and wreckage, floated past. A tangle of hair and netting caught her eye. She kicked over to grab the woman.

All at once, the current released its hold. Isiilde broke free with her burden. She drifted into an eddy, and finally slapped a hand against a slick rock.

Dark pillars rose along the cave wall. They were natural, like the pillars along the cliffs. In the dim, she saw the outline of a ledge. Keeping one hand on the rock, she wrapped the other arm around the feral woman's shoulder and turned her over. Kasja stared at the stony sky, a shard of wood protruding from her breast.

A slippery swift movement bumped Isiilde's leg. She jerked back, nearly losing her grip. The water broke, and a black eel wiggled on Kasja, slithering towards her wound with a needle-filled mouth.

Isiilde ripped the eel off the woman, and threw it as far as she could, then pulled herself on to the ledge. She tried to pull Kasja out of the water, but she was too heavy.

Something large splashed in the water. The cave was dark, and the back of her throat went dry. She tugged and heaved at the woman with in terror. A man broke the surface with a gasp.

"Rivan!" she breathed.

He grabbed for the shore. Half out of the water, he panted against the rock. His eyes strayed to the woman in the water.

"Help me get her on land," Isiilde said.

With a weak nod, he assisted, and while he pushed from below, Isiilde pulled. When Kasja's body had flopped on the rock, Rivan scraped and pulled himself up after.

As soon as he was out of the water, he wrapped his arms around Kasja's stomach, and lifted. Water gushed from her mouth and nose, but no breath came. Two more heaves and the sea poured out of her lungs. He rolled her over, and waited. Nothing.

Isiilde drew her knife to slice through netting and rope, cutting around the stake protruding from her chest.

Rivan put his hands over the wound, bowed his head, and began to pray. His hands glowed with radiant power, and a spark of hope filled Isiilde's heart. But that spark quickly died.

Rivan broke the link, sitting back, hard. "She's dead."

An eel was sucking on Kasja's leg. Isiilde ripped it off and threw it with a curse. She wanted to scream at the sea.

Rivan shuddered with cold. He looked as battered as she felt. "Are you all right?"

Isiilde showed him her hands. "Only cuts." The cold numbed the pain. "I grabbed onto the leviathan. It dragged me out of the current. What about the others?"

"I don't know. The wave tossed our boat, too."

A knot twisted her gut as she looked at the channel. Flotsam and wreckage swirled past. And bodies. Her gaze skipped from one to the next, searching for white hair, or a giant with a black beard. But the passengers in the other longboats had long floated past. These were sailors from the tall ship.

It took effort to look away. But there was nothing she could do for them now. Isiilde crouched beside Kasja, salvaging what supplies she could. Anger rose in her throat. If Kasja and Elam had only stayed in Mearcentia, they would be alive.

Rivan watched her desecration without a word. She dumped the belongings beside him: a pack, a decorated pouch, and several knives, including a sling. He wiped his eyes, then gathered Kasja's things. He had lost his own pack, shield, and longsword, but the arming sword he had found in Vaylin was still in his baldric.

Isiilde summoned a flame, but it sizzled and spat on her bloody palm. She whispered to the flameling, urging it to grow, and it obeyed her command, illuminating the sea cave.

Carcasses littered the rocks. Rotting sharks and older bones of whales, picked clean and white. A massive turtle shell was wedged in a tide pool.

The sea had carved a path through the middle of the cave, leaving a ledge on either side. Balancing carefully on the slick rocks, she followed its path, her flame hissing in the wet air. The cave kept going, deep into the cliff.

"Isiilde?"

Rivan's whisper brought her around. He stood on a rock that jutted into the channel. Sea spray misted his body with every crashing wave. When he removed his baldric and started unbuckling his breastplate, she hurried back.

Rivan pointed across the water. A wash of debris floated by: barrels from the *Squall* and other more ominous remains. But she barely glanced at the wreckage. Her gaze was fixed on the opposite cliff wall where a boy was clinging to the rock. Elam.

Rivan reached for the laces of his boots.

She grabbed his arm. "You can't."

"We can't leave him there."

"Look at the water." It was swarming with scavengers feasting on flesh.

"I can make it," he said through his teeth. Rivan would not leave a child in trouble. No matter the risk. And neither would she.

Isiilde eyed the black sea. "I'll get him."

"You're not going in there," Rivan argued. His voice boomed in the cave, and he flinched, lowering his voice. "I won't let you."

Before Rivan could dive in, she summoned the Lore with a chant. She disliked the sound of it. The language was coarse and guttural—so human. Sick of its sound, Isiilde changed her tune, nearly singing, weaving new words. Power lay in the breath between thought; words were the consequence, not the heart.

Focusing, she wove a feather rune, bound it to the boy, and sent it drifting across the water. Air and spirit followed, traveling along her ethereal tether. Words flowed from her lips like music, a captivating song that held her attention.

With a deft hand, she plucked Elam from the rock, and with a gesture, lifted him over the water. The boy screamed as he tried to claw his way back to the cliff. But when the water beneath him began churning with eels, he went limp.

Isiilde tugged at the tether. But she moved too quickly. The weave tore like a fraying rope. Each strand began to unwind, and her control slipped. Elam splashed into the sea.

Rivan dove into the water. He swam to him with powerful strokes, grabbed his collar, and dragged him back into the sea cave. Isiilde hauled Elam onto the rock.

The water turned white around the paladin. Rivan bit back a cry, and hauled himself onto a rock. Long black eels hung from his legs. He began tearing them off in panic, and Isiilde ran over to help, kicking them all back into the sea.

Elam kissed the ground, then spotted his sister. Everything that had come before vanished. He crawled towards her, taking her face in his hands, yelling at her to wake up, shaking her body. His grief filled the cave.

"*Quiet*," she hissed.

Elam kept shouting.

Isiilde clamped a hand over the boy's mouth. Tears ran over her hand, and she pulled Elam towards her. He fought for a moment, then went limp, sobbing against her breast.

As she held the shaking boy, she stared numbly at Kasja's body. There was nothing to do but shiver and breathe the stench of rotting fish.

CHAPTER 24

Footsteps whispered in a narrow hallway. It was nowhere and everywhere. It was endless time; the vast sea; a maze of moments. A lone man dragged his long fingers over stone. Pebbles cracked and flaked, skittering on the floor under his bare feet. The stones were as soft as ash, and cool—a snowfall of destruction. His fingertips brushed a door, one of a multitude.

The door was as bright as spring, and he smiled at the emotion that pulsed from its wood. A festival and a fiery-haired nymph whispered in his mind. The door was locked, not to keep the moment inside, but to keep the outside from entering.

Memories had a way of escaping. And few were innocent.

The traveler looked up at the shimmering water. The ceiling was endless, a brilliant ocean that flowed from nowhere. It cast the dark hallways with light—a peaceful, soothing blue that deepened shadows.

The man who stared back wore a white robe, tattered and torn, singed with fire and time, and streaked with blood. His long hair gleamed white in the reflection.

The man remembered his name. "Marsais," he whispered.

Having a name helped. He closed his eyes, feeling the ash beneath his bare soles. Why ash, why stones? He had no answers, so he continued down the long hallway. At the end, the path split. His fingers stilled. Right or left?

Marsais turned left. Another lonely, door-lined hallway stretched into the dim. He passed a rusted door that creaked with age; a rough door hewn from bark that sprouted leaves; a steel one that pulsed and clanged, throwing off rage.

His memories were endless.

Marsais stopped in front of an ivory door. The handle gleamed gold. He pressed his palm against its surface, listening. Whispers returned. This door was not a vision, but a memory. In a flash, he saw a river rock and a swirl of runes—Vaylin.

Marsais opened the door, and stepped into the recent past.

SUNLIGHT PIERCED HIS SKULL. Half of his vision was cloudy. Marsais tried to wipe the cloud away, but his head gave a mighty throb. He sucked in a pained breath, but gagged on a rotting stench.

Where was he? He had been talking with the Guardian of Life. Vaylin? No, he blinked, reeling, searching for some sign of place and time.

Sand was under his fingers. Where were the rock and river and the silver-eyed god? What had happened to the moon? Was this a vision? Most visions did not have him staring at sand. Mearcentia? A girl?

Marsais gave a shake of his head. But instead of knocking loose his memory, pain stabbed at his temple. Apparently, something had already kicked him, and it hadn't helped.

Marsais pushed himself up, but stopped. His legs were pinned. Stench, sea, sand, rot; the words tumbled around his scattered brain in a sing-song fashion. He might have drummed his fingers to the tune if every fiber of his body had not been shouting at him to play dead.

He glanced over a shoulder. A massive wall of barnacles filled his vision. When it did not disappear, crush him, or sprout a portal and pour out fiends, he tentatively touched the wall. It was breathing.

Marsais closed his eyes, counted to twenty, and opened them. He was still trapped under a sea monster on a putrid beach.

Not a vision, he decided. But a blink later, the beach fell away. A gust of wind brought a howling sandstorm. He squinted against the grit, but a part of him was aware he could breathe without issue.

Three paladins strode from the storm with a horde of Fomorri at their backs. They were chopped down like wheat.

The sands of Time shifted. A severed head rolled into view and came to a stop under his gaze. It was Oenghus. His eyes were missing, picked clean. Marsais considered his friend's head with cool detachment. He saw at least three such visions every day. Oenghus had a knack for escaping certain doom.

He looked back at the sandstorm.

It was ripping the Fomorri apart. Definitely a vision. The sand fell, the air settled, and a crab replaced the severed head. Marsais squinted at the creature. He held himself still, waiting, wondering what the crab would transform into. A fiend?

It reached out a claw and snapped his nose. His eyes watered with pain as he jerked back. Not a vision. He ripped the crab off, and tossed it as far as he could manage. It started coming back for him.

"Blast it," he muttered, clawing at the sand. But he was pinned—not crushed, only stuck. The wall of barnacles shifted.

Not crushed *yet*, Marsais corrected.

He stopped struggling. Slowly, he twisted to the side. The sea lapped at the narrow beach, and the wall of barnacles disappeared under the water.

Memory flooded back. He remembered being battered, churning in the sea, rolled by waves, and frantically tracing a weave, binding air to his lips. Something had knocked him, and then darkness.

And now here he was, washed up on a beach, surrounded by dead things and trapped under a leviathan's tail. The crab returned, and Marsais groaned, planting his face back in the sand.

CHAPTER 25

"We can't stay here," Rivan whispered.

He was right, but Isiilde cringed at the thought of dragging Elam away from his sister's body. The boy had run out of tears, and now he sat holding his sister's lifeless hand in a kind of trance.

The tide was rising. They couldn't stay here for much longer, but the sea was swarming with flesh-eating eels.

"Maybe there's a way out." Her voice was calm, but her heart galloped. The back of the cave was pitch black and the sound of dripping water echoed in her ears. It reminded her of the washroom. Of Stievin. And that thought brought rage.

Isiilde leapt to her feet with clenched fists.

"Can't you just float us up to the top?" Rivan gestured towards the opposite cliff.

"It's not as simple as that. A weave like that would take considerable concentration."

"Then concentrate."

She glared at the man. "Can you juggle?"

"No."

"Why don't you just concentrate, then?"

"It's harder than that."

"Exactly," she said. "You're asking me to juggle three large objects. I dropped Elam in the water, and he's only a boy. Marsais makes the weave look easy, but it isn't. Most Wise Ones can barely levitate a rock." Isiilde turned to Elam. "We have to go."

The boy did not move. She reached for his hand, but he threw himself on his dead sister.

Rivan set down Kasja's things, then took out his Sacred Sun, clasping the symbol between his hands. The emblem glowed gold between his fingers. "May Chaim guide her spirit safely to the ol'River. May she find peace. Be at rest."

"May she piss in it and claw her way back," Isiilde added with strength.

Elam looked up at her. The boy wasn't fluent in common, but he recognized Oenghus' words.

"We have to go, Elam," she said, pointing down the tunnel. "I'm sorry."

The boy frowned. With a sigh, he rummaged through her gear, and unsheathed a knife. He spoke softly, a litany of words that held the weight of ritual. Then he sliced a lock of her hair—one interwoven with beads and bone. He tucked it under his shirt, close to his heart.

Still speaking in his lilting tongue, he rubbed his hand over the grimy rock, collecting mud. Elam smeared the mud over her face, then dipped his fingers in her wound. Fighting back tears, he drew lines of mud and blood on his own cheeks and nose.

Elam slung her pack over his shoulder, and stood. His brown eyes were sad, but resigned. Together, they pushed her body into the sea.

"WHY ARE THERE STAIRS?" Rivan asked.

Paladin, nymph, and boy stared at the stone stairway.

"They look old," Isiilde noted. "Maybe they've been forgotten."

No one held out much hope.

Rivan drew his sword and Isiilde whispered to the flameling in her hand, feeding it with her voice. It expanded, growing into a palm-sized fireball. On a whim, she wove an air rune around the fireball, and bound it together. Isiilde stopped humming. The flame held. But only for a moment. The wet air choked her fire, and without her voice, it spluttered and died. It'd been worth a try.

Before she could weave an Orb of Light, Rivan touched the Sacred Sun symbol around his neck. "May Zahra guide us," he murmured.

Isiilde snorted. "Doubtful."

Rivan gave her a smug look when light flared from the sun. "It's glowing."

Isiilde stuck out her tongue. But before Rivan could take the lead, she slipped past him to bound up the stairs. She had her fire. She didn't need a lumbering paladin in front of her.

The slick stairway was cut into the rock. Someone or something had formed this tunnel, and while that thought made her uneasy, it also meant that it likely led to the surface.

As she climbed, the wash of sea faded, leaving a dim purr of its presence. Eventually, the stairs gave way to a narrow passage that rose sharply into darkness. She summoned her flame.

"I'm not sure how much air we have in here," Rivan whispered at her back.

He was right. She closed her fist, snuffing the flameling, and kept walking. With no sun or stars, time lost meaning in the dark. She did not know how long they walked, but when her calves began to burn, Rivan's divine light touched a dead end. A cave-in blocked the tunnel.

"Blood and ashes," she cursed.

"There weren't any side passages..."

"Are you going to ask Zahra to move the rocks?"

Rivan sheathed his sword. "No, but I might be able to manage. Can you weave one of those bobbing lights?"

With a murmur, she traced an Orb of Light, and it flared blue in the dark. As soon as Rivan let go of his holy symbol, the ritual light blinked out.

Rivan started to squeeze past her, but hesitated. She was in the way. "Don't set me on fire," he said.

She rolled her eyes as he squeezed past.

Rivan climbed up the rocks to the top of the ceiling. "There's a gap here. Maybe a passage. Stand back."

Isiilde pulled Elam away as Rivan wrestled with debris. Boulders and earth tumbled down the steep passage. He was soon sweating, and covered in grime.

Rivan threw his weight against a large rock, his muscles straining. The rock gave. Rivan fell forward, nearly rolling away with the stone.

Isiilde and Elam choked on the dust clogging the air. When it cleared, Rivan looked down at the two. "I think I can make it through." He slithered into the space. And when his feet disappeared, Elam quickly followed.

Isiilde frowned at the narrow gap between ceiling and rock. What if there was another cave-in? The thought nearly froze her. Being buried alive was not high on her list of ways to die.

Before she could ponder the weight of stone, she sent her orb ahead and scurried in after. She coughed and choked on dust as she crawled through the passage. There was enough room for her to turn around, but Rivan must have had to squeeze through. The tunnel opened, and she slid down a slope of scree, coming to an abrupt stop on a tunnel floor.

Rivan offered a hand, and she took it without thinking, letting him pull her up. The touch of his skin froze her. She looked into his eyes, and he met her gaze, then looked down at their joined hands.

"Sorry, I..." he hesitated, dropping her hand. "I can't imagine a life like yours."

"What do you mean?"

Rivan shrugged, dusting the earth from his hair. "Always having to be so cautious, even of a helping hand."

"A mere touch can drive a man insane," she quoted.

"That explains what happened to Marsais and Oenghus, I suppose."

A smile cracked her lips. "It's not really the truth."

"No?"

"Nymphs bring out the true nature of a man. Maybe women, too," she mused, thinking of Zianna. "We cut through lies."

"What does that make me?"

"A kind and courageous man."

Rivan seemed to stand a little straighter as he drew his sword and moved in front of her.

"Stay behind us," she said to Elam.

The air was dry on this side of the cave-in. And the farther they walked, the hotter and drier it became. The tunnel wound its way upwards, but Isiilde couldn't tell if they walked a mile or ten.

Eventually, the passage widened. Insects skittered across the ground with clicking steps, diving into cracks. Dust gave way to sand, and the tunnel opened to a chamber. Pillars lay toppled, etched with scenes of pain and horror.

The carvings made her shiver.

There was light ahead. A dim slash of sunlight that illuminated the chamber floor. The ground was moving—a writhing mass of bodies slithered over the stone. All scaled and sand-colored, with little horns on top of their flat heads. Snakes.

Rivan took a step back, knocking into her. Elam drew his blade.

"Are you afraid of snakes?" she whispered.

"Everything in Fomorri is poisonous," Rivan explained.

Scorpions and centipedes crawled over the twisting mass. It looked like they were all hurrying away on an errand. It reminded her of the Wise One's castle.

With a quirk of lips, she whispered to her flame, humming as she formed it into an orb. Rivan quickly pulled Elam back into the tunnel. When the flame roiled between her hands, she whispered her desire. A wave of fire swept over the floor. It ripped a path through the snakes, parting them like water.

Isiilde's breath caught. She could have watched her fire all day long. The crackle and hiss, the softly licking flame over flesh, was hypnotic.

Rivan and Elam raced through the path of flame. After they reached the other side, Isiilde followed, brushing tendrils of fire with her fingertips.

Stones and sand spilled down the wide stairs, but there was a crack above, one that let in a line of light. Isiilde squeezed through a narrow opening.

A city of ruin sweltered under the sun. Its stones were bleached white with time, and seemed to melt into the sands. She breathed in the heat of the day, feeling alive and free.

Elam shielded his eyes from the brightness, and asked something in his lilting tongue. His meaning was clear.

"I don't know where we are," she admitted. One direction looked the same as the next.

Rivan squeezed through the opening, and when the stone released him, he stumbled forward, thudding onto the sand with a grunt. He climbed to his feet with sword in hand.

"Do you know what side of the cliff we're on?" Rivan asked, blinking against the sunlight.

Unaffected by the brightness, Isiilde climbed a stone wall, and balanced out onto a tilted pillar. She frowned, searching the ruins. "I don't even see the sea." Or Marsais and Oenghus. She tried not to worry about them, but was failing.

Elam pointed to a taller ruin in the distance.

"Good idea," she said, summoning a flame. It leapt to her palm, and danced under the blistering sun with relish. It wanted to grow, it wanted to burn, but she shushed it with a whisper. This time, when she bound air to its dance, the flame remained without her voice.

"How do you do that?"

"What?"

"Are you talking with the fire?"

"I suppose." She hopped down.

"You don't know?" Rivan asked.

Isiilde cocked her head. "Do you know how you breathe?"

Rivan opened his mouth to reply, but caught himself. He frowned in thought. "It's that easy?"

"Now it is."

As they walked towards the toppled ruin, Isiilde kept her fireball at the ready. She had little experience with ruins, but she'd learned that things usually lurked in them. Very unpleasant things.

The ruins opened to a raised dais. A greenish statue lay toppled in the middle. It looked like a bull, but larger: an Auroch. Underneath, the stone was cracked and covered in sand.

Drawn to the metal husk, Isiilde stepped onto the dais. The statue lay on its side. She touched the statue's horns, running her fingers over the corroded copper. Its nostrils and mouth were hollow, and it smelled of char and cooked flesh. A hatch lay open and gaping on its side like a dark portal into its belly.

Isiilde shuddered and stepped back, hurrying across the dais to the other side. Without waiting for the others, she climbed up a partially intact wall.

Remembering her bright hair, she pulled her hood farther forward, and crouched at the top of the perch to survey the land. A city had stood here at one time, but most of it had long been buried in sand.

To the west, the stones stopped suddenly. Although she couldn't see the chasm, she was sure the cliffs were there. She looked east. Sand-colored rock wavered beneath the sun, and to the northeast, a distant mountain range rose starkly in the sky. The land reminded her of a worn painting.

Isiilde was about to whisper down to Rivan when movement caught her eye. It was on the outskirts of the ruins, blending with the terrain. Isiilde dropped to her stomach, knocking loose sand and pebbles as she clung to the top of the wall. Slowly, she edged her way down, and joined Rivan and Elam in the shadows.

"I saw a cloaked figure, to the west, towards the cliffs."

"Could it be one of the Elite?"

Isiilde shook her head. "It wasn't walking like a human."

"Can you send a Whisper to Marsais and Oenghus?" Rivan asked.

Color rose to her freckled cheeks. She hadn't thought of that. But she'd only ever watched Marsais weave a Whisper. And it wasn't an easy one.

Isiilde closed her eyes, trying to recall the runes. But her thoughts were a jumble of memories. Of Marsais. She shoved the whirlpool of emotions and sensations aside—the feel of his muscles under her hands, his lean body over hers, the heat of his skin, the gentleness of his touch. The love in his eyes.

Isiilde traced a spirit rune, spoke his name, and bound the whisper to air. But instead of narrowing in focus, it unraveled, blossoming into an explosion. A single word snapped in the air like thunder: *Marsais?*

Rivan flinched.

"At least we didn't explode," she said with a grimace.

Without warning, Rivan dragged her into a half-toppled ruin. Elam darted in after.

"Something's out there," Rivan hissed in her ear.

Isiilde heard a soft scuffing sound. She glanced at Rivan. His sword was shaking in his hand. The scuff of boots grew louder. Someone or something was trying to be stealthy. The sound moved around back, towards a crumbled wall. And Rivan edged them into deeper shadows.

Isiilde bit her lip. Footprints. It wouldn't take a skilled tracker to notice their tracks in the sand. Should they run? Or...

A sudden idea flared in her mind. Her fingers moved quickly, nowhere as fast as Marsais, but where she failed, her whispering voice wove what her fingers could not: fire around stone, adding water to the wispy threads, then a pinch of spirit to draw an image from her mind.

With a final breath, she bound the image to all three of them, and pressed Rivan and Elam against the wall.

Elam gasped in surprise. He could not see her, and she could not see him; they all looked like stone. Her mirror weave reflected the wall at their backs.

Another thought kicked her dull wits. The Whisper—she should have drawn out the memory of Marsais with the spirit rune. No wonder the message had had nowhere to go.

Light shifted outside the doorway. She held her breath, and hoped Rivan would have the sense to do the same. The boy's hand clutched her own tightly, and he was as still as the stone they resembled.

A figure appeared on the half-tumbled wall. Sand-colored cloth covered him from head to toe. He clutched a curved sword, its metal notched and dented, but the edge looked sharp.

The cloaked intruder hopped onto the sand and moved into the small ruin. He seemed to sniff the air. As he edged farther into the building, maggots fell from the folds of his cloak. A Fomorri.

He looked directly at the trio.

A guttural voice called from the outside, catching the man's attention. He hesitated, then stalked out, leaving them shaking in the ruin.

TIME WAS MEASURED in heartbeats as the soft hiss of footsteps faded. No one dared move; not at first.

A swirl of sand tickled Isiilde's nose. She squeezed her eyes shut until tears came. It was useless. She sneezed. Her head hit the stone, fire burst from her ears, and the illusion unraveled.

Rivan patted out the fire on his arm while Elam crept towards the doorway to peek out. The boy glanced over his shoulder and flashed a crude gesture he'd learned from Oenghus. She supposed he meant it as an 'all clear' sign.

Rivan moved to the crumbled wall to peer over, then relaxed at what he didn't find on the other side. "That was close," he whispered. "But there might be more on the way."

Isiilde eyed the small, squirming white maggots burrowing aimlessly on the ground. With disgust, she kicked sand over the larvae. Legend claimed the Fomorri were formed from the maggots of the dead. Before today, she'd always doubted that claim.

"We need to leave," she said.

"But where will we go? There's nothing in Fomorri but sand and sun."

"We need to find the others." *If they're alive.* She closed her eyes, picturing Marsais, then traced an air rune in front of her lips. It drifted, ethereal and wavering, like a wisp of thread on a breeze.

"Wait—"

Isiilde shot him a glare. "Marsais, where are you?" she whispered into the rune. This time, instead of binding the Whisper to air, she traced a spirit rune, drew the vision of Marsais from her mind, as she had done with the illusion, and bound the trio together.

The weave shot off with a puff of air.

Rivan clutched his sword, waiting. When her question did not crack in the ruin, she relaxed, and so did the paladin. Isiilde straightened, feeling accomplished. She repeated a Whisper for Oenghus, knowing he had no way to answer. He'd never mastered the art of whispering in any form.

Isiilde edged to the doorway, and peeked into the bright day. From her vantage point, she could see the bronze bull. "I suppose we should scout."

"And if we're discovered?" Rivan asked.

"We'll have to be very quiet."

Elam spoke in hushed tones. He sounded like a bird, but the gist of his words got through as he pointed at himself and mimed walking over the sand with two fingers.

"I don't think that's a good..." The boy zipped out the doorway. "... idea," Rivan finished with a sigh. He made to follow, but Isiilde grabbed his arm.

"Elam grew up in the Vaylin wilds. He knows what he's doing." She hoped so, at any rate.

They both waited for the boy to return. And for a Whisper from Marsais. It seemed like an eternity. To keep from worrying, she examined the surrounding stones. Fire had scorched some ruins, while deep ruts marred other parts. Claws.

Whatever had made those marks was massive. Isiilde hoped it was far away.

Elam silently slipped in through a broken wall. He held up seven fingers, then drew an odd shape in the sand. Some long-legged, long-necked form with a big hump on its back.

Isiilde's eyes widened. "A Voidspawn?"

Rivan looked at her. "You really don't get out much, do you?"

Her eyes flashed with anger.

"It's a camel," he said, taking a hasty step back.

"Oh."

Elam held up two fingers.

"Two camels." Rivan looked thoughtful.

"Are they dangerous?" Isiilde asked.

"No more than a horse. But they're extremely useful, especially in deserts."

"I've only ever seen a drawing of one." Isiilde looked at the fallen statue of the bull. Hideously bloated, tarnished and tainted with the lives it had taken. "How useful are the camels?"

"A matter of life and death in a desert. But we don't stand a chance against seven Fomorri."

"Don't worry, I have a plan."

CHAPTER 26

Marsais, where are you?

That was an excellent question. His head still throbbed, and the light still hurt. Marsais coughed into the sand, and squinted. Ah, yes, he thought, the leviathan.

Movement caught his eye. He shifted, and the world lurched. Fighting down nausea, he looked past dancing spots and focused on a point near the cliffs. A boat in the water. The crew of two hugged the rock, inching towards the crescent of sand where he lay.

Acacia and Lucas.

The longboat was damaged, but it was floating. Barely. And although the paladins had lost their oars, they dragged themselves and the boat, hand over hand, along the rocks.

Moving slowly, Marsais stretched his arms, sinking his fingers into the sand. He pulled, trying to wiggle out from beneath the behemoth, but the wet sand sucked at his legs. Clawing at it was about as useless as climbing water.

His skull gave a pulse of pain that threatened to send him back into the darkness. He dropped his head, panting into the sand. When the world stopped spinning, he cracked open an eye.

The boat had touched shore. Acacia climbed out, gazing uneasily at the slumbering leviathan's tail. There wasn't much one could do against a man-eating mountain, but pray it did not wake.

"Isiilde! Isiilde!" A voice boomed down the channel.

Oenghus was alive. For the time being. As always, the berserker seemed determined to be noticed.

The leviathan stirred. Barnacles dug into Marsais' back as the monstrosity shifted. He bit down on his arm, stifling a scream, but the tail dragged over his body. This time, he could not hold back the pain. It left his lips. And then he was being dragged, pulled by the leviathan.

Heedless of the monster, Acacia sprinted forward, grabbed his wrists, and dug in her heels. Even when he had been half-dragged into the water, she did not let go. Something gave—a bootlace.

As he broke free, Acacia tugged, tripping over the body of an Elite warrior. She scrambled to her feet and helped him find his own. The world lurched. He nearly fell back to his knees, but she caught him under the arms.

As the leviathan swam towards the booming voice, the sea retreated, exposing the beach. The sheer size of the thing controlled the tides.

Acacia put a shoulder under Marsais, and wrapped another around his waist. Together, they limped towards the waiting boat. As soon as Acacia had settled him inside, she and Lucas pushed it back out into the water.

His coins chimed, signaling a vision of the near future. A familiar roar rose from the south. The leviathan burst from the channel. Then the vision crumbled. But he knew that roar, and he knew his crazed berserking friend.

Without thought, Marsais' fingers flashed: stone and light and a quick bind. When Time caught up to the seer, he had the weave on his fingertips. Again, he heard the roar. But it was no vision. And again, the leviathan burst from the sea.

Marsais hurled a weave at the creature. A burst of light smacked into its eyes. In that same instant, Oenghus leapt from the cliff to the crown of its head. Confused and blinded, the leviathan rose, ever higher, like a cobra. When it started to fall, Oenghus leapt back onto the rock face.

"By the gods," Lucas hissed. "That man is insane."

"The rope," Acacia ordered.

Lucas tugged on a rope that dipped into the water. The slack was instantly gathered, and the boat was dragged forward at a rapid pace.

The leviathan crashed back into the sea. A wave rose and consumed their boat. Wood splintered and cracked, and he was thrown into the water. He came up for air with a gasp.

Acacia wrapped an arm around his waist. She held the rope in her other hand. They were being dragged towards a staircase carved into the cliff. The Elite stood on the steps with the other end of the rope.

Another wave crashed. He slammed against the rocks, but Acacia kept a hold of him. When the tide ebbed, he sucked in another breath. The Elite yanked him onto solid ground.

"Go!" Nimlesh hissed.

Two Elite ushered him up the stairway as the others reached for the paladins. Marsais tried to focus on putting one foot in front of the other, but his head felt like he'd guzzled a keg.

When the crash of waves faded, Marsais slumped against the rock-face to catch his breath.

"What did you do?" Acacia asked from a lower step.

"I wove an illusion to confuse its senses," he said with a chatter of teeth.

"Do you think Oenghus survived?"

The question reminded him of Isiilde's Whisper. Marsais sat heavily on the step. Gathering his strength, he traced a Whisper, speaking into the weave. *'I should ask the same of you, Isiilde.'*

'Are you all right? What took you so long?' she answered immediately. *'You sound hurt.'*

'You sound exhausted.'

'I'm alive. Rivan is with me, and so is Elam. Kasja is dead.'

'Are you safe?'

'We found a sea cave with a stairway that led up to the surface. There are Fomorri in the ruins on the east side. They have camels.'

This gave him pause. His gaze strayed in that direction, on the opposite side of the channel. *'Keep clear of them. They're formidable fighters.'*

'Where are you? Is Oenghus with you?'

'We're on the west side. Stay hidden. We'll meet you there. And no, Oenghus is not here, but he was alive last I saw.'

'I have a plan. It doesn't involve waiting.'

'Isiilde,' he warned. But she did not reply.

Acacia stood at his shoulder, waiting for the other half of the conversation. But he didn't fill her in; instead, he traced a Whisper to Oenghus. *'Isiilde is with Rivan and Elam on the east side. We'll meet you at the top.'*

Acacia's shoulders sagged with relief.

Marsais traced a final message. *'Thank you for distracting the leviathan. You make splendid bait.'*

They climbed out of the mist and into charred ruins. At the top of the stairway, Marsais dropped to his knees. A shadow neared, blocking out the sun, and he glanced up to find Oenghus baring his teeth in a grin.

"I won."

"You sound winded," Marsais wheezed.

"Not at all."

"You took a shortcut," Acacia said, climbing the last step.

Relief softened his eyes. Oenghus caught her in a hug, crushing her against his chest.

Acacia gasped. She could not breathe.

Oenghus set her down, color rising above his beard.

"I'm glad you're alive, too," she said, gripping his arm.

He cleared his throat. "Aye, well, I leave the Scarecrow with you for a few hours and he comes back looking like a lion had its way with him."

"I found him pinned under the leviathan."

"I would have left him," Oenghus snorted.

"We were napping together," Marsais corrected.

"I'd offer you a healing, but we need to find Isiilde."

"She said there are Fomorri in the ruins."

Nimlesh heard this last. "These ruins look like they were attacked and abandoned long ago," the sergeant noted.

Lucas touched a deep gouge in a stone wall. "By something large and clawed."

"Let's hope it's not the leviathan's land dwelling cousin," Acacia said.

Oenghus looked at the remaining warriors. "Is this it?" His voice was rough with emotion.

Nimlesh gave a jerk of his head.

Marsais counted the remaining Elite. Only fifteen had survived. Cas, the dark-haired woman whom Oenghus had been knocking against the walls, was not among the living.

The warriors stared back at him. There was accusation in their eyes, but he felt no guilt—he could not. A sea of blood already stained his hands, and if they failed, the realm would drown in an ocean of it. These were warriors, not children. They knew their Fate, and so did Oenghus.

"I need a weapon," he growled.

"Did you lose yours again?" Marsais sighed.

Oenghus did not answer. He stomped away, but returned shortly, carrying the jawbone of some long dead creature. He slapped the bone against his palm. "Better than Kilnish steel."

"You could've bought a kingdom with the war hammer you lost," Marsais said, climbing to his feet. It had been a gift from King Syre to replace his own.

"Well, now I have a bone."

"Shall I throw it to get you walking?"

"Har, har, you skinny bastard."

CHAPTER 27

BEFORE AGE and neglect had tinted its skin green, the brazen bull must have glowed like molten metal under the sun. Isiilde tried not to think of the screams that lingered inside its belly.

"Are you sure this is a good idea?" Rivan asked from his hiding place beside a fallen pillar.

"I used to do things like this all the time on the Isle."

"This isn't the Isle."

Isiilde shrugged. "Danger is danger."

In the Wise Ones' castle, knowledge was power, and a lack of it killed. Out here, in the wilds, so much was unknown to her. But there was only one way to learn.

Isiilde rubbed her hands together, flexing her fingers and preparing her mind. What would come, would come.

Two Fomorri shambled into view. One was hunched, walking with a horrible limp, sniffing at the ground like a dog. From the way they were picking through the ruins, she thought they might be scavengers rather than scouts.

With a soft voice, she began to weave, calling to her flame. It sprang to life in her palm, and she coaxed it with a touch, causing the flameling to swirl. She bound air and power to the flame, then whispered her desire: the bull.

The fireball leapt to the beast's hollow belly. She sang softly, weaving her voice through the air like the hiss of flame on a cool night. As the fire grew and danced, she wove a spirit rune, and whispered into the weave, then bound the Whisper to the air. It boomed to life, coming from nowhere and everywhere in a voice that was not her own.

"Long have I lay abandoned!"

Isiilde nearly squealed with delight. Elam pointed at himself, and then gestured towards his own lips.

Why not?

She repeated the weave. Only this time, Elam spoke in his own tongue. Maybe the Fomorri would mistake it for Abyssal.

It did not really matter what the creatures thought. Elam's voice hit the air like a flight of birds screeching their way into the sky. And as the bull glowed with her fire, all seven of the Fomorri gathered around their fallen idol.

Another quick weave. *"Abandoned. Forgotten. Starving."* She drew out the last word until it hissed on the wind.

The Fomorri retreated a step. Worried they would flee, she changed tactics. *"Stand me upright so I may gaze on the faithful."*

The Fomorri stopped to gaze at the glowing bull.

"Set me right so I may repay your devotion," she urged.

This was the final hook. They shuffled forward, edging into the fire's glow. Isiilde smiled with a cool twist of her lips. She started singing, pouring her rage into the fire. It was trapped in a shell and she gave it release. The weakened bull exploded with a roar of fire.

Glowing metal rained from the sky. Isiilde tucked herself under a fallen stone. When the wreckage had settled, and the glowing shards of copper dimmed, Isiilde peeked from her hiding place. Seven burnt bodies lay on the charred dais.

Isiilde grinned. "That was gorgeous!"

Rivan and Elam slowly climbed from their own cover. The two looked stunned, and more than a little fearful of the beaming nymph.

'*By the gods, what was that?*' Marsais whispered in her mind, but there was no time to answer.

"Let's find the camels before they bolt," Rivan said.

Elam led the way through the stone maze to the camels. The long-legged animals stood on the outskirts of the ruins, near a half-covered well and an overturned bucket.

The scene pricked her instincts. Something was wrong. A moment later steel glinted in the sunlight and a Fomorri sprang from behind a crumbled wall. Rivan threw himself in front of her, ramming the veiled-figure.

Both men fell in a cloud of dirt and grunts. Rivan scrambled free, reaching for his fallen sword. The Fomorri raised his own, and Isiilde hurled a grease weave at his feet. He slipped. Rivan brought his blade down. The falchion fell to the ground along with a severed arm, but the attacker's cloak flew open, revealing three more hands: one with a dagger, one with a shortsword, and the last all clawed and curving.

Rivan screamed with rage, and swung. But the Fomorri deflected his attack with a shortsword and claws. That left a third arm. The Fomorri thrust a dagger into Rivan's thigh. He reeled backward, hitting a stone wall.

The Fomorri hopped to his feet with a hiss, and Isiilde shouted, calling to her fire. Flames shot from her hand. It wrapped around the Fomorri, but he didn't slow.

Rivan charged with a bellow. His blade sliced across the creature's neck. With gurgling, rasping breaths, the Fomorri sank to his knees, and fell forward.

Rivan wrenched his sword free. He was breathing hard, glaring at the dead creature. With a growl, he drove his boot into the Fomorri, and then again, jerking the body with force. Next came his sword, rising and falling, hacking at the corpse. Tears streamed from his eyes, blow after blow fell, until blood pooled in the sand.

The camels tugged on their reins, trying to flee.

"Rivan!" she hissed.

When he did not stop, she gripped his shoulder. He raised his sword as if to attack, but the moment he saw the nymph, reason returned. Rivan tossed the weapon away as if it were tainted.

Isiilde bent to retrieve his sword. It was warm, the leather wet with sweat and fear, and the blade covered in ichor. "Does it help?" she asked.

Rivan shook his head. "My family is still dead."

Isiilde held out his sword. He eyed it for a moment before accepting, then cleaned the blade on the tattered remains of the Fomorri's cloak.

"You have a dagger in your thigh," she said.

Rivan nodded numbly. A moment later, her words caught up with his mind, and he looked down. "I think it caught on my armor."

He reached for the dagger, and wrenched it free. Blood dribbled out, but not enough to cause alarm. He dropped the blade, and walked away to see to his injury and collect himself.

Elam's eyes were wide. He had either counted wrong or missed a Fomorri while he was scouting.

"It wasn't your fault," Isiilde soothed.

Elam grunted, then trotted over to calm the camels in a trilling tongue. The animals seemed to respond. And she was glad for it—animals generally distrusted her.

Isiilde turned to the corpse. She nudged his cloak aside and rolled him over with her boot. A human male. But not quite. Bone horns protruded from his skull, and his face was a mottled mix of scale and skin. The scales covered most of his sun-baked face, but the edges around the scales were red and swollen, and yellow sores circled his lips. He smelled of rotten meat.

Careful not to touch his blood, she examined the extra arms. One looked more suited to a child. The arms were stitched on, and the wounds underneath were festering with maggots. Both arms were covered with scars—neat slices that had too much rhythm to be coincidence.

'*Isiilde?*' Marsais whispered. There was fear in that Whisper. And heart-ache.

The rush of battle had left her drained. She sat beside the bucket and wove a short but proud reply. '*We have camels and a well of water.*'

CHAPTER 28

A DUST cloud heralded new arrivals. A large man led the pack, speeding ahead of the rest. Her heart swelled with relief.

As soon as Elam recognized the leader of the pack, he burst from his hiding place. "Oenghus! Bastard!"

Oenghus ruffled the boy's hair. "I need to teach you more Common."

Isiilde eyed her father. Dried blood crusted his beard, chest, and arms. It looked like he'd had a rough time of it. Before she could protest, he pulled into a fierce hug. She returned the gesture with all her strength.

Only half of the Elite remained. She was relieved to see Acacia, and even Lucas, in the group. She gave them all a passing nod, and looked to the lone straggler. Blood marred Marsais' white hair, and his clothes were torn. He staggered to a stop and sat down, hard.

"You look terrible." She carefully probed his skull, finding a large, swollen knot, then tilted his head upwards, searching his eyes. He flinched at the light.

"You have a concussion," she noted.

"I managed to weave an air rune before I was knocked out underwater."

His words struck her. The desert, the camels, and warriors fell away.

There were only his eyes. And they anchored her. He took her hand, and pressed his lips to her knuckles. "It takes more than an ancient leviathan to kill the likes of me. And apparently you're hard to kill, too."

Isiilde squeezed his hand and turned to the ruins. "There are seven dead Fomorri over there—there isn't much left of them. The eighth surprised us, but Rivan handled him."

They found Oenghus looting the dead Fomorri for weapons and cloak. The thought of wearing anything on that maggot-infested thing made her sick.

"I've worn worse," Oenghus said, slapping her on the back. "Another tale for the mead hall." He beamed at her with pride, then strutted over to the camels. No doubt to loot them as well.

Marsais knelt beside the Fomorri. He swayed, nearly pitching forward, but Isiilde grabbed his shoulder, steadying him.

"It will pass." He waved a tired hand.

"I didn't expect the Fomorri to be human."

"Hmm." He studied the man for a moment. "Fomorri alter themselves using a combination of Blood Magic and Void Rituals."

"But why?"

"It's part of their worship of Karbonek. They aspire to fiendish heights. But it's more than that—the thirst for power is an addiction." He plucked a wiggling maggot from the corpse and held it up for her study. But even a nymph's curiosity had limits.

"The ultimate victors of all life," he mused. "Maggots eat rotting flesh, so the Fomorri place them in grafts to help the healing process. They also use leeches to aid blood flow." Marsais dropped the reigning monarch into the sand. "This man is a mere nomad."

"How do you know?"

"His grafts are sloppy. He likely did it himself. True Grafters, as they are known, are like artists. They strive for horrific perfection. A warrior shaped by a Grafter is formidable."

"That arm—it looks like a child's. Is it?"

Grey eyes, misty with pain, met her own. "Yes. They harvest the dead. And the living."

"Do they experiment on their captives, too? As a kind of canvas for practicing?"

"Yes," he said flatly.

Isiilde's hands curled into fists. "And Karbonek is their god?"

"The very god that Tharios seeks to release."

"This will happen on the Isle, won't it?"

"Not if we can stop it."

Isiilde suspected he'd foreseen the outcome—the mutilated bodies and harvested limbs of children on the Isle. One path in a multitude of horrors.

"I wish the Shattering had destroyed this realm," she whispered.

"Gods no, please, my... Isiilde," he corrected. His eyes were pleading, and his hand encompassed hers, beseeching. "We're all that stands between the Void."

"How do you know?"

"I know how you love puzzles..." His eyes flashed with a silver light. "I wouldn't want to spoil one for you."

CHAPTER 29

STEP, *scoot*, *step*; Zoshi paused to shake out his tired arms. His ankle throbbed, and his backside hurt from scooting down the long stairway. He didn't dare wobble down in the dark.

Crumpet clicked his disapproval.

"I need to rest. I don't have wings like you."

Zoshi didn't know how long he'd been scooting down the spiraling stairs. He'd slept and woken in darkness. And done it all over again. His provisions were nearly gone.

The stairway seemed to go on forever.

Zoshi unwound the bloodied bandages on his hands. The skin had been scraped raw on the rough stone. He flexed his fingers, then fished around his pockets for a crust of bread. It was as hard as a rock. He'd run out of water... when?

Time moved strangely in this place.

Crumpet returned with a flutter of wings. And a gift. A fresh piece of moss. While Zoshi exchanged this new one for his old, the bird pecked at the moss, then the bread.

"Can I eat it?"

The bird croaked out a *yes*. Zoshi made a face. The sound of trickling water saved him from sampling the moss. It brushed his ear like a feather, and he perked up, listening hard; it was not his imagination. A thrill washed away his fatigue.

Taking care with his swollen ankle, he gathered his things and scooted down the steps, listening for the noise. When it was at its loudest, he touched the wall. Cool water dripped over his fingertips. Zoshi put his lips to the stream, and slurped at the rivulets.

It took awhile, but he drank his fill, and then pressed the mouth of his waterskin to the wall. It didn't matter how long it took to fill. He needed water.

The stairway curved, round and round. There were no landings or corners, just an endless spiral. But there *must* be an end. He only hoped it didn't lead to the Nine Halls.

CHAPTER 30

Morigan stared at her shield-sister. A thin layer of snow covered Brinehilde like a white veil for the dead. The bailey was littered with the dead.

"She died with the hunt in her blood," Rashk said.

Morigan did not answer.

Rashk hissed in pain as she crouched. The bandage on her leg was soaked with blood. She was missing a chunk of her ear and a deep gash cut across her face. She'd come close to losing an eye.

Morigan didn't have the energy to heal. Her helm lay on the ground, along with her axe. Both were covered and caked with gore.

"She wounded Tharios," Rashk said into the silence. "Foolish but brave. Her sacrifice will be remembered."

Morigan looked over the field at the countless dead. All brave; all foolish. Courage stank like piss and desperation. She was tired of its stench. But there was still more to come. Eiji and Tharios had retreated to the Spine—a large, fortified and warded hole, with rot in its bowels.

Rashk dropped into the snow. "Your Whisper saved us. And Brinehilde put fire in our hearts. Seeing you on the battlefield... I did not know you were a warrior."

Morigan met Rashk's slitted gaze. "When I go to the ol'River, I don't want to be known as a butcher; only a healer."

At the intensity of those words, Rashk dipped her chin. "What can I do to help, Healer?"

"Help me carry Brinehilde on her shield," Morigan said, climbing to her feet. "She should be buried in her grove."

It was a foolish notion. Drivel was hours away, and the battle not yet won, but grief clouded her reason. She needed to bury her shield-sister.

"There is an old oak in Coven," Rashk offered. "Its leaves sing and its roots go deep."

Morigan closed her eyes, and nodded.

"I'll find a cart."

Being carried on a shield was poetic. But a cart was practical.

MORIGAN TRUDGED THROUGH THE SNOW, dragging the cart while Rashk kept it steady, slowing its descent on the slippery road. They stopped under a twisted old oak at the edge of town.

There were no footprints in the freshly fallen snow. And frozen corpses littered the main road. Coven looked to be abandoned.

It put her on edge.

Morigan reached for her axe. "You can come out now," she called. "The fog is gone."

No answer.

"It's Morigan Freyr," she added.

A door to the pleasure house cracked, and a big man with a shock of blond hair poked his head outside. "*Morigan?*"

"Aye, Breeman," she said, walking to the steps. The Nuthaanian stared at her, mouth slightly agape. Few on the Isle had seen her fitted for battle. "Are your ladies all right?"

Breeman stepped outside. He held an axe in his hand. "Scared witless, but we're better off than the ones caught in the fog. There wasn't much of an enemy to fight."

"No," she agreed. "Are there wounded?"

"Not in my house. We've all kept inside—away from that bloody fog." He joined her on the road, and gripped her shoulder in greeting. "What happened in the castle? You look dead on your feet."

"Tharios is a Bloodmagi. There's a cabal of them holed up in the Spine. They have a mind to invite a fiendish god into the realm."

"Void."

"Aye."

"Did that bloody new Archlord kill Oenghus and Marsais, then?"

"Oenghus and Isiilde are alive. I'd imagine Marsais is, too."

"I never believed the lies. Not for a second. But I tossed out a good number who did."

Their voices carried in the quiet, and doors began to crack open. A few brave souls peeked out of their shelter. They were all pale and worn, with a haunted look about them. Two armed Nuthaanians standing in the open gave them courage. And soon enough, Morigan was surrounded by a barrage of people clamoring for answers she didn't have.

"Quiet," she ordered. The townsfolk fell silent. "You there…" She recognized the man as the reeve. "Knock on every door, search out the wounded, and bring them to Isadora's. I'll send a healer from the castle. And start gathering the dead before they thaw."

It gave the survivors purpose. She left the reeve to organize the search, and strode quickly back to the oak tree.

Breeman followed on her heels. "What do you need of me?"

In answer, she yanked back the tarp covering the cart. The sight of Brinehilde was like a kick to the man's gut. "Blood and ashes."

"Help me bury her, Breeman. The battle isn't over."

When Morigan stabbed her shovel into the near-frozen earth, her vision blurred. The world swayed and lost focus.

"Mori," a voice rumbled. "You're about to keel over. Leave this to me."

For a joyous moment, she thought it was Oenghus. But when she looked up to find a man with a shock of blond hair and a trim beard, her hope shattered.

Morigan ignored his order—she only occasionally took them from Oenghus—and tossed a shovel full of earth out of the shallow grave.

Breeman muttered, but kept digging. His powerful shoulders made quick work of the ground. Rashk had run off to summon a healer, and with work to be done, a semblance of normality had returned to Coven.

"If Oenghus was 'ere. He'd sit you down on your lovely arse and hold you down 'til you slept."

"He's not here," she said, jabbing her shovel back into the earth. Thoughts of the man led to worry and ache. By the gods, he was irksome.

"Aye, but if anything happens to you, he'll have my hide."

Morigan pinned the man with a glare. "If you try anything so foolish Breeman Mchamish, I'll set your bollocks to boiling so thoroughly that you'll wish your tender bits were buried in ice."

He paled and went back to digging.

When the ground was deep and their muscles numb, they lowered Brinehilde into her cradle. She lay on her shield.

"Piss in the ol'River, Hilde," Breeman said with a sniff.

Both Nuthaanians spat for good measure.

Morigan placed a hand on the oak. "May she give life to many."

The roots shifted as vines grew from the earth, wrapping the body in a cocoon. Breeman took a step back, but Morigan held her ground, watching the earth swallow the priestess.

"Zemoch's bollocks," Breeman breathed. "Did you do that?"

Morigan shook her head. "The Sylph."

Breeman scratched his beard. "Would've been nice if she gave us a hand with the digging." Nuthaanians weren't known for their reverence.

Morigan began shoveling the dirt back into the empty grave. When it was flat and black against the snow, she set her shovel aside.

"Come in for a drink," Breeman said. "I'll warm you up if you like."

"I've a mind to sit and be for a bit."

"I'll miss her," Breeman sighed.

"So will I."

Breeman tugged his cloak from a branch and draped it over her shoulders. "My shield stands ready for you—whatever you need."

When he walked away, Morigan slumped against the oak tree. How long had she been on her feet? The height of the snowdrifts, the frozen dead, the thin faces of the townsfolk. It seemed only a few days, but... Time seemed to move strangely in the fog. She couldn't be sure. And she was too exhausted to think.

Morigan let her head fall against the bark. Her gaze traveled up, through a tangle of branches, to the darkening sky. She closed her eyes. Only for a moment, or so she thought. But when she opened them, night had fallen, and the Keeper's moon was casting its ruddy light over the earth.

Morigan felt the touch of eyes. Someone was watching her. She reached for her axe, and stood.

"The fog seems to 'ave cleared." It was a deep, velvety voice, and it came from behind. She spun, but could only make out shadows. Then her gaze traveled up, and she saw a small figure sitting on a branch. He looked like a child wearing a broad-brimmed hat.

A woman stepped into the moonlight with a shift of shadow. "I told you not to startle her." Her voice was pleasant, but her eyes were hard. Her curly black hair was pulled back, exposing pointed ears. A Kamberian. They weren't residents of the Isle. Morigan was sure of it.

"Can I help you two? It's been a long day of killing and I've just buried my shield-sister."

The gnome in the tree fell back, flipped off the branch, and landed easily on both feet. He swept off his hat and bowed with a flourish. "My condolences, m'lady. And apologies for startling you. The name is Bram. And this here is my lovely Evie."

The woman smiled, a slash of white across her dark brown skin. "We're looking for a healer by the name of Morigan Freyr."

Morigan eyed the two strangers. The gnome had blades on his person, and the woman wore leather armor. A bow was slung on her back, and a quiver rested against her thigh. She moved like a snake coiling for the strike.

"I am that healer."

Evie looked dubiously at Morigan's armor and axe.

"Ah, I told you, Evie. Didn't I say?" Bram crowed.

"I didn't hear your squeak."

"Like a purring panther, isn't that what you always say?"

The woman rolled her eyes. Amusement had melted the hard edge of her gaze. "We're here to help. The Guardian of Life himself sent us."

"That's a high claim that needs more proof than words," Morigan said.

The gnome sighed. "We're never believed."

"You don't look much like a Wraith Guard, love."

"As if you do—all supple and lovely, and delicious as chocolate," Bram shot back. The little man did sound like a purring cat.

"That's because I'm not," Evie explained to Morigan. "I'm a Valkyrie, not a Guard, and really, love, you're more of a scout."

"Am I now?"

"More rogue, even."

"Iilenshar requires all," he said grandly.

"More words," Morigan growled, knocking the two on track. She had no patience tonight.

Evie sobered, her eyes softening with kindness. "A seer by the name of Marsais told the man himself that we could trust you," she explained. "The fog delayed us—nasty that—and from what we've heard, this Marsais and Oenghus got tossed to Vaylin."

Morigan shuddered with relief. Vaylin was on the other side of the realm. But at least it was *in* Fyrsta. And Marsais had gotten word to Iilenshar. It gave her hope. They were no longer alone.

"I think some food and a warm fire are in order," Bram said gently.

Morigan did not argue.

CHAPTER 31

Soldiers were collecting the dead into wagons, and taking them through the gates to a long line of pyres waiting on the hillside.

"War is a terrible thing," she whispered.

"That it is," Evie agreed.

"I've seen too much of it. And yet I'll never understand it. What drives men and women to such madness?"

"The Void does it," Evie said.

"And boredom," added Bram.

They both shrugged.

Morigan agreed. Puzzling over power-mad fools was a road to insanity. She turned, and walked through the open gates, nodding to the guards.

Thira had been busy. The lower bailey bustled with activity. Tents had been erected, cooking fires lit, and a long line of horses stood by the ramparts. The Blessed Order had arrived.

Last night, after the pair had seen her fed and settled by a fire with a mug of ale, they'd joined her for a chat.

"Let's keep our arrival under our hats, shall we?" Bram had suggested.

"And best to leave out the 'sent from Chaim' part," added Evie.

"Why?"

The gnome sighed. "No one ever believes us."

"And Marsais is unjustly wanted by the Blessed Order."

Morigan smiled at this. Valkyrie and Wraith Guard could be as rigid as the Blessed Order. But not these two, it seemed.

"And before you think that all Himself sent you was a scrawny gnome and a charming woman—we're not alone," Bram confided.

"Did you bring an army?" Morigan asked with hope.

"Erm... no." Bram blushed.

"Twelve Wraith Guards," Evie supplied. "We thought we were sneaking into an open castle; not one under siege with a mad Blood-magi in charge."

Twelve Wraith Guards were better than none—they were the elite warriors of the Guardians.

Presently, Morigan was leading her companions across the field and through the long tunnel that led to the outer bailey. Workers were busy fortifying the Fire Gates. The castle had been designed to defend against attackers from the outside, not the inside.

Eldred stopped barking orders long enough to nod at Morigan. "Thira's in the tower over there with his Holiness, the most righteous prick."

The trio walked towards the tall tower. In contrast to the lower bailey, the outer bailey where the battle had raged was empty save for a line of guards on the ground, keeping watch on the closed bailey gates. They stood out of bow range. No invading force had ever made it past those gates. The walls were formidable.

Raised voices echoed from a second-story window. Morigan sighed. Although she had slept, her body was battered and bruised, and the long walk to the castle had left her thinking of a warm bed. The last thing she wanted to do was deal with High Inquisitor Multist.

Morigan bullied her way past a pair of paladins at the entrance, and marched up the stairs. The High Inquisitor was in a high temper.

"...the lot of you! If you had allowed the Blessed Order a Chapter-house inside the walls, this would have never happened." His fervor was lost on the rail-thin woman in the room. Thira took a bored sip of her tea.

"If you had arrived sooner, instead of hiding like cowards, we could have defeated him," Rashk hissed.

"My duty is to Drivel," Multist defended. "I sent scouts. They couldn't penetrate that Void-cursed Fog."

Thira looked to the new arrivals. "Morigan." There was very nearly relief in that clipped tone.

"This is Evie and Bram—friends of mine," Morigan explained.

Thira looked thoughtfully at her *friends,* but thankfully kept those thoughts to herself. The High Inquisitor was another matter.

Multist drew himself up. "You're intruding on my meeting. Leave at once. You kept company with that berserker—the Bloodmagi."

The days had been long, and full of pain. And she had no patience left for incompetence. Morigan shoved the man against the closest wall, and pinned him there. "Oenghus is *no* Bloodmagi. If you say that word with his name again, you'll discover why berserkers fear Nuthaanian women."

Everyone in the room froze. Even the Inquisitor. Few knew of her history, but it didn't matter—the look in her eyes said it all.

A timid sound entered the tension. "Inquisitor," Tulipin spoke up. "I was sorely mistaken. Marsais and Oenghus are *not* Bloodmagi. Tharios is the threat, and he alone."

Morigan gave the man a final shove before taking a step back.

Thira cleared her throat, and set down her tea. "Tharios fooled us all," she said. The confession seemed to leave a foul taste on her lips.

"While he was lining the pockets of others," Morigan added. There was no need to name the Inquisitor. The twitch in his eye said it all. "Now, let's put all that behind us and figure out how to get at the bastard."

Lord General Ielequithe unfurled a map on the table. The corners were weighted, and those assembled drew near, bending over to study the maze-like map.

"Even before Tharios was named Archlord, he was bringing in recruits," Ielequithe admitted. "After his Confirmation, we saw an influx of fresh faces. We now know that the Quartermaster was loyal to him. He positioned those loyal to Tharios in key places. Most of those men were placed in the Spine. Presently, Tharios holds everything beyond the Bailey Gates. Thanks to your Whisper, a good number of castle residents escaped during the battle in the bailey."

"What about Leiman and the other healers?" she asked.

"I've not seen them."

Morigan frowned. A myriad of choices; a fountain of regret. It was useless to ponder what might have been if she'd remained to help Leiman. She eyed the map, searching for the tunnel barracks. "Tharios has been emptying the dock districts and using others from the castle to dig in the Underneath."

"Digging for what?" Thira asked.

"Brinehilde and I captured an Unspoken by the name of Fallon Able. He said Tharios plans on bringing Karbonek to this realm."

Silence was tangible for a full minute.

"His true prey," Rashk finally hissed.

"What are you talking about?" Multist demanded.

"Thedus told me the fog was the Fey," Thira explained. "Rashk and I think they were imprisoned in the Nameless chamber—that Tharios released them to buy himself time to complete his ultimate goal. The fog was a mere distraction."

The Inquisitor's eyes narrowed. "Are you telling me that the God of the Fomorri is under this castle?"

"We do not know," Rashk said. "Tharios has an artifact that can open portals. We think it is Soisskeli's Stave."

"The stave *binds* creatures; it doesn't open portals," Multist said.

"We have a witness who saw Tharios open a Gateway with a stave."

"Why would Tharios be digging if he has an artifact that can open a portal?" Multist's question was a good one.

Morigan placed her palms flat on the map. "There are places where the veil between realms is thinner."

"The Isle of Blight," Thira said.

Morigan gave her a nod. "And also on this island."

"What?" Multist asked in shock. Even the Wise Ones looked at her in question.

"A portal to the Nine Halls was opened long before the Shattering. Ulfhidhin and Hengist Heartfang battled the fiendish god to close it."

Multist clutched his Sacred Sun emblem. "I've sensed evil on this

Isle since the day I first graced its shores," he announced with an overly righteous air.

Thira studied Morigan like she was a frog on a novice's dissection block. "That knowledge isn't in our Lore."

"It's Nuthaanian legend," she lied.

Oenghus had never slept easy. And through their many Oaths together, his night terrors became worse with each passing year. She'd never betray him—that included what he said in his sleep.

"Are these maps complete?" Evie asked.

Morigan shook her head. "There's a maze under the castle."

"I suspect the *Archlord* has a complete map," Thira said with contempt.

"The map may very well be why Tharios wanted the throne so badly," Morigan agreed.

Thira straightened, and took her tea to the window, gazing at the looming Spine. "The Order's scouts keep petitioning to explore the Drakenwood, but no one has any interest in what's under our feet."

"Ah, well," Bram sighed. "Wanderlust never takes me to the cellar, either."

"Do you remember where the tunnels were?" Ielequithe asked.

Starting at the infirmary, Morigan traced a finger over the path, exchanging maps as needed. The farther down she went, the less detailed the maps. And when she reached the last section, she slid over a piece of parchment and dipped a quill in ink. The result was a rough sketch, with an X marking the makeshift barracks.

"Now, how do we get inside?" Bram asked.

"The time-honored way," Morigan said. "We knock, good and bloody hard."

CHAPTER 32

A LINE of soldiers marched under a merciless sun. Their heads were bowed and their faces covered, leaving a narrow slit for scorched eyes. The horizon wavered with a mirage that teased their tongues.

Although the sun hadn't reached its peak, it consumed the world, and every human sweltered, save for one cheerful nymph.

Isiilde tilted her uncovered face to the sky. She had shed every piece of clothing possible, stopping just shy of indecent, and now she basked in the heat. It was utter bliss.

Overcome, she stopped, and spread her arms. Joy filled her heart, and she twirled with a laugh.

"Keep walking, Sprite," Oenghus rasped, taking out a pillaged waterskin. He squeezed it to his lips, and the pebble that he kept in his mouth clicked on his teeth.

When he wasn't drinking, he sucked on it, as did every other man and woman. The group was well-versed in desert survival, but humans had a low tolerance for heat.

"I can always catch up."

A camel stopped to lick her ear. It was Spot, named for the mark on his tongue. He tried to lick everything. She reached up to rub his velvety nose and he leaned into her touch. Most animals were wary of the combustible nymph, but these two were comfortable with her. Maybe because they were used to heat.

Elam was draped over the bags and blankets. The boy looked like he was melting. And Marsais rode the second camel, which she'd named Red.

Marsais was lost in another vision. Rather than lead him around, Oenghus had healed his injuries and stuck him on a camel. At least he wouldn't wander off into the desert again.

Acacia and Rivan stopped beside the nymph, each taking a draught of water. "I'm dry as a bone," Rivan said, eyeing her. "How can you be enjoying this?" Her hair was fire, and her skin wavered like a dream.

"It's wonderful here."

"Except at night," Acacia pointed out.

Isiilde had spent the night shivering.

"Aye, that, and the Fomorri roaming the desert," Oenghus grunted.

His remark sobered her. She gave Spot a gentle nudge, and fell in step with her friends.

"I didn't mean to put a cloud over you, Sprite."

"You're right. It's not a wonderful place." She glanced at Rivan, who'd barely spoken since his fight with the Fomorri, and then to Elam, who had lost his sister.

"I, for one, would rather rejoice at a mug half-full than despair over one half-empty," a voice mused from above.

Isiilde looked up to find Marsais focused and clear-eyed. He slipped off the camel with his usual nimble grace, and took cover in Oenghus' shadow. "The darker the place, the more joy should be treasured."

"Are you bloody done making up proverbs? Gods, you sound like a walking prayer book."

"You quote me often enough," Marsais said.

Isiilde smiled, and brushed his fingers, welcoming him back from wherever his mind had thrown him.

"Void," Oenghus spat. Then, without warning, he surged forward, descending on a scorpion that blended with the sand. He plucked the barbed creature from the ground, and held it up, triumphant. "Flat tail. Extremely deadly," he explained for her benefit and Rivan's.

So far, he'd declared every single creature as venomous. He then ate every one. The flat tail was no exception. With quick efficiency, he drew his knife, pressed the scorpion to the ground, and cut off its stinger. Then shoved the insect into his mouth.

Isiilde looked away.

"You really should try one," he said with a crunch. "It's more like crab than meat. You'd be fine."

"I have strawberries."

"You need to save your rations," he argued. The Fomorri supplies had supplemented the ones that were lost in the landing, but it would not be enough.

"I'll pass."

"I suppose I'll try one," Rivan said. But from the color of his cheeks, his stomach was not thrilled with the idea.

Oenghus gave the paladin an approving slap on the back. A chattering voice joined the fray. Elam had stirred from his nap.

"He would like the next one," Marsais translated. "He thinks you're so big because you ate scorpions."

"That's right." Oenghus thumped his chest. "Grows hair on your chest."

"The last thing you want in this land," Acacia said.

"Not when the sun goes down." Oenghus waggled his brows at the woman. "Feel free to curl up to me."

The edge of Acacia's lip quirked. "I prefer the camels."

A CLUSTER of date palms stood out starkly on the horizon. Isiilde blinked at the distant trees, wondering when they had appeared. The distant mountains to the east looked no closer.

Elam tipped back a waterskin, careful not to spill a drop. Marsais spoke to the boy in Lome, puffing out his cheeks. The boy corked the skin and held the water in his mouth.

"Water lasts longer that way," Oenghus explained, sucking on the pebble in his mouth. He gestured the boy closer, and reached under Red, gently gripping her teat. A skilled squeeze squirted out milk. He licked it from his fingers. "Good and filling."

"You've been here before," Acacia noted.

"Aye, the Scarecrow and me got stranded in the Great Expanse. Things got rough."

Marsais snorted. "Just a tad."

"How'd you find your way out?" Rivan asked.

"We walked."

"No," Oenghus corrected, "I *carried* your bony carcass."

"Ah, that's right. You make for an excellent pack animal. Your shoulder is far more comfortable than a camel's back."

"You can bloody walk next time, you ol'bastard."

There seemed to be a lot of walking in Fomorri. The group had walked through the night, and now, at the peak of the next day, Nimlesh called a halt under the trees.

Without a word, the Elite fell into practiced routine, setting up camp. An agile woman named Nalani scurried up the palms, tossing down clusters of small round dates from the crown, while the other soldiers dug deep bowl-shaped holes in the sand. Palm leaves and shrubs were tossed inside, and then each soldier pissed into the hole. The paladins did the same.

Isiilde watched, puzzled. When bladders were emptied, a cup, or pan was placed in the center of the hole. After that, each hole was covered with a thin oilskin, then a rock was placed on top of it.

Humans, she decided, were odd.

Curiosity got the better of the nymph. She stepped beside Marsais, who was lacing up his own trousers. "Why is everyone pissing into a hole?"

"The sun heats the oilskin, drawing water from the leaves and urine. The water rises like mist, and then it gathers on the oilskin, and because of the rock—"

"It drips into the cup," she realized.

"Precisely. Every drop of water is precious here."

"I brought water runes," she said. "There was an entire cabinet of the runes in my chambers on Mearcentia." It was worth a fortune. She wasn't sure how she felt about Finn Syre II, but she felt bad about looting his palace for supplies.

"Thoughtful," he said, bending to pick up a rock. "But you'll find that the runes won't produce as much water here. Water runes aren't much different from the holes. They simply pull water from the air."

"Oh." Her waterskin was nearly empty.

"Use the rune stones at night," Marsais suggested. "Dew still gathers in the desert."

She looked at the hole, then at the humans. Sensing her thoughts, Marsais obliged, tracing a quick mirror weave. If anyone looked her way, they'd see desert. She added her own piss into the hole, and helped Marsais lay the oilskin and rock back over the pit, pushing sand over the edges of skin to hold it in place.

A triumphant grunt drew her gaze. Oenghus, Elam, and Lucas were gathered around a shrub, poking it with sticks and swords. A long, tan snake slithered out of the underbrush. It had horns on its head.

Lucas pinned it with his shield and hacked off the head.

"One drop of venom from its fangs and you're dead, but the meat is worth the risk," Oenghus said, picking up the still twitching serpent.

As they buried the head, and rolled the skin down its pink body, the soldiers dug narrow trenches beneath the palm trees in the shade. Each soldier lay in the cool sand, breaking out rations to wait out the hottest part of the day. A small fire had already been lit with camel dung to cook the snake.

Isiilde turned away from the smell, the humans, and the piss pits, and walked out onto the sand, in the full light of day. Heat rippled off the rocks.

The temptation was too great.

Without a care, she tugged off the last of her clothes, and lay down, stretching beneath the fiery bliss. In less than a minute, the nymph was asleep.

THEY WALKED through the evening until nightfall and beyond, keeping the distant mountains in sight. The temperature dropped with the sun. And despite her layers of clothing, she was shivering.

Oenghus slowed to walk beside her. He was leading Spot. Isiilde scratched the camel's nose, and buried her fingers in his warm hair.

"Are you sure you don't want to ride?"

"If I stop moving, I'll freeze," she chattered.

The moon and stars were bright, but she kept her eyes on the shadows. Scorpions and beetles roamed the night, and other, larger things. Somewhere, far off, a jackal was howling to its pack.

"Marsais could weave a heat rune... once he comes to."

"I don't think he's up to that."

Marsais had his own problems. He'd been staring at the moon for most of the night and murmuring in a strange tongue. They tried to coax him back onto a camel, but he'd grown agitated. And dangerous. So Rivan was watching him—from a distance.

"Besides, I don't need help. I can manage on my own."

"Look here, Isiilde. You don't need to prove anything. Everyone needs help. That's what friends are for."

"I'm here to help, not to be a burden."

Oenghus snorted. "You don't think the ol'bastard there is a burden half the time?"

At that moment, Marsais tripped over a rock. Rivan grabbed his arm, but Marsais shook off the hand and returned to his restless mutterings.

"What is he saying?" Isiilde asked. She didn't even recognize the language.

"Void if I know." Oenghus scratched at his beard. "Probably garbling all his languages together again. He does that sometimes."

"Not when we were bonded."

"You weren't bonded long."

"No, but even when I was his apprentice, he seemed more coherent."

"You weren't with him all the time. Why do you think he disappeared for days on end?"

Her lips parted in surprise. She never considered the possibility that he was unwell. She'd always assumed he was busy with his Archlord duties.

"This is his life," Oenghus said. "He's been like this for a long time."

"But when we were bonded, and even before, it seemed like I could reach him—pull him back from wherever he went."

"I don't doubt it." Oenghus kicked at a rock, sending it flying off into the night. "Speaking of that... Are you, erm... still bonded?"

"I already told you."

"But maybe you don't realize it's still there."

"You don't think I'd notice something like that?"

"There's no connection at all?" Her father looked down at her, face obscured by shadow, but his eyes were bright as sapphires.

"Our bond was..." She hesitated, searching for a word that fit. "Untangled, I suppose."

Oenghus fell silent, but she could sense him brooding.

"What is it?" she pressed.

Oenghus looked towards the silver moon. His shoulders seemed to sag for a moment. "Er, well, sometimes a bond can be, erm... dormant."

He looked as uncomfortable as the time she'd asked how babies got into a woman's stomach. He'd shoved her towards Morigan, and promptly left.

"Tell me what you know," she demanded.

"There's nothing simple about a bond. Granted, if it's forced, then it's like a collar."

The thought made her sick.

"But your mother... she could control her bond. Shape it, even. I don't really know. I think it was her age."

"How old was she?"

"I don't know."

"Then why would you think her age was involved?"

Oenghus ignored her question. "She could choose who she gave her bond to, and could keep it intact when she wanted. I think a bond, for some nymphs, is like love—no matter what happens, it never goes away. Take me and Morigan, for example."

They loved each other. It was written on their faces, and in their eyes. Oenghus never looked at anyone the way he looked at Morigan. And yet... they both took other lovers.

"We've taken more than one Oath together. Sometimes for forty years. Sometimes for twenty. But that doesn't mean we've ever stopped loving each other. It's that simple. I love her. She loves me."

"You hope," Isiilde said dryly.

"Don't think it doesn't surprise me," Oenghus grunted. "But it doesn't mean there isn't room for others. Nuthaanians aren't like the other races. We have a uhm... broader view of love."

"And the mating habits of rabbits," Marsais called over his shoulder. It seemed he had returned to the present.

Oenghus directed a crude gesture at his back. Before the two started bickering, Isiilde slowed, falling behind the group, and her father followed suit, until they were out of earshot.

"The ol'bastard is right," Oenghus admitted. "That's how the other races view us. We're not like most who only take one Oath at a time. Men are just the peckerheads who spread the seed, but a woman is the soil. Without her, every man dies. That's why a woman can have as many Oathbound as she wants in Nuthaan."

"How many Oathbound does Morigan have? She almost never leaves her infirmary."

"Aye, well, she had a rough time in the Fell Wastes." He tugged savagely on his beard. "We both did. And then you came along and... Well, it's complicated. What I'm trying to get at is that I love her, and she loves me; we come and go as we please, but the love is still there. It's just not urgent."

"I think I'd know if I were still bonded to Marsais."

Oenghus shrugged, and fell silent. He was brooding again.

"Was that how your bond with my mother was?" she finally asked.

"Aye, our bond would fade in and out, but it was always there. Didn't matter when—" He caught himself. "When the Emperor took her."

She narrowed her eyes. "You mean by force?"

"Aye." There was an unbearable pain in that single word. And there was something more he wasn't telling her. A whole lot of something.

Before she could press him further, he stomped away, moving to the front of the line. And there he stayed, far ahead of the others, walking in a pool of silver moonlight.

CHAPTER 33

MARSAIS WALKED in a maze of memory. His footsteps whispering in his own ears. The hallway was dark; the ash thick.

He brushed a groove in the stone, tracing its path. Claw marks. At his careful touch, the stone flaked off, swirling in the air, clouding his vision.

Marsais frowned at the marks. The ocean that drifted over his head did not penetrate this corridor. It was all shadow and haze and clogged with ash.

Stone did not turn to ash. Why was it here? The question puzzled him.

Marsais frowned, gazing down at his body. He wore a white robe stained with blood, and his feet were black with soot, marred by time and age. He curled his toes in the ash. The ground was warm.

Marsais squeezed his eyes shut, willing himself to wake. Once, he could walk the maze as he pleased, and leave when he desired. But not now. Marsais was only a shadow, a phantom drifting in ruin.

He pressed his palm against the crumbling wall. The stone vibrated, and his heart quickened, pounding against his ears like a drum. Squaring his shoulders, he walked into the deepening darkness.

This was his realm: all of Time. Why was the maze darkening? The ash, the soot, the crumbling walls—

You're dying.

The thought gave him comfort.

The path split ahead. Marsais hesitated for a moment, then went left. An endless line of doors stretched down the hallway.

The first door was plain: teak with a simple, rusted lock. He trailed his fingers over the old wood. The smell of pine and gentle fire filled his senses. The memory inside the door beckoned, but he walked on to the next. Splintered wood lay at the threshold, and when he looked inside, everything was ashy ruin.

Marsais swallowed down the urge to lie down and weep. He quickened his pace, walking past the other doors, the other memories, not daring to touch their surface.

"The past is as hard to chart as the future," he'd once confided to Isiilde. Those words were never truer than now. His past was crumbling, his mind was in ruin. Time was unraveling. And he was lost in a maze of his own making.

He thought of Isiilde and her fire, and the force of chaos that created her. Was that her purpose—to burn the threads of time?

Marsais had no answers.

He glanced up, daring to look in the ocean's reflection. The dead floated there. He shook the vision from his eyes, and hurried on, turning left. It seemed the right way.

Marsais chuckled at his pun, and somewhere, a madman laughed, too. But he was alone. Wasn't he? Both possibilities unnerved him.

Another hallway, more doors. The corridors became a blur. He turned a corner and stopped. A metal door waited at the end of a long hallway. It was a chained, monstrous iron thing covered with locks.

He did not like the look of it.

Marsais took a hasty step backwards. But that was always a mistake with Time. He fell through the ash and landed with a bone-jarring thud.

Coughing, Marsais put an arm over his mouth, trying not to breathe in the choking air. He staggered to his feet and fell against the wall, searching the haze.

The ocean still drifted above, but this time, his reflection stared back. It wasn't a vision. That was good. But the sound he heard was not.

A door banged open. He spun and his throat went dry. A single door stood at the end of the corridor. It was draped in shadow. He didn't remember it.

Marsais edged towards this strange new door. There was no handle, but it whispered, not with memory but of the future.

Stone rubble was strewn across the floor, poking through the ash. He side-stepped a collapsed section of wall, and stopped in front of the door. Shadows clung to it like a shroud and claw marks marred its surface. He traced a finger over the marks.

The door bulged with a thud that knocked him back a step. Marsais thrust a hand into his pocket and brought out three small discs. Bright light flooded the corridor, illuminating the door.

The wood warped and rippled, pulsing like a heartbeat. Dark ichor ran from the seams, and the coppery scent of blood filled his senses. It pooled on the floor, reaching towards his bare feet. He took another step back, and another, timed with the thuds and knocks.

Marsais fled. He turned left.

The hallways of Time were a blur, and he walked briskly past countless forgotten moments, until his heart slowed. But he felt the touch of eyes on his neck. Footsteps whispered to his own. He was not alone.

Marsais looked over his shoulder. A snatch of shadow detached itself from the wall. Two pinpricks of ice stared back. His mind shouted Reaper, but his instincts disagreed.

"Who are you?" he asked instead.

"I saw you die." It was a rasping, damaged sound, but underneath the pain was the voice of a girl.

"Did you?"

"Yes."

"I have seen many deaths," he replied.

"I have only seen one."

"Ah." Such a simple sound for a pronouncement of death. The single syllable had gotten him through worse.

"You don't know who I am?" she asked.

"Should I?"

"We've met before."

"Have we?"

"Yes."

"I see." And he did. "Time," he gestured at the ceiling, "is an ocean—one moment brushing against the next. This is a moment. One that still doesn't answer my question: who are you?"

"You named me yourself, Marsais," the girl replied, taking a step towards him. The shadows seemed to open like a cloak and fall behind her. Light touched inky scales. "I am the bird over the sea."

"Impossible," he breathed.

The girl-creature smiled, revealing pearlescent fangs. "As you see, it is not."

A sound cut through the maze, a grinding, ear-rending scrape. Pain shook his bones. Marsais clutched his ears and fear entered the girl-creature's glowing blue eyes. "Go!" she hissed, and then darted away, swift as a bird.

Marsais sprinted after her. The hallways shook, the ocean of Time rippled, and the ground heaved. His scar burned. And the pain dropped him to his knees. As he struggled to breathe, darkness and sound washed over him—a grating scrape, and the steady gait of crashing steps.

The darkness spewed a nightmare from its depths. Claw and shadow, and screeching heads. Marsais forced himself to move, to stagger to his feet, and run. He turned left.

The Nightmare turned right, its cloak reaching towards him with a snap of teeth. He didn't know where he ran, or for how long, but he ran until his ribs ached and his breath came in panting gasps. Eventually, the quaking stopped, and so did he.

Marsais steadied himself on a wall, and as he struggled to get his breathing under control, he heard a whisper. It touched his fingers. His head snapped up, and his eyes grew wide. He wasn't leaning against a wall, but a door—a chained metal door covered in locks and misery.

No, he thought desperately, not here, not now. He had fled this memory.

The whispers grew, the iron bulged, revealing screaming faces in the metal. Time snapped, dragging him inside. His realm quaked with terror. Mountains fell, castles collapsed, and the ground swallowed it all. Time lay in ruin.

"Father!"

A desperate scream jerked him awake. Marsais was being shaken, not by the earth, but by a frightened girl. "You can't leave. I've stopped the bleeding. You can't go. Not yet. *Please.*"

His heart responded to that voice. He forced his eyes open and blinked at the face hovering over him—his daughter. Tears streaked her ash-covered cheeks. He tried to comfort her, tried to speak reassuring words, but his body was so very distant.

The shaking stopped. She touched his cheek with a bloody hand, and his head fell to the side. A pair of fingers filled his vision—lifeless, still, caught in the act of reaching.

But this was no vision; it was memory and heartache.

A face came into focus next. He knew that face, and he reached towards the dead woman—his Oathbound. But when he moved, a scalding brand sliced his chest and a multitude of screams took flight.

They came from his own throat.

MARSAIS SCREAMED. His body arched, and his back bent like a bow with his head and heels anchored to the earth. All at once, he collapsed.

"Marsais."

The voice soothed his mind. A cool hand rested on his chest, buried under robes, pressed flat against his flesh. He blinked. An ethereal face framed by fire stared back. It was not his daughter from memory, nor the scaled girl running through Time. It was a nymph.

"Who?" Talking was difficult. His swollen tongue bumped against his teeth.

"Isiilde."

The name was familiar. He squeezed his eyes shut, searching the crumbling maze of his mind. Future and past clamored, all mixed up and turned over, jumbled like the ruins of his home after the Shattering. And his slaughtered family.

Tears burned a path down his cheeks.

"We're in Fomorri, traveling to Finnow's Spire," the voice whispered. "We're not bonded."

How did he know that voice? A door clicked open, and a memory stepped into the light. "Isiilde," he rasped, seizing her hand.

She anchored him to the present. Not altogether sure he wanted to know the where or when, he squinted at his surroundings. There were no ruins, no ash, no lifeless shell of his once Oathbound. No dead children nor a beautiful daughter who would die all too slowly.

Marsais lay in the shadow of a boulder. A ring of watchful soldiers had abandoned their shade to escape the raving lunatic. He closed his eyes, feeling cool sand beneath his back. He was lying in a trench.

"How like a grave," he murmured.

"Aye, well, I was about to bury you and leave. Scream any louder and you'll bring a horde on us." A giant of a man spat in the sand.

"Oenghus."

"No, I'm your bloody mother. On your feet, ol'bastard. We need to move."

A woman knelt by his side. Her eyes were caring, and her face weathered. She slipped a hand behind his head, and pressed a waterskin to his parched lips. It tasted like sand.

Marsais struggled to sit up, but eventually managed, taking the waterskin. "Thank you."

"Acacia," the woman reminded.

The name snapped his mind fully into focus. "Ah, yes, of course." He had to save the realm. Again. A never-ending job of his. Why couldn't humans stay out of trouble for one bloody century?

Marsais stood too quickly. He nearly toppled, but Oenghus caught his arm in an iron grip. "Get on a bloody camel, or I'll knock you out and toss you over it."

Marsais did not have the energy to argue.

A boy nudged the camel's knee, and it knelt. But by the time he climbed onto its back, he was lost again—racing through a maze of doors, of memories and visions, searching for the girl-creature who roamed his realm.

CHAPTER 34

Camels were not smooth mounts. And they stank, too. Along with the humans. Everyone smelled of sweat and unwashed bodies. Except Marsais.

Isiilde buried her nose against his back. She liked the way he smelled—even at his worst. He was slumped in front of her, weak with exhaustion, and her arms were the only thing holding him in place.

Not that he would notice falling to the ground. His heart had slowed, but he was still lost. She had her hand pressed over the scar on his chest. It seemed to help.

Isiilde was worried. But so were the others. His screams had echoed across the desert. The soldiers thought a scorpion had bitten him. But his eyes were milky white and his body rigid with anguish. She'd ordered them away to preserve his dignity as he convulsed.

Oenghus and Rivan now walked on either side of her camel, ready to catch Marsais if he slipped off.

The distant mountains wavered beneath the sun. But they were unlike anything Isiilde had seen. Their peaks were flat like a table top. Acacia had called them plateaus.

They looked no closer.

"Is he heavy?" Rivan asked. "I can take a turn if you need to rest."

Isiilde shifted on the packs. "I'm fine, but I'll switch if I get tired," she promised. Truth be told, her back ached, and her arms hurt, but she didn't want to take her hand away from his chest.

"Why do you always put your hand over that scar?" Acacia had drifted back to walk with them.

"It seems to help," she confided.

Her cryptic answer was not enough. "How so?"

Isiilde took a breath. "The scar is always painful. On most days, it feels like a brand against his flesh. I don't know how he tolerates it. When I touch it—the pain leaves."

"How did he get that wound?" Acacia asked.

"The Shattering."

Acacia's brows shot up. "But it's fresh. The scar barely looks a year old." She looked to Oenghus for an answer.

He shrugged. "I can't heal it. And don't try to heal it, or him, unless you're feeling reckless."

"I healed him in Vaylin. His spirit is... I've never seen anything like it." Acacia shivered despite the heat. "I got out of there as soon as I could."

"Aye, it's like looking into a broken mirror. It's easy to lose your way."

"Why is that?" Acacia asked.

Oenghus adjusted his turban with a jerk. "Have you ever healed a madman before?"

"Aren't all men mad?"

Oenghus rumbled out a laugh. "Point taken. But I've healed mad men and women before. Their mind is fractured. Sometimes I can mend it, depending on the cause, but it drives a wedge through their spirit, too. As ancient as his spirit is... let's just say there's a whole lot of him to break."

Isiilde tightened her hold on Marsais. He wasn't broken. He was wounded—in mind and spirit. There was a difference.

Long hours passed before Marsais stirred. "You must be exhausted," he murmured.

"Are you feeling any better?" she asked against his ear.

"Your breasts feel nice against my back."

She snorted, and he shifted, taking his weight off of her. He looked over his shoulder, lips twitching upwards.

"You look terrible, Marsais."

"I'm alive," he sighed.

"Did you have another vision?"

He was silent for a time. And she feared the window of clarity had shut on her again. "I'm not sure," he finally said. And nothing more.

Marsais placed a hand over her own. And his touch awakened her senses as he traced her knuckles, every line and curve, and the tender hollow of her wrist.

Her fire was intense, but his touch was different—like a warmth that wrapped around her bones. She wanted to melt into the man.

At sunset, Nimlesh ordered his men to make camp. Oenghus had claimed he was tired of walking, but Isiilde knew it was so Marsais could rest for a night. Her father could outrun a horse.

Fire flickered under the stars. It smelled like camel dung, but it was warm. Marsais reclined on a blanket, studying a spiral of runestones. It was the set Isiilde had made to teach Rivan how to play King's Folly.

Isiilde nudged the life rune into an inner circle. "It's your move."

"Hmm?"

She pointed at the game. Voices came and went in the dark, with occasional snatches of laughter. The soldiers had their own island of firelight, giving the seer and nymph a wide berth.

"We don't have to finish," she said.

Marsais shook his head. He placed an exacting finger on the steel rune and slid it towards a power rune. "Earlier today, you asked me if I'd had a vision."

"You said you weren't sure." The confusion was plain in her words.

"Not precisely a vision, but many things." Marsais hesitated, and when he spoke again, his voice was thready—a whisper that she strained to catch. "After the Shattering, as I've told you before, I went mad. There was no law or order for a long time. I was—" His voice caught with pain. "There was a tribe of sorts. Terrible men who took what they wanted and slaughtered those who resisted. They killed my daughter, eventually..." His voice faded, his eyes dimmed, and he looked so very far away. "I was the leader's pet seer, like the girl kept chained in the Ardmoor's fortress."

Marsais did not need pity; he needed her to listen. And so she did, biting her tongue to keep from raging against men who were long dead. To give him time, she swept in, stealing the power rune with her stone. It swirled to life, binding together to create something more.

"Eventually, a cleric rescued me. He removed my collar, fed me, clothed me, restored my dignity, but my mind... I didn't even know my name, or that I was a man and not a beast."

He touched a stone, tracing the rune that swirled on top of it. Spirit. Spotting a better move, he switched runes, moving steel from an inner circle, a stronger cycle, to her outer, crushing her powered stone.

Isiilde reassessed the cycles. He had left her fire rune wide open.

"But even under the cleric's care, I drifted in visions: past, present, future. I couldn't tell one from the other."

"How did you find your way back?" she asked, moving her fire rune and stacking it with wind—a powerful combination, and her favorite strategy.

"The cleric helped me build a place to catalog memories and visions. A mental exercise of a sort."

Of a sort. It sounded like when he said *ill occurrences*. The two words really did not convey the extent of destruction that a mishandled weave caused. Isiilde knew this well. A single *Hmm* from Marsais could mean the realm was coming to an end.

"A place?"

"A maze of hallways lined with doors." His eyes flickered to her, gauging her reaction to what sounded like madness. "Each door holds a memory, a moment, or vision. When I need to retrieve a memory, I find the correct hallway, and open the door."

"You imagine it, then?"

"No," he said. "I see the future and the past as clearly as I see you now."

"Like a scrying mirror," she realized.

"But I can also touch things—*feel* the stones underfoot."

"That's where you go when you're lost."

"Yes." He moved his ice over steel. It slid to the side, falling on the life rune. The cycles shifted. His ice rune was poised to take her Queen. "Only now, the maze is crumbling. I don't know how much time I have left."

Isiilde's heart stopped. And then lurched, trying to gallop out of her chest. She swallowed down her panic. "Time for what?"

"Who knows?"

"You're a seer, Marsais."

He raised a brow in a kind of shrug. "A life of madness is no life. One day, I fear, I will not find my way out."

Isiilde pressed her lips together. She placed a finger on her roaring fire rune, and ruthlessly melted his ice rune. But the move cost her. It weakened her runes, separating the wind from fire.

Marsais merged water with her wind, capturing the rune stone and adding it to his own cycle. Her fire was surrounded.

"Can this cleric help you again?"

"I don't know."

"Doubtful," she agreed.

He looked up, surprised.

"You're quite mad. You always have been."

Marsais laughed. It was a rasping chuckle at first, then it bubbled like a brook. "You smooth-tongued fiend." He clucked his tongue, but the mention of fiend cast a shadow over his mirth.

The reminder of Saavedra filled her with anger—directed at the fiend.

In the past, Isiilde would have charged his steel rune with her fire, giving it the strength to flee, and that's what he counted on—that she would leave her Queen vulnerable.

Isiilde pushed her fire rune towards his wind and water. The runes sizzled and steamed, then dissolved with a hiss. A steam rune materialized, and the wind blew it to another cycle—in the path of his Queen. Steam hit flesh, and the rune dissolved.

Marsais stiffened. Slowly, he sat up, replaying the sequence of defeat in his mind. He met her gaze, his eyes wide and full of disbelief. "You sacrificed your fire rune."

"No," she corrected. "I won."

Isiilde reached over the cycle of runes, and grabbed what was left of his severed goatee. The three coins woven into the hair were warm to the touch. She leaned forward until her nose was nearly touching his.

"Listen to me, Marsais. You *are* mad. I've always known that. And I love that about you, because when we're together, I feel normal—everyone stares at the madman instead of the nymph."

Marsais blinked rapidly. His lips parted, slack-jawed. She had robbed him of the ability to speak. A rare thing.

"You might forget things, but I don't. You told me that what I want matters. I still want you."

"I will not inflict this on you," he whispered.

"Does your word no longer mean anything?"

"Did it ever?"

"Now you're being childish."

"Blast it, Isiilde, I've given you freedom! You're not bound to me, or any other man."

"I never asked to be released from our bond."

"I had to protect you."

"You made that choice for me."

"To spare you the suffering to come."

"I wanted *you*. I *chose* you. You said it was *my* choice."

"I'm already dead!" he snapped.

There it was.

Isiilde shrugged off his claim. "Then I'm madly in love with a dead lunatic."

Marsais was shaking his head. "You're only attracted to me because I'm—"

"Don't say old," she warned.

"I wasn't going to."

"Then what?"

"God-like in age."

She snorted.

"Nymphs are attracted to experience," he argued.

"And yet you told me some nymphs refused to bond with the druids. You weren't the only long-lived man on the Isle," she pointed out.

He couldn't argue with that.

"Marsais," she growled. "We're friends. Talk to me. Why are you trying to shove me away?"

"I'm not—"

She arched a brow. "Then kiss me."

He took a deep breath. "You deserve better than me."

"But I want you."

"Dammit, Isiilde," he growled. "I forget my own name. I don't know where or *when* I am half the time. I need to be led about like a simpleton and cared for like an old toothless fool. I need to be put out of my misery."

He believed it. She could see it in his eyes—all the pain, the hopelessness, the plea for relief.

Isiilde reached for his hand. "Do you think so little of yourself?" she whispered. "Can you see no hope in your future?"

"I cannot," he rasped.

She smiled, sadly. "Then let me imagine it for you."

"I'm not meant for you, Isiilde."

"I'm free," she said. "I make my own Fate. Your visions mean nothing to me. So damn your visions and stop trying to protect me."

Marsais did not answer immediately. His eyes grew distant, and when he spoke, his voice was like gravel. "I can't ignore them. No matter how hard I try."

"Then I'll make you forget them," she purred, her eyes dancing with mischief. She kissed him, hard and long, until the realm fell away.

Marsais shuddered against her lips. She caressed his pointed ear, then let her finger trail down his chest as she kissed his neck. "With your vast control and superior mind, I'm sure you'll have no trouble resisting me," she whispered.

"You're cruel."

"I know," she preened, sitting back.

The rest of the camp had stopped, eyes on the elf and nymph. She did not care.

Marsais shook himself, then lent forward, rising on all fours, until his lips were tantalizing close to hers. His white hair fell forward, veiling the two from prying eyes. "You're wrong, you know." His voice was rough with passion.

"What about?"

"The reason people stare at me."

Her lip quirked in a smile. "Enlighten me."

His gaze drifted to that spot, the corner that held her smile. "People don't stare at me because I'm mad. They're jealous of my radiant hair."

Isiilde laughed, a sound that trickled like cool water over the sands. "I don't think so," she said with a grin. Although it was glowing white in the moonlight.

"Why, then?" His voice was light and teasing, and she sorely missed the sound of his happiness.

"I think they're staring at your fine backside."

"That must be it," he said dryly, sitting back to study the cycle of runes. The twinkle in his eyes faded."Why did you sacrifice your fire rune?"

"I didn't sacrifice it; I let it go."

MARSAIS SAT CROSS-LEGGED BY A CAMPFIRE. He stared into the flames, aware of Isiilde sleeping nearby. Some part of him was always aware of her. But he missed their bond. For a brief time, he hadn't felt so alone.

His gaze drifted to her. Isiilde had taken hot stones from the fire and placed them in the sand to ward against the chill.

The surrounding air rippled. And in his eyes, those stones sprang up like a wall. It towered over the camp, casting a long shadow over the humans—over the entire realm.

In that instant, the nymph goddess was alone with her fire. A moment passed. The wall broke into pieces, raining down ash and brimstone.

It was a vision. He often drifted in and out of time, and he'd learned not to react. But they *looked* real, they *felt* real, and it'd taken him centuries to recognize one.

Madness dreaming, he thought, as he sat watching the storm of embers.

When the brimstone touched his nose, it melted, dripping down his skin to pool on the ground. Ice spread over the sand, creaking towards the mountains.

Marsais leapt to his feet, and ran into the night, over ice and brimstone, through visions that shifted like dunes.

The ice cracked and shattered, then vanished. He stopped. A barren land stretched into darkness under a silver moon. His mind rippled like a mirage. He waited for a span of heartbeats. Nothing changed. *This* was the now and where, with a silver moon hanging over a desert.

A presence brushed his shoulder, and he spun. Campfires dotted the distant horizon. How far had he run?

Visions roared on the edges of his sight. Darkness burned; death, screams, ruin; a blade poised against his throat. The ground opened, and swallowed him whole. He fell into an ocean. Waves rose, devouring cities, drowning life. The water receded, revealing a forest of frozen humans. And over it all, a nymph sat on a black throne, serene, and so very cold. A heart of ice beat in her breast.

Marsais sank to his knees.

The visions battered his defenses. He fought to breathe and clutched his head, trying to keep the last thread of his sanity from unraveling.

"Grant me peace," he begged, as fear and grief washed over him. Marsais fell to the sand, and wept.

A hand rested on his shoulder. It was familiar and calm, and a haven in the storm of visions. Eventually, his tears ran dry and his visions stilled. And Oenghus remained long after, as steady and patient as the earth.

CHAPTER 35

Zoshi clutched the wall. His backside was too sore to scoot, so he risked hobbling down. Step, hop, steady; step hop, steady—*ping*. Zoshi stopped, listening. Had he imagined the sound?

Zoshi took a pebble from his pocket and dropped it over the edge. Seconds ticked by. *Ping*. He nearly shouted in triumph, but swallowed it back.

He poked his head over the edge of the stairway, but the glowing moss in his hand was too bright. He tucked the moss away, and tried again. A faint blue light glowed in the blackness. It was like looking down a deep well.

Blowing out a breath of relief, he put his back against the wall. He was close, so very close, to—something.

What would he find at the bottom of the well? Hopefully a door. But Zoshi didn't want to hope too much. Hope had never done a thing for him.

Zoshi rummaged in his pockets for some dried moss. It was barely edible, but he'd had worse. He ate every last bit of the moss. It had filled his belly these past... How many days had he spent here?

It didn't matter, he told himself.

For the first time since falling into this place, he could see an outline of stairs. They stretched down and around in a spiral.

Zoshi steadied himself on the wall. The swelling in his ankle had gone down enough to lace up his boot. Gritting his teeth, he put weight on the foot. The pain wasn't sharp; he was on the mend.

Moving cautiously, he limped on his way, descending into the light. It grew bright, so bright that he could see the bottom. The rough walls were covered with the glowing moss, and the vast cavern was round as if a spear had been thrust into the ground and yanked back out.

For the first time, in a long time, he stepped down to find earth underfoot. Moss clung to a mound by the stairs. Zoshi began tugging at the moss, and when he'd uncovered a patch, he rubbed the underlying surface. It was rusty metal.

That was odd.

Zoshi pulled away more moss, then stepped back to study his work. It was an overturned mining cart. Twisted metal tracks ran away from the overturned cart.

Crumpet was squawking at him impatiently, hopping back and forth on the tracks. The crow wanted him to follow.

Maybe there was a way out.

Zoshi followed the crow, edging further into a cave. Debris littered the path: a pickaxe, a twisted piece of metal, and a rusty chain. And bones. Skeletons lay in the wreckage. A lot of skeletons.

His mum always said that the dead should be left alone, but Zoshi figured he'd be one of them soon, so he might as well get familiar with his solemn friends.

He crouched beside the first skeleton. Decayed leather and rusty chain clung to the dry remains, and a sword and shield lay nearby. These were not miners, but soldiers.

Curious, the boy moved from one to another in the dim light. A white form caught his eye. Zoshi froze, staring at the whiteness until he could make sense of it. It wasn't a skeleton, but a pale white warrior. The man almost looked alive.

Zoshi was caught between curiosity and fear. Finally, he tiptoed closer.

Calling the man human didn't seem quite right. His face was too angular, the cheekbones too high, and the ears too sharp. Even for a Kamberian.

Zoshi watched the man's chest. But it didn't rise. Gathering his courage, he crouched and crabbed-walked closer. The strange man held a shortsword that didn't have a spot of rust on it.

Swallowing, he reached out his arm as far as it would go, and leant forward. With a trembling finger, he poked the pale creature. The body was stiff. It didn't move. Definitely dead.

With a shiver, he backed away, leaving the strange corpse and his sword alone. It seemed wrong to take something from the man's hand.

Zoshi turned to the rubble and claimed what items he could find: a dried leather belt, a small tin box, and a knife still in its sheath. It was a large knife with a curving blade, and although its hilt was frayed, the blade was sharp.

The tin box was empty, but he didn't mind. He had other ideas for it. Using the knife, he poked holes all over the tin. When he was satisfied, he stuffed a heaping pile of moss inside the box. Blue light burst from the holes. It wasn't perfect, but it'd do.

Clutching his new lantern, he limped around the giant cavern. And all the while, Crumpet hopped from track to track, rasping what could only be bird curses.

Finally, when Zoshi had satisfied his curiosity, he limped back to a twisted track, and held up his lantern. The path disappeared straight into a gaping tunnel that swallowed his light.

Zoshi felt like an ant gazing into a snake's burrow. But the crow flew in, leaving him no choice but to follow.

CHAPTER 36

THARIOS leant over a railing to study the castle grounds. A sharp wind battered his bare chest, but he seemed unaffected by the cold. And his precarious perch. He held the barbed relic in his hand. Soisskeli's stave. The Archlord never set it down.

Eiji eyed the raw wound on his torso. Several tattoos were missing—powerful rituals that had been applied to his flesh. One was working now. A ghostly spider spun a web of inky threads over his wounds. The surrounding flesh twitched.

Anger rippled off Tharios in waves, but Eiji wasn't worried—he wasn't the type of leader to toss a gnome off a balcony. He was the type to torture them first.

Eiji stepped up to a gnomish crystal, and put her eye to the lens. The net of wards covering the castle burst into view. Eiji fiddled with the knobs, then hopped on the railing and tilted the telescope as far as it would go. The camp came into focus.

"Progress?" Tharios asked.

"Slow," she admitted.

His hand tightened on the barbed stave. A trickle of blood leaked onto the stone. In the glowing light, he looked even paler than usual, and there was a kind of tautness to his skin, like a stretched piece of leather.

"Can we use the stave to reach the chamber?" she asked.

"What did the runes on the Titan Gates once say?"

"They cautioned any who dared to enter with ill intent."

"The wards were never meant to protect the Archlord," he confided. "They guard the chamber where Pyrderi Har'Feydd opened a portal. The tear in the veil between realms is heavily warded, more so than the wards surrounding the Spine. In order for me to reopen the Gateway, I need to be inside the chamber."

"Are you sure we have the right tunnel?" Eiji asked.

His knuckles went white, and more blood seeped from his palm. "The Fey showed me the path."

Eiji pointed her telescope towards the arena. The fog swirled in the domed shield. Easy enough to deactivate, but now that Thira and the other Wise Ones knew the mist could be contained, it was a pointless weapon.

Eiji missed the Fey spirits. She rather liked them.

"Don't fret," Tharios purred. "These walls have never been breached."

Eiji eyed the patchy, incomplete ward that shimmered around the open air garden. Everyone, herself included, had believed the guardian statues protected the Spine from invaders. But now they knew better. The Barrier was a cage.

Would it kill someone who tried to leave? She planned on shoving a prisoner through first. But there was nothing threatening about a prisoner. Given the warning on the Titan Gates, a person's intent might trigger the ward.

For now, there was a convenient tear in the weave that let them come and go as they pleased.

"There's been no word from N'Jalss," she said.

Tharios had sent him to kill Marsais and Oenghus, and bring back the nymph. But N'Jalss hadn't returned. His silence was troubling.

"It doesn't matter," Tharios said, stepping away from the railing. "By the time Marsais and Oenghus limp back here, they'll be facing a god."

Eiji turned to face her master. Pain etched his face. Despite all his wards, the priestess had sliced through them and nearly killed him. Without his Rituals he would be dead.

"Where is the traitor?" Tharios asked.

"I lost sight of him after the elemental attacked us. I can't find a trace of the man. He's likely halfway to the Bastardlands by now."

It grated on her professional pride. Eiji was a skilled, and therefore, unknown assassin. How had Isek Beirnuckle slipped through her network of informants? It was like trying to track a wraith.

"I can't stand a turncoat," he muttered. "What does your spy in Thira's camp say?"

"The Blessed Order arrived. And more soldiers from Drivel are on their way. Rashk is building a battering ram. She's covering it with enchantments."

"How many Devout remain?"

"Twelve."

A muscle in his jaw twitched. The Unspoken's numbers had dwindled. "We could use the prisoners..." Eiji began, but stopped when he shook his head.

"We'll sit behind our walls. Once the Shadowed Dawn arrives, nothing in this realm or the next can stop us."

"It's the getting there that has me worried. Thira, Rashk, and Morigan are resourceful."

Eiji stopped short of saying formidable. She didn't want to test the limits of his temper. The battle in the bailey had put a dent in their numbers.

As if sensing her thoughts, Tharios began to laugh. But madness lurked in that sound.

"Who knew the healer and priestess were so dangerous? I should have had them gutted in the dungeon." Tharios glanced down at the Forsaken Orb Weaver spinning its inky threads over his flesh. "But perhaps you're right, Eiji... We shouldn't wait. Gather the dead."

FLURRIES STIRRED FITFULLY in silence as Tharios walked over the frozen dead. He was a slash of crimson against white, with a small leather-clad form trotting beside him. The pair joined six figures standing in the middle of the bailey. They were arranged in a circle. The Unspoken did not speak; they waited.

Tharios looked at each faithful. No sacrifice was too great for their god. Without ceremony, Tharios drew a curved knife. Forbidden words washed over the dead. Words that grated on the ears and scratched at the throats of the archers on the rampart walls.

Tharios sliced the blade across his arm, and blood dripped, spattering on snow.

A guard dragged a Wise One onto the field. Leiman was stripped to the waist and covered in bruises and cuts. Who else would have let the priestess into the fold?

When Leiman saw the six Unspoken and their leader, he fought. It was useless. A steel gauntlet to the jaw stilled his struggle.

Tharios grabbed the young healer by the hair, and sliced his throat with one clean jerk. Steam rose in the chill as his life pulsed from an artery. Tharios began to chant. Power thrummed in the air. He let the ritual blade fall, and teased a scarab from his chest. It fought and chattered in his hand, eager to be free. Tharios dropped the hungry spirit into Leiman's blood. One became a multitude. The insects swarmed the dead, slipping between lips and burrowing into wounds, settling like maggots in a new home.

Bones cracked, bodies shifted, and the dead soldiers of the Isle rose as smoothly as puppets on strings. A forest of dead awaited the Archlord's command.

Tharios looked to his Unspoken. Each drew a ritual blade and plunged the tip into their hearts. Tharios and Eiji retreated as the screeching spirits were torn from their bodies. Shadowy forms took flight, beating on the air, hungry and alive.

"Slaughter them. Scatter them," Tharios ordered. "Open the gates!"

CHAPTER 37

SHEER RED ROCK rose from the desert. Bits of greenery stood out starkly in the crevices and birds circled the plateau. Not vultures, but something much larger.

Isiilde didn't like the look of the creatures.

Marsais walked beside her. Days had passed since their game of King's Folly. He'd hardly spoken.

Isiilde touched his hand. "We're nearing the mountain range."

"Hmm." He didn't take his eyes off the rocky ground and his scuffing footsteps.

Oenghus nudged Elam off a camel. "Stay behind the camels and use them for cover. That goes for you too, Scarecrow."

The words sparked the laughter of a madman, and a chiming of coins. "They've been watching us approach for days. A camel won't save us."

"Have you seen an ambush in your visions, Seer?" Lucas asked.

"Does it really take the *gift* of foresight to answer that?" Marsais asked. "Where there is water, there is life."

"Is Finnow's Spire on the other side?" Isiilde asked, reaching for his hand. He let her hold it, and she drew him over to the camels as Oenghus had suggested.

"It is."

"How will we pass?" she asked.

"There's a pass," Marsais said dryly.

"With the way Fomorri tribes fight over territory, it's probably more like a trap," Acacia noted. "Do we even know where the pass is?"

The plateaus looked like a solid wall that stretched from the tip of north to the end of south.

Nimlesh brought out his spyglass. "We could climb over, but I don't like the look of those birds."

"Bone vultures?" Oenghus asked.

"More like flying reptiles." The Elite sergeant handed over his spyglass. Oenghus looked, and grunted, passing it to Acacia.

"They might be grafted Fomorri," Acacia said.

Isiilde frowned at the distant blots in the sky. Humans with wings. The Afarim lived on the Isle of Winds, but they more resembled humans than flying reptiles.

"What do you know of this, Seer?" Lucas asked.

"I'm uncertain it matters anymore." Marsais sounded defeated, and that gave her pause. He'd schemed and manipulated her Fate with one goal in mind—that she remain in Mearcentia. He had walked that path through his visions, and now, despite all his careful navigating, she was here. Had she thrown his plans into disarray, or was there more? The distance between them felt like an impassable chasm.

"Do you know anything about the mountains?" Acacia asked, gently.

"Only from a bird's point of view," Marsais said, rubbing at his temple. "There are wadis and cracks through the mountain range. Beyond are sand dunes, and after that, Finnow's Spire. You can't miss it."

"A bird's point of view?" Lucas asked. "You said a Guardian told you where the Spire is—was it Yvesa?"

The Guardian of Peace, a sprite, had a reputation as a prankster. Small wonder Lucas was suspicious.

Marsais arched a brow. "Did I say that?"

"Yes," Acacia said through her teeth.

"I warned you, Seer," Lucas growled. "I'll have no more of your games."

"A game?" Marsais gave a sharp bark of laughter. "I assure you, this is not a game. Would you like the truth?"

"Yes," Lucas bit out.

"A dragon told me. Does that make you feel better? Is that more reassuring? Isn't that what you all want me to be?" Marsais threw out his arms and shouted at the sun. "Marsais zar'Vaylin—the ancient who knows and sees all!"

His voice thundered over the sand. And when the echo of his mad raving faded, Rivan asked a hesitant question, "A... dragon?"

Marsais turned on the paladin. "Yes, an old apprentice of mine, if you must know. She had a sleek body and beautiful scales."

"Oh, gods, shut it, ol'bastard," Oenghus said, tugging on his beard.

Isiilde tilted her head. "How many odd notches in your belt do you have?"

Marsais looked thoughtful, but before he could reply, Lucas grabbed him by the robe. "Tell us what you know," he demanded.

Marsais did not resist the paladin; instead, he sobered and seemed to shrink with despair. "I don't know what we'll find. My visions stop at Finnow's Spire. Perhaps I'll die there and save you the trouble of killing me. I don't really care. There are Fomorri in these mountains, that much I know, but all of you know that already."

Lucas let Marsais go with a shove.

"Are you two done arguing?" Oenghus asked, cracking his knuckles. It wasn't really a question; more of a threat to the paladin.

Lucas spat. "I don't argue with madmen."

"I would not trust the Trickster's word anyway," Nimlesh admitted, collapsing his glass. "We'll approach between wadis and scout from there."

"Void, I hate scouting," Oenghus grumbled. "Let's just march in and bash their heads."

Even Isiilde thought that was a bad idea. But then, berserkers weren't known for their brains.

The open ground between was daunting, a sea of heat with no end. And definitely no cover. Isiilde half expected to find a sailing ship coasting over the sands. A bit of air stirred her hair, snatching up sand. The haze obscured the mountain range like a dry fog.

"Would it help if the Fomorri couldn't watch our approach, or see what wadi we entered?" she asked no one in particular.

"There's always an advantage with stealth," Acacia said. "Do you have an idea?"

"We're far enough away that we need a spyglass to see the birds. What if we all disappeared—here and now? Would they think us a mirage?"

"Hmm, excellent idea, my dear." Marsais did not notice the slip, and she did not correct him. "But in my current state, I can't weave invisibility around the camels *and* these men." A bone deep weariness laced his words. She looked into his eyes, ringed by dark circles, and haunted by something more. "Not without Blood Magic, at any rate," he added.

"Not an option," Acacia bit out.

Isiilde had to agree. "Something simpler?" she suggested.

"I can try."

"Try what?" Nimlesh asked.

"A mirror." Marsais gestured at the soldiers. "Have your men group together. Closer... *more!* Blast it, I can't keep track of all of you."

The warriors closed in, and when the group was clustered around the camels, he seemed satisfied.

"Would it help if I made it appear more natural?" Isiilde asked, gesturing towards the haze.

"I believe it would. Can you manage *not* to whip up a storm?"

"Probably not, but I can try." She gave him a lop-sided smile. "Will you be able to hold the weave long enough to reach the cliffs?"

Weaving a mirror rune on an inert object was akin to setting a mirror in front of it and leaving it there. But weaving a rune around a person who moved—well, that was the equivalent of running around with multiple mirrors and trying to keep the reflection in place for each person.

Isiilde had managed it in the ruins because Elam and Rivan had not moved. But even then, it had taxed her.

"We shall see," he said.

She wanted to pull him into a feather bed, wrap her arms around him, and let him sleep for days. But that was part of the issue: Marsais did not rest easy.

"You start. I'll finish," he said.

Isiilde turned to the cliffs. She needed a breeze, not a storm. A light touch was required, more like a whisper than a word. She focused on the haze and the light mist of sand swirling over a baked earth. For a moment, she closed her eyes, picturing the runes, and then softly, she sang. A whisper insinuated itself into the air. Her fingers traced the runes, but her voice brought them to life. First air, then a breath of wind.

A strong breeze snatched her hair, blowing sand into the eyes of the group. Everyone tucked a scarf around mouth and nose, but Isiilde had forgotten that part. She nearly choked on the sand. Three puffs of flame shot out of her ears. She scrambled to cover her nose and mouth, but her weave unraveled. The sand, however, continued to stir. It had only needed a nudge.

Marsais was already weaving. Grit clogged her vision, and she averted her gaze, wishing the scarf covered her eyes.

When the sand pattered back to the earth, the haze remained, like a stirred pond, all cloudy with mud. A ripple of gasps surrounded her. She looked at the soldiers, but could no longer see them.

"Now that's better," Lucas grunted.

"Isiilde did this to us when the Fomorri came. Elam and I looked like stone." Rivan's voice was right at her shoulder.

"Quick thinking," Acacia said.

The air rippled whenever someone moved, but it was still hazy. It would take a sharp eye to see through the weave.

"How long can you keep this up?" Acacia asked.

"I suggest we start walking."

THEY WERE NEARLY to the cliffs. The rocks had spent a full day under the sun and threw off heat like a kiln. Isiilde basked in that heat.

A wet tongue licked her cheek. She opened her eyes in surprise. Spot was walking beside her, and so was the rest of the group. The mirror weave had unraveled.

A cry of alarm echoed off the rocks.

"Void," Oenghus spat. "Get to the cliffs." But instead of following his own order, he sprinted in the opposite direction.

Marsais had fallen behind. He stood staring at the sun, arms spread, fingers splayed as if he were taking flight. It reminded her of Thedus, and that thought terrified her.

"Oenghus will get him." Acacia pushed her towards the rocks.

Overhead, a black cloud of winged creatures gathered. And to the north, a cyclone of dust rose on the horizon. Riders. She heard their horns in the distance.

The Elite drew their weapons and ran for the cliffs, making for a narrow crevice. She ran too, glancing over a shoulder.

Oenghus had Marsais by the arm, dragging him in his wake. A shadow swooped at the pair. It was swift and leathery, and had the face of a man, but the wings of a bat, with scaly skin and talons instead of fingers and toes.

Oenghus swung his club at the Fomorri. It reeled from the blow, falling to the ground. Another swooped. But an arrow pierced its shoulder. The wings spasmed, and it spiraled down.

Isiilde looked to the riders coming from the north. The Fomorri were closer, bearing down with a fury; some rode camels, while others looked like beasts themselves. She stopped running and began to weave. Runes flared to life. A wind swept from the cliffs, hitting the winged Fomorri and sending them off course. When her weave brushed over the ground, it plucked up sand, and she hurled the sandstorm at the approaching riders. A wall of sand swallowed them.

Isiilde dropped the weave, and raced through the storm towards Marsais. Acacia was close on her heels.

The Fomorri who'd been hurled to the ground had a strangely human face. It charged her, hopping and flapping, talons stretching. Acacia shouldered her out of the way, caught the attack with a shield, and plunged her sword through the Fomorri.

In the sand and grit and swooping forms, Isiilde grabbed Marsais' hand, freeing Oenghus to fight. She pulled Marsais towards the waiting Elite. Halfway there, she felt him tense.

"Run!" she ordered.

There was no recognition in his eyes, but he ran, following her without protest. They rushed into the safety of the cliffs, and Oenghus and Acacia came pounding in after.

The air cleared in the crevice. The rocks nearly touching above, creating a ceiling of stone. Only a sliver of light shone through the crack.

With a quick gesture from Nimlesh, four warriors dropped back to bring up the rear. Alert and ready, the group filed through the narrow crevice.

There were whorls of red, copper, and orange in the stone. It'd been blasted by wind and sand, and smoothed by time. It reminded her of the Spine.

Marsais was staring at the slice of sky. She squeezed his hand, and he focused on her. "Are you with me?"

"You're holding my hand, aren't you?"

"I am," she agreed. "Another vision?"

"Isn't this one?"

"No."

"Hmm." He blinked at their surroundings, then focused on her again. "Isiilde?"

"Yes?"

"You're not shivering."

"Should I be?"

"Aren't we in a glacier?"

Isiilde pressed her lips together. "Just hold on to my hand," she said softly.

Marsais tightened his grip.

"We could be walking into a dead end," an archer whispered. His name was Coen, and he had broad shoulders that were always hunched, ready to draw and fire the bow in his hands.

As the group ventured farther into the crevice, the camels scraped the walls. Nimlesh ordered the gear stripped from them.

While the dwindling supplies were being redistributed through the ranks, Oenghus laid a hand on the rock and closed his eyes. Covered in sand and grit, and bulging with muscle, he looked like an extension of the stone. After a minute, he opened his eyes.

"It's like a honeycomb. There's a lot of movement in this hive."

"How can you tell?" Acacia asked.

Oenghus shrugged. "Vibrations in the rock."

A shadow passed over them and everyone tensed, but nothing swooped through the crack overhead.

Lucas frowned at the sky. "I feel like a fish in a barrel."

"Let's find a place to make a stand," Nimlesh said grimly.

Oenghus slapped the jawbone against his palm. He liked that plan.

PILLARS OF RED hemmed in the group, herding them single-file through a maze of stone. Every time a shadow passed overhead, Isiilde summoned her flame. But she was penned in, unable to get to the back of the line.

A clash of steel sounded from the rear. Grunts came next, and distant horns. The last two soldiers in line fought a desperate battle as the group trudged forward, unable to help in the narrow crevice.

Through moving legs and arms, she caught snatches of battle. The Elite at the end of the line wielded a short, stabbing sword and shield, while the second soldier wielded a long spear. The two men worked together, one fending and blocking while the other stabbed, backing up, step by step.

Isiilde did not know how many Fomorri had fallen, or how many crowded the passage.

When the crevice widened, winged Fomorri swooped down, shooting arrows.

As one, the Elite raised and locked their shields with the paladins. Isiilde yanked Marsais down as arrows bounced off the metal. At a signal, shields were lowered, and the Elite answered with arrows of their own. A winged Fomorri crashed from the sky, thudding on an Elite with a sickening crunch. The impact broke the soldier's arm.

"Marsais," she shouted in his ear. "You need to weave armor." But he was lost, and she didn't want to risk weaving one for him. She wove a quick armor weave for herself, adding fire, and peeked through the cracks in the shields.

Nimlesh barked an order, and the Elite rose as one. The sky was clear, and the line of soldiers moved to the next crevice.

That was the rhythm for a long while: a rush of battle followed by tense waiting. Isiilde felt like they were being herded by a pack of dogs, but eventually, the wait turned into a long stretch of silence.

At nightfall, the crevice spilled into a natural hollow and silver moonlight streamed into the grotto. Tense and ready, the warriors edged into the open, searching the tall bushes that grew along a dry stream bed. Nothing moved; nothing stirred. Until finally, Oenghus had had enough. He marched out into the middle of the grotto and slapped his club against a pillaged shield. No one answered his challenge.

Oenghus walked beneath an overhang. It was spacious and tall. But more importantly, it offered protection from an attack from above.

Nimlesh signaled his men, and the Elite fanned out to scout, each returning with a shake of the head.

Camp fires were lit, sentries posted, and Isiilde was soon sitting with Marsais in the shallow cave. Nearby, the camels lay down with a groan. She didn't know how long they could go without water, but it already seemed too long, even for a camel.

Isiilde handed Marsais a half-empty waterskin, and he nearly drank it dry. Her supply of water runes was running low.

"I couldn't hold the weave, could I?"

"You're tired, Marsais. It wasn't an easy weave." She was happy to see that he had returned to himself.

He violently stuffed the cork back on the top. She handed him a strawberry, but he shook his head.

"Eat it. You'll feel better," she ordered.

Marsais gave her a sideways glance, then with great ceremony, plucked it from her hand. He slowly tore each leaf off the stem, letting it fall to the ground. The flutter of green captivated him, and he seemed to forget about the berry in his hand.

Isiilde sighed. She wanted to stuff the berry in his mouth; instead, she ate a dozen of her own, and watched Rivan and Elam digging in wet sand at the base of a rock. They gathered sand in a handkerchief, and twisted, squeezing out the water into their mouths.

Isiilde cocked her head. Abruptly she stood and thrust her arm inside her enchanted pouch, searching for a runestone.

"Get the pot that was on the camel," she said to Elam with broad gestures.

The boy darted to a soldier who carried some supplies. When Elam returned with the pot, she set a water rune inside, and activated it with a tap.

"This should gather more water here," she explained. But it did more than that—it gathered so much water that the pot overfilled. The three quickly caught the overflow in their waterskins, and when those were filled, Elam ran to each soldier, taking their skins to fill. Even after all the waterskins were bursting, the water kept bubbling from the ground like an underground spring.

Isiilde ran to fetch the camels. She led Spot and Red back to the pool, and watched the camels happily drink their fill.

"Is Marsais all right?" Rivan asked in a hushed voice.

Marsais was still staring at the strawberry leaves while he held the forgotten berry. "I don't think so," she admitted.

"What a life..." Rivan shook himself. "I would never want to know the future."

"He doesn't just see *one* future—he sees *every* possible future." And then some. "Do you think the Fomorri will come tonight?"

Rivan considered her question. "I think the Fomorri know these mountains. If it were me, I'd bide my time and wear us down."

Isiilde sighed. "I hate waiting."

Oenghus chuckled from where he leant on a rock, watching the grotto. "Might as well make the best of it. Are you up to setting wards, Scarecrow?"

"Hmm?"

"Gah, never mind."

"I can." Isiilde hopped to her feet. "But I don't think I can weave a stone rune over everyone's boots."

Oenghus grunted at her in agreement. "Make it strong, and tell them to keep clear of it."

Rivan walked beside her as she made her way down a narrow passage. An Elite stood watch in the shadows. "I'm going to set a ward—a powerful lightning strike. If you walk past it, you'll die," she explained.

The sentry approved of the plan.

She tapped her lips in thought. Why lightning? She was far more skilled with fire. A slow smile spread over her lips. "Something powerful, at any rate."

Rivan glanced nervously at her. His sword was in hand, steady and very ready. "Don't burn us," he muttered.

"It will only burn Fomorri, unless someone is foolish enough to trigger the ward."

He muttered a prayer under his breath.

The Elite backed up, and Rivan took a long step, too. Isiilde stood in the narrow canyon of dark rock. It was still hot from the long day. Marsais had taught her how to trace a lightning weave onto a small stone, set a perimeter around the camp, and bind each stone to the other, like a string that would be tripped if someone passed over it.

Before she worried over the outcome, she closed her eyes and began to hum, slowly at first, and then with rising confidence, tracing a fire rune over the rock on either side. The weave glowed red in the night, and the nymph thought it was beautiful, so she left it, binding it just as it was.

Rivan looked warily at the pulsing rune. "What will it do?"

"I'm not sure," she admitted. "But I can't do anything for the open sky."

At each passage, she repeated the process. And on the last, when she turned, a voice spoke from the shadows. "You've changed the Lore."

She started in surprise. Rivan stabbed his sword at the shadows, but a quick hand batted the blade to the side, and it went wide, scraping the rock. A moment later, realization came. It was Marsais. He stood tall and slim in the dark passage, white hair gleaming in the reddish glow. It gave him a fiendish air.

"Gods, I'm so sorry," Rivan said in a rush.

Marsais silenced the paladin with a gesture, his gaze intent on the nymph.

"I didn't change it," she corrected. "I made it prettier."

"It's beautiful, Isiilde."

"The wards?"

He shook his head, coins chiming softly in the night. "The Lore is a crude voice. It drags the Gift into the light of day, but your voice..." he trailed off, ending with a sigh. "May I talk with her alone, Rivan?"

"Erm, yes, of course, sorry."

Rivan tried to get by, but the crevice was narrow and he ended up having to squeeze his way past Marsais, their bodies pressing together. "I hope you feel better," Rivan murmured, breathlessly.

Marsais turned to watch him leave. When he looked at Isiilde, his features were thoughtful, almost amused. "Hmm, I see why Acacia chose him."

"He's very nice," she agreed.

"Even more so around nymphs." His lips twitched.

"What do you mean? Rivan's been nothing but a gentleman to me."

"Indeed. A wonderful and rare thing. I don't think any woman has to worry about her virtue around Rivan."

Before she could ask, he waved a hand at the ward and stepped closer, studying the rune.

"What happened in the desert?" she asked.

"I drifted." He shivered in the night. She had brought a cloak; he had not. She took a step closer, leaning against his body, sharing her own heat.

"You seem... distracted. More so than usual." Her words were soft, and she felt him shrug.

"As apprentice and master, we didn't spend so much time together. I visited you on my more lucid days."

"Were you embarrassed?"

"I didn't want to frighten you. Save for Isek and Oen, you saw more than most."

"I think you were always more focused with me."

"I was," he admitted.

"It's been difficult on you—severing our bond."

"It has."

"I miss it."

He looked down at her, eyes shining silver in the moonlight. "I miss it, too," he whispered, caressing her cheek. "I'm cracking, Isiilde. I'm not sure what it would do to you."

Her eyes blazed. "Fire does not crack."

"It can be smothered."

"Only to spring to life in another place. It both kills and gives life. I should be more worried about what I would do to you."

"That's the least of my worries."

"You seem to welcome it—death."

"I do."

The two words were like a dagger twisting in her heart. "You want it, then? You're not even going to *try*, are you?" she demanded. "You saw your death and now you're going to lie down and wait for it."

"I am tired."

Isiilde shoved him, hard. He hit the rock, and she stepped forward, standing on her toes to glare into his eyes. "*I* did not give up when Stievin had me trapped."

He opened his mouth, but thought better of his words and closed it with a click.

"*Please*, I beg you," she said, placing her hand on his chest. "I've never asked anything of you, Marsais. *Never*. But I am asking this..." She choked to a stop.

His strong arms wrapped around her, and she leaned into his heat, wanting to stay there forever. "I'll try, but I can't make promises," he whispered into her hair. "I don't know how long I have left."

Isiilde looked up into his eyes. "I only ask that you try."

He nodded.

"What have you done in the past to stop the visions? Or is it worse than usual?"

"It's everything. As I said, I'm cracking."

"Why now?"

"That's an excellent question," he said with a shudder. And with that shudder, Isiilde realized Marsais was clinging to her as tightly as she clung to him. He was terrified.

A GARBLED, half-choking bellow shattered the moment. The pair jerked away from each other, alert for danger. A moment later, she realized the cry came from a camel. The sound was full of panic and pain.

She raced back to the grotto to find three men standing over Spot, hacking and cutting at his corpse. Another dagger flashed, and Red fell next.

"No!" she screamed.

The camp fires surged. Soldiers and paladins scrambled backwards. Fire blazed from her clenched fists, licking at her sleeves.

A hulking shadow blocked her view. "We need food, Sprite!" The growling voice and endearment conflicted strangely. It gave her pause.

The men near the camels were frozen, still gripping the dagger, red with the camel's blood. Death filled her senses, and bile rose in her throat. The gurgling stopped, and Red's hoof went still. In the after echo of Red's death cries, the nymph moved forward, taking a step, and another, until she stood over the slaughtered animals.

Animals. The word mocked her. She looked at the soldiers—the humans. What was a nymph to humans but an animal?

The Elite edged back. All but one. She turned on the sergeant, her fire aching for release, to lick his flesh and boil his blood. Her hands shook with rage.

Nimlesh stiffened to attention. "It is the way of the desert, Princess Isiilde. I ordered it."

In the blinding rage that threatened, she was vaguely aware of another presence, a familiar man who stood at her side, grim and watchful. No, not a human man, another faerie.

Marsais said nothing. He simply watched, and waited with a slightly curious air. And she had the impression that no matter what she did, he would not interfere.

"Isiilde." Acacia's voice cut through the thunder beating against her ears. "The camels would have slowed us down. They can't climb the rocks."

"You could have set them free!" she snapped.

"Nothing will go to waste," Nimlesh assured.

Her eyes blazed at the man. "Not even a *hair?*"

There was something in her voice; not a growl or a threat, but a cold void that made the commander take a step back. A heavy hand settled on her shoulder, but she shook it off, and moved towards the camels.

"The Fomorri drive their animals into the ground," Acacia continued. "There's no room for mercy out here. The Fomorri would've found the camels and rode them until they dropped dead."

"You're no different from every other human." A muscle in her jaw twitched. "You've killed them already. Get on with your harvest."

In the dim light, she stood still as stone and cold as ice, watching the humans gut and skin her friends. True to the sergeant's word, nothing went to waste.

The smell of cooking flesh drove her to the other side of the grotto, across the dry stream, through the bushes, and past a group of boulders. In the quiet, she sat with her back against the cliff. It wasn't long before Marsais joined her there. He sat, watching the glow of fire burn through the bushes. He said nothing.

"Humans take, and take more—anything they see. But they never give back." There was a quiet fury in her voice.

Marsais rested his head against the rock, and closed his eyes, a tired sigh sweeping past his lips.

A shadow moved in the night, between the rocks, and Rivan edged into the little clearing. "I'm not hungry," he said, hesitant. "Am I interrupting?"

She shook her head.

The paladin sat beside her at arm's length. "I'm sorry, Isiilde."

How many times had she apologized to humans? Looking back, she was no longer sorry for any of it. Humans slaughtered each other and animals without remorse. Why should she feel anything for them?

"Sorry has never fixed anything," she said.

Rivan fiddled with a greave strap. "No, I suppose it doesn't," he said softly. "An apology is more like a bridge to someone's pain—an offer, really. It doesn't mean you have to walk over it. Not unless you want to."

His words struck her. Rivan was right: pain was like an island, and right now, it was all her own. She had no intention of sharing it.

CHAPTER 38

Stars shone in the pool of night overhead, but Marsais felt no wonder as he gazed at the heavens. He was tired. And weak with grief.

Isiilde had finally drifted off to sleep. Rage had rippled off her in waves. Despite all his careful plotting, she had defied her nature, and appeared on deck.

She was on the verge of slipping down a dark path. He did not know what to do.

He searched the stars for portents, a whisper of what was to come, but all was silent. For now.

The Fomorri might attack at dawn. Or not. They liked to torture their prey—mentally and physically. But he couldn't wait. He had little time left. His mind was crumbling, and he needed to know why.

Marsais idly rubbed the coins threaded through his goatee. Their song soothed his thoughts. There was little choice left to him: he could wait to die, or walk towards his death.

This might be his last chance.

Feeling his age, he climbed to his feet and limped across the grotto, aware of the sentries watching him from the shadows. When he disappeared between the shrubs and rocks, the sentries lost interest.

A pair of boulders offered some privacy. He began weaving, layering one rune over the other, creating an orb of drifting threads.

When the weave took shape, he stepped into a space between time; the pause between up and down, right and left, the catch in a breath. Neither light nor dark, only the vague in-between. It was nowhere and everywhere, and he paced restlessly.

Another figure, cowled in a gleaming white robe, joined him in the space. The new arrival lifted his hands. His fingers were long and fine: a musician's hands. He pushed back his cowl. The Guardian of Life resembled the dark mahogany statues that littered the realm in his honor.

"You look like you've climbed out of the Pits o'Mourn," Chaim said.

Marsais glanced down at himself. Unfortunately, the state of his mind reflected his appearance: battered and bloodied.

"Aren't you full of compliments." He ran a hand over his hair, sweeping it back, and noticed the lines creasing the god's brow. "I take it the war in Somnial's Realm is not going well?"

"No," Chaim sighed. "An upstart tried to take the Dreaming God's throne. There's a civil war within a war raging now. Nightmares have been running rampant. I pity the children."

The word nightmare triggered a thought. "The ol'River was raided."

"Yes," the god whispered. "But how did you know? Did you have a vision?"

"Hmm, more like a logical conclusion based on pieces of an unknown puzzle, which I do not yet fully understand."

Chaim opened his mouth, but Marsais interrupted. He was not ready to discuss the how or why. "Have you received word from Bram and Evie?"

"I have," Chaim said. "Tharios released the Fey. The Isle was obscured by an unnatural fog that delayed their arrival."

"The *entire* island?" he asked in surprise. "Why weren't the castle wards activated?"

"According to Evie, there are holes in the shield—frayed edges. The Fey seeped through the cracks."

Marsais frowned, studying his toes. They were covered in ash. "That should be impossible."

"That was my thought, too. But who knows—as old as that power is, the wards may have deteriorated."

"Hengist sacrificed his spirit to guard the Spine," Marsais said, more to himself than the god.

"Spirits *do* fade over time," Chaim said. "It makes me wonder about the wards surrounding the Bastardlands. Despite the Keeper's sacrifice, will they deteriorate, too?"

"Hmm."

"You've had no visions about the Fey?"

"Erm... not precisely. The Fey dwell *outside* of Time. They're like dreams drifting through a fog—just as they are in the Ways. Time has no meaning in a dream. How did your guards get through?"

"Three Wise Ones trapped the fog under the arena Barrier."

"Ah! Tulipin, I'd wager; goaded by Thira, no doubt."

"That's what I heard," Chaim confirmed his guess. "Tharios and his Unspoken barricaded themselves inside the Spine. My scouts are trying to get into the fortress, but that may take time. Are you still in Vaylin?"

"Fomorri."

Chaim blinked. "How?"

Marsais waved a hand. "I'm sure you don't want to know."

The god narrowed his silver eyes. "Have you remembered how to open a Runic Gateway?"

"Although useful, I'm afraid not."

"Did you use Bloodmagic again?"

"Not I." Marsais cleared his throat.

"You had a Bloodmagi open a portal from Vaylin to Fomorri?"

"To Mearcentia."

A muscle in the god's jaw twitched. "How many 'cattle' did you slaughter for that portal?"

Marsais arched a brow. "So little faith in me."

"I have faith that you'll do whatever needs doing," Chaim said with clipped tones.

Marsais' lips twitched upwards. "Instead of sacrificing lives, I betrayed a trust. I gave the Bloodmagi a single vial of blood."

"Only a single vial... That's impossible."

"Is it?"

"You would need—" Chaim stopped. Marsais could see the thoughts churning in his eyes. "You haven't been completely honest with me, have you?"

"Honesty is relative to time."

"Marsais," the god warned.

"Your word."

Chaim tilted his head slightly. "You're wondering if you can trust me."

"Do you really want this burden that I have for you?"

Chaim sighed. "Why not? I already have the Dracken Wood, the Isle of Blight, and Somnial's Realm that I'm dealing with. What's one more issue?"

"Well, this one is... delicate. Your mother can't know."

"My word, then."

"The moment I bonded with Isiilde, I discovered that she's the true daughter of the Sylph—power in its rawest form flows through her veins."

Chaim nearly choked. "*What?*"

"I know... surprise," Marsais said, dryly.

"How?"

"Aren't you a little old for that talk, my boy?"

Chaim glared. "You know what I mean. It shouldn't be possible. The Sylph would have to..."

Marsais waited for him to work through the full gravity of the situation.

"Why would she risk it?" Chaim finally asked.

"From what I gather... desperation."

The blood drained from the god's face.

"You can see why I hesitated to tell you," Marsais pressed on. "The daughter of the Sylph is a prize that would tempt the noblest of hearts —even you, Chaim. Isek betrayed me because he discovered the truth. He overheard a conversation I had with her father."

"The berserker?"

"Yes."

"He's more than he seems, isn't he?"

"Of course." Marsais frowned at the god. "Why else would I drag him out of a gutter?"

"Amusement? A death wish? Madness? Take your pick. Who is he, then?"

"He is Ulfhidhin reborn. Don't you keep track of your spirits, my boy?"

Chaim rolled his eyes. "Legends are prone to exaggeration."

"So they are," Marsais agreed. "If the realms knew how truly clueless we were, it would scare them witless."

"Still, it's comforting to know he's here."

"He's a shadow of what he was. As am I."

"You've managed so far."

"If by managing you mean failing, then yes. Despite my efforts, Isiilde is here in Fomorri."

Chaim grimaced.

"Ah, I see you grasp the danger. I assure you, I had no intention of taking something so precious into the heart of evil. I tried to leave her with Syre on Mearcentia."

"What happened?"

"She snuck aboard the ship." Marsais gave a slight shake of his head. "I thought I knew her; I was wrong. She surprised me."

"I didn't think anyone surprised you."

His lip quirked with irony. "I weary of what is already written, and when something new comes along, I groan and complain like a tired old man set in his ways."

Chaim grinned. "Perhaps you need to be shaken."

"She's more akin to the Shattering. I fear what she may become."

"And what is that?"

"You know the story of Pyrderi Har'Feydd, and why he went against his nature. I fear the same will happen to Isiilde. Humans have... wounded her. Severely. And I made matters worse—I betrayed her trust. She's bonded to her fire, and the divide between human and faerie grows each day."

Chaim rubbed the bridge of his nose. "What do you mean, she's bonded to her fire? I thought she was with you."

"We're no longer bonded. I don't want to talk about it."

Chaim had every intention of pressing him for answers, but one look at Marsais stilled his tongue. Instead, he nodded to the scar beneath his robes. "Do you think she may be part of some greater plan?"

Marsais barked out a laugh. "Her very nature is chaos—the plan is that there is no plan."

"I suppose she can't go against her nature, then."

Marsais mulled over his words. "I suppose not," he finally admitted. "But I still worry."

He was tired; he wanted to sit—to rest there in nothingness.

"Chaim…"

"Yes?"

"If anything should happen to me… swear you'll find her. I beg you. Please. Help her." His whisper was more fervent than intended. The immense weight of responsibility settled on his shoulders, and he felt crushed.

"I swear I'll find her, now and in the future."

A bit of weight lifted off his shoulders. "Thank you."

Chaim frowned, taking a step closer. "I saw you with the Gravedigger. I thought it odd to find you dreaming of death while bonded to a nymph, but this explains it. You lost your bond with her."

"How is my maggoty old friend?"

"Temperamental and territorial as ever. There was a raid on his Graveyard. He didn't take it well."

"If only we could convince him to fight against the rebels in Somnial's Realm."

Chaim smiled wryly. "Life and Death serve no one."

Words drifted to his mind—words that Isiilde had spoken: *Fire can bring life and death*.

"And neither does Time," Chaim added.

"Hmm."

"What will you do?"

"Nothing. What comes will come. That's why I'm here."

"And here I thought you simply missed me."

"I do, actually—miss you, that is. What I wouldn't give for your steady mind right now." Marsais shuddered, and Chaim waited, his eyes softening with concern. "I'm cracking, Chaim," he said abruptly. "I don't know how long before this shell is swept away by madness."

"But your realm—"

"Is crumbling. And *this* realm is unraveling."

Chaim swallowed, brow furrowed in thought, mind grasping at implications and the unknown on the horizon.

"I saw something in the maze: a girl and a monster. Both of the Void."

Chaim's eyes widened a fraction. He looked as grey as the air around.

"You know something," Marsais stated.

Chaim pressed his lips together.

Marsais tilted his head. "Oh, let me guess—the Sylph?"

Chaim looked at his boots. "This girl... what did she look like?"

"She looked like a Reaper, only—" Marsais cut off, searching the hallways of Time, and all of possibility. "The Sylph isn't involved in this, is she?"

Chaim shook his head, and when he looked up, tears shimmered in his eyes.

"The raid on the ol'River—you don't watch every spirit, but you watch some, don't you?" Marsais asked, already knowing the answer.

"Yes."

"What happened?"

"I did not..." The words got stuck and Chaim swallowed down the lump. "I didn't know what else to do. I kept the child separate from the others."

"What child?" Marsais demanded.

"I swore to her—to Raven. She came to me after the Shattering. I couldn't deny a mother's love."

When Marsais spoke, his voice carried the weight of his timeless power. "Tell me, Chaim." Not even the Guardian of Life would ignore that command.

Chaim closed his eyes, took a breath and told Marsais of events long ago, and a beginning that would not end for years to come.

Marsais opened his eyes to a quiet night. He stood in a circle of swirling runes while visions churned at the edges of his awareness. The visions were a mash of pieces, all shattered and broken, reflecting light in fragments. Cursed with foresight, and yet utterly blind. He saw *too* much.

His gaze drifted upwards, to the heavens and the silver moon. The Sylph was watching—waiting for his next move.

Marsais unlaced his robe, shed his shirt, and knelt bare-chested in the sand. He drew a knife from his sash, and calmly brought the blade to his throat. There, he paused.

Two choices lay before him. Which path would he take?

Absolute stillness—the camp, the night, even the fires seemed to freeze. The realm held its breath. It waited for his answer.

"Grant me peace," he whispered, pushing the blade into his neck. Blood slipped from the cut. He tightened his grip for the stroke that would end his days.

At the last moment, Marsais changed his mind—he sliced off his goatee. Three coins fell to the ground. He dropped the knife, untied them from the severed braids, and curled his fingers around the coins.

Sweat glistened on his flesh, his heart beat erratically, his mind screamed in terror. There'd be no going back.

The Fate of the realm rested on his shoulders.

Marsais took a deep breath, and focused on the coins in his fist, unraveling Witman's illusion. When he opened his fingers, three pearlescent discs glowed like the sun—fragments from an artifact long shattered.

Marsais looked to the moon. "You want chaos?" he asked. "I will give you chaos, Yasine."

It was time to let go. And he did.

Marsais squeezed the discs until their edges drew blood. A burst of pure light exploded from his fist, and he began to chant—words that had not been spoken since before the Shattering. The light grew. A shock wave of power that washed over the camp and beyond.

Marsais slapped the fragments against his scar. His body burst with pain—every nerve-ending was on fire. He clenched his jaw, forcing out each word as a chaotic power churned in the grotto. He was the eye of the storm. And he fought to bring it under control.

With a final word, Marsais pushed the last fragments of the Orb into his flesh, and the storm reversed itself, flooding into his body.

Cries of alarm echoed in the grotto, fire roared into the sky, and in its red glow, he looked down at his palm. The fragments were gone. For better or worse, two relics of a shattered age were now one.

Marsais fell forward into the sand.

CHAPTER 39

FIRE ROARED INTO THE SKY, spitting upwards and outwards, funneling through cracks and open air. It shot into the grotto with a *Whoompf* of heat, consuming the sentries who failed to dive under the blast.

Isiilde stared, awestruck. It was beautiful. But that meant—

A dozen ropes unfurled from above. Fomorri slid down the lines. Her wards had been triggered.

Isiilde tore her eyes from the blaze. There were others too—dark shapes that crawled down the rock face like spiders over a web.

Arrows flew from both sides. She dove for cover, pulling Elam down as a hail of missiles cut towards the overhang. One shattered on the rock by her ear.

A bellow rose over the song of fire, drowning out the other battle cries. She poked her head around the rock.

Oenghus barreled into a knot of Fomorri, swinging his club. Bones crunched and bodies flew, and her father kept swinging, crushing everyone who stood in his path.

The Fomorri scattered, but few escaped the berserker's fury. Coen stood behind a rock, releasing one arrow after another in quick succession, dropping shadows like flies. But where was Marsais?

Isiilde quickly wove an armor ward, then pressed Elam against the boulder. "Stay here."

Before she could stop to think, she darted across an open patch of sand. Arrows hissed over her shoulder, and she dove behind another rock. Keeping low, she searched the chaos.

The paladins fought in a cohesive knot. Acacia slammed her shield into a Fomorri with four legs, stunning the monstrosity. Lucas stepped forward and swung his axe, cleaving its skull in two.

"Where's Marsais?" Isiilde yelled.

Acacia searched for him in the chaos, but it was Lucas who answered. "He walked across the grotto before the attack!"

Isiilde darted into the fray. An arrow whizzed over her head. A heavy blade stirred the air, and she ducked, rolling and scrambling beneath a jumble of feet. She came up running, darting behind her father. He stood alone, at the largest break in the rock, holding the floodgates with brutal strength. A pile of Fomorri lay at his feet.

She raced through a mass of bushes, and slipped between boulders. Marsais was sprawled in the sand, his white hair gleaming in the predawn light. He was partially undressed, his robe hanging around his waist, displaying all the scars that crisscrossed his flesh.

The chaos of battle fell away—the noise, the clash of steel and cries of death. Her world consisted of his body, lying so still.

The ground seemed to drop from under her, and she slid to a stop on her knees to roll him over. Her heart skipped. His chest was covered in blood and sand. With shaking hands, she probed the area, searching for a wound. But there was none. His heart beat and his breath came evenly.

Isiilde dusted off the sand, revealing the long, gash-like scar. She blinked. It was no longer raw, but puckered and pale. Her brows knitted with confusion. How—

A soft thud, more felt than heard, spun her around. She thrust out a hand and fire leapt from her fingertips to a Fomorri. His cloak went up like a torch. Scales glistened, and eyes burned with rage. He kept coming.

Another thud vibrated the sand at her back. Heedless of her own safety, she drew her knife, hopped over Marsais, and charged the flaming creature.

There was leather in her palm, darkness, sweat, and blood. And pain. Isiilde was no longer in Fomorri; she was in a washroom with a man. She screamed with rage, and struck.

Her knife slid beneath scales, and she threw her weight behind the thrust, pressing hard. Flesh parted and blood warmed her hand, filling her senses.

The two went down in a tangle of limbs. A ball of flame illuminated the Fomorri's face, and her fire's light was reflected in six eyes. Those eyes were full of fear and shock—each surprised by death. The thought made her laugh. In a veil of flame, she watched the life drain from those eyes, until every unnatural curve of the Fomorri went limp.

Isiilde climbed to her feet as more Fomorri landed on in the grotto. She unleashed a wave of flame, and the creatures were blown off their feet.

The paladins rushed into the carnage. Steel glinted in the heat. Blades rose and fell, and a clash of battle surrounded her.

Isiilde stood over Marsais, inside a protective knot of armor. She caressed the fire roiling between her fingertips, fed it rage and pain, and set it free.

A dragon of fire took shape. It soared through the air with a beat of wings and lashed over the battlefield with a roar of death.

Desperate lips pressed against hers. For a moment, she struggled, pushing at the man, but the lips were persistent. And familiar. Isiilde stopped struggling.

The kiss stole her breath and rage, and will. Robbed of her voice, the fire dimmed and died, and the flames roiling over her flesh traveled to her veins, clouding her mind. Her teeth ached with need.

The man broke the kiss, and she gulped in air. Marsais held her against his body, his fingers buried in her hair.

A few wispy flames clung to his warded flesh. His silver eyes were as bright as stars, and she saw herself in their reflection.

"I swore I wouldn't take your fire, but I said nothing about stealing your breath," he whispered.

"Yes." One word was all she could manage as she stretched towards his lips. She kissed him again. Her head swam, her toes left the sand. She ached for him.

But pain burned away desire. It lashed through her body and her knees went weak. Marsais caught her, one hand on the small of her back, the other pressed to her side. Blood seeped between his fingers. Her blood.

Isiilde came back to herself.

Sunlight peeked over red rock. Charred bodies smoldered in the grotto. A moment of panic clutched her. The paladins had been fighting beside her—

She searched for the others. Acacia, Rivan, and Lucas stood in the wreckage, armor singed, clothing crispy, smudged with ash and blood.

Isiilde shuddered with relief, and sat down hard in the ashy sand. Somewhere, off in the distance, she heard Nimlesh shouting orders.

Oenghus stomped into view. "Get some clothes—" His gaze flickered to her ribs. "Void, lay her down." He reached for his flask and knelt as Marsais eased her down.

Isiilde was too exhausted to even think of resisting. The moment she hit the sand, he poured Brimgrog on her wound. It tickled.

Oenghus frowned at the slash. "You'll live," he grunted.

"Summoning her fire took a lot out of her. It's mostly exhaustion," Marsais said. He looked exhausted, too.

Oenghus placed a hand on her forehead and another over her stomach. But Isiilde growled and batted his hand away. "I will not be carried. Bandage it."

Her father paused, then bared his teeth. Brain and gore were stuck in his beard. "Aye." There was pride in his voice and approval in his eye. "I'll do a quick stitch."

"Gods, no," Marsais said. "Your needle work is appalling. I'll tend to her." He reached into his pack. "Leave your Brimgrog."

Oenghus eyed him suspiciously. He started to pass the flask to

Marsais, thought better of it, then thrust it into her hands before stalking away to pillage the dead.

Isiilde shivered in the early morning light. The aftermath of the battle left her empty and cold. She rummaged through her enchanted pouch for clothing. Before leaving Mearcentia, she'd raided the wardrobe in her room.

Marsais wrapped a cloak around her shoulders before pulling out needle and thread from his own pouch. With infinite care, he cleaned the wound, and began to sew.

The needle bit and thread tugged flesh. She distracted herself by studying Marsais. There was something different about him.

He was not burned, thank the gods. He'd had sense enough to weave a fire ward before kissing her. Her gaze strayed to his chin. The coins. His coins were gone, and what remained of his goatee was short and uneven.

"I found you lying here," she said through her teeth. "There was blood on your chest. What happened?"

Marsais glanced up from his sewing. "I bought myself time."

"Time for what?"

"Until I fall."

"How?"

"I let go," he said simply.

"Where are your coins?"

"They were annoying me. I put them somewhere else."

Isiilde eyed his loose clothing. "Your scar looked different."

"Did it?" he asked.

"It looked healed."

Marsais kept his eyes on his needlework. And when he said nothing more, she tugged on the remaining scruff. "It seems madmen like to butcher your hair."

"Hmm."

"You need a shave, Marsais."

"Are you offering?"

"In a hot bath, yes."

A smile played at the corner of his long lips. "I'll see what I can do."

When the last knot was cinched, he sliced the thread and covered the line with a bandage. It burned and tugged, but she managed to dress. Isiilde turned to where Acacia had been tending to a gash on Rivan's arm.

"Thank you," she said to the trio. "I'm glad you're not burned."

Lucas looked at her. He was always unreadable and disagreeable, but this time, his eyes glittered with something close to approval. "Your dragon passed over us."

Acacia slapped her on the shoulder, reminding Isiilde that she was covered with bruises. "Well done. Are you sure you can manage?"

"I'll have to."

IN THE MAD dash to the grotto, one Elite had fallen, and four more in the recent attack. Of the thirty-six souls who'd entered the leviathan's lair, only seventeen remained.

When wounds were bandaged and dead comrades plundered and buried, Oenghus secured his weapons and adjusted a rope on his back. They would attempt to traverse the maze from higher ground.

Oenghus began to climb. He looked a part of the stone, just another edge jutting from a crag. He stuck to a crack that ran up the rock face, climbing it as swiftly as a ladder.

Elam asked something at her side.

"He wonders how you'll manage the climb with your injury," Marsais translated. A spot of blood had soaked through her bandage and shirt.

"I was wondering the same," Rivan admitted, testing his arm. "About me."

Isiilde flashed him a smile. "I'm going to fly," she answered, flapping a hand.

Marsais shaded his eyes, gauging the distance to the top. Although he didn't voice his worry, she could see it in his posture. The height would be a stretch for her nearly five-second record.

"I'll give you a boost," Marsais offered.

"Uhm... are you sure?" Rivan hesitated, leaving the last unsaid: *Are you sure you won't have a vision and drop me?*

Lucas slapped the soldier on the shoulder. "If he drops you, I'm taking your sword."

"All clear," Oenghus called from the top.

Marsais nodded to Isiilde, and she sang, weaving her voice through the runes, filling the gaps in the levitation weave. A feather rune, a bind to her, and around that, air and spirit, creating wind. That part required concentration.

With a breath, she looked up. The ground fell away, and the top of the rock neared—at an alarming rate. She sped towards the sun.

Isiilde dropped the weave. It unraveled. Momentum waned, and her stomach dropped. She lunged for the rock. Too far; too late. She was falling.

A hard force slammed into her back. She hit the cliff, and clawed at the rock face, her fingernails scraping over stone.

A grip like iron locked around her wrist.

Isiilde looked up to find the face of her father. She smiled at his scowl. He hoisted her to safety and set her on her feet. Color heated her cheeks. It didn't take a far stretch of thought to realize that Marsais had given her a push, and Oenghus had caught her.

"I need to work on that," she admitted.

Oenghus grunted in agreement.

Rivan came next. He drifted softly to the rock, eyes brimming with excitement. "By the gods, that was amazing!" When Marsais joined them a moment later, Rivan looked like he might hug the man. "Thank you."

Marsais nudged the distracted paladin back a step before he fell off the edge. Isiilde tugged Rivan down, following a scout's urgent hand signal. Rivan was too excited to notice.

Next came Elam. Quick as a lizard, he scampered up the rope, and crouched, sling held at the ready.

The top of the plateau was pitted with crevices and cracks. There was no straight path to their goal. They'd have to navigate the maze of chasms. But at least up here, they could see their enemy coming.

Isiilde greedily soaked up the sun. Here, under a blistering sun, the power in her blood was not as draining as it had been in Vaylin. Was it the heat, or had she grown stronger?

As Isiilde mulled over the possibilities, another question came to mind. "Where's Finnow's Spire?"

Marsais pointed northeast. "There." Crags and wind-shaped pillars stretched to the horizon. "Beyond the rocks."

"That's a long way."

"It is."

"We could fly there... just the two of us."

"We *could*." There was always a catch. "But it would be risky. Fomorri grafters might recognize a weave. And we'd be at the mercy of every predator in the Great Expanse, to say nothing of our arrival. We'd be vulnerable during the transformation. I think we'd need Oenghus."

"Can you turn him into a bird?"

"I doubt he'd leave the ground as a bird. He's terrified of heights, unless he's climbing stone."

"I suppose a pig wouldn't do in this case," she mused.

"No," he agreed.

"It wasn't a pig," Oenghus growled. "You turned me into a bloody boar."

CHAPTER 40

How long had he been in darkness? There were so many passages, so many dark holes that he could not remember what the sun looked like. He wondered if there ever had been a sun. But mostly, he wondered where was *here*?

Zoshi slumped against a stalagmite. Why did it matter if he found a way out? No one would remember him except his mother. And he couldn't face her without his brothers.

Crumpet rattled in annoyance. When Zoshi didn't immediately move, the crow nipped his hand.

"Ow." He snatched his hand away and glared at the bird. "You're as lost as I am."

The crow turned his beak up and to the side, looking at the boy with an imperious eye. *Of course I'm not. Don't be stupid.*

Zoshi sighed, gathering a fistful of moss from the stone. He frowned at the stuff, and before his stomach completed its roll, he shoved it into his mouth. The moss was slimy with moisture. It reminded him of a slug.

The crow flapped off, leaving him to his meal. When his belly had quieted its grumble, Zoshi closed his eyes and let sleep take him. But his dreams were far from restful. He dreamed of a shadow. It sprouted wings, and he chased it endlessly. Always a step ahead; always a corner away. And eventually, he tripped and fell and broke his head. That last bit didn't scare him as much as it should.

Zoshi woke up to a soft blue light. Something was poking his head. He waved off the offending crow to sit up.

Crumpet nudged his makeshift lantern. It had gone dull, but the moss glowed brightly from the surrounding walls. Zoshi reached inside the tin lantern to empty it, but instead of dried moss, his fingers touched slippery movement. He jerked his hand away. That was not moss. He tilted the can and peeked inside. Thick white worms wiggled at the bottom.

Crumpet hissed, and waited.

"No." Zoshi shook his head. "I won't eat that." Even street rats had standards.

The crow dipped his beak in the tin, and emerged with a wiggling fat worm. He gulped it down whole, then gave a rattling caw.

Zoshi's stomach grumbled. He looked from the moss to the worms. He'd eaten worse. Closing his eyes, he plucked out a worm at random. Before he thought better of it, he popped it into his mouth. He didn't chew. That would be gross.

Zoshi gulped and gagged it down, and as he reached for a second, he told himself that it wasn't half bad.

CHAPTER 41

MORIGAN WATCHED the fog through the shimmering shield. If fear had a form, this would be it. She took a step closer.

A shadowy Fey drifted on the other side of the Barrier. Anger burned from its eyes. It wavered and shifted, and for a moment, an angular face took shape. It smiled like a cat with a secret. When she blinked, it was gone.

Instead of drifting in the ol'River after death, the Fey had been trapped in the Spine—in the Nameless chamber. What cold silence had those spirits endured?

She felt no pity for them.

Morigan stepped away. She was bone-tired, and found a bench to collapse on. She lay on the bench, staring at the winter sky, thinking of Oenghus and Isiilde.

Tharios had sent a horde of Flesh Puppets and Forsaken Furies through the gates. Oenghus would've enjoyed the battle, and their side would've fared better with him here.

She tried not to think of the lives lost. Victory had come at a steep cost.

"You sent a Whisper," Thira stated.

Morigan jerked upright. She hadn't heard the other woman approach. She nodded to the bench, scooting over to make room.

Thira sat down with care. She looked as haggard as Morigan felt. And lost without her dog. Her fingers unconsciously stroked the fabric of her longcoat. It was strange to see the woman without her dog—her only friend, as far as Morigan knew.

"Using the arena shield was brilliant."

"I require answers, not compliments," Thira snapped.

And that's why she didn't have any friends, Morigan thought.

"Why did you want to see me? Rashk's battering ram is nearly finished."

Morigan nodded towards the Archlord's private balcony. The curtain was swept aside to reveal a gnome lounging on the throne.

Thira stood with a weave on her fingertips. And Bram lifted his hat, flashing a grin.

"You remember my friends," Morigan said. A second figure stepped from the shadows. "Well, they have friends, too."

Twelve warriors stepped from various places of concealment around the arena. Each gave a nod before fading back into darkness. There was a reason they were called Wraith Guards.

Bram skipped from bench to bench until he stood before the women. "We've been sent from Iilenshar," he explained with a sweep of his hat. "Though we were sent to infiltrate an open castle, not a closed one."

"More than himself thought was needed," Evie added.

Thira looked from Bram and Evie to the cloaked figures above. "Wraith Guards," she realized.

Evie sighed. "I'm a Valkyrie."

"Marsais and the others are alive. He sent a message to Chaim," Morigan said. "They were in Vaylin."

"I'm still going to strangle that absent-minded fool," Thira huffed.

"All in good time." Bram paused as if he expected laughter. When all he got was a smirk from Evie, he cleared his throat and went on. "We asked Morigan to keep our identity under her hat. As things are, we've a mind to keep our plans to ourselves."

"And just what are your plans?" Thira asked.

"According to the seer, we have until the Shadowed Dawn," Bram said. "That's when the portal can be opened."

"According to the *seer*," Thira repeated with distaste. "Seers are notoriously mistaken."

Evie narrowed dark eyes at the woman. "We don't plan on standin' around twiddling our thumbs until then."

"So what we'd like to know..." Bram cut in. "Is whether there's a back way into that beast?"

"Preferably not the sewers," Evie said, wrinkling her nose.

"It's always the sewers," Bram agreed.

"Even if we break through the bailey gate with the battering ram, Tharios can seal the King's Walk," Morigan said. "If the gates in the Walk are sealed, our only option is to go through the elemental. I think we'd have better luck chipping through stone. At any rate, we're looking at a long siege if we don't take them by surprise."

"Agreed," Thira said. "I've discussed our options with Ielequithe."

"Without me?" Morigan asked.

"And without Rashk and Eldred," Thira defended. "The last thing we wanted was to draw Multist's attention. He wants me to deactivate this shield so he can banish the Fey with Zahra's grace."

Morigan snorted. "Good luck with that."

"It did spark an idea," Thira said, looking to the shimmering Barrier. "We could use the mist as a weapon—channel it into the Spine to confuse the Unspoken."

The idea made Morigan queasy. "The dead don't rest easy in this realm. There's no telling what will happen. I think these spirits have grown stronger since their release."

"I thought the same," Thira admitted. "But it's an option. And we don't have many."

"There *are* the sewers," Morigan mused. "But we'd have to scale the sea cliffs to get to the grates."

"I'm deathly afraid of heights," Evie quickly said.

Bram chuckled. "Terrible place to live, being on a floating city like Iilenshar, love."

"That's why I'm hardly there," the Valkyrie defended. "Now what of that shimmering net of runes over the big ol' tower? Can we pass through it safely?"

Thira shook her head. "I don't know. The castle wards have never been activated. And even if we hadn't left Thedus in Rashk's tower, I'm not sure he could have told us."

"Thedus?" Bram asked.

"A madman who's wandered these halls longer than any of us can remember," Morigan explained.

"He activated the wards," Thira said.

Evie sighed. "Right, there's that." It was looking more and more like the sewers.

"There *are* gaps in the ward," Thira mused. "The one we passed through in King's Walk, and there..." She pointed to the Spine's pinnacle and its open garden. "The Storm Gates aren't fully closed. I think the elemental interfered with the wards, but I'm not sure how wide the gap is—not with the ice coating the gates."

Bram drummed his fingers on his belt. "Definitely the ol' Iiisikle Spirit."

Evie nodded in agreement. "Not something I'm keen to mess with."

"Nor a thing that should be loose in the realm." Bram clucked his tongue with disapproval.

"We had no choice," Thira defended.

"I'm not saying it wasn't brilliant, but we'll have a time dealing with it," Bram said.

"Can you bind the elemental again?" Morigan asked.

Thira shook her head. "It was already bound. I simply nudged the bind that was in place—as filthy as it was. Tharios mixed the bind with Bloodmagic. The gods only know how he managed."

"Or who stuffed a glacier in a bottle to begin with," Evie said.

"Marsais could manage it," Thira said with grudging respect. "His skill far surpasses my own."

"We can't wait for him to show up," Morigan said. "Do we know how to deactivate the wards?"

No one answered.

After a minute, Thira sighed. "I fear we gave too much power to the Archlord—too many secrets. Tharios wanted that throne for a reason."

"Thedus knows something..." Morigan said.

"Yes," Thira agreed. "But of the two, I think we have a better chance of asking our current Archlord to open the gates than getting a word out of Thedus."

Morigan had to agree. "You said you left him in Rashk's tower?"

"That doesn't mean he's still there."

"But there's a chance." Morigan might get him to talk. Aside from Marsais and Isiilde, he responded best to her.

"We'll still need to get inside," Thira pointed out.

"Do you have another option?" Morigan asked.

"As a matter of fact," Thira said, looking to the Spine, "I do."

CHAPTER 42

Arrows lit the sky. For a second, each flaming tip was caught in time, then they screamed, crashing into an armored thing. The boots beneath the shields trampled the snow, and rushed the gates. Runes flared, the battering ram's serpent-shaped figurehead boomed, and the gates rocked the soldiers back.

Morigan watched as burning oil poured from the rampart spouts, splattering over the covered ram. A few warriors fell, but most were saved by their stoneskin weave. The ram struck again, and this time, the gates groaned.

Rashk watched her creation with obvious pride. "It will break the gates," she announced.

Morigan nodded to Thira, and the two women left Rashk, keeping to the shadow of the rampart wall.

"I still think you should stay," Thira said. "They need healers here."

"Most of my healers are inside the Spine. Besides, you'll need help with Tharios," she said, putting on her helm.

They joined the waiting group of Wraith Guards (and one Valkyrie). The Guardians' Elite stood solid and grim-faced. Formidable warriors, each and every one. Except, of course, the carrot-haired gnome.

"This may not work," Tulipin reminded them all for the dozenth time.

"And I may trip over a rock and die," Morigan said. "We've been through this already."

As the battering ram drummed and crackled in the distance, the group made their way around the outer bailey. They kept to the rampart wall, circling the keep and moving to the back of the Spine's base.

The castle ward pulsed with runes. But there was a tear in the weave, its threads fluttering in the air. Morigan wondered what would happen if it unraveled completely. The backlash might level the entire island. And beyond.

"So there's an open garden all the way up there?" Evie asked.

It was impossible to see the top of the Spine while standing at its base, no matter how far back one craned their neck.

"And a rookery a few floors below," Morigan said.

"You could always go through the sewers, love," Bram offered.

The woman shot her mate a withering glare. "I'd rather fall from the sky than drown in filth."

"Ah, the choices we make."

Thira dropped a neatly packed bundle onto the ground. She removed a slim vial, and unhooked her cloak. It slid from her naked shoulders. The woman was all skin and bone, but she did not shiver. She tipped the vial to her lips. It fell from her fingertips, runes swirled, bones cracked, and a beady-eyed raven stood in the fading light. With a lift of powerful wings, the raven took flight, grabbing the bundle from the snow.

"I always figured her for a vulture," Morigan admitted.

Bram laughed, but Tulipin was not amused. He hugged himself, and rocked back and forth. "Maybe *one* of you, but not *all*."

"If we fall, we fall," Morigan said.

Evie gave a wistful sigh. "Shame she can't do that for all of us."

"Transformation is dangerous if you can't weave," Morigan explained. "Not many Wise Ones can transform others—takes a strong and sure hand. She used to do it, but not anymore. The last novice she transformed never returned to human form."

"What if there's no tear in the shield farther up?" Tulipin's voice was as high-pitched as a squeak.

Bram smiled. "You'll just 'ave to put us down real soft like."

"She'll send a Whisper if there's a hole," Morigan reminded.

Every minute they waited, Tulipin grew more nervous, and Morigan worried he'd work himself into a faint. She wasn't looking forward to being levitated, either. She took a slow, calming breath, resisting the urge to slap some sense into the man.

"That fellow must be freezing," Evie said with a note of caution.

Morigan followed the Valkyrie's gaze. She blinked in surprise and hurried over to the naked man who stood at the base of the Spine.

"How did you get out here, Thedus?" she asked.

Slowly, like a stone being turned, Thedus looked at Morigan, and for a moment, he focused on her. She was so shocked to find clarity in his eyes that she failed to notice his hand.

Thedus reached up to touch the shimmering ward.

Morigan bit back a cry of alarm. She surged forward, but before she could stop him, he pushed his hand through the ward to touch the stone underneath.

Nothing happened.

Morigan remembered to breathe. The stone beneath his palm pulsed with a teleportation rune. But how? Only the Archlord could grant permission to use the Runic Eye. She'd used them when Marsais was Archlord, but Tharios had taken away her privileges. That only left one possibility.

Morigan motioned the others over.

"It appears we won't be needing you, Tulipin." And with that, Morigan walked through the shimmering net of runes.

It was like diving into a mountain river. Her heart sped and leapt, and her senses came alive; a sharp breath later, the stone reached for her, pulling her in with the familiar tug of a teleportation weave. The stone pushed her out into a cobweb.

Morigan batted at the sticky threads, searching for the elusive spider that she'd never seen. She quickly stepped aside, and peeked around the dusty tapestry. The hallway was empty.

The Wraith Guards and Valkyrie came seconds later, their cloaks blending with the stone as they slipped into the hallway.

Thedus stepped out from behind the tapestry, and Morigan nearly hugged the man. "You were an Archlord, weren't you?" she asked, softly.

But his eyes were unfocused again. Thedus shuffled down the corridor. Morigan let him be.

"Do you know where we are?" Evie whispered.

It took a moment to find the Valkyrie. Their cloaks were enchanted with a chameleon-like power, but she could sense no lingering weave. Such were the mysteries of Iilenshar.

"I do." They weren't far from Oenghus' rooms. She led the way to the rookery.

Morigan motioned the Wraith Guards to wait outside, and poked her head through the door. Thira had the falconer cornered and his tongue bound with a weave. They couldn't afford to trust anyone at the moment.

Thira joined her at the door. "I'm relieved you're all here."

"Thedus activated a teleportation rune for us—the Archlord's private entrance."

Thira blinked. "Those runes only work for the Archlord and his trusted few."

Morigan shrugged. "We're all here." She looked to the roosting owls and hawks. "Any sign of Crumpet?"

Thira gave a sharp shake of her head. "Where's Thedus?"

"He wandered off."

Anger flashed in her eyes, but Morigan silenced it. "He knows what he's about. And he's no traitor. Let's be on with it."

THEY WERE CLOSE. Morigan signaled to Thira, who began to weave, thin fingers moving like knife strokes. At the final slash of runes, a mirror weave settled on the pair.

Morigan eyed the long hallway, noting each ripple of air against stone: the Wraith Guards were in position. She poked her head around a corner.

A squad of red-banded soldiers guarded the entrance to the King's Walk—a long corridor that connected the castle to the Spine.

Morigan no longer felt the rush of battle in her blood or heard its song in her ears. It was simply work to be done. And the sooner it was over, the better.

When Bram tapped the stone, a whisper of a signal, she calmly stepped out of the doorway. Wraith Guards fired their bows, arrows zipping past her ears. A knot of red-banded soldiers rushed from a guardroom to raise their shields.

Morigan waded over the dead and dying soldiers to add more to the pile. A soldier stepped forward with sword raised. She hurled a weave into the man. Bones snapped, one after another, and he crumpled like an accordion. His agony filled her ears.

In the chaos of battle, in the cries and swinging steel, she calmly applied the edge of her axe to his neck, silencing his cries.

Her next swing took another by surprise. The beard of her axe slipped around his neck and caught him under the chin. With a tug, she jerked him off his feet and raised her shield to catch another sword stroke. A quick bash, a side-step, and she caught the next soldier on the back of the knee. He buckled, but she left his death to another, hewing a path through a knot of steel, towards a chanting voice.

Evie's arrow whispered past her shoulder and sank into the weaving Wise One. He slumped, and Bram dropped two more soldiers who stood by a lever.

Morigan looked at Thira. "Open the bailey gates. I'll stay and hold the Walk." Even as she spoke, the Wraith Guards were dragging the corpses behind the statues that lined the long corridor.

Morigan glanced at the blood in the hallway. With a practiced hand, she wove a water rune and mixed it with ice, scrubbing the floor clean with cold water. With luck, no one would notice the change of guard.

"We'll go, too," Bram said.

Evie ordered the others to stay and defend. But before Thira entered the Walk, she stiffened in alarm.

Morigan followed her gaze to a patchy, flickering break in the castle ward. It was the hole they had fled through after releasing the elemental. Precisely in the center of the hallway.

But now that Morigan had walked, unharmed, through the shimmering Barrier, she knew that the castle wards were for the Fey spirits, not for flesh and bone.

That hole troubled her, too. Thira met her eyes, their thoughts traveling in the same direction. The tear was too much of a coincidence. But there was no time to worry over it.

Thira shivered, and left with the Wraith Guards, while Morigan picked up a spear and planted herself in front of the mechanism that sealed the King's Walk—a lever connected to a maze of gears and pulleys and a tangle of enchantments. It had never been activated, and if she had her way, it never would be.

CHAPTER 43

THE AIR WAS COLD, but not a normal cold. Zoshi was used to that. He'd been down here for—

The boy did not know.

The air had changed, though. Empty, he decided, and then shook his head, trying to dislodge a hiding thought. The whole place was empty. But this was different, like fingers crawling up his spine.

He stopped and looked down at a skeleton. Black hollows stared back. It looked like it was laughing at him. Zoshi wished he could laugh, too. But he only felt like crying.

"*Hurry,*" the crow screeched. He was a harsh taskmaster, and he was hopping in front of a wide tunnel.

Zoshi frowned at the passage. It gave him pause. It didn't look any different from the others. But it *felt* wrong. His instincts told him to run in the opposite direction.

The tunnels were endless. He even thought he'd heard the ocean down one passage. But the crow had nipped and pecked at him until he steered away.

What was special about *this* tunnel?

Crumpet squawked again. It grated on his ears. With little else to do, Zoshi plodded onwards. The crow was his only hope.

Bones crunched under his boots. He'd found more weapons, another sack, and coins—lots of coins that he didn't recognize. The thought of dying rich appealed to the street rat, so he'd collected the coins. But never from the skeletons—it felt wrong.

No moss grew in this tunnel. Odd. Zoshi raised his lantern. A river of bones stretched as far as his blue light dared to go. The bones were all mangled and twisted, with rusted weapons and armor laid bare.

Crumpet hopped on a crushed skull, and cawed. There was a promise to the sound. The end was near. Still, his legs wouldn't move. It was like staring down Death herself.

Zoshi recalled every legend he had ever heard about the Guardian of Death. Pale as a grave worm, quick as a viper, cold as snow, and blue eyes that froze a heart. The Lady Death stalked the shadows, gathering them like a cloak.

Would she grant him a quick death, or would she toy with him like a cat with a mouse?

"I think we should go another way," he whispered. His voice bounced and shattered in the desolation. He sounded tiny.

The crow flapped to his shoulder. This time, the bird's talons dug into his flesh.

"Ow!" Zoshi jerked, but it was hard to get away from something on your own shoulder. A sharp beak nipped his ear. "Stop it!" The more he struggled, the deeper the claws dug, so he took a step forward.

Crumpet gave an approving caw.

"You're a terrible guide." He kept walking, picking his way over the river of bones. Then he heard screams—whispering ones like memories. As if the strange stillness had captured the death cries and never let go.

Zoshi edged along the rough-hewn stone. He kept his hand on a wall, afraid to let go. It felt like he was drifting into nothing.

The rush of blood in his ears was deafening. The stillness sucked at his breath. He wanted to stop and never move again.

Even the bird was tense, stiff and alert, like a stuffed parrot he'd once seen on a crazed old sailor. Zoshi shuffled forward through the dark until his little light touched a corner. But when he tried to follow it around, the crow bit his ear.

Zoshi didn't want to step into the void. But he did. He let go of the wall, holding up his light and edging forward. More bones, more fallen warriors mixed with the pale sleeping dead.

The light wavered with his shaking. Zoshi gripped his own arm, trying to keep it still. He was falling; he was sure of it, and his stomach had been left at the cave wall.

Tears slipped down his cheeks and piss seeped down his leg—the smell of courage. It was strangely reassuring in the void of time and space.

He did not know how long he walked, but he stopped when his toe knocked against something hard. Metal glinted in the blue light. A war hammer, all etched with bright markings, just like new. It reminded him of his friend—the giant Oenghus.

A massive skeleton lay nearby. Its hand was outstretched, reaching towards the weapon in death.

Zoshi hesitated. He didn't know how to use a sword, but a hammer looked like a simple thing. But the owner had died reaching for it. Did that count as taking something from the dead?

It was so shiny, though. He didn't feel so afraid with it there. Zoshi bent to touch the shiny hammer, but a sound sent his heart into his throat. A rasp, a creak of metal on stone. It stopped. And then came again like a long, rattling breath.

The crow was shaking, but only because his perch could barely stand. Something slithered beyond the light. Zoshi clamped his teeth together to keep them from knocking. He thrust his arm out as far as it would go. The light touched upon the rattle. It was a chain, a great barbed and rusted thing. It moved again, then stopped.

Zoshi stood like a statue, watching the chain rasp against the stone with the rhythm of breath.

He didn't care if the bird turned his flesh into shreds. He wouldn't follow that chain, not for any life. He'd rather die right there. But when he looked at his guide, the bird was pointing his beak to the right.

Zoshi didn't argue. He darted in that direction, hopping over bones and twining his way around rusted mining equipment. He ran until he found a cave wall.

Out of breath and dizzy with fear, he slumped, pressing his back against the solid stone. He was all alone under the earth with a breathing chain and a lost bird. Life, he was sure, could not get much worse than this.

CHAPTER 44

WATER WAS LIFE. And Isiilde had none left. The water runes were gone. And the rock overhead had run out, too. It had forced them to climb down into a wide wadi full of nooks and crannies.

Isiilde popped another strawberry into her mouth. They should've run out by now. But then Oenghus never seemed to run out of Brimgrog either. One answer came to mind, but she couldn't deal with the implications at the moment.

She peeked around her concealment. Pillars of red rock stretched like a petrified forest. It was a maze of threat. And the perfect spot for an ambush.

Two Elite scouts crept over the open terrain. A shift here, another there. The pair were good. Even knowing they were there, she could barely see them.

Unfortunately, the Fomorri were also skilled hunters—they'd been hounding the group's every step. Their tactics reminded her of Mousebane. Her cat used to toy with his meal, goading a mouse and batting it until it fell over with exhaustion. Isiilde was close to that, and so was everyone else, even her father.

Rivan shifted by her side. "This looks familiar," he croaked.

"Everything looks the same," Lucas whispered.

Elam pointed at a distant rock, speaking in his fluttering tongue. His youthful voice sounded like sand between cogs.

Marsais squinted at the spot. His lips were dry and cracked, but his eyes were sharp. He hadn't lost focus since the attack in the grotto. "Elam says he has not seen that rock before. It looks like a hairless mammoth."

The rock formation had a long wide arch with a shorter one that looked like a trunk. A barely perceptible movement caught her eye, far across the pillared space. It was the scout's signal for all clear. Nimlesh rose from his concealment and signaled to the rest.

For now, it was safe.

As the group walked in the shadows between pillars, she eyed the sky, searching for the winged heralds of the Fomorri.

"I feel like we're a flock of sheep," she murmured to Marsais.

"*Baaah,* said the lamb to slaughter."

"You're not very reassuring."

"Most sheep don't know where they're headed. At least we're prepared."

She narrowed her eyes. "How do you know the sheep don't know?"

"I speak sheep."

"Do you?"

"*Baaah.*"

Isiilde snorted. "What does that mean?"

"We are insulted that you haven't learned our tongue yet."

"That's rather complicated for an animal that doesn't know where it's headed."

Marsais lifted a shoulder. "I don't know where I'm headed half the time."

A scout crouched at the entrance to a crevice ahead. He motioned them forward, and put a finger to his lips. Isiilde followed the others into the narrow passage.

The second scout knelt in the shadow of the high rocks. She gestured at them to keep low. Isiilde dropped to her knees, and slithered forward, coming to a stop on the edge of a rock. Her breath caught.

The ground dropped sharply, spilling into a canyon with high cliffs and a snake of green cutting through its center. An eye-shaped oasis sat in the middle of the canyon.

Isiilde blinked, cleared the exhaustion from her mind, and looked again. It wasn't a mirage. Camels dotted the canyon floor, roaming free, drinking the water. Caves, roughly hewn stairs, and crude doorways dotted the canyon sides. But instead of reminding her of the Lome's underground city, it brought to mind a hive of wasps.

Nimlesh removed his spyglass and ran it over the gorge. "There are a handful of sentries and a gate at the end of the canyon."

The spyglass was passed down the line, and eventually Isiilde got a turn. The caves were impenetrable. They looked like black eyes and a feeling of being watched prickled the back of her neck.

She pointed the spyglass down the canyon to the strange gate. Two high pillars of rock guarded a narrow opening that was blocked by a large stone. It looked like a flat disc that rolled into the canyon wall. She counted six sentries, including a hunched figure tending to the camels.

"There's only six sentries… Isn't that odd?" she asked the man stretched beside her.

Marsais grunted.

"I'll wager they're waiting for us to get at the water."

"I'll not wager against that," he murmured.

Isiilde passed the glass to him. "I thought an ambush was supposed to be a surprise. Isn't it all a bit obvious?"

"Not when we need the water," Acacia answered.

Oenghus spat. "I hate ambushes."

"Maybe we killed the rest?" No one bothered responding to Rivan's optimism. "Could we backtrack and search for another route through the mountains?"

"We still need water," Acacia said.

"The others might be out looking for us," he pressed.

"They've been herding us," Lucas said.

"Right, I'll draw out the ambush while the rest of you get water and open that gate. I'll catch up." Oenghus started to rise, but Acacia clapped a hand on his shoulder and bullied him back down.

"*That* is one of the worst ideas I've ever heard," Acacia said.

"Do you have a better one?" he shot back.

"Anything that doesn't end with you being disemboweled by the Fomorri."

"So you do care?" He was all cocky grin and brows.

"Yes," Acacia said flatly.

Oenghus opened his mouth.

"No," the captain interrupted. "I don't want to see what's under your kilt."

"I wasn't—"

Marsais cut him off. "She's right, Oen, it's a terrible plan."

"Then you come up with a better one," he growled. "I'm tired of sitting on a fence like some cockless bastard with two fingers."

That was a new one. Isiilde glanced at Marsais in question, who gave a shake of his head. Best not to wonder.

"At least wait until dark to plow the Fomorri," Acacia said dryly.

Oenghus bared his teeth. "I love it when you use words I understand."

"I try to keep things simple for you."

"We'll wait until dark," Nimlesh said. "It's close to their camp, but more defensible than the terrain we passed. Set a watch on both ends of the crevice."

No one argued with that logic.

Guards were posted, and the rest of the group moved away from the canyon and settled into wait.

Oenghus prowled around their camp for a time. Finally, he planted himself on the sand with his back to a rock. Acacia moved beside him.

"Are you all right?"

"I hate waiting," he growled.

"For death?"

He grunted. "I'd rather charge her."

"All in good time."

"At least I get to wait by you."

"The only time I'll sleep with you." Acacia drew her sword, and laid it across her knees, keeping a hand on the hilt.

Oenghus started to say something, but closed his mouth when Acacia leaned into him, resting her head on his arm.

"Wake me when it's dark," she whispered.

CHAPTER 45

THE SUN HAD FALLEN, coldness crept over the desert, and nothing stirred but the faint ripple of moonlight on water.

It was time.

Marsais wove stoneskin weaves for the warriors, and Isiilde wove her own, adding fire. He eyed the weave as it melted into her skin.

Isiilde arched a brow at him. *Yes*, that brow said, *my weave is perfect. What else did you expect?*

"Finnow's Spire is sacred to the Fomorri. It lies beyond that gate," Marsais told the group. "No matter the cost, we must recover the final piece of Soisskeli's stave, and take it to Iilenshar."

The warriors nodded, each grim save for Oenghus, whose eyes gleamed with expectation.

"Hold the weave, Seer." Nimlesh said.

"I will." Marsais began to layer runes over the group. As each shimmered, Isiilde took Elam's hand. The boy squeezed it back, holding on tight.

The slope was steep to the canyon floor, and with every careful step, bits of sand and scree tumbled loose. She hoped the darkness would conceal the disturbance.

Mirror rune or not, she crouched at the bottom of the slope, waiting for the word to move forward. She could not see the others, but she could sense their mirror weave.

Could the Fomorri Grafters do the same? She held her breath, eyeing the caves. Were they watching, even now?

A soft whistle signaled her group to move. She walked, boots crunching in the stillness. Silent sentries stood at the faraway gates. Something was wrong. Her senses tingled with a warning. Every inch of this place was vile.

Isiilde wanted to forget the water, run straight to the gates, and take her chances with whatever lay beyond. But she held her ground, keeping her fire close, ready, on the tip of her tongue.

The air cooled near the oasis. A breeze stirred the water, creating ripples that disturbed the moon's reflection. One of the group crouched at the edge. A slosh of water signaled a waterskin dipping into the pool.

Isiilde held her breath, willing all her strength to Marsais, hoping he could hold the weave before a vision shattered his focus.

Three more blurred shapes bent to fill their own skins. The wind picked up, kicking up sand. Holding back a sneeze, she quickly buried her face behind a scarf. The mirror weave would not conceal a flaming burst of fire. But that was not what gave them away.

As the sand blew, it gathered on clothing, outlining each person in their group. Isiilde's eyes widened, and she swallowed down a cry of alarm. It was too late.

A horn shattered the silence. Fires sprang along the canyon walls and cliff base, lighting the caves like a myriad of gleaming eyes. Fomorri charged from their holes.

"If you attack, I'll poison your water!" Marsais' voice boomed like a thunderclap.

The Fomorri who'd rushed from their holes skidded to a stop, and the bowmen on the high ledges hesitated.

Isiilde looked to the source of their fear. Their mirror weaves had unraveled, and Marsais stood knee deep in the pool, his arm outstretched, a vial poised to tip over.

"Widow's Mark venom," he drawled. "A drop will taint your water supply." He repeated the words in Abyssal, a harsh, grating tongue that slithered from his lips.

Weapons bristled on both sides, but no one dared move. She could feel the fires in the braziers that lit the caves. The flames whispered to her, begging to be set free. She looked to Marsais, but he gave a slight shake of his head.

A line of Fomorri shifted, making way for a single cowled figure who walked from a cave into the night. He lowered his scarf, revealing a scaled face and slitted eyes that glinted in the fire's light. He looked like a horned snake.

The leader bared a row of sharp teeth. "We have other wells, Magi."

"If that were the case, then I'd be dead," Marsais called back. "We seek Finnow's Spire. That is all."

"Then walk there. It is beyond those gates."

"Your word is as fleeting as a drop in the sands, Grafter."

The man laughed. "No, it is as fleeting as the pillars. That is where my word will run out. After that, no more words. We Fomorri like games, Magi."

As they talked, Elam continued to fill the waterskins, but Isiilde did not share the boy's optimism.

"I will even give you time to pray to your weak gods," the Grafter offered. "You can beg them for a swift death."

They were surrounded and outnumbered—seventeen humans facing hundreds of Fomorri.

Marsais considered the distance, then looked at the others. "Walk to the gates. I'll join you there."

"They'll attack as soon as you're clear of the water," Oenghus growled. "Let me take the vial."

"We'll need you at the gates, Oen."

"Then I'll take it," Acacia said.

Marsais sighed. "Everyone is so eager to die."

"As if you're not?" Isiilde growled.

"The seer has a plan," he said with a wink. His fingers flashed, and a moment later, he released the vial. It remained in the air. A levitation weave. In a louder voice, he stated his ultimatum. "If anyone approaches, the vial will fall; if you attack, it will fall; if you block my view... I believe you get the point. Need I go on?"

The Grafter said nothing.

Slowly, Marsais backed up, keeping his hand stretched towards the vial. The Elite and paladins closed in, and Isiilde and Elam were herded into the center of a tight knot of warriors, protected on all sides by armor and shields.

Oenghus stood at the fore, his fingers flexing and curling around his bone club as the group walked towards the gates.

The Fomorri parted, slowly. Some were hidden in robes with only eyes glinting from dark cowls. Others were not; the ones she'd rather forget.

Some had faces stitched to bare chests. Others had eyes, everywhere; heads sharing one body; too many legs and a patchwork of limbs; scales and the skin of serpents and beasts—the Fomorri grafted human and animal pieces onto themselves like a jester's motley. The stench of rotting flesh made her gag.

Isiilde could feel hungry eyes lingering on her. Obscenities were thrown at the women, and threats of torture at the men. She closed her ears to what the Fomorri planned.

"That one is mine," a giant of a man pointed his spear at her. With curling horns and gleaming bronze skin, he looked like the brazen bull statue. His armor was his flesh.

Oenghus growled at the hulking Fomorri. He was on the verge of losing control.

"*Oenghus*," Marsais warned.

Their leader fell in step, walking on a ledge that skirted the cliff base. "If you reach the Spire, what do you think you will do?" he called.

"Oh, I don't know," Marsais replied. "Take in the sun; enjoy the scenery."

"Funny, Magi." The Grafter did not laugh. "Do you run fast, eh? A child, women, and a few warriors will outrun Fomorri? We will see if you are so carefree on a Cradle."

Isiilde clutched Elam's hand, and she could feel the boy's trembling. Beside her, Rivan's knuckles were white on his hilt and the blade quivered. She stilled her own heart, reaching for the raging fire in her breast. It washed over her, leaving her cold with clarity, and imagining every single Fomorri in flames.

"We have a strong sense of preservation," Marsais replied easily. "As

I'm sure your warriors have discovered. Pitiful, really. How many warriors did you throw at us? How many were lost?"

The Grafter spread his hands. "Merely fodder. The weak die; the strong live. And don't worry, we will let your women live to breed, and raise the boy as one of us."

Isiilde snorted, eyeing the braziers. Elam would not spend a moment with these men.

"Not yet," Marsais murmured to her.

The Fomorri closed in, forming a wide semi-circle around the group, matching them step for step. They passed the pillars into a narrow bit of rock, and there, the Grafter joined his men on the canyon floor. The Fomorri warriors parted for their leader.

"Remember," Marsais called. "If I cannot see the vial; it will fall."

The Grafter jerked his pointed chin. His men left space, a straight line to the pool and the suspended vial. "What do you want with the Spire?"

"A visit."

The Grafter laughed, a disturbingly high-pitched sound. "A visit— do you plan on knocking and asking to enter?"

"That was my plan."

"It would be entertaining to watch you try."

"If it would add to your amusement, I could juggle while I knock," Marsais offered.

"Only if it's with the heads of your friends. Maybe we will let you try after we toy with you." He looked to his men. "Keep his hands intact, so the Magi can knock."

A ripple of laughter passed over the Fomorri. It was not a pleasant sound.

"He does not need hands. He can knock with his skull," the giant bull of a man roared.

More laughter followed them as they came to the gate. Isiilde turned towards the mass, all glinting eyes and tensed muscles. Blood lust filled the night.

"Open the gate," Marsais called.

"Remove the vial," the Grafter ordered.

The gate was as solid as it had appeared from the crevice. The round stone sat on a track that disappeared into a narrow slot in the cliff. High above, on the canyon wall, a heavy winch sat on a ledge where three Fomorri stood at the ready.

"Your word," Marsais said.

"My word," the Grafter agreed.

Marsais gestured. In the dim firelight, the vial drifted to the side, and toppled safely in the sand. "Open the gate," he said again.

The Grafter bared his fangs. "My word is not worth much, Magi."

Marsais shrugged. "The vial was empty." He looked to Oenghus. "Bring down the mountain."

Oenghus reached for his flask.

"Preserve them!" the Grafter hissed.

As the horde charged, Oenghus chugged the sacred brew—more than Isiilde had ever seen.

"Now," Marsais hissed.

Isiilde called to her fire. It leapt from braziers, surged from tunnels and gushed from the holes. Red flame spilled into the canyon, devouring the archers and their arrows.

Another roar cut through the flame, stealing her breath and stopping her heart. Oenghus stepped in front of the charging Fomorri, arms spread, bellowing into the night.

The earth shook, the ground cracked, and the cliffs fell. Isiilde was knocked off her feet. Sand and rock choked the air, smothering her voice and fire.

Marsais thrust out his hands. The air snapped, and a raw surge of energy hit the first wave of Fomorri, blasting bodies, severing heads and limbs, and tossing others aside like rag-dolls.

The giant, bull-like Fomorri climbed to his feet, and roared a challenge that the berserker could not ignore. Oenghus charged.

"The gate!" Marsais yelled.

But the berserker was caught in the moment. The two brutes clashed, muscle against muscle. Both staggered back from the impact and were swallowed in a rush of fighters.

Isiilde could not see her father, but she could hear his rage over the clash of steel. It shook her bones.

Grunts and howls filled the canyon. A Fomorri broke free from the haze, sword raised, and Rivan appeared, slamming her attacker with his shield. Another four-legged creature rushed forward, nearly trampling the nymph. She scrambled back, flinging a bolt of energy at the second. His body jerked, and he stumbled. Lucas finished him.

In the confusion, she backed into something solid: the gate.

"Give me a boost, Nymph!" It was Lucas, wounded and bleeding. He pointed up towards the ledge where the guards stood, and slung his shield over his back.

Isiilde coughed out the Lore as her fingers wove. With a gesture, the paladin shot upwards, but her hand was too heavy. Isiilde focused, willing the paladin to slow. When he did not, she let the levitation weave unravel. He flailed for a moment in midair, then caught the ledge.

An archer spotted Lucas, and his bow swung down, arrow pointing at the paladin's head. Lucas grabbed the Fomorri's ankle, and pulled. The arrow went wide, bouncing off his pauldron.

Isiilde hurled an energy bolt at the archer. The weave was big and sloppy, and knocked him off the ledge.

Lucas scrambled up, ramming his shoulder into another Fomorri, swinging his axe with both hands. He cleaved and cut his way through the knot, and when the last fell, he threw his weight against the gate's lever.

A sizzling crack drew her attention. Blue energy shot from Marsais' fingertips. Lightning collided with a Barrier of swirling black. The energy bounced off the Grafter, spiraling into a mass of fighters. Ten men fell where they stood, their charred flesh mingling with sweat and fear.

The Grafter held a knife in his hand, but he didn't use it to attack Marsais. The Fomorri leader slashed his own arm, and the air rippled around the scaled man. An inky tendril lashed at Marsais. His own Barrier flared, sending the whip of darkness into a nearby Fomorri. The man fell to the ground howling.

Marsais' fingers flashed, and a burst of light lit the sky, blinding the Fomorri closest to him. Isiilde blinked away the spots, unable to follow the flurry of deadly weaves.

As the two fought, power thrummed in the air with a clash of weaves that tore through flesh. Death rained on the surrounding fighters. Fomorri trampled each other, trying to escape the backlash of force, giving the two magi room to fight.

A grinding sound jarred her bones. The stone at her back moved, and the gate rolled into the rock. Above, on the ledge, more Fomorri rushed Lucas. He abandoned the wheel, swinging his axe.

"The gate is open!" Isiilde yelled. Only two feet, but it was enough.

"Go!" Acacia ordered.

Isiilde hesitated, searching for her father in the chaos. He stood at the forefront, holding back a horde. She summoned a flame, but it sputtered on her palm, dying out. The air was too clogged with sand for her fire to burn.

Isiilde grabbed Elam, and dragged the sling-wielding boy through the opening. They rushed through the gap, stumbling into the open desert.

A monstrous shape rose from the sand—a giant scorpion with the head and torso of a man. The abomination wielded pinchers and a deadly tail that dripped with ooze.

Elam screamed, letting a stone fly from his sling. The missile pegged the monster in its human, shell-encased head. The eyes blinked, but the monster advanced with a snap of massive claws.

Isiilde hurled fire and bolts, but its armor was like stone. The Fomorri grinned down at her.

An Elite slipped through the gate, weapon in hand. The Gate Guard struck, catching the Elite in a pincher. The man was snapped in two.

Isiilde shoved Elam back, stepping in front of the boy. With a shout of fury, she thrust out her hands, hurling a fireball at the Fomorri. But it was a creature of the sand and sun, and it walked through unscathed.

A pincher opened, the tail quivered. Death flashed in her eyes, but the snapping blow never came. The flames of her armor weave flared, halting the killing blow. She was plucked off her feet, but the Fomorri struggled to break her armor weave.

Isiilde could not breathe. In the cocoon of her flaming shield, she pushed and pulled, struggling to pry the vise-like pinchers apart. The tail came up, curled and poised, and the scorpion raised her for the killing blow. The tip was as long and sharp as a sword.

With her remaining breath, she gasped out the Lore, tracing a crude earth rune with trembling fingers. When the last thread was cinched, she slapped her hand against the pincher's apex.

The weave seeped into the creature; earth and stone, all sloppy and haphazard. The pinchers turned grey, and cracked. Isiilde slipped through, falling to the sand. The Fomorri's human head looked at her, eyes wild with rage.

She quickly scrambled away.

With a shout, Lucas Cutter leapt off the ledge. He landed on the scorpion's back, swinging his axe. The blade sunk into the human head, cleaving it in two, but some life remained; some instinct, headless or not. The tail stabbed at the paladin. It pierced armor, and burst from his stomach, impaling Lucas on the end.

The scorpion lurched forward. Isiilde threw herself to the side, dodging the six stamping legs as a swift form ran past. Acacia twisted and dodged the remaining pincher, hacking at the legs and vulnerable underbelly.

The scorpion reared, and Isiilde rolled away from the thrashing beast. A wave of force zipped over her head, leaving her hair frizzed. The scorpion crashed forward, twitching in the sand.

Isiilde staggered to her feet as Acacia hacked at the quivering tail. It broke free, and Lucas fell. Acacia caught her lieutenant, and Rivan rushed forward to help. They lowered the man onto the ground. Acacia abandoned shield and sword, laying her hands on the warrior. She bowed her head, but no light flared; no power warmed his dying body.

Acacia drove her fist into the sand. "Damn you, Seer—save him!"

Marsais slid to his knees in the sand, and placed his hands on the impaled paladin.

"Go now, all of you!" Acacia shouted. She was clutching her leg, blood seeping from between her fingertips.

Rivan nudged Elam towards the desert, but Isiilde took a step towards the gate. Oenghus was still beyond the barrier. Screams and death filled the night, and a roar stopped her heart. The ground began to shake, trembling and quaking beneath her feet.

Nimlesh and three of his Elite squeezed through the gap in the gate. Marsais opened his eyes, and Lucas took his last, rattling breath.

Thunder cracked in the clear night, and a moment later, lightning crackled from the sky. A jagged, razor-white streak struck the stone gate. Forks of energy reached out, pounding the earth.

Isiilde lay on her back. She did not remember getting there. Fire flickered around her flesh. Acacia and Marsais bent over her. She blinked, reeling. Her skin felt charged.

Acacia was shouting, but all she could hear was ringing. She scrambled to her feet, and was pushed towards darkness.

Acacia staggered beside her. Isiilde shook the buzzing from her ears, and put a shoulder under the wounded woman.

Together, they limped forward, following the fleeting shadow of Elam over the sand, away from the carnage into the cool endless night.

CHAPTER 46

The ground was shaking—a great rumbling earthquake that drowned out the cries of battle. With every step, Isiilde slipped and sank in the sand.

An explosive crack tripped her into the sand. She looked over her shoulder. The gate had collapsed. Fomorri staggered from the rubble, and the Elite archer Coen picked them off like flies. Marsais was a blur, his arms moving snake-like in the haze, gathering force.

Oenghus charged from the dust, and a lash of inky darkness reached towards her father's back, whipping the legs from under him. He crashed into the sand. Oenghus crawled forward, tried to stand, and fell.

Marsais released his weave. A white hot arc sliced through the air, rippling over Oenghus' head, cutting Fomorri down like wheat.

Isiilde ran towards the gate—towards her father, but Marsais got there first. But he kept his distance, shouting at Oenghus and goading him with words.

Caught in a berserker's frenzy, Oenghus didn't recognize him. He attacked. Marsais narrowly dodged the club.

There was no reasoning with him. Marsais ran for his life. Oenghus chased after, limping but picking up speed. Even wounded, he could outrun a horse.

Would Oenghus recognize her? She didn't want to find out. She turned and raced after the others, catching them in no time.

"Stop!" Rivan shouted.

Isiilde tried to do just that, but she slipped. A void stretched beneath her feet, and she skidded right over the edge.

Sand poured after her like a waterfall. She was falling. In darkness, it felt like an eternity. Then it ended. She hit something hard, rolled, and fell off another edge.

Isiilde clawed at the air. Her fingers dug into stone, and she hit a wall, dangling over an abyss. A lash of pain split the wound at her side as the sutures tore. It nearly knocked her senseless.

Frantic, she gasped out the Lore, tracing a trembling rune, but her grip on the edge slipped. Isiilde fell again. But not before she'd finished her weave. The air caught her. For a moment, she levitated, then her sloppy weave unraveled. The ground came quick—she hit the sand with a *thump*.

There was a stone wall in front of her. She scrambled forward and put her back to the solid surface.

Isiilde gulped in air, trying to get her bearings. How far had she fallen? She looked up to find a star-strewn sky. She was not underground. But somewhere far above, the battle still raged.

"*Isiilde?*" Acacia hissed from above.

"Yes?"

"Thank the gods," Acacia breathed.

A light flared. It came from Rivan's hand. He shone the light down, bathing the nymph in a golden flare. Isiilde rather wished he had not. She sat on a ledge, on the brink of a void. If the earth had a throat, this would be it.

"Are you alright?" Rivan stood twenty feet up, at an angle. There must be another ledge farther up—the first one she'd hit.

Isiilde winced at the question. Every inch of her ached. She was sure something was broken, but she was only bruised and bloodied from her reopened wound.

"I'll live," she said.

Isiilde wove an Orb of Light, then stepped to the edge of the ledge, sending it into the darkness at her feet. It touched on another ledge, one that hugged the cliff and curved upwards. One ledge above, and one below, each ten feet tall. They were like steps for a titan.

"What is this place?" she asked.

"I think it's the Spire," Acacia replied.

She blinked. The Spire? The famed Unicorn's Horn? She had expected a mountain or tower, something that went up, not a hole in the sand.

She heard footsteps above. "Isiilde?" Marsais called, his voice echoing in the void.

"I'm here," she called, softly.

Oenghus loomed overhead. His face was in shadow, and she could hear his growling breath. He turned from the edge, and roared. It was like thunder, and it was followed by an arc of lightning that split the night.

The Fomorri were on their heels.

"Hurry!" Marsais ordered.

As the others climbed down, Isiilde pulled another set of clothes from her pouch and quickly dressed. Elam hung from the ledge above her for a moment, then let go, landing easily.

Another roar shook loose stone, and she cringed, waiting for the rock to slide out from under her feet.

Elam grinned, and pointed. "Oenghus." But Isiilde did not share his optimism. Her father was not invincible, and he was far from careful.

As sounds of fierce fighting raged above, Rivan helped lower Acacia down. Isiilde tried to soften her fall, but the captain bit back a cry, and crumpled to the stone.

Isiilde directed the orb over her. Blood saturated her clothing, seeping beneath armor and cloth. Acacia tried to unbuckle a greave on her thigh, but her fingers shook with weakness. Isiilde quickly helped. The wound beneath gaped.

Acacia tossed her greave over the edge. "Bind it."

Isiilde pulled out a bandage from her pouch, and cinched it around the wound. Rivan joined them on the ledge.

A scream pierced the din of battle, a flash blinded and spots danced in her vision. The air went taut, charged like a storm about to snap.

"Oen, no!" Marsais barked, but his cry was drowned in an earthquake. Rock cracked and tumbled loose, and sand poured over the edge. Isiilde started slipping. She threw herself against the rock face and grabbed Acacia's pauldron to keep her from falling.

The two women hugged the stone. Sand clogged Isiilde's nose and mouth, and her light was snuffed, plunging them into darkness. Sand flowed over their heads as the earth kept shaking. She was being pulled towards the edge.

All at once, the quaking stopped. Sand clogged her eyes, her nose, her skin and clothes. There was nowhere to wipe the grit from her eyes.

She summoned another Orb of Light with a coughing voice. Acacia's pale eyes blinked in the haze. The paladin looked like she was sculpted from sand. Another mound shifted. It was Rivan. He lowered his salvaged shield, dislodging a pile of sand on the boy who'd taken cover with him.

Isiilde climbed to her feet, and took a cautious step towards the edge, peering upwards. All was silent. Something heavy dropped on the ledge above, then a massive form stepped over the next edge.

Oenghus landed with a snarl.

Fury beat around him. One eye was swollen shut, and the one that remained was wild and savage. He was covered in gore and sand, clothes torn and shredded from more wounds than she cared to count.

When he looked at Isiilde, there was no recognition; only a glint of death. He bared his teeth, stained with blood, and gripped his club. But she wasn't afraid.

Isiilde laid a hand on his forearm. "Father," she whispered. His eyes focused, and he saw her then. A long, violent shudder swept through his body.

"Go!" Marsais snapped from above.

Oenghus stepped towards Acacia, and Rivan raised his sword, preparing to defend his captain. Isiilde gave a sharp shake of her head.

"Oenghus—" Acacia warned, but he ignored her. Without asking, he simply hoisted the injured captain over one broad shoulder as if she were a child, and stalked down the path, ignoring her protests.

Rivan followed, but Isiilde stayed, eyes on Marsais. He stood on the lip of the Spire, weaving. A flash of power left his fingertips, and he stepped back, off the edge.

Marsais did not fall; the air caught him, and he drifted down beside her.

"Cover our backs," he ordered the three remaining Elite: Nimlesh, Coen the archer, and Nalani, who fought like a dervish with twin scimitars.

Isiilde extinguished her light with a snap of fingers.

"Careful now," Marsais whispered. Her hand found his own, and he squeezed it back. She could not see, so she felt along the rock wall, hoping the path would not abandon her feet.

As they hurried down the winding ledge, shouts and torches drifted on the rim. Arrows were loosed, zipping and whizzing through the dark. Some missed their mark by yards, and others brushed her hair.

In a futile attempt to illuminate the pit, one of the Fomorri tossed down a torch. She watched it fall, tumbling end over end, slowly drifting, and then fading until the fire was swallowed by darkness.

A part of her was relieved she couldn't see.

EVENTUALLY, the torches faded, and nothing moved on the rim of the Spire. At least, not that she could see. Isiilde felt as if she were falling, slowly. With every step, the moon drifted farther from reach. The scuff of boots was the only thing marking time.

Soon, the air turned frigid. She started shivering, and Oenghus sounded like he was on the verge of collapse; his Brimgrog had finally worn off.

"We should stop," Rivan whispered. "The captain—"

"The Fomorri may regroup," Nimlesh said from the rear.

Marsais nodded in the dim. "Make it quick."

"An Orb," Oenghus growled.

Marsais summoned a small one, barely a wisp. In the soft blue light, Oenghus lowered the captain onto the ledge. Acacia's face was pale and etched with pain, and Isiilde thought her father looked little better.

When he crouched to heal the captain, he swayed, nearly falling off the edge.

Acacia grabbed his wrist. "I'll live. Let me walk."

"I could heal you," Marsais offered.

"No," she snapped. "Unless I'm dead, I'll not be left helpless in this gods' forsaken place."

Isiilde understood. A healing rendered the wounded unconscious. The thought of waking up in Fomorri hands was too much to contemplate. Better to die fighting.

Oenghus uncorked his sacred flask and took a long, fortifying swig. It seemed to revive him. He unwrapped the bandage around Acacia's thigh. "This will sting."

Acacia braced herself. Her muffled cry was worse than a scream as smoke hissed from the wound.

"How do you drink that?" Acacia gasped.

"The first time, it feels like the flesh is being pulled from your bones." Oenghus worked quickly, hands sure and now steady, re-wrapping the gaping wound. When it was bound and cinched, he drew his knife and applied the tip to his own shoulder, digging after an arrowhead.

The sight made her queasy. Isiilde turned to Marsais. His heart was steady and his arms sure, and she closed her eyes, thinking of Lucas and his sacrifice.

Would he have saved her over again, knowing the cost? Her heart said yes, but her mind churned with confusion. Lucas had hated her. Hadn't he? Why would he protect her—a mere nymph?

"What's at the bottom?" she asked, pulling away.

"A door."

Isiilde waited for more.

"That's all I've seen."

"Isn't that strange?"

"Perhaps. Maybe not. I hadn't really..." he trailed off, frowning in thought. "Hmm."

In all the years that Isiilde had known Marsais, that sound had never filled her with so much dread. "Hmm?" she asked.

"I may have overlooked something."

"What?"

"Have you ever stepped on broken glass?"

"I love my feet too much."

"Well, I have. There's a shock of pain, and it's so distracting that one never wonders."

"About what?"

"Whether the shards were all from the same glass."

CHAPTER 47

Tap, *tap, tap*. Something knocked on his skull like a woodpecker. A weight left his shoulder, and Zoshi's eyes snapped open. The crow. Had Crumpet left?

Zoshi couldn't bear the thought of being left alone—not here. But the crow was close. Crumpet hopped out of the pool of blue light, and disappeared.

Zoshi scrambled to his feet, snatched up his lantern, and followed. He sighed with relief when he spotted the crow. But for every step, the bird hopped two more, keeping just on the edge of light, always out of reach.

Crumpet was in a hurry. But for what?

He tried to ignore the rattling chain—that rasping, shuddering breath. A whisper of metal on stone; of rust and age; of something old and worn, biding its time.

Zoshi would follow Crumpet anywhere, except back, towards that chain. He would never go near it again.

Crumpet stopped in the darkness. Zoshi raised his light, and screamed. His fingers lost their strength, and the lantern fell. All the moss tumbled onto the stone.

Zoshi stumbled back. A rush of fury and feathers flew at his face. His boots got caught in a hip bone, and he tripped, falling hard on his backside.

Crumpet thudded onto his chest. The crow was angry. Zoshi batted at the bird, trying to knock him off as he craned his neck to look back at what he'd seen.

The man was still sitting there—pinned by a spear like an insect on a corkboard, right through the chest. Crumpet flapped into the air, and swooped, perching lightly on that spear.

Zoshi scrambled to find his lantern. He stuffed the moss back inside the tin as if he were gathering his wits.

The man had not moved. He was like the other not-quite-human corpses that were perfectly preserved: sharp ears, high cheekbones, tall and thin, and pale as snow. A curved sword rested across his thighs, and an elegant hand rested lightly on its hilt. It looked like the man was waiting to be nudged awake.

"*Remove the spear,*" Crumpet rattled.

Zoshi shook his head—too lost and lonely in the dark to wonder when he'd started speaking crow.

"Spear," the bird croaked.

Again, Zoshi shook his head, edging away. But Crumpet flew right at him. He threw his arms over his head. Talons latched onto his little lantern, and ripped it from his hand.

The blue light bobbed and finally disappeared, leaving him in the dark. His breath caught. The rasping, breathing chain filled the stillness.

"Crumpet?" he squeaked.

Aware of the dead man at his back, he glanced that way, and wished he hadn't. He could see the man perfectly in the blackness. Even the shadows were too afraid to touch that bone-white skin.

Terror bubbled from his throat. "Crumpet!" he screamed, and kept screaming, until his voice went hoarse.

Zoshi started to run, but stopped. He couldn't remember a direction, even up or down.

"Spear," a voice croaked from the dark.

Desperate and confused, he no longer cared—he *needed* light. He couldn't lose his guide.

"Come back and I will." His voice was a thready whisper, but the bird heard it.

A dim blue light wavered in the void. It grew closer, and Zoshi nearly wept when Crumpet landed by the dead man, lantern still clutched in his beak.

"Please don't do that again." Zoshi hurried closer. "I'll take the spear, and we can leave, is that it? It's a key?"

"*Yes*," Crumpet hissed.

The boy believed him. He had no choice.

Keeping as far away from the man as he could, Zoshi gripped the very end of the spear haft, and tugged. The spear slid free.

The next moment landed him on his back. Pain came next. He brought up his hands, all raw and dark. Before the burns could settle in his thoughts, a heavy weight thudded onto his chest. Stunned, he looked up at the crow. A beak filled his vision, stabbing at his face. Something popped. Terror screamed through his body, and he thrashed, clutching his face. Warm liquid leaked between his fingers. All his nerves were aflame.

Zoshi pressed a hand over his eye. He staggered, and fell, shocked and betrayed. He smelled blood; felt it on his hand.

He couldn't see. At least not out of one eye. He blinked. One eye worked. The bird hadn't taken both.

In the blurred light, Zoshi saw the crow stuff a bloody mess between the man's pale lips. It was *his* eye.

As soon as the gift was delivered, Crumpet burst into cool blue flames. A wind swept through the cave, and a howl of triumph followed. The angular man sucked in a long, savoring breath.

Wreathed in blue fire, the man stood, unbuckling his breastplate. The armor with the hole over his heart fell to the ground, and the remnants of his tattered padding turned to ash.

Zoshi watched in a dream-like haze as the hole in the man's chest knitted together. When flesh was mended, a flawless man towered over him. He was tall and lithe and perfectly formed—pale and hard as a statue.

Zoshi could not breathe. He tried to move, but he was frozen. The man's eyes held him in place—two silver pinpricks ringed with blue.

The man smiled, a slow curving of his long lips. He stepped forward, closer to the boy, until he stood right over him.

"The blood of innocents is ever so potent, human."

It was a voice from dreams, of nightmares, and the faint whispers that lingered under beds. Long fingers reached towards the boy, and shock finally rescued him. Zoshi's one remaining eye rolled back in his head.

CHAPTER 48

"The gate will break soon," Eiji reported.

Tharios stood in a wide tunnel. The steady clink of pickaxes and shovels filled the hollow passage. He watched their progress under the lights in silence.

A ragged, dirt-covered man staggered behind a mining cart. Eiji recognized the Wise One as Jaelin Featherpalm. He was little more than a scribe. His hands were now bloodied from hard labor.

The wheels squealed, and her fingers twitched. She'd like to slit the man's throat for not oiling them. Jaelin quickly looked away from the two. Even if he hadn't been silenced with a weave, the man was too cowardly to lift a finger against them.

Eiji hated what the Wise Ones had become. But she and Tharios were so close. Soon, the Order would be respected—and feared.

Tharios waited until the squeaky wheels faded. "Draw back and seal the King's Walk. It doesn't matter if they breach the bailey gates. We can pick them off in the hallways."

Blood curled down the barbed stave in his hands. Powerful artifacts often came with a price. This one was no exception.

"And if they breach the King's Walk before the Shadowed Dawn?" she asked.

Tharios looked at her then, his face illuminated by an Orb of Light. She swallowed back a gasp. His face was no longer impassive, but stretched and worn. The priestess had wounded him, and raising the dead had exacted its own price, but this was more.

Eiji rocked to the balls of her feet, ready to skip back and dodge the madness lurking in his sunken eyes.

"*If*," he stressed, "that should occur, then we will move more provisions into the tunnels and seal the entry points. Let them wander in the maze."

Eiji glanced at the darkness. She was a gnome, and most of her kind labored underground as slaves. She held no love of the dark. The thought unsettled her, but she obeyed, sending a Whisper fluttering to the ears of Yasimina.

Abandon the gate, fall back and seal the King's Walk. And to be thorough, she ordered a guard to relay the message.

As the guard disappeared up the tunnel, a horribly scarred human female hurried from the dark.

"The diggers have broken through, Archlord," Zianna said. Her croaking words were like a crossbow trigger, shooting Tharios towards the end of the tunnel.

Ragged, filthy slaves watched Tharios passing in silence. The tunnel sloped sharply, and then narrowed. At its end stood a solid wall of stone—but not quite.

Tharios gestured, directing an Orb of Light closer. A single crack opened to darkness. "Break it," he ordered.

"Sir, we need to shore up the sides first," the overseer said.

"*Open it*," Tharios repeated. His tone left no room for argument.

The overseer hopped forward, grabbed a pickaxe from a slave, and started widening the crack himself. Dust and rock choked the air. Eiji wove a quick rune, summoning a breeze.

Hours passed, rock fell away, and for the first time in over three thousand years, a path was cleared. When the dust settled, Eiji cocked her head. Something whispered from the darkness.

Tharios gestured at the Orb of Light. It drifted forward, pushing back the darkness. A man stood in the tunnel. Pale and ethereal and angular in every way. His white hair gleamed in the orb's light.

Eiji threw a knife, but it never hit the man. He stepped to the side, faster than she could follow, and plucked her blade out of the air. Impossible.

The man's lips curved in a smile. She'd thought it was Marsais. But she was mistaken. This was not the madman returned, but a Fey—a phantom come to life.

"Tharios." The Fey's voice lilted from the dark like a song as he stepped fully into the light.

Tharios slapped his hand on a fiery tattoo. Flames sped down his arms in a flash, and a wave of heat arced towards the pale man. In the fire's wake, Tharios unleashed another volley. Inky tendrils of energy twisted in the air: Bloodmagic and the Gift hissed and spit at each other.

The devastating weaves hit the Fey, but the runes shattered, drifting in front of him like frayed threads. Defying the laws of power, the Fey gathered up the mangled remains, and thrust out a hand.

Eiji dove to the side. Tharios threw up a Barrier. The tunnel shook, and rocks tumbled from the ceiling. Eiji rolled into a ball, covering her head.

In the settling dust, the Fey laughed. It was like ice slipping down her spine. Eiji swallowed down a cough, and sprang to her feet, knives in hand.

The Fey looked at her with cold eyes. He shook his head. The message was clear. Slowly, Eiji lowered her weapons.

Tharios staggered to his feet. He was bent over double, clutching his stomach, coughing and gagging. Black bruises outlined every vein of his body.

"Is this all that is left of humans?" the Fey asked. "All they have learned in over three thousand years?" He gave an odd trilling of his tongue, the human equivalent of a cluck.

Slow realization dawned, and the rising light stilled her tongue. Tharios reached the conclusion before she did.

"Forgive me, I thought you were an enemy," Tharios gasped.

"I'm sure," the Fey purred, taking a step forward. "Not even a thought for me. Not *one* thought."

With every word he neared, and Eiji and Tharios retreated. Everyone else had run. The Fey's bare feet whispered over stone, and the remnants of flame and crackle of power clung to his flawless skin.

"Who whispered to you, who taught you, who fed your dreams?"

"I thought you were dead," Tharios defended. There was a note of begging in his tone. "Forgive my oversight."

"Dead, no; broken, yes. A small matter for a god."

"Let me serve you," Tharios said, dropping to his knees. He held out the stave—an offering of power.

The Fey leaned close. "Oh, you have already done my bidding, Tharios." His voice chilled, and his words whispered like a breeze through the tunnel. "Your thirst for power blinded you, and I played you like a puppet."

The Fey moved his fingers in a whimsical fashion, and Tharios twitched with realization.

"Yes," the Fey hissed. "As Karbonek once used me; I used you." Quick as a snake, the Fey wrapped long fingers around Tharios' hand—the same that clutched the stave. "A lesson from the wise, human. There is *always* someone stronger."

The Fey squeezed, driving Tharios' flesh into the barbs. Blood activated the stave, and Tharios screamed.

A howl of wind stole her breath. A portal snapped to life in the tunnel. Eiji squinted past the dust, and looked through the crackling vortex of energy. It wasn't the Nine Halls, it wasn't the Isle of Blight, or Somnial's realm—it was the arena pit.

Sickly, greenish fog rushed through, and with it came a barrage of gleeful whispers. The arena shield crackled and twisted, and surged through the portal.

The backlash traveled through Tharios, and the Archlord of the Isle dropped dead, a burnt and blackened crisp. The Fey plucked the stave from a brittle hand, and gave it a twirl, stepping towards the gnome.

Eiji dropped to one knee and bowed her head.

"Wise of you, Eiji." Looking up, her eyes betrayed surprise. "Oh, yes, I know you. I know every breathing thing in this cursed prison—every crack and crevice. And now, my dear gnome, we will clear this infestation of humans. Do you have any objections?"

She shook her head.

"I thought not. You and I will get along splendidly. And don't worry, we'll have help."

Eiji looked to the fog. It flowed down the tunnel, into the black, as if blown by a wind. "Who are you, sir?" she asked. Her voice was thready with fear, and it made her sick to hear.

"Pyrderi. Pyrderi Har'Feydd."

With a twirl of the stave, the very first Fey, the defiler who had tainted the Lindale and spit in the Sylph's face, swaggered out of his prison.

CHAPTER 49

The sound of marching footsteps echoed in the hallway. Soldiers were coming from inside the Spine. Morigan glanced at the other Wraith Guards, whose cloaks had shifted to resemble the red-banded guards.

With luck, the traitors would march right past, never suspecting that the King's Walk had been taken.

Yasimina led the pack. "Prepare to close the gates," she ordered.

Morigan cursed the Fates. The traitors were falling back. She half-turned towards the lever, trying to keep her face averted. Her helm offered some cover, but if Yasimina were to look, she'd recognize her old mentor.

A long line of soldiers marched past. The river of armor ended with the Quartermaster at the rear. He stepped into the guardroom. "Close it," Kreem ordered.

Morigan turned fully towards the lever. It was likely her braid that gave her away, because a sharp intake of air signaled recognition. But Morigan was already spinning. She jabbed her spear at Yasimina. The tip hit a stoneskin weave, sliding to the side of the woman.

Yasimina skipped back, and Kreem rushed forward. Morigan brought up her shield, deflecting a sword stroke that jarred her bones.

Kreem was a large man, and she used that to her advantage. She stepped into his long reach, catching him under the chin with her shield. The big man staggered back and a Wraith Guard took up the fight.

Off to the side, she heard Yasimina chanting. Morigan hurled her spear at a charging attacker, then shouted the Lore, tracing a crude water rune. A fine mist formed, drifting into the wide hall.

On the tail of that simple weave, she hurled a bind that bounced off Yasimina's Barrier. With a deft stroke, Morigan severed the bind midway. The mist churned like a whirlpool. With a gesture, she pushed the water towards Yasimina.

The mist was harmless enough. Or so it seemed. Yasmina was too busy weaving to adjust her shield. It passed through her Barrier and soaked her to the bone.

A split second after, a barrage of weaves flew through the air—as sharp and lethal as a scythe. Morigan shifted her focus, adjusting her Barrier. But the weaves came one after another, slicing her skin. A lightning bolt rocked her back a step. She absorbed the energy with a grunt, unhooked her axe, and charged.

Morigan swung her axe. It hit the slower woman, but the edge didn't bite. Yasimina's armor weave caught the blow. That was all Morigan needed. She let her axe fall, and with a word and a weave behind her shield, touched the air over Yasimina's skin.

The air chilled instantly.

Morigan's weave crept over the woman, seeping through the runic Barrier and into her flesh. The water on Yasimina's skin froze, and she gasped, heart racing and sputtering with cold. The Unspoken screamed out a final word to cinch her own weave, hurling a backlash that shattered Morigan's Barrier. An inky whip caught Morigan around the throat. It squeezed and tugged, and she drove her head into the woman's face.

Yasimina fell to the floor, her skin frostbitten and black, but the lash held tight. Morigan staggered, fighting for breath, tugging at the filth around her neck. Spots danced in her eyes, and all around, a battle raged. A blade flashed, but it wasn't for her. A Wraith Guard plunged his sword through Yasimina's heart.The Blood Ritual unraveled.

Morigan sucked in a sharp breath, snatched up her axe, and joined the other Wraith Guards against a flood of red-banded soldiers.

Battle was chaos. The air reeked of piss and bowels, of blood and death, and time slowed to the immediate. But Morigan was no novice. She hewed and hacked until the floor ran red with blood.

In the blur of movement and screams, a note inserted itself into the song of battle: the sound of running soldiers.

The red-banded guards looked to the King's Walk, to Thira leading a line of reinforcements, and every traitor turned and fled.

The bailey gates had fallen.

CHAPTER 50

IN THE DAWNING light of a new day, Isiilde stopped to catch her breath. But stopping reminded her of every bruise she'd collected through the long night. And that she was freezing.

She walked on.

The group was ragged and tired, and grief hung heavy around the humans. The dead left a void; silence brought them out of the shadows.

Isiilde could almost see Kasja walking beside her forlorn brother. And Lucas shadowing his captain. Did spirits linger? Or was it this place?

It was an unsettling thought. But then so was this place.

The spire pierced the earth for miles. The path hugged the rock, around and around, spiraling down. Isiilde risked a peek over the edge. Even under the rising sun, the titan's stairway stretched into darkness. It made her dizzy.

Marsais clamped a hand over her shoulder.

"What is this place?" she whispered.

"A madman's obsession."

"Obsession for what?"

Marsais looked across the vast, open space towards the spiraling ledge on the opposite side. They'd traversed it hours ago. He craned his neck to gaze at the perfect circle that made up the sky. A narrow slab of stone jutted into the abyss, and sand drifted over the edges, swirling down into the throat of this… *What*? A ruin, a wonder, or a nightmare?

"There are many myths," he explained quietly. "Some stories claim this was a diamond mine. Others say it was a vault, or a weapon, or the tomb of a god. When I was a boy, there was a legend about a madman who tried to capture the sun. But even then, in my youth, the legend was ancient."

Isiilde could feel the Spire's weight; it was like a wound in the earth that never healed. "Which story is true?"

"I don't know."

"You don't know, or you can't remember?" she asked.

Marsais pinned her with a searching gaze. Most shifted under the intensity of it. But Isiilde simply stared back, waiting. Marsais was vast. His eyes were the stars, warm and comforting, but unreachable.

The corner of his lip quirked. "You ask all the right questions," he whispered. "Both are correct. I can't remember if I *should* know."

She started walking again. "Do you remember anything about Finnow, the man who built this?"

"I don't think Finnow was a man at all."

"A woman?"

"A word." She glanced back, curious, and he obliged. "All tongues change over time. Words are mangled and shift, taking on new meanings from one age to the next. As old as this place is, the spire may have been built by the Lindale, or at the very least, named by them."

"Finnow is a word in the old tongue?"

"A mangled version, I think. It stems from the legends about catching the sun. The original word in ancient Lindale means futile, or folly—a fool's task."

"Do you think spire was originally *spiral*?"

"It could very well have started that way. Time has a way of muddling things."

"Fool's Spiral," she murmured. A thought pricked the back of her mind, but when she tried to grasp the intangible thread, it fluttered out of reach.

Isiilde looked towards the sky. The sun had not yet peeked over the rim, but the sky was blue and clear. "I'm not sure this would capture a falling sun, but I'm fairly sure the Fomorri intend to capture us." She pointed at a dark blot in the sky: the faithful herald of an impending attack.

As Isiilde and the group descended, the walls closed in, until the opposite side was a mere forty feet away. All was dark down below, but overhead, the sky was blinding white. Around and around, until the first in the line of travelers could see the last on the opposite path.

Isiilde climbed over a fallen pillar. Down in the basin, arches had been carved into the rock, faded and pitted with time. A single mark repeated itself, carved into every surface: a spiral pattern, worn and nearly smoothed to obscurity.

Isiilde traced a carving. It was exactly like the Spire itself, narrowing to a pinpoint. Ahead, Oenghus stopped on the path, squinting into the dark. He grunted at Marsais and pointed down. Speech, it seemed, was still beyond his reach.

Marsais fed light into his Orb, and the blue glow brightened, filling the frigid basin. The pathway plunged beneath the sand.

Oenghus crouched to brush away the sand. There was ice underneath. It looked like a frozen pond.

"Void," he spat.

Isiilde peered over his shoulder. There was something under the ice. A skull, bones—lots of bones. She looked up towards the top, to where that arch of stone jutted from the edge. Was it a sacrificial altar, or a testing ground for Fomorri and their newly grafted wings? She did not really want to know.

"You said there was a door," Nimlesh stated.

They all looked to the pathway that disappeared under the ice.

Rivan gulped. "Do we have to swim down there?"

Isiilde shared his worry. The idea of swimming beneath the ice through freezing, bone-riddled water in search of a door did not sit well with her, either.

"You want me to break it?" Oenghus raised his club, but Marsais stilled him with a gesture.

"This is a madman's dream. Let's take things slowly."

"The Fomorri are on their way," Coen said.

Even now, a long line of warriors raced down the spiral path. The quickest would arrive within the hour.

There was nowhere to go, no defensible position. Down here, at the bottom of the basin, the group would be ripe for the picking. They were cornered.

"Move the light closer to the edges," Acacia ordered. Marsais obliged, illuminating the rock above the ice. "Are those bore holes?"

Small holes ringed the basin, just above the frozen surface. Isiilde knelt on the path and bent over the edge, studying the rock beneath her. She stuck her finger inside of one.

"Sprite!" Oenghus hissed.

"What?" She withdrew her finger. "It's just a hole."

"Don't bloody touch anything here. Ruins are riddled with traps and wards."

Isiilde ignored him. "The hole slopes downwards."

Marsais joined her on the ledge for a closer look. "There's no lingering weave around the hole. And it's not large enough for a spear." Upside down as he was, his voice was muffled.

"Maybe it blows poison darts at anyone dumb enough to stick his face in it," Oenghus grunted.

"Are you referring to the time you got pegged in the forehead by a poisonous dart?"

Oenghus raised his foot to shove Marsais over the edge, but Isiilde grabbed his leg, keeping the kick at bay.

"I think they're drains," Marsais stated, oblivious to the foot aimed at his backside. "During the stormy season, this basin would make for an excellent well." He pulled out his dagger and began chipping at the ice directly under the drain.

Oenghus lost his balance, and yanked his foot free. Isiilde stuck her tongue at the brute.

"But why block the door?" Acacia asked. "Unless the entrance is farther up and we missed it."

Everyone looked in that direction, searching the crumbling arches. But the sky, far overhead, caught Isiilde's eye. The sun wasn't yet visible in that perfect circle of light.

The thought sparked an idea. "Do you think something happens when the ice melts? Maybe the holes are here to keep the water at a certain level? Like a bathing tub."

Marsais considered the sheet of ice. "I think you're right," he murmured. "There's a trigger—a faint weave—that's aligned with the layer of ice."

Isiilde bent over the rim. She traced a runic eye and studied the rune. Quicksilver—a catalyst used in alchemy. The element was sensitive to changes in temperature.

"Before the Shattering, water was used as a source of power. Even in this era, it's used to run mills and such."

"So when the sun is at its peak, it melts the ice, triggers the weave, and a ward is activated?" Oenghus asked.

Isiilde frowned at the skeletons beneath the ice. It seemed plausible.

"It could also open the door." Acacia said. "Think about it... a perfect defense against unwanted intruders. No need for guards at night and early dawn."

"Do you think the water is poisoned, then?" Nimlesh asked.

"Perhaps," Marsais said.

"Can you test its purity?" Oenghus asked Acacia.

She looked away. "Rivan can perform the ritual."

Rivan blinked in surprise. "I've only done it once—"

"Do it," Acacia ordered. "My prayers are worthless."

Rivan gaped for a moment. Then hopped forward, crouching at the end of the path. As Oenghus smashed a hole in the ice, the paladin pulled out a stone from his ritual pouch.

But Isiilde wasn't watching Rivan; her eyes were on Acacia. She'd tried to heal Lucas, and failed. Not once, in all these long days since Mearcentia, had the Knight Captain used any of her rituals—not even a light.

Marsais watched her, too, but Acacia pointedly ignored him. The tension in the air was tangible, and it had nothing to do with their surroundings.

Isiilde sat beside Acacia, and rested her back against the stone. "What happened?" she asked.

Acacia clenched her jaw. "I failed Lucas. That's what happened."

"There was poison in his blood," Marsais said. "I doubt Oenghus could have saved him."

"I might have, Seer," Acacia bit out. "But the Guardians have abandoned me."

At her words, Rivan nearly dropped his stone. His concentration broke, and he looked at his captain in shock.

Isiilde tilted her head. "Did you piss off Zahra, too?" she asked Marsais.

He raised a shoulder. "Doesn't everyone?"

"Was it *you* who sent the Whisper in the guise of Chaim?" Acacia abruptly accused Marsais. "It was, wasn't it? You tricked me into following you."

Isiilde blinked at Acacia.

"Would you believe me if I denied it?" Marsais asked.

Acacia shook her head.

"But why would he do that?" asked Isiilde.

"He needed the Blessed Order's support for your trial."

Oenghus looked at his old friend. "Did you?"

"No."

"Right then," Oenghus growled. "It's settled. You're exhausted, is all."

"He's lying, Oenghus, as he always does. Why else would I fail even the simplest of rituals?" Acacia's pale gaze burned into the seer.

"Are you sure you haven't lost faith in yourself?" Marsais asked, gently.

Acacia did not answer. The silence stretched until Rivan broke it. "The water isn't poisoned," he muttered. He cleared his throat, and raised his voice. "But I wouldn't drink it without a purification ritual first."

Rivan replaced the Sacred Sun around his neck, and tucked away his implements.

"So what now?" Oenghus asked. "Do we break the ice under each hole, or do we wait for the sun to melt it?"

"We don't know what will happen to the water once the triggers are activated. But if we wait for the sun, the Fomorri will be on us," Nimlesh said from the ledge above.

What was left of his Elite, were spread out: Coen hunkered down in an archway, bow held at the ready, and Nalani stood on the path, scimitars in hand, watching the Fomorri with keen eyes.

Isiilde studied what remained of the ragged band. Even her father looked deflated. She was tired of fighting Fomorri, and wasn't keen on fighting more.

That thought sparked action. "I'll melt the ice," she said.

Marsais looked at her. "Are you sure?"

She flashed him a cheeky smile. "I'll wager you a hundred crowns."

"I believe I owe you as much."

"A chance to even your debt."

"I'll take that wager."

Isiilde stepped to the end of the path. With a whisper, she summoned her flame, and the fire in her blood responded. Her bond flared to life, leaping to her palm. The flameling flickered, small and steady, eager to do her bidding.

She sang, gently at first, wrapping the flame to her will. Her voice was the soft hiss, the smolder of a low burn, throwing heat in the air until it sweltered.

The nymph whispered her desire. The ball of fire surged from her hands, rippling outwards, spreading over the ice. It caressed the cool sheet. Her voice grew. Power soared in the air, beating around her like wings.

The Spire fell away, the humans, her father, and even Marsais. Bound in a cycle of allure, one fed off the other, the nymph and her fire. The seductive quiver of flame captivated her, and she ached to feel its touch on her skin.

Isiilde moaned.

A deluge of water hit her. The fire hissed, and steam rose from her skin. Isiilde spluttered and turned, fury rising in her veins. Her eyes flashed at her father.

"There is no way in the Nine Halls that I'm going to stand here and watch—" Words failed him, so he changed tack. "You're running out of clothes," he growled instead.

Isiilde seethed. "That water is filthy!"

"Well, now you are, too." He bared his teeth.

Isiilde punched his gut, and instantly regretted it. Pain lanced up her arm. It was like hitting a rock.

As Oenghus snickered, she shook out her hand and the others watched warily. They'd all retreated to an upper tier. Except for Marsais. He was crouched on the edge of the path, gazing into the pool.

"You owe me two hundred crowns," she said to his back.

Marsais flashed a crooked smile over his shoulder. "An invigorating defeat."

Oenghus grumbled, and Isiilde ignored him, moving beside Marsais to watch the water. A grating rasp filled the basin. The water began to turn, creating a whirlpool. Marsais gripped her arm and pulled her away from the edge.

Bones churned in the terrifying swirl, a continuation of the spire itself. The water level dropped, revealing toppled pillars and faded carvings. And as the last drop disappeared through a rusty grate, the bones settled in the center.

Water dripped from stone, pattering on tiles and running rivulets through moss and slime towards the drain. The tiles underneath were patterned in the same dizzying design as the spire.

"Door!" Elam pointed excitedly at a segment of stone. He nearly hopped from the path to the basin, but Rivan held him back.

The door was hard to spot. A faint outline of seams in the stone was the only revealing mark.

Marsais moved to the end of the path and murmured the Lore, layering the Runic Eye over a spirit rune. The weave took shape, and a gossamer net fell softly on the tiles. He eyed the ground suspiciously. After a minute of inspection, he stepped on the first tile.

Isiilde held her breath. Nothing happened.

"Don't touch anything. Any of you," he said, looking first at Isiilde, then at her father.

Oenghus answered with a rude gesture.

Marsais stepped beside the grate, and the others moved into the basin. It was a perfect circle that was a mere twenty feet across.

Isiilde wrinkled her nose at the slime and bones. She looked through the rusty grate and down into the hole; it swallowed her heart. She shivered, retreating from the edge.

"What is it?" Marsais asked.

"I don't know. This place is... watchful. Malevolent."

"Hmm," he agreed, glancing at the golden sky blazing high overhead. "At midday, the sun will be directly over the Spire, and the ice would ordinarily melt."

He directed his Orb of Light towards the grate. The little orb slipped through and descended into darkness. Its light was lost. He snuffed it out with a quick gesture.

"So every day the drain is triggered," she mused. "It doesn't rain much, so the water must come back."

"That's what I fear." Marsais turned abruptly to the door.

As he wove a Runic Eye, she traced yet another worn mark on the stone. The spiral pattern was repeated, over and over, all around, as if a mad child had taken chalk and marked the walls. "Marsais, did this symbol have a meaning before the Shattering?"

"Not to my knowledge," he replied. "If the end were connected to the beginning, then yes, it would. But unattached as it is, the symbol is simply a spiral."

"It reminds me of the cycles in King's Folly," Rivan said at her shoulder.

A light flared in her mind, and her ears stiffened with excitement. She looked at the paladin, eyes wide. "You are brilliant!" Her voice echoed off the stone, and then soared. She was sure it would burst from the rim and pour into the desert, but the nymph didn't care. In her exuberance, she stood on her toes and kissed Rivan on the cheek.

Rivan blushed. "I'm not sure about that."

"Yes, you are, even if you don't know it. You see sun melts ice, and water moves stone. This is a giant game!"

Marsais slowly turned his gaze on her. There was worry there. "I think you're right. But not quite a game—not when *we* are the runes."

Isiilde waved off his concern. "We are not runes, Marsais. We are the *players*."

He rubbed his goatee in thought. "No, not the players, but an opponent. We're on one side of the board, Isiilde. We could very well be playing the builders."

That thought hung heavy over the group.

"Hmm," she said.

"Indeed."

"That means there will only be one winner," Acacia noted without enthusiasm.

"Bollocks," Oenghus spat. But Isiilde thought it was brilliant. She studied the spire with new eyes.

"If it's a game, then how do we begin?" Nimlesh asked.

"I don't know," Marsais admitted. "This is where my vision stopped."

The others blinked in surprise. Marsais never mentioned his visions. But no one looked reassured by his honesty.

"The Fomorri will be in bow range soon," Coen called down from his perch.

"Let me try," Oenghus said, stepping up to the door. He placed his hands on the stone, palms flat. Muscles strained as he tried to push, and then slide. Finally, closing his eyes, he concentrated as if he were listening to the stone.

Isiilde glanced over her shoulder at the pile of bones. She stepped over to the grate, to the last tile that spiraled into the metal. Wrinkling her nose, she swept the bones out of the way.

There was a perfectly round hole in the grate, only two inches across. Trying not to gag, she picked up what looked like the haft of a broken spear and thrust it into the hole.

It fit.

Quivering with excitement, she pushed the spear forward. The entire grate turned with a grinding that tore at her ears. She hopped back, covering her ears.

"What the Void did you do, Sprite?"

Heat rose in her cheeks, and she spluttered, pointing at the turning grate.

"Marsais said *not* to touch anything," Oenghus growled, dragging her away from the mechanism.

The others backed away too, watching the center. Stone rasped on stone, and the ground beneath their feet quivered.

The door swung open.

Everyone turned from the grate to the opening, and Oenghus quickly moved to the forefront, hoisting targe and club.

When nothing charged out of the blackness, Isiilde raised her chin. "I opened the door," she said.

Oenghus muttered something rude.

"Next time, some warning would be appreciated." Acacia took a breath, and unslung her shield, putting some weight on her bad leg.

"Remember," Marsais said, gravely. "We're looking for a spiked sun, the end piece to Soisskeli's stave."

Isiilde rubbed her hands together, nearly hopping with anticipation. "Let's begin."

CHAPTER 51

The air inside smelled surprisingly fresh. With a gesture, Marsais sent his light bobbing ahead. Cool blue light filled the chamber, illuminating a stairway. They spiraled upwards in a circular room that was covered in vibrant green moss.

Isiilde stopped to gape at the ceiling. A scintillating spiral of tiles continued the pattern of stairs. When light touched the ceiling, it threw back prisms.

"I'm glad I haven't eaten," Rivan groaned, focusing on the solid steps.

Isiilde had not eaten all night. She reached into her pouch and popped a strawberry in her mouth. The berry burst against her tongue, chasing away hunger and the long, bloody night.

"How many of those do you have?" Rivan asked.

That was an excellent question. Far more than she started out with. She knew that much. Instead of pondering that conundrum, she handed him a strawberry.

"That looks like a door up there." Acacia pointed at the top of the spiral, some forty feet up.

"There's nothing to brace the door, Scarecrow."

"Hmm, that would be cheating."

Oenghus grumbled as he wedged his club in the groove. When he stepped over the threshold, the stone door fell, turning his bone club into dust. A second after, the floor slid open.

Nalani leapt towards the stairs, catching an edge, but Oenghus fell, disappearing down a hole. Isiilde pushed her way past Nalani, rushing to the edge. Water bubbled upwards, touching her boots. A pool of brackish water sloshed where the floor had once been.

A head burst from the surface.

Isiilde reached for her father, tugging at his arm. He handed over his targe, then hoisted himself out. The water brushed her ankles. It was rising.

"Up!" Marsais barked.

Oenghus nudged her up the stairs, and she bolted past the others, swift and light of foot. She beat Marsais to the door, which was only halfway up the stairs. The door was a piece of solid round stone: no handle, no lever, no adornment.

Isiilde only glanced at it. The ceiling was far more interesting. She continued to the top, where the stairway disappeared, touching the beginning of the same tiled pattern.

Something caught her eye on the stair. The stone dipped near the wall. She crouched to inspect the indentation. It was a small, half-moon basin with grooves etched into its curve, similar to Saavedra's ritual chamber.

"Marsais," she called. He sprinted up the stairs and was at her side in an instant.

"A Bloodmagi's ritual stone," he murmured, running his fingertips over the grooves. She took a step back.

"We don't have much time!" Oenghus called from the door.

Isiilde looked over the edge. The water was rising, fast. Her father was braced in front of the upper-story door, trying to push, slide, or pry it open. None of it was working.

"Sun, ice, water... blood. It requires a sacrifice." Marsais pulled back his wide sleeve, exposing a wrist.

Isiilde grabbed his hand. "No!"

"We don't have time," he said, drawing a curved blade from his sash.

"Wait one moment." She thought furiously, glancing up at the spiral tiles. The light threw back its reflection, shimmering on the black water. "This is the second cycle of King's Folly: ice, sun, water and stone."

"And we need life to move into the third cycle. It requires blood."

"But water moves stone," she argued.

"Scarecrow," Oenghus shouted. "I'm about to crack this door open!"

The water was a foot below the others.

Marsais shook off her hand, and brought the knife to his wrist.

"You're wrong," she said.

He paused, blade poised to slice a vein.

"Death bridges the cycles, too," she blurted out. "The door will open when the water touches this basin. But before that, it will drown the intruder." Isiilde uncorked her waterskin and looked into his eyes.

"Do it," he said.

She poured water onto the stone. It ran rivulets down the grooves and pooled in the basin. A grating sound signaled her triumph. The door rolled open. The water was now level with the opening.

"Get down here," Oenghus said.

Isiilde flew down the steps, and Marsais followed. A long, terrible slope of stone dived down the tunnel. Stairs were etched into the stone on either side of a deep channel. Water began draining down its center like a river.

"Hurry, but be careful," Oenghus ordered.

A roar filled the passage, and they followed the stairway to its source: a waterfall plunged onto a grate of spikes. Skeletons were impaled on their tips.

Isiilde stopped at the bottom of the slope. The deadly trap had collected an assortment of victims: humans, gnomes, and a great many Fomorri—all long dead.

Marsais drew her back from the edge.

"See," she said. "Death."

He arched a brow at her. "You're enjoying this, aren't you?"

The Spire was fiendish and ingenious, and she was loving every minute of it. "Aren't you, too?"

"Oh, my dear," he said, pressing her hand to his lips. "The tombs we could plunder." It was the first time he'd spoken of a future at all.

As the cool water rushed over the edge, it hit the warmer air in the cave. Steam rose and hissed, rising towards the darkness above. Two narrow walkways skirted the deadly drain, circling the pit to meet on the other side. There was no door, but a long, narrow passage covered in pristine tiles. Condensation gathered on the tiles.

"What bloody now?" Oenghus asked.

Marsais squeezed his way to the front, and Isiilde followed, peering down the strange corridor. *Ominous* was the word that came to mind.

Marsais tossed a weave into the hallway. Runes flared, but none clung to the tiles. He directed his Orb of Light into the passage, and the moment it entered the corridor, the light weave unraveled.

"What is it?" Isiilde asked.

"Power."

Marsais tossed his dagger into the hallway, and a web of crackling energy slammed into the blade, knocking it from the air. It fell to the floor and was zapped again and again, skidding its way to the end. Finally, the ward let go and the blade slid out of sight.

"Give me an arrow."

The archer handed one to Marsais. He snapped the metal head off, and tossed in the wooden shaft. The wood clattered on the ground, unharmed.

Oenghus frowned at the smoking dagger. "Give me a stone weave, and I'll test it." He had an affinity with lightning, but how many bolts could he withstand?

Marsais layered a stone rune over air and bound it loosely to Oenghus. It was a delicate weave that required skill; a stronger bind would turn her father to stone.

Oenghus stepped into the steam. It swirled around his body like a hungry thing, but no sparks flew. Oenghus disappeared down the hallway. "There's some kind of chamber beyond. All full of mirrors. Watch out for the bones."

Marsais traced a weave for each of the Elite and paladins. When it came to Isiilde, he hesitated. "I don't want to risk a feather rune here." He always added a feather to her armor so it wouldn't suffocate her.

"Do it."

He bound stone to her flesh, and it was every bit as suffocating as before. The weave crawled over her body. She could barely breathe.

Isiilde quickly picked her way over skeletons. And Marsais was close on her heels. As soon as they were clear, he plucked the weave from her body. But the weave's lingering touch continued to shake her bones.

Marsais put a comforting hand on her back, and turned to look at the next puzzle—the fourth cycle.

Alcoves ringed the chamber of stone. The same swirling pattern covered every inch of rock, etched and repeated until her mind spun. There were no bones on the floor, but a mirror stood in each alcove.

Oenghus stood in front of one, gazing at his grizzled, blood-smeared reflection. It wasn't glass, but a thin, crystal sheet of water that threw his image back. Elam stood in front of another, mesmerized by the effect. She stepped behind the boy, and blinked in surprise. Elam was there, but she was not.

"We're not there," Acacia said. The Knight Captain stood at her shoulder, but wasn't in the reflection.

"Elam, come over here," Oenghus ordered. The boy went, but his reflection remained.

"He's still in this mirror," Isiilde said.

"And he's not reflected here," said Oenghus.

Isiilde wove a Runic Eye, layering it over spirit. When the weave touched the water, a mirror rune flared to life. She looked over her shoulder at Marsais, but he was nearly lost in the steam. Sweat beaded on his brow.

"It's getting hot in here," Nimlesh called. "Where do we go?"

Marsais stepped in front of an empty alcove and frowned at his battered reflection. He leaned right, then left, watching the movement. The steam thickened, pouring out of the hallway, until Isiilde could barely see the others.

Elam strayed too close, and the steam brushed his arm. The boy yelped, jumping back. He hugged the arch, clutching his burned arm.

"Go, Oenghus," Marsais said.

The berserker drew his heavy falchion and stepped through the waterfall. He disappeared, but his reflection remained. Nimlesh followed on his heels.

A hiss filled the chamber, and the air snapped. A lash of force slammed into Nimlesh, knocking him clear off his feet and across the room. He disappeared into the steam.

His screams filled the chamber.

Coen and Nalani started forward, but when the scalding steam touched their skin, both jumped back, their faces red and burnt.

Marsais threw an air weave into the mass, parting the steam. For a split second, they saw the sergeant. Nimlesh writhed and twisted on the ground, burnt and red, down to the bone.

Coen started forward, but the steam slithered through the weave, and it unraveled. Before the air closed in, he loosed an arrow, silencing his commander's agony.

Coen retreated, grim-faced, and Nalani nodded to her kinsman. It needed to be done. But Isiilde felt little pity for the man. Nimlesh had killed Spot without a second thought. Shouldn't she feel something more? Her lack of empathy disturbed her more than his screams.

"Walk through your reflection, and *only* yours," Marsais ordered the others.

When they did not immediately move, Acacia spurred them with a sharp word. Rivan stepped through his archway, and Coen and Nalani walked into their reflections.

Marsais steered Elam to his reflection. He gripped the boy's shoulder, said something in Lome, and turned him towards the sheet of water. Elam straightened his shoulders, and walked bravely through.

Isiilde tore her eyes from where Nimlesh had lain. The steam thickened, and even she, with her affinity for fire, could not linger.

"What did you say to him?" Acacia asked.

"That he cannot die because I've foreseen a long life."

"Did you?" Steam hissed and spit, rolling towards the trio.

Marsais' lips twitched. "Some lies are kind, are they not?"

Acacia shook her head. "Not to me." She stepped through the water.

Isiilde's heart hammered in her breast, but the nymph in the reflection seemed distant. She did not recognize herself. "Marsais," she whispered.

"Hmm?"

Isiilde touched the water. It was as cold as the nymph who stared back. "This isn't me," she said for his ears.

"Mirrors always tell the truth."

"I think this one is lying."

He looked at his own reflection. The steam touched his back, and he flinched, stepping forward. "Ladies first."

"As long as you're second."

"I always come last."

Isiilde snorted, and stepped through.

CHAPTER 52

Isiilde stood in an empty corridor. Tiles spiraled along the floor, ceiling, and walls. It made her head spin. The world tipped her towards a door.

She turned to find a mirror instead of a sheen of water. A dripping wet nymph stared back, her face smeared with blood and grime. The dripping water gathered in spiraling grooves to flow towards the door at the other end. Once again, it reminded her of a ritual chamber.

She shook the thought from her mind, and hurried down the corridor. The dizzying pattern threw her off balance, and she had to steady herself on a wall to keep from falling.

At least the water was draining under the door. As far as doors went, this was a simple one: plain wood with a metal handle. Isiilde traced a Runic Eye to inspect it, but nothing flared to life.

Everything about this place felt like a trap, but she couldn't find one. With a shrug, Isiilde pulled open the door. It led into yet another circular chamber. When she stepped over the threshold, the door closed on her heels.

There were no spirals, no doors, no markings, save for a ring of alcoves along the wall and a round fountain in the center of the room. Water flowed from a basin of stone, trickling peacefully into the pool below. The tiles were polished and white, and the entire room seemed far too bright.

Isiilde was not alone. Oenghus, Marsais, Elam, Acacia, Rivan, and the two Elite stood in front of their arches—all looking wary and perplexed.

"That was easy," said Rivan.

Oenghus grunted.

"Is everyone all right?" Acacia asked.

Everyone nodded. The others moved towards the fountain, but Isiilde stood her ground. Something was horribly wrong; every fiber of her body screamed out danger.

Marsais noticed her unease. "What is it, Isiilde?" He took a step towards her, but she stepped away until her back hit the door.

Marsais stopped. "Isiilde?"

The room was serene, and so very clean and fresh. What had her on edge? Her gaze darted around the chamber, from the pristine tiles, to the trickling fountain, and at each of her companions.

Elam asked something in his native tongue. Marsais answered with a shrug.

"What's the matter, Sprite?"

She did not know. It was a feeling of fear.

"Maybe it's the water," Rivan said, taking out his ritual stone. With a prayer, he summoned the light to the stone and placed it in the fountain. After a full minute, he proclaimed the water clean. "Should I try it?"

"It seems to be the only thing in here," Marsais said.

"Aye, you might as well be the cupbearer. If you keel over, I'll heal you." Oenghus rubbed his hands together.

Rivan dipped a hand in the water, bending forward to drink. Isiilde held her breath. "It's good," he announced. But when he straightened, his eyes went wide, staring into the fountain. The paladin drew his sword, and spun. He looked straight at Oenghus, then stabbed him through the gut.

Oenghus dropped to the floor.

"No!" Isiilde screamed.

Acacia stepped forward, swinging, but her leg was weak and her balance off. Rivan deflected the blow, answering with a swing. It caught her between neck and shoulder.

Isiilde summoned her fire, but before she could attack, Marsais drew his knife and plunged it into Rivan's back. The paladin dropped to his knees. Marsais wrenched his blade free, raising it to strike again—in his left hand.

Everything clicked. At the last moment, Isiilde adjusted her focus, sending a flaming burst at Marsais' chest. The blow knocked him back against the wall.

Pain sliced across her shoulder, and another arrow ripped her clothes, thudding into the door. She whirled, sending a barrage of flame into the Elite. Both fell.

With a screeching cry, Elam charged Rivan. The paladin caught the boy, hurling him against the stone. Elam landed with a crack.

Rivan scrambled for his sword, twisting around to point the tip at her. There were tears in his eyes, and pain on his face. He held his arm close to his body.

"Stay back!" he shouted.

Isiilde shook out her flame, and put a hand to the arrow wound. Blood seeped between her fingers. "Put the sword down, Rivan."

"How do I know you're not one of them?"

"Acacia's bandage is on the wrong leg. Marsais is right-handed, not left. And Oenghus is quicker than that... thing. I think it's some kind of mirrored illusion."

"How do you know it's me?"

"You're holding the sword in the correct hand. A mirror reverses everything. What about me?"

"You used fire," Rivan rasped. Slowly, he lowered his sword. But the act pitched him forward. Isiilde raced to his side. Blood seeped from his back. She pressed a hand to the wound, but it felt odd—dry. Something protruded from his back.

Trusting her instincts, she drank the water from the fountain. The illusion around the dead unraveled, revealing dried, thread-like husks—humanoid shapes that looked like they were spun from finely woven silk.

The illusion of stone shattered, too. The same silken threads covered the walls and floor like a spider's cocoon. Isiilde shuddered at the sight.

Rivan was struggling to breathe. There was a yellowish-bone horn, like a fang or talon, stuck in his flesh. The threads were spreading.

Isiilde probed her own shoulder. It wasn't blood. Frantically, she unlaced her shirt. Threads crept from the wound. She focused on her bond. It stirred, and fire roared to life, surging through her veins. She concentrated on that spot, on the pain and dryness, on the intrusion of poison. Her body heated, her clothes grew hot, and a thin line of smoke rose from the gash.

The threads curled back, burning to ash.

Isiilde gripped the horn in Rivan's back with both hands. It was dry and sticky, and a wave of revulsion churned her gut. With a jerk, she tugged the horn free and tossed it as far as she could. She peeled off his armor and cut at his clothing with her knife, exposing the wound.

Isiilde bit back a cry. The silky threads were spreading, weaving in and out of his skin. The taint was stitching his flesh anew.

She glanced at the husk of Marsais. Did the poison claim him before her arrival? Surely there hadn't been time.

Isiilde pushed the thought aside. Rivan still lived; she'd focus on him. She raised her dagger, summoning flame to her palm. Fire engulfed the blade. In seconds, the steel glowed red.

"I'm sorry, Rivan."

The threads had spread, reaching towards his eyes and mouth. He gasped and sucked in air. She pressed the blade over the wound. Rivan arched and screamed, clawing at the ground.

The silky threads curled into ash. But instead of blood, a thick black substance bubbled from the hole in his back.

Isiilde bit back a cry. She took his face in her hands. His eyes were alert, but the pale, silken threads reached out of his nose, and stretched from the corners of his mouth. "It didn't work."

"Heal me," he choked.

"I can't!"

"Try."

"I'll burn you," she whispered.

Rivan shook his head. "I don't want this." He coughed and gagged, and his eyes slid sideways, to where a husk lay. "I like your fire." With trembling fingers, he fumbled for his pouch. "Horse... for you."

Isiilde's eyes itched. She blinked away tears, and retrieved the small, wooden horse he'd worked on every night during their journey.

Rivan's hand locked around the Sacred Sun on his neck and his lips moved, but no sound came. *Acacia.*

Isiilde laid one hand on his forehead and slipped the other over the thread-like skin of his chest. She could feel the warmth and the taut muscles beneath.

There was still time.

Isiilde closed her eyes, summoned the Lore, and plunged into Rivan's spirit, leaving the physical realm behind. She went straight for the source. She didn't have to take on his pain; only burn away the poison.

She touched each thread, so carefully, so gently, following the thready strands in her mind's eye, each one curling into blackness and ash.

Isiilde felt his heart stop. Her healing was too slow. Desperate, she sent a pulse of the Gift into his body. Rivan jerked, his heart began to beat, but the source of her Gift was not life; it was chaos.

Fire surged from her fingertips, washing over his spirit, setting it alight. The threads burned, the poison fled, and Rivan's flesh burst into flames.

She broke the link, falling back with a cry. Unnatural fire consumed his clothes, his face, and burned away his hair, leaving a cairn of smoke and char. The flames spread, eating at the cocoon of silky threads.

For a long time, Isiilde stared at the remains of Rivan: a husk of char and bone. Ash swirled around her like gentle snow. She looked at her hands—so small and ethereal, and yet so destructive.

The nymph sat until the ash settled, until nothing stirred but a slow trickle of water. She blinked, eyes burning, and then blinked again. Slowly, she forced Rivan's hand open. Brittle bones cracked, and the Sacred Sun came free. She rubbed the soot from the golden symbol, and tucked it in her palm.

There should be words to say, but none came. Rivan had crossed a bridge that no one could breach.

With a numb, stony heart, she stood and turned her back on the dead paladin. The walls were all blackened stone. The only door was still the one she'd walked through.

A shape caught her eye in the ashes. She nudged it with her toe, and knocked loose the soot: Rivan's sword. Isiilde picked it up. It was lighter than she'd imagined, and although the hilt was blackened, the steel was bright. She glanced back at the paladin's burnt husk. He no longer needed it.

With nowhere to store it, she thrust the sword through her sash and walked to the only remaining thing in the chamber: the fountain. Ash floated on the surface of the water. Her heart hurt, so she turned it off and focused on the puzzle.

This was a cruel trap. A ward had mirrored each companion, and each had entered a different alcove. But there was one cruel twist: not all were mirrored husks. The first to drink the water would be the first to see through the illusion. When Rivan attacked, she'd first thought him poisoned or mad. What would Oenghus do if Marsais had suddenly killed her mirrored twin? Friends would kill friends. That was the intent.

Isiilde hit the water with her fist. A hazy, rippling reflection stared back, and the puzzle clicked. Through water she had entered, and through water she would leave.

Isiilde stepped into the fountain.

The stone underfoot clicked. A stone hatch slid to the side, revealing a spiral of stairs. The water flowed gently down its slope, trickling peacefully into the dark. Without looking back, she summoned a spark, and followed the path.

CHAPTER 53

Isiilde stood on the last step. Water drained through tiny holes in the floor, and a short corridor stretched beneath her feet. Everflame flickered steadily in a sconce, illuminating a mirror at the very end.

She walked to the mirror. Full of silence and empty of fear, she felt the powerful weave clinging to it. A teleportation rune.

Isiilde touched the rune. The mirror tugged her in and spewed her out into a great hall. It was round, ringed by pillars and a large spiraling floor. The columns reached towards a dome, but there was no queasy pattern on the tiles above. It was shadow and air.

She swallowed down an urge to hide, and stepped into the hollow chamber. The shift in perception offered a new view. She was not alone.

Oenghus stood on the far side, gripping sword and shield. Marsais stood with Elam to the right. Acacia and Nalani stood together, clutching their own weapons. Eight had entered, and six now stood. More trickery? Another game?

Oenghus charged across the spiraling tile. She tensed, taking a step back, fire erupting from her hands.

"Oen!" Marsais hissed.

Oenghus slowed. "Sprite?"

"What are you to me?" she asked.

He blinked at the threat in her voice, and stopped. "I'm your father," he whispered.

No weave would know that; no imposter. She shook out her flame, and he rushed forward, catching her up with one arm. He smelled of blood, and she pulled back, searching for the source.

"You're hurt."

"Aye, well..." he faltered, face grim. "The archer and I didn't get on too well in there." He put her down. Blood leaked from his chest, and he held his arm stiffly.

Relief warmed Marsais' eyes, and Elam smiled, but the boy's excitement faded when he saw Rivan's sword thrust through her sash.

Acacia was pale and drawn, and looked dead on her feet, but her gaze was fixed on the sword. "Rivan?" she asked.

Words caught in Isiilde's throat. "The poison... the threads... I tried to heal him, but..." Isiilde held out his sword and holy symbol.

Acacia bit back a sound. Her hand went to her stomach as if she'd been run through. She made for the mirror, but Oenghus stepped in her path.

"Get out of my way," Acacia growled.

"You can't," Oenghus said.

"I won't leave him in there!"

Oenghus grabbed her arms, but Acacia drove a fist into his wounded chest and he staggered back. Acacia limped past.

"I burned him!" Isiilde shouted.

It brought Acacia up short. Isiilde expected anger, ached for fury, wanted the warrior to run her through, but there was only shock.

"There's nothing left of him," Isiilde whispered. "He didn't turn into... one of those things."

Rivan's gentle voice drifted in her memory, about two simple words bridging someone's pain. She spoke those words now. "I'm sorry." Not for herself, not for the burden of blood that she carried, but for another's loss.

Acacia closed her eyes. Despite the woman's steely visage, tears leaked down her cheeks. For a moment the paladin swayed, and then she stepped towards the nymph, not with anger but grief.

Acacia pulled her into a hug. "Thank you for trying," she whispered. Isiilde clutched the woman back.

"Coen?" Nalani asked.

Oenghus shook his head. "I was the first to drink. He thought I'd gone berserk."

"Cruelty at its finest," Acacia said, stepping back.

Isiilde held out the Sacred Sun. "He wanted you to have this."

Acacia's fingers trembled when she took the blackened symbol. She hung it around her own neck, tucking it beneath her armor. When Isiilde tried to hand over his sword, Acacia shook her head. "Keep it." Her voice cracked.

Isiilde gazed at the sword. She saw darkness in the blade's reflection, and looked up. The dome was completely obscured.

"The darkness on the ceiling—it's spreading."

Marsais eyed the shadows. "Hmm, there's a wide corridor that way." He pointed in the direction.

Isiilde fell in step beside him. "Did you know?" she whispered.

"I told you," he said. "My visions stopped at Finnow's Spire, the door to be specific. If I had known..."

"I'm not asking about your visions." Her gentle words soothed his irritation.

"Forgive me," he sighed. "Who better to blame than a seer?"

She brushed his fingers with her own, and he grasped her hand in return, holding on tight. "What were those things?"

"Husks," he rasped. "I didn't know what they were at first, but I've learned not to react to everything I see. And when you attacked me with your dagger instead of your fire, I knew it wasn't you. During the battle that followed, Elam dove into the fountain. A hatch opened. And I assumed he was who he appeared to be."

"I thought the same when your husk attacked Rivan with a dagger. Left-handed. You could've easily slaughtered us all with a weave."

He smirked. "I am not as deadly as you think—only exceptionally clever."

"Only sometimes," she said.

"Let's hope this is the 'some' in that time. I dislike those shadows."

"Agreed."

The urge to hurry itched at her legs, but Acacia could barely walk, and even Oenghus was lagging. What scheme was their long-dead opponent planning next?

A shadow rune could be many things. The rune changed and freely slid from one cycle to the next. Light kept it at bay, but not if the shadow was cornered.

"We're going to find a dead end," she said.

"Yes, I think so." Marsais had drawn the same conclusion.

"I'm not going to worry about it," she stated.

"If only I could be so brave."

Isiilde cocked her head. "You ordered me not to worry."

"I could hardly forget that."

A shift of shadow in a faraway corner caught her eye. The air was grey and tattered, and when she looked at the movement, it sank further into darkness. Coldness and misery prickled her skin. "We're not alone," she said.

"Ruins are rarely uninhabited."

"How do you fight the Forsaken?"

"It depends on what severed their spirit. And what they want."

"What do most want?"

"Revenge."

Their footsteps echoed in the corridor. It was wide and lined with arched pillars, leading to countless branches. Marsais ignored the intersecting corridors, and focused on the large door at the end.

Isiilde glanced over a shoulder. The darkness was spreading, blocking their retreat. She wasn't the only one to notice. Marsais broke into a run, climbing a series of stairs that led to a dais and the large double doors. Symbols and runes spiraled up its length. There were no handles.

Marsais wove a Runic Eye, and the door flared to life. He stepped back, eyes intent, murmuring under his breath as he tried to decipher the writing.

Isiilde recognized the markings. "Is that the old tongue?"

Marsais nodded. "Very, *very* old. With one exception." He pointed towards a symbol: three circles intertwined, each with the others. It reminded her of the ol'Father's symbol, except the wolves were missing. Where had she seen that mark before?

"The Sylph," she said. "I've seen it around Brinehilde's neck."

"Yes."

"Why would the symbol of the Sylph be in a place like this?"

"It's newer than the other writing. Added much later, I think. We're not the first to break into this ruin."

"Of course," she realized. "You said this ruin was ancient when you were young, but Soisskeli's stave was used during the Chaos Wars. Why would the end piece be here?"

"Because it needs protecting."

"Who placed it here?"

"The Keeper."

Isiilde blinked in surprise. The Keeper was legendary—the man entrusted with the Orb to fight the Void. The leader of the Guardians who sacrificed himself to create the gates, cutting off Dagenir the Betrayer and the Guardians of Morchaint.

"What now?" Nalani asked. She stood at the bottom of the dais with Oenghus, facing the approaching wall of shadow.

"Do your light thing, Acacia," Oenghus said, hoisting falchion and targe.

"I've told you, my prayers are worthless." There was no anger, only defeat. It was worse than her earlier fury.

"Void," Oenghus spat.

Isiilde hated waiting. She stepped forward, summoned her fire with a breath, and fed it with her voice. A fireball roiled between her hands, its roar singing in her ears. She set it free.

Fire swept over the great hall. For a moment, she banished the creeping black, but it slipped between the currents of heat, and gathered anew.

Slowly, the shadows crept towards them. Shades of grey fluttered in the dark, and a whisper hissed in her ears. Isiilde's throat went dry.

"Keep singing," Oenghus urged. "Give him time."

Isiilde braced herself, raising her voice until the air beat with her power. An arc of flame sliced through the great hall. But the shadows shifted like water, opening and closing in the fire's path. For every lash of flame, the shadows came back stronger than before.

There was no fuel, nothing for her fire to feed on, save her voice. With a final note, a fireball exploded, sending sparks raining down on the floor. When the last ember faded, the shadows remained.

"I think it's darker than before," Acacia said.

Oenghus grunted in agreement. Elam ran up the stairs. He got out his sling, and sent a rock spiraling into the mass. It disappeared with a puff. The boy loaded another stone.

"Acacia," Marsais called. "I need you up here." He did not take his eyes off the doors.

The captain looked about to hold her ground, but after a moment, she sheathed her sword. Isiilde quickly put a shoulder under her arm, helping her up the stairs.

As soon as Acacia reached the doors, Marsais abandoned his inspection and stepped in front of the paladin. His gaze flickered over her shoulder—at the approaching darkness—and when he spoke, there was a note of desperation in his voice. "Listen, please, I beg of you. You believe that the Guardians have abandoned you because of my actions—"

"I allowed it," Acacia bit out.

"Your own choices, then. Which is even better, my dear Captain. So listen to me if you are brave enough. I only ask that you listen."

"We don't have time for this," Acacia said. "*I* can't do anything. You can, however. In Vaylin, the Forsaken fled from you."

Isiilde could hear the captain's teeth grinding, and did not like the way she gripped the hilt of her sword.

"I cannot banish *that*." His eyes flashed to the gathering darkness. "We triggered a ward—a powerful and complicated series of traps. There's no stopping the reaction and ultimate conclusion." He paused, letting that sink in.

The darkness was closer, and the shapes were taking form—phantoms drifting in torment.

"Listen to me," he begged. "Even the undisciplined can tap into the Gift. Prayers are but errant whispers—crude and unformed. And a few are desperate enough to touch the ears of the Guardians. You could just as easily pray to a beggar in the gutters, Acacia. Your rituals are a discipline that allows you to wield the Gift, just as the Wise Ones use runes. The power lies in the Gift; not the Guardians."

"More lies from a heretic," Acacia growled. "If you're hoping to restore my faith in myself, you are sadly mistaken. I am a Knight Captain of the Blessed Order—I have given my *life* to the Guardians of Iilenshar, and now you tell me it's a grand jest."

"No jest. Only misplaced knowledge. There is one who listens, who works through her favored few." He thrust a finger towards the symbol on the door. "*That* symbol is new. We are not the first tomb raiders."

"Scarecrow," Oenghus growled.

Shadows approached like mist, bringing an icy chill that creeped over Isiilde's heart.

"The Keeper placed the end piece in that vault," Marsais continued. "He put that symbol there. Only someone pure of heart and motive can open the door—a devotee of the Sylph."

Oenghus roared, swinging at the shadows. His sword passed through a grey phantom. It retreated, and grew, and when the phantom emerged next, it towered over the berserker.

Marsais kept Acacia pinned with the sheer intensity of his gaze. "I'm far from pure. And I'm definitely not favored—quite the opposite. I don't know if the Keeper unraveled the original ward. It requires a sacrifice. And I don't know what will happen if you touch that symbol."

"What the Void, Scarecrow?" Oenghus bellowed, sending a stream of lightning into the giant phantom. The air scattered, and when it reformed, two stood in its place.

Nalani fought, too. But for every strike, another phantom formed. They were multiplying.

"Don't you dare, Acacia," Oenghus urged as he fought. "I'll break the bloody door down."

"And bring the mountain down on our heads!" Marsais snapped.

Oenghus and Nalani were forced back, up the stairs, one step at a time. Isiilde sent a wave of flame over their heads. It pushed the darkness back, but when it gathered again, the grey, indistinct wraiths stood in a tight mass. They were nearly tangible now, growing in strength. She could feel their eyes, hear the malevolent whispers coming from beneath their tattered veils. Their presence tugged at her heart, seeking to rip it from her breast.

"I think they're feeding off us," she whispered. "Feeding off our attacks."

"We can't just stand here and do nothing," Nalani said.

Marsais chanted, tracing runes. As Oenghus and the woman retreated, he stepped to the forefront, down to the first step, and spread his arms. A white hot pulse of light stabbed at a knot of wraiths. The air gathered and burst with an implosion of force.

Isiilde's heart skipped, and stuttered at the sheer power of his weave. It bought them time, nothing more.

The air was stale and cold, and a shadow reached from the step. A wraith-like hand appeared, and then a face—all malformed and tortured, caught in an eternal scream. Elam and Isiilde put their backs to the wall.

"You think me a heretic?" Marsais shouted over the hissing multitude.

"I do not *think*," Acacia said through clenched teeth. "You plow fiends and use Bloodmagic!" She swung her sword at an emerging phantom. It retreated, and two more appeared, climbing from the stone.

Icy fingers brushed the back of Isiilde's neck. Her knees went weak, and she spun, sending a burst of flame at the phantom. The air rippled, and the fire shot through the incorporeal form, slamming against the stone above Elam's head. The boy's eyes went wide.

The whispers laughed.

"I do, and worse," Marsais confirmed. "I have knowledge, Acacia. As do the Guardians. If you will not listen, then look!"

Marsais chanted, but it wasn't the Lore, it was another language, both foreign and familiar, a language that stirred something deep in Isiilde's blood; of earth and fire; of air and water. It was the sky, and the sun, and each sliver of grass. Marsais opened his hand, and a pure, white light flared to life, swirling over his palm with a hypnotic pulse. The aura of his spirit.

Acacia's breath caught. "*Who* are you?" she whispered in shock.

"Trust me," he said softly. "You *are* favored by the Sylph. Oenghus is drawn to her priestesses like a moth to flame."

And then, like those very moths, the phantoms surged towards Marsais. A great howling agony filled the chamber: madness and fury, and every pain ever inflicted in a lifetime, focused on that single man.

They swarmed him and swallowed his light. Marsais screamed with pain.

Oenghus roared with fury. He reached into the mass, and pulled Marsais away from the phantoms. Isiilde caught him as his knees buckled. He was pale and his skin was like ice to the touch.

Oenghus stepped to the forefront, lighting crackling over his skin like a shield. He would fight to the death. Even if it was useless.

Isiilde looked at Acacia with a plea in her eyes. But the paladin had already made a choice. Her face was serene, her eyes focused. Acacia touched her blade to her forehead. The steel flared to life—pure and silver—and then it hummed through the air.

A silver Orb formed around the group. It shimmered with light and the shadows retreated, but did not flee. They stayed just out of reach, beyond the mercurial shield.

"The door!" Marsais gasped.

Acacia slapped her palm against the triune of rings. The multitude screamed with rage, and the door swung open.

Acacia's fingers relaxed. Her sword clattered to the stone and she fell with the blade. The silver shield vanished.

A wave of shadows rose over the dais. Isiilde shoved Marsais through the titan doorway, grabbed Elam by the wrist, and pulled him in her wake.

Oenghus seized Acacia's collar and dragged her through, and as soon as Nalani entered, he threw his weight against the door. It slammed shut with a deafening boom.

CHAPTER 54

A FOUNTAIN SPLASHED in the silence. She nearly wept with relief. They'd made it through the doors and into a vast chamber filled with gold and jewels. No one cared about the treasure.

"Acacia!" Oenghus dropped to his knees. She wasn't breathing. He placed one hand on her forehead, slipped the other over her stomach, and closed his eyes.

Isiilde willed the woman to breathe. But she was as still as stone—not even a flicker of a lash.

Oenghus broke the link. Blood trickled from his nose and ears, and he planted his hands on his thighs, panting. His broad shoulders slumped.

Marsais turned and walked away. At first she thought he feared a berserker's building rage, but Oenghus was still, and so incredibly quiet. It was worse than fury. Her father looked old and fragile, kneeling beside Acacia's body.

Isiilde placed a hand on his shoulder. It seemed a cruel dream. At least Acacia was at peace.

An hour might have passed, or a few seconds, she wasn't sure. Marsais came hurrying back, holding a drinking horn in his hands. He knelt beside the dead paladin and put a hand under her head, lifting her lips to the rim of the horn. Water splashed over her mouth, trickling down her throat. Color returned, flesh mended, and Acacia gulped in a breath as if she had been under water too long.

"Aha, I thought so!" Marsais grinned, and Oenghus grabbed the woman, crushing her to his chest.

Acacia spluttered. "Oen, I can't breathe," she gasped.

Oenghus loosened his hold. "Sorry." He did not entirely let go, however.

"What happened?" Acacia asked.

"The Unicorn's Horn," Isiilde realized.

Marsais turned the legendary artifact over in his hands. "I didn't think the Keeper would allow a sacrifice without some means to revive a priestess of the Sylph."

"You still bloody risked her life," Oenghus growled.

Acacia laid a hand on his broad chest. "It was my choice." She untangled herself from his arms. A light entered her eyes. "We need to go back. I'll use the horn on Rivan."

"I'm afraid that's not possible," Marsais said. "Its power is limited. Both water and horn are needed, and it takes a hundred years to replenish the power."

Hope died in Acacia's eyes. Her mouth worked, and finally she found the words. "And you wasted it on me?"

"I do not consider it a waste," he said.

For a moment, Isiilde thought Acacia would strike him, but she closed her eyes and sighed.

"Rivan was a noble young man," Marsais said. "I am truly sorry."

"And a friend," Isiilde added.

Silence fell over the survivors, each turning to look at this new chamber, wondering what tricks lurked in the golden splendor.

Oenghus shattered the lull with a growl. "A hundred years? How the Void did you know it'd be full?" He snatched the horn from Marsais.

"I didn't know," Marsais admitted.

Disgusted, Oenghus stalked to the fountain, and replaced the horn in its cradle. The group joined him at the basin.

Isiilde's mind worked through the puzzle. "The vault requires a sacrifice... The Keeper changed it to be someone pure of heart. But before that, the thief would have had to choose between a life and removing the horn."

"Possibly his own," Marsais added. "The ward likely works differently if only one person enters."

Isiilde considered this, but shook her head. "I think two need to enter. The mirrors, the husks, it's all designed for two. Sacrifice one to save another; a common enough ploy in King's Folly, only now... with lives."

"Whatever it is, I don't think it's over," said Nalani, nodding towards a far wall. "Something moved over there."

Isiilde barely heard the woman; she was lured to the side by a flicker of light. Voices faded as she walked through an archway.

A wide patch of stone floor was void of treasure, empty save for a single skeleton in its center. The skeleton's spine was bent at a breaking angle, and tattered robes still adorned its frame. Isiilde looked up. A whirlpool of chaotic energy churned high overhead. Her mouth fell open.

"How the Void are we going to leave this cursed place?" Oenghus rumbled as the others followed.

Isiilde laughed. "Did you know?" she asked Marsais.

"Names have meaning, my dear."

"Wait, is that..." Oenghus trailed off, gawking.

"What?" Nalani asked.

Acacia stared. "That looks like the... thing in the Spine."

"Lispen's Folly," Isiilde said. "You *are* clever, Marsais."

He gave an elegant gesture of dismissal. "I was merely hopeful."

"Is that the crazed bastard himself?" Oenghus asked, studying the broken skeleton.

"It appears so," Marsais said.

"Is it a Portal?" Acacia asked.

"Hmm, yes and no," he answered. "Lispen was obsessed with rare artifacts, especially the Unicorn's Horn; he took great risks in the pursuit of wealth."

"But fiends have fallen through the portal in the Spine," Isiilde pointed out. Gods, she hoped there weren't fiends in here.

"It's far from stable."

Acacia sighed. "I am sick of working Portals, let alone broken ones."

Elam nodded in agreement.

"Let's find the end piece and get out of here," Oenghus said.

Isiilde thought that was a wise idea. The gold, gems, and treasures of arms and armor made her ears twitch and her skin crawl. She said as much to Marsais.

"Where there is treasure, there is blood. Greedy spirits often linger over the very gilt that slew them."

"I'm not sure that's it," she whispered. "Something is holding its breath."

"Whatever that something may be—touch nothing," he stressed, and repeated the order to Elam in Lome. The boy thrust his hands in his pockets, and Isiilde did the same.

"We touched the Horn," Acacia said.

"Let's hope it was part of the puzzle," Marsais muttered.

"A Queen was not taken," Isiilde observed.

Marsais frowned at her. "You're right. The game is still in play."

Isiilde gazed at the swirl of energy overhead. "Then it's time to cheat," she whispered for his ears alone.

"Hmm," he agreed. "Spread out, look for the end piece. Elam, come with me. Isiilde, stick with Acacia. Yell if you find something, and meet back here."

Each pair walked in a different direction. The hoard of treasure made Isiilde's head spin. So much wealth; all useless. She wasn't even tempted to touch any of it—all of it carried the stink of death and greed.

"Gold is the weakest rune in King's Folly, but it's also the most resilient," she said to Acacia. "Water only moves it; fire can melt it, but only when surrounded; power can move through it, but gold is never destroyed."

A gold coin tumbled from a hill of treasure. It hit the floor with a soft *tink* and rolled to a stop at her boot. Isiilde stared down at the little coin. She tilted her head, and slowly looked up to the top of the mound. The air above wavered like a mirage. Heat rippled from the pile of gold.

"It's getting hotter," Isiilde said.

"I think we're overstaying our welcome. We need to hurry."

The two broke into a trot. Isiilde looked from one mound of treasure to the next, searching for the jagged sun she'd glimpsed in Marsais' study—it seemed a lifetime ago. Time, she decided, was not constant, but a fickle, moody thing that slipped through fingers, or clung for far too long.

Isiilde wanted to shout at time to stop, to freeze and let her think. "Wait."

"What is it?"

"The Keeper brought an artifact here to hide—where would he hide it?"

"I don't know the Keeper."

"He didn't destroy it," Isiilde said quickly. "He placed it here and altered the original puzzle, so that only someone with a pure heart could find it. The Keeper believed it might be useful one day. Where would you put it?"

Acacia eyed the mounds of heated treasure. "Others would be lured by gold, but a servant of the Sylph would have a purpose. And he wouldn't want that person killed in this trap—the door."

"Marsais!" Isiilde shouted.

Far away, across the great hall, Marsais spun, and tensed to run to her. "Look by the door!" He was closer.

Without question, Marsais turned and ran with Elam on his heels. He moved swiftly through the sweltering maze, until he disappeared behind a hill of gold.

"Go back to the Portal," Isiilde said. "As long as I don't touch anything, I'll be fine in the heat."

Acacia did not argue. She wiped the sweat from her brow, and trotted back the way she'd come. Isiilde didn't want to abandon the search on a hunch. She ran on, searching the treasure with a quick eye, until she heard a triumphant shout.

Marsais had found something. She raced back to the portal. The others were there, all drenched in sweat and licking parched lips. The great hall felt like a kettle.

Marsais raced back across the hall with the spiked sun in hand. Steam rose from the metal, but she sensed a weave lingering on him: an ice rune.

"That portal is looking bloody good," Oenghus panted.

Elam nodded in agreement. His lids were heavy, and he looked sleepy.

"How do we control it?" Isiilde asked.

Marsais stepped directly beneath the whirlpool of energy. When nothing snatched him up, or blew him to pieces, the rest followed.

"When you weave a Whisper," he explained. "You keep an image of the recipient in your mind's eye. Much like an illusion."

"If the same applies to Gateways, then how did Lispen open one here?" Isiilde asked. "Had he been here before?"

"A name will work for the talented, or desperate. Even a sketch will do."

"We could bloody end up anywhere," Oenghus said. He nudged the remains of Lispen the Louse with his boot.

"We will be fortunate if we end up *somewhere* and not *everywhere*," Marsais murmured.

Oenghus groaned. He hated dangerous things he couldn't bash.

Marsais studied the artifact in his hand. It was a nasty, bristling thing, all green-tinged and dark. A light entered his eyes; one Isiilde knew well. "Perhaps this is the key."

"What do you mean?" Acacia asked. "Isn't that the binding part?"

"It is. But it's also warm."

"Everything is warm in here, Scarecrow," Oenghus said, pushing his sopping hair away from his face.

"Not like that—it's vibrating. It *wants* to be reunited." He looked at Isiilde. "You'll need to go first."

"She does not need to go first," Oenghus argued.

"It's fifty feet off the ground, Oen. Even you would break your thick neck."

The full implication slammed into her. She would have to weave levitation. Not only for herself, but for each one to fall through the portal. Lispen the Louse seemed to mock her from the floor. Marsais was placing their lives in her hands.

"Can you do it?"

Isiilde looked into his eyes. "I have to."

"Yes, you do," he said, flatly.

There was no choice.

"I know you will."

She arched a brow. "Did you foresee it?"

"No." No lies, no false assurances, only truth. He smiled, a wolfish half grin that made her want to kiss the man. "I've always said you're brilliant, have I not?"

He did not give her time to answer. Marsais thrust the spiked sun towards the portal, his fingers tightening around its jagged edges. Blood trickled down his forearm. He began to chant, not in the language of the Wise Ones, but in that grating, hissing echo that could only be Abyssal.

The portal slowed, and shimmered, moving like a sluggish stream. The air thrummed with power and the Gateway fought and bucked like a stallion bound by a fragile thread.

Isiilde did not think; she did not worry. Her fingers flashed, and she sang the Lore in her own, flowing tongue. A feather rune, a layer of air, a spirit, and a binding tether to herself. Isiilde shot upwards like an arrow, leaving Lispen on the floor of his greatest and last success.

Energy crackled in her ears, hummed through her bones, and set her nerves on fire. All the hours she'd spent staring at the portal in the Spine, wondering, dreaming, aching to know—the time was finally here. Her heart swelled, not with fear, but with pure, unbridled excitement.

The portal reached out and snatched her from the air.

CHAPTER 55

ZOSHI HUGGED HIS KNEES. His empty eye socket throbbed, and the wad of cloth he'd pressed over it was crusty with blood.

He wondered when he would die.

At least the man was gone. But now he was alone in the void with that Chain. It was like a living, breathing thing—a sound that sent his knees knocking.

He could stay here and die of hunger, or he could get off his arse and try. But his body didn't want to move. It shook, and rooted him to the stone like a twitching fish on land.

Start small, his mum would say. But the thought of her made him want to cry, and crying never did anyone any good.

Zoshi tried to think of something else. And he did. He thought of his friend Oenghus. He imagined the giant man standing beside him right there in the dark.

With that thought, Zoshi moved an arm, then a leg. His head throbbed, so he didn't try to stand, only felt around the darkness for his sack of supplies. The feel of something familiar and solid under his hand gave him strength.

After he'd slung it over a shoulder, Zoshi began to crawl—back the way he'd come. The breathing Chain filled his ears. And then the emptiness came. That great expanse of nothing, the sea of bones and dead, and the lair of the Chain.

His arms and legs turned to stone, and the image of Oenghus shattered. He was rooted in place. Everything hurt. Blood and tears streamed down his cheeks.

He didn't want to die near that Chain.

Gasping for breath, he sang his favorite song: *The Mule King*. At first the words came so faintly that they might have never been, and then he sucked in a breath, and sang through the rawness of his throat.

"*The young king's son, a foppish dandy, strode 'long the lane in lacy finery...*" Zoshi darted forward, singing louder. "*Cursing the laborers, dodging the mud...*" The rasping Chain faded. "*Slipped on a slurry left by a pig—*"

Something cool and wet touched his cheek. Mist. A greenish light filled his eye. He shook his head, thinking that he imagined it, but when he looked again, the light was still there. The cavern took shape.

The Chain slithered in the bones and bodies, and now, shadows moved in the strange light. He could see enough to tease and terrify. This was a nightmare; death would wake him soon.

A shadow stood in front of him, smiling. It came like a flash of light that seared itself in the back of his eyeball. He blinked the spots away, and watched as the shadow fell into a pale, perfectly preserved corpse. The fingers curled, and the non-human inhaled. The man sat up, and cocked his head at the boy.

Zoshi bolted in terror, and promptly tripped. He threw his hand out to catch himself and felt cold steel. It instantly warmed at his touch. Crackling runes flared to life on a war hammer. His hair stood on end as light flooded the cavern. He clung to that light, and scrambled to his feet, clutching the war hammer like a lifeline.

Everywhere, all around, the dead were rising, and the creatures surrounded him, eyes burning with hate. Life could, it turned out, get much worse.

The thought pushed him over the brink. He laughed, a mad chortle that echoed in the vastness. The war hammer pulsed with a white light. It filled him with power.

Zoshi raised the hammer, and roared. It came out as a squeak, but the challenge was there.

The newly risen warriors edged back from the jagged light. A few cracked their necks and flexed fingers, giving their elegant swords an easy twirl. With amusement dancing in their cold eyes, they turned their backs on the boy and marched out of the cavern in a quick line.

It was so sudden, so swift, that he wondered if he'd imagined it. But no, the hammer still thrummed in his hands.

Zoshi looked to that breathing Chain. His new sense of power filled him with courage. And curiosity. He was no longer afraid of the Chain.

With nothing left to lose, he followed the Chain. The hammer's light pushed back the dark. And that light met a hole in the cave. The Chain disappeared into nothing. It wasn't dark; it wasn't lightless; it was... an absence.

Between the rattle and rasp, Zoshi could hear a beating heart. Not his own, but a slow, ponderous thud. He edged forward, and thrust the hammer closer to the void. It swallowed the light whole.

It was like standing on the edge of a cliff.

His feet moved; one step, two, and another. It put him on the precipice of a hole in the realm. The war hammer went cold in his palm, its light fading.

Zoshi sucked in a breath, and staggered back. The cavern spun, all twisted and shadowed, and he ran—away from the great void, and away from the Chain to follow the dead.

CHAPTER 56

BATTLE RAGED THROUGH THE CORRIDORS. Brutally but steadily, loyal guards pushed the traitors back, and the red-banded soldiers scattered like rats in a sewer.

The tide had turned.

Ielequithe called her troops to a halt. Morigan paused to catch her breath, and Thira and Rashk found her. Bram and Evie were not far behind.

"We need to get to the tunnels," Thira said.

Morigan took the lead. And Ielequithe ordered her soldiers to fall in line. They'd retaken the castle and the Spine. Now they needed to kill Tharios.

With Wraith Guards, paladins, and the Isle Guard at her back, Morigan kept to the wider corridors, wary of ambushes. But in the armory, the vast hall of ancient armor, she held up a hand. Her silent order stilled the advance.

Fog swirled at the far end. Soldiers lined up on either side of her, facing an impossible foe.

"Ah Void," Evie sighed.

"Language, love," Bram chided.

"How is this possible?" Rashk hissed. "We trapped the Fog in the arena."

Thira murmured the Lore and wove a deft breeze. It stirred the ancient tapestries, and brushed relics from before the Shattering. She gestured, and the wind picked up, pushing at the mist. It parted.

A pale, angular man stood solid and real in the center. Sharp ears poked from long white hair that fell past his shoulders. Ethereal and perfectly sculpted, he stood like a dream.

At first glance, Morigan thought it was Marsais, but his eyes—those silver pinprick eyes gleamed with hate. He was not alone. As the mists parted, ranks of pale warriors mirrored their own line. The Fey, in the flesh.

"Zahra protect us," a paladin whispered.

"Your Archlord is dead," the Fey stated from across the great hall. He caressed a barbed staff capped with a jagged sun. Soisskeli's Stave.

The similarities he shared with Marsais and Isiilde gave her pause. His appearance and voice, the way he moved in and out of reality like a dream. It was unnerving.

Thira stepped forward. "Who are you?"

"The rightful ruler of this Isle," he replied. "I ask that you leave now. Every man, woman, and child. You have three days to vacate my island."

"*Who* are you?" Thira repeated.

"I am the shadow under your beds; the creak on the roof; I am nightmares and horrors. And here I stand, a myth, a tale, a god in the flesh. You call me Pyrderi Har'Feydd."

A ripple traveled through the ranks behind Morigan, and across the way, Eiji smirked, twirling a blade in her hand.

Thira's only reaction was a twitch of a brow. "And you just expect us to leave? Is that an ultimatum, Har'Feydd?"

"It is."

"Or what?"

"What does one do with rats in a home?" He idly studied the jagged sun on the stave, turning it this way and that. "There are two choices: drive them out or slaughter the vermin. I offer you a chance to save yourselves."

The Fey alongside Har'Feydd did not move. The men were like ice, cold and remorseless, eyes burning with hunger. Morigan had seen that lust before—in hordes of Wedamen. The Fey's stillness, however, was far more unnerving than a raging mass of crazed berserkers.

Pyrderi turned to leave, but stopped. He cocked his head, and turned. "There is *one* small matter—it's not a request." Gleaming eyes settled on her. "You, Morigan Freyr, will remain as my guest."

The blood in her veins went cold. "Why me?" she asked.

"I'd like to dine with that nymph who suckled on your teat."

In answer, Morigan snatched a spear from a soldier, and threw it at the god.

THE SPEAR FLEW TRUE. One moment Pyrderi was there, and then he was not—he stood three feet to the side and snatched her spear from the air.

Morigan hadn't seen him move.

The Fey warriors charged. Not with battle cries, but in silence. The mist swept over the fighters.

"Get out," Bram shouted to Evie. "Warn Chaim!" The Valkyrie did not argue. Even as arrows flew, she sprinted away, weaving through the Isle Guards.

The next minutes were frantic. Chants and prayers rose in the air; weaves crackled and steel clashed; grunts and cries and blood filled the great hall. The Fey moved like Forsaken, swift and silent, with one lethal difference: their blades hit.

"Fall back!" Ielequithe shouted.

The tide shifted once again. This time, Morigan found herself on the run. Soldiers funneled into the wide hallways, and the Fey came at them from all sides. The enemy knew the castle—every twisting corridor and forgotten passage. And they came not with a roar, but with smiles plastered on cold faces.

Morigan cleaved one Fey after another. Screams howled in her ears, and the scents of blood and bowels clogged the air. But she was as calm as a butcher hacking at meat. One foe replaced the next, until her arm stopped aching and all went numb.

"Fall back!" There was desperation in that order.

Bit by bit, in the mad chaos, the Isle Guards gave ground. In a haze of blood and an explosion of weaves, a thought pricked her calm: the King's Walk and that perfect tear in the castle wards. Already, soldiers were funneling through the long tunnel.

The Fey had driven them here.

"The tear, Thira!" Morigan shouted over the din of battle.

Thira stepped beside Morigan, unleashing a chain of lightning that crackled with red heat. Fey dropped, and more came. Blood seeped from Thira's nose and ears, and Morigan shoved the woman back into the King's Walk. The retreating soldiers caught her up as they fled towards the castle.

Morigan stood with Rashk and the remaining Wraith Guards, holding the narrow space, giving the others time to clear the passage. The Fey weren't trying to drive them out; they were trying to escape through the hole in the prison wards.

And then it happened. While Morigan was lost in the moment, one axe swing after another, cleaving skulls and deflecting blows, a small gnome slipped behind her.

A searing pain sliced across her leg. Morigan spun, but her attacker leapt back. Eiji. There was blood on her blade and a triumphant smirk on her lips. She always coated her weapons with poison.

Rashk leapt in front of Morigan, landing in a defensive crouch. It robbed Eiji of her shorter advantage. Rashk rushed the gnome with a flurry of blades.

A Fey's sword bit into Morigan's shoulder. Unable to hold her shield, she let it slide from her arm, and turned, bringing down her axe. It sunk into the Fey's skull with a crunch. She wrenched it free, and staggered forward, towards a lever on the wall.

Morigan dropped her axe and yanked on the lever that would seal the King's Walk. Soundless gears turned, teeth met teeth, and she bit out the Lore, feeding the Gift into dormant wards. The gates fell, one after another, crashing down on the unlucky who were caught fighting in the corridor.

She bound a powerful combination of stone and water to the lever, then bent to pick up her axe. The realm tipped and spun, but she had one final task to finish. Gathering her strength, fighting the burn of Eiji's poison, she brought her axe down on the lever. It shattered.

Her ears rang with silence.

Morigan blinked through a haze of blood. She slumped against the wall. The Fey surrounded her. And on the floor lay a twisted tangle of bodies: Eiji, a good number of Fey, and more allies than she'd care to count. Her gaze swept over Rashk and Bram and all the Wraith Guards who'd stayed behind. She was the only defender standing. And she was trapped in the Spine with the Fey.

The silent warriors parted, making way for their god. His cold eyes flickered from the broken lever to the gleaming wards pulsing on the first gate.

Morigan wiped the blood from her eyes, and attempted to stand, but her muscles twitched from Eiji's poisoned blade.

"Humans never change," Har'Feydd sighed. An odd chirp issued from his throat, like a cluck of a tongue. "You've delayed me, nothing more." He twirled his stave and swaggered forward. "This is such a useful little artifact. It was so kind of Tharios to retrieve it for me."

Pushing aside pain and summoning strength, Morigan charged. She swung her axe, but Pyrderi leapt back with casual grace. Wood slammed into her face, and the thorns ripped her flesh. She struck again. But the god moved like the wind.

In a blink, he swept her legs from under her, and slammed her onto the floor. Pyrderi speared her thigh with the jagged sun, pinning her to the stone.

Morigan swung at the shaft, but he gave a twist of the stave. She screamed in agony. Pyrderi casually plucked the axe from her numb fingers.

She writhed on the slick ground, reaching for the barbed staff burning in her thigh. Pyrderi tossed her axe aside, and ran a finger over the line she'd carved across his gut. Only a scratch; not nearly deep enough. He licked the blood from his fingertips.

"Ah, Morigan," he purred. "Mate to my old foe, Ulfhidhin." He grabbed her by the braid and yanked her head off the floor.

Agony shot from her thigh to her skull. She couldn't even scream.

"What do you call him now—Oenghus? In my tongue, Oen means blockhead. Fitting, I think."

The god bent closer. She could feel his breath on her cheek. It was as cold as the Fell Wind. Her entire body trembled and darkness crept into her vision.

"If I were human, I would rape and torture you, then hang your mutilated corpse from the gates."

Pyrderi jerked the stave from her thigh. Morigan clenched her teeth, nostrils flaring, staring through a sheen of tears. But he kept a hand on her braid; she was like a dog on a leash hanging over the ground.

He set down the stave and drew a blade. Whispered words flowed from his perfect lips—the language of fire and steel. The blade glowed hot with eagerness.

"You're a healer. You know what happens when a wound is cauterized. That is what humans did to my heart. Revenge is like a brand." He pressed the glowing blade to her wounded thigh.

Morigan growled through her teeth. The blade left, the pain remained.

"There, all better now." That angular face swam into view, amusement gleaming in his eyes. "It hurts now—I know—but soon the wound will heal and scar over, and you will never feel anything in that spot again. I've given you a gift."

In reply, Morigan spit blood in his face.

He licked it from his lips. "Ah, humans. I offer civility and you answer with barbarity. You know, I am not an animal. I only want Ulfhidhin."

Pyrderi released her braid. Reduced to a trembling lump of flesh, Morigan flopped to the floor, hitting her head.

A high-pitched scream filled the chamber. Swimming in confusion, Morigan thought it came from her own throat, but a moment later, a small, dirt-covered boy charged from the line of distracted Fey. The enraged boy flew at Pyrderi with the war hammer raised. His blow struck Pyrderi's back.

Lightning crackled and splintered, and Pyrderi staggered from the shock. Zoshi raised the hammer to strike again, but the Fey was too fast. Pyrderi delivered a brutal kick to the boy.

Zoshi flew backwards, dropping the war hammer and landing on a heap of bodies.

Morigan *knew* that war hammer. She knew its name from the whispered dreaming of a man whose bed she'd shared for most of her life. She thrust a hand towards the hammer, and called its true name.

The war hammer of Ulfhidhin leapt to her hand, warm and willing, and with a roar, she brought the head down on the spiked sun. Stone cracked, light flared, and the powerful artifact was rendered to ash, unleashing its violent energy.

A wave of force rippled outwards. Fey and god were blasted off their feet.

Morigan hit a wall, tried to rise, but only floundered. She could not see, could not hear, but she felt herself smile. At last, she'd get to rest.

CHAPTER 57

Isiilde fell headfirst into a realm of ice. Her levitation weave had unraveled. She screamed, twisting in midair like a frantic cat, and threw a sloppy weave at the floor.

She hit the ice, hard. Isiilde couldn't breathe. She was sure her ribs were shattered—she was dying. The others would die, too. With that desperate thought, she gulped in a breath.

Isiilde scrambled to her feet. The portal had spit her out into an ice cave. There was no time to worry about it—she had to catch the others. But what had caught her?

She spun to inspect her hasty weave. It reminded her of a grease enchantment, only this one wasn't slippery—it was a cloud of feather runes. She'd woven an ethereal mattress.

The Gateway crackled and spit out Oenghus. He twisted in midair with a bellow, then hit her weave and slowed, dropping to the floor.

"That was a very high-pitched scream," she said as he climbed to his feet.

Oenghus grunted as he hoisted his shield and sword. "Did we bloody end up in Isiikle?"

That thought terrified her. And then a noise pricked her ears: ice shifting against ice with a creaking rasp. The air temperature dropped. It hurt to breathe.

"Bollocks," Oenghus croaked, reaching for his Brimgrog.

Isiilde kept her focus on the weave as the portal spit out Elam. Behind her, Oenghus roared in challenge. It shook the ground, cracking ice. She glanced over a shoulder, and a blizzard flew at her face, stinging her cheeks. Oenghus charged into the white.

Fighting for breath, she wove a Barrier of Fire. It snapped into focus and pushed at the chill. Keeping one hand stretched towards the white-out, she extended the other towards her feather weave.

Acacia fell through next. Isiilde shifted the weave under the falling knight, and as soon as Acacia landed, the paladin pulled Elam behind her shield.

Oenghus roared again. Spear-like icicles crashed from the high ceiling, but her Fire Barrier turned them to water. Ice and snow swirled with steam, parting for a split second. She glimpsed her father. Energy crackled over his body as he faced a titan of ice.

The elemental answered his roar with a bellow and a spear. Oenghus stepped to the side, swinging his falchion. A crackle of blue lightning shattered the ice spear.

The Gateway churned overhead. Isiilde tore her eyes from the fight to shift her weave. It caught Nalani, but Isiilde couldn't concentrate on two weaves at once.

Ice blasted through her Barrier of Fire, and a deathly chill crawled over her flesh. It was unlike anything she'd ever felt. An element in its purest form, utterly raw. It threatened to freeze her solid.

Isiilde couldn't breathe, couldn't move her lips. She focused on her bond. It stirred at her silent plea. Fire bubbled in her breast, warming her throat. Desperate, she screamed. Flames surged from her fingertips.

It ignited her Barrier and snapped it back into place, but her fire surged from her other hand, too. Her feather weave burst into flames.

Marsais fell from the portal into a blaze. There was no time to think. She dropped her Barrier and focused on the flaming feather weave. With a shout, and a bind, she sent the whole burning mass hurling into the ice storm.

Hot air clashed with cold, and the impact rippled outwards. Isiilde hit the ground. Steam hissed, fire swirled, and ice knocked together, creating its own thundercloud. Jagged lightning streaked over her head, throwing off thunderclaps.

The air was charged. All was blinding and wild, and Isiilde fought through the storm, crawling to where Marsais had landed. He lay on his back. The twisted sun was half-buried in the snow by his limp hand. She shielded him from the pelting ice with her own body. A heart beat in his chest. He wasn't dead.

Isiilde reached for the twisted sun. But when she grabbed the artifact, filth crawled along her flesh. Every instinct screamed at her to throw it into the storm. She quickly stuffed it inside her pouch.

Marsais sucked in a breath of air. He blinked at the hail and crackling bolts, and his fingers began to weave. A Barrier flared to life. He climbed to his knees and stretched out his hand, holding back the onslaught of forces.

"Sever the Bind!" he shouted in her ear.

Isiilde looked at the tangled runes, twisting and bumping against one another. She sang, calling to her flame, untangling it from the weave. When a sinuous line blazed through the air, she stepped from the safety of the Barrier, and gathered the fire to her hands. Her voice rose, feeding it, shaping it, until it roiled and spit with molten heat.

The ice elemental roared, something crunched, and Oenghus sailed through the air. He smacked onto the ice and slid. The elemental charged after him with steps like cracking earth.

Isiilde was shaken off her feet. But before she hit the ice, she threw her fireball at the enraged elemental. Enormous slabs of ice cracked and fell, and she rolled to the side.

Through the storm, she spotted a shimmer of blue and a hole in the ice wall. Isiilde dove for the opening. It was a cave entrance covered by a runic shield. She slithered through the hole with Marsais on her heels.

When she touched the shimmering shield, her mind cleared and her senses came alive. There was no time to wonder about it. She turned to help Marsais through the narrow gap.

The air was warmer inside, and quiet. She smelled blood. Lingering flashes of lightning lit the darkness, illuminating a small cave of ice.

Through a chatter of teeth, she wove a small light. The firefly-sized orb glowed softly, enough to see the shivering man beside her. He was covered in frost.

"We need to help Oen." She started to move, but Marsais grabbed her arm.

"Listen."

Ice creaked and a few flashes lit the dark, but the earthquake had quieted. Something breathed, slow and rasping, in the aftermath. The elemental had either killed Oenghus, or he'd taken refuge.

Marsais traced an air rune, then whispered into the weave. *Isiilde is safe. Are you?* With a gesture, he sent it fluttering through the air.

"He can't Whisper back," she reminded.

"We're all here in some sort of tunnel," Oenghus shouted. "Where the Void are we?"

His voice roused the elemental. It shifted in irritation, knocking slabs of ice from the ceiling. Marsais shielded her with his body, and after the ground stopped moving, he wove another Whisper.

Isiilde didn't pay attention to his message. She'd spotted a pattern in the ice. It looked... familiar. She crawled towards it. With a whisper, she summoned a flame. It danced and twirled on her palm as she held it up to the wall. The ice melted. And with every drop, a portion of the pattern was revealed. It was a twining image of vines and leaves.

Marsais crawled to her side. "We're in the Nameless chamber in the Spine. It's the gate to the throne room," she whispered.

Marsais looked from the vines to the black ice. He quickly traced another Whisper.

"What happened here?" she asked.

"When we were captured, Tharios wanted directions to a tomb."

"You told him where the map was."

"Yes. In a flask. The elemental was guarding the map, but I don't know how it ended up here."

"Does that mean he's found the tomb?"

"If I were the optimistic sort, I'd say Tharios was likely killed."

"You *are* optimistic... only very practical, too."

"A seer's lot in life, I'm afraid."

"You said we have until the Shadowed Dawn. We have time." It was more question than statement.

"According to my visions... But I'm not sure I can trust them anymore."

"Why?"

Marsais glanced back to the gap in the ice. His eyes were as troubled as a storm-tossed sea.

Isiilde took his hand. "We'll sort this out."

"We have no choice."

"I know," she whispered, leaning into his shoulder. "If I had one, I'd find a feather bed. All I want to do is sleep."

"I've finally exhausted you." His breath was warm on her temple.

Isiilde smirked. "There are more pleasurable ways to do that than with Fomorri, ice elementals, and power hungry madmen."

"Such is my life."

"I'll never be bored again." She sat back and cocked an ear, listening. The elemental rasped its glacial breath. "What is Oen going to do?"

"Likely the opposite of what I suggested."

"Which is?"

"Something extremely foolish."

"Is that part of the castle wards?" She nodded to the shimmering shield.

"Yes."

"Can the elemental pass through it?"

"I'm not sure," he admitted.

Isiilde climbed to her feet, and helped Marsais find his own. He looked as tired and battered as she felt. One foot in front of the other, she silently reminded herself. That's all that was needed.

"Sorry I dropped you."

"You had enough to worry about," he said with a grimace. "I caught myself. Barely."

There was no other exit in their ice cave. The gate to the throne room was iced over. Without thinking, she sang a quiet, lilting song. Isiilde traced a fire rune, adding her own flourish to it. The metal glowed molten.

As the ice melted, it puddled around their feet, and she stepped closer to the glow, warming herself in the heat.

Isiilde pondered her fire rune.

"That would be extremely unwise," Marsais said, sensing her thoughts.

"How did you know what I was thinking?"

"Your ears are thoughtful."

Isiilde narrowed her eyes.

"In order to melt *that* elemental, you'd need to trace your rune directly onto it. And even then, it would only turn into a liquid state. An elemental that old and powerful would likely reform."

"It would give us time."

"Are you cold now?"

"Freezing," she chattered.

"Imagine touching the essence of ice."

Isiilde pursed her lips. She'd rather not.

When a section of the gate had been revealed, Isiilde poked the ice, and a slab slid off, shattering on the ground. She looked through the gap. The throne room was dark and misty, and her ears twitched with unease. But then, the throne room had always made her queasy.

"Can you still open this gate?"

Marsais glanced at his palm, but nothing flared to life. The Archlord's Runic Eye had passed to another.

She eyed the gaps between the vines. "I used to squeeze through all the time."

There was a warded panel near the throne that opened the gate for when the Archlord wasn't present.

Before Marsais could answer, the floor under their feet shuddered. The elemental was on the move. Oenghus bellowed, lightning cracked, and a spear-like stalactite fell on the elemental. The wall of ice gave way.

"Blast it, Oen," Marsais hissed.

Acacia, Nalani, and Elam ran towards the Nameless chamber. When they saw the shimmering blue shield, the three skidded to a stop, but Marsais motioned them through. A look of dismay filled Elam's face when he saw the half-frozen gate.

"Oenghus thought we could sneak through." Acacia blinked at the gate of twining vines. "We *are* in the Spine."

Marsais began weaving, his fingers a blur of movement. But no weave, no matter how complex, would open the gate. They were trapped.

Isiilde didn't wait for permission. She squeezed through a gap between the metal vines.

The throne room was shrouded in mist. It twined around a forest of columns that rose like ancient trees, their tops lost in darkness.

Isiilde hurried to the first column. A tendril touched her hand, and another slithered around her leg. It felt like filth. With a murmur, she wove an armor weave, and added her fire. Her skin began to glow, and the mist hissed, retreating like a wounded animal.

She glanced back at the gate. The ice had nearly melted. She could see Marsais and the others, and beyond, her father racing towards the Nameless with a glacier on his heels.

There wasn't much time.

Isiilde sprinted through the mist. Only she didn't get far. She hit something solid, bounced off, and fell on her backside.

"Pardon me," said a voice like a dream.

CHAPTER 58

A MAN STOOD in the mist. "Shall I calm the old one?" he asked. He was tall and angular, and his snowy hair brushed past his slim shoulders. He reminded her of Marsais in so many ways—except for his eyes. No emotion touched the pinprick of silver that gleamed coldly inside.

He was not alone.

There were other Fey standing in the fog, hundreds of beautiful warriors, all like this pale man. Their stillness unnerved her.

Isiilde climbed to her feet. Fire danced in her palms, licking at her sleeves, and waiting for release. She hesitated. Marsais had woven a Barrier, and he kept the raging elemental at bay. But her friends were still trapped between a gate and looming death. His arm shook with the effort it took to keep the elemental from freezing the air in their lungs.

"Please do," she said.

"So polite."

He walked towards her, and she tensed, backing up, but he didn't look her way, only stepped up to the gate. He was beautiful and ethereal, and he moved like water over the ground. Her mind reeled.

"Ulfhidhin," the man purred.

Oenghus staggered at the name. He grabbed the bars of the gate to keep himself upright. Veins throbbed along his temple and his knuckles turned white—he looked like he was in pain.

Marsais glanced over his shoulder and nearly dropped his weave in shock.

"Whatever you're doing, stop it," Isiilde demanded.

"I'm not doing a thing," the man said. "Names take on a power of their own."

"And what is your name?" she asked.

"He's Pyrderi Har'Feydd," Marsais answered through his teeth.

The name knocked her back a step. How was that possible?

Pyrderi bowed deeply to her. He seemed a dream—not an actual part of this realm. Was that how humans saw her?

When he straightened, there was a smile on his long lips. "I've longed to meet you Isiilde Jaal'*Yasine*." He drew out her mother's name, tasting every syllable. "I'm at your service."

"Then call off your elemental."

Pyrderi stepped up to the gate and spoke in an old tongue. It was a soft song, a gentle lullaby, and the sound of his voice nearly made her weep. She *knew* it, but had never heard it—it was the language of her heart.

The elemental retreated with a scrape of ice. It moved to the center of the great hall and shifted into a quiet mountain of crystal. A deep, blue glow emanated from the elemental's core. When light touched the slumbering creature, its multitude of facets threw off prisms, bathing the cold chamber in beauty.

Marsais lowered his arm. The two men stood at arm's length, their eyes locked.

"Now open the gate," she said to Pyrderi's back. Fire flickered around her fists. Unfortunately, Pyrderi now stood between her and the exit. The other Fey surrounded her, not crowding, but waiting. For what, she did not know.

"I'm afraid I can't," Pyrderi admitted. He stepped away, and turned to face her. "Humans need cages to stop their butchery. As soon as that gate opens, what do you imagine Ulfhidhin will do?"

The name was like a dagger in her father's temple. Pain blossomed on his face, and he shook the gate with a growl. Acacia put a hand on his shoulder, but he shrugged off her touch.

Isiilde did not know why Pyrderi used that name—the name of the Wild God who abducted the Sylph. Or why a faerie three thousands years dead was standing in front of her. Along with his army of Fey.

She wasn't sure the *why* of it mattered. Only that they were here. But one detail was worth noting: a slice marred his flawless skin. He bled. That meant the Fey could be killed.

"What have you done with the other residents?" she asked, shifting slightly to the side, so she'd have a better view of Marsais. There was a gleam in his eyes. Isiilde knew that look—she'd seen it every time they played King's Folly as he worked through possible strategies.

"I did nothing with them," Pyrderi said. "I simply asked them to leave my home. But the humans refused and attacked us, so we drove them out like the rats they are."

"Alive?"

"Some." He lifted a shoulder. "This island is ours, you know. Humans took it from the faerie long ago. They take and they take, and when you think they've finally quenched their thirst... they demand more."

The words caught in her mind. They were her own thoughts. He'd only given them a voice. And what a beautiful voice. A part of her ached to hear more.

"Breathtaking, isn't it?" He gestured towards the resting elemental. "That spirit is as old as this realm. The first Wise Ones captured it and bound it to a flask to guard the key to my prison. That poor, beautiful spirit has spent *thirty-five hundred years* in a prison. Now it's free. And what do humans do but torment it again? Humans never think to talk. And that is what I desire, Isiilde—to speak with you without a raging beast frothing at the mouth." He gestured at her father, who currently looked every bit the beast.

"Speaking of cages," Marsais said in a casual tone. "How did you find your way back?"

"I never left."

"We killed you," Oenghus growled.

"I *lingered* until someone was kind enough to release me."

"And where is Tharios now?" Marsais asked.

"Tharios is dead," Pyrderi stated. "I did not care for his treatment of you." His gaze settled on her, and in that coldness, she saw a glimmer of heat. "We faerie must look out for one another."

"My friends look out for me. If you truly cared, you would open the gate."

"Your friends would try to kill me, and I would be forced to defend myself. Just as humans have forced your hand."

"What do you want with me?"

"Want? Nothing. To talk, if you like."

"What could we possibly talk about?" she asked.

"Ah—I see. Your friends have filled your head with horrors of the Fey. No doubt they told you I tortured humans and gave myself over to obscene rituals." He stepped towards her, slowly, casually, without threat.

"Stay away from her," Oenghus snarled.

"I will not hurt her, Ulfhidhin." He gave a dismissive gesture, one she'd seen a thousand times before.

The similarities between Pyrderi and Marsais struck her anew. Their mannerisms, their appearance, even their hands: long and fine and so very eloquent. What was more, she believed him.

Isiilde released her fire. The sparks bounced on the floor, sputtering out. A thin line of black smoke rose between the two faerie.

"Then you didn't do those things?" she asked.

"Oh, I did," Pyrderi admitted without guile. "But what no human ever tells is the *why* of it. Isn't that what you always ache to know, Isiilde? The *why* of everything?"

"Does it matter? I've seen your creations—the Fomorri. They're twisted and foul."

"They were never meant to be that way—I was interrupted before I could shape my children. That happens when you slaughter parents. Children grow into monsters."

"He twists everything, Isiilde. Don't listen to him," Acacia said from behind the gate.

"Aah, the noble paladin." Pyrderi smiled sadly. "The essence of everything wrong with humanity. Lies, hypocrisy, and atrocities committed in the name of good. I do not defend my answers, Paladin. I simply state the truth."

"Truth has many facets," Acacia said. "Depending on the angle, each is unique."

"She speaks philosophy with a mere animal. Is that not what your Blessed Order calls us? Every living faerie is but an animal to be treated as humans see fit."

No one could deny it. No one tried. It was the truth.

"You see, Isiilde," Pyrderi continued, turning to her. "Those humans are not in a cage. They can leave; I cannot."

"I can't either."

"You are free." He held out his hand towards the gate. "Go, crawl back through, and stare at the animals here. I had hoped the humans hadn't broken you yet, but it seems I was mistaken."

He turned to walk away. And the other Fey seemed to meld into the mist, but curiosity burned in her breast, and it could not be denied.

"Why?" she asked, suddenly. "Why did you do it?"

Pyrderi spun on his heel to look at Marsais. "Tell her what humans did to our people. To *your* people."

"I've told you some, Isiilde. Humans did what you might expect. *Some* murdered, raped, and pillaged the Lindale."

"They wanted our forests, our lands, and after they burned our trees to the ground, their hearts filled with fear. *Humans* slaughtered my family. But it wasn't enough to slit their throats. Do you see these scars?" Pyrderi thrust out his arms, palms up. There were thick, scarred circles in the center of those palms. "They nailed me to a tree and raped and tortured my mate, my daughters, and my young sons in front of my eyes." There was no emotion, no pain, or hate. Only coldness. A raw truth that was like ice scraping against her skin.

"Is it true, Marsais?" she asked.

"Monsters and gods are molded by humans," he replied without hesitation.

Pyrderi took another step towards her; she did not retreat. "I did everything humans have said of me. And more. Hate creates the very thing it fears. But what I ask you, Isiilde, is what would you do if Stievin stood before you now in the flesh?"

His question hit her like a punch to the gut. She took a hasty step back, fists flexing.

"I am so sorry," he whispered. "I could not stop him—my spirit has drifted through this cold stone for millennia, watching but never acting."

The throne room spun. Having a witness, knowing another had watched her assault unseen, shook her to the core. It made it more real, and for a moment, she was there again, trapped beneath his leering eyes with the stone biting at her back.

Pyrderi inclined his head towards the gate. "Even now, they plot and conspire to slaughter the animal in its cage."

She glanced over her shoulder. They had their heads bent together. Oenghus looked up with hate in his eyes, then with a warning growl, he turned and left with Acacia on his heels.

Pyrderi glanced at his warriors, and through some unspoken command a large number faded back into the mists.

"What purpose does this serve?" Marsais asked.

"I want her to know the truth. I want her to understand our history." Pyrderi snapped his fingers and the Fey split ranks in perfect unison. Not a step out of place. Two Fey emerged from the mist, marching a horribly scarred woman between them. Zianna.

Pyrderi leaned in close. His breath was cold as he whispered in her ear. "I cannot bring you Stievin, but I can bring you *this* human. She hated you without cause; insulted and mocked your every move, goading you to attack. She's the reason you were dragged to that wash-room. And now look at her." Pyrderi circled Zianna like a slinking panther. "She should be begging for forgiveness."

"I'll never grovel in front of this creature," Zianna said.

"Of course she won't," Pyrderi purred. "She's human. Vengeance burns in her heart. What can you do in the face of such hatred?" At a nod from Pyrderi, the fey let Zianna go. She stumbled forward, caught herself, then straightened.

"Look at me, *nymph*!" Zianna spat.

Isiilde met her eyes. They burned with hate.

"You've ruined me. Taal is dead... *Your* friends killed him. I only want one thing—the chance to slit your throat."

The nymph's hands flexed.

"Isiilde," Marsais called, gently.

She looked at him.

That moment nearly killed her. Zianna drew a blade and charged with a dagger raised, the very same that Isek had once held to her throat. With a shout, Isiilde called to her fire, blasting the woman off her feet. The blade slid across the floor as Zianna writhed and screamed, batting at the flames.

"*That* is how humans repay faerie," Pyrderi said. "Now here she lies in agony. Will you show her mercy, or watch her suffer?"

Isiilde was rooted to the spot. She watched, still as a statue, mind reeling, thoughts all aflutter with confusion. A small part of her relished that suffering. Repayment for all the pain Zianna had caused. And yet another part curled back with revulsion.

"Why are you doing this?" she demanded.

"So you know the choices I was faced with."

"I would help her." But her words felt hollow. It was a lie.

"Then help her," he said. "But know she'll try to kill you again. And given the chance, she'll try to kill your friends, too—everyone you love. Because that is what humans do. They *never* stop."

Indecision turned her stomach.

"Now, who is the torturer?" Pyrderi asked.

The screams, the whimpers, the agony—Isiilde couldn't take it. She drew her sword and plunged the tip through the dying woman's breast.

Everything stopped. Zianna fell silent, and still. And a coldness crept over Isiilde's own heart. The sword fell from her limp fingertips.

"Now you know why," Pyrderi whispered.

CHAPTER 59

ULFHIDHIN RAN OVER THE ICE. Heart pumping, blood rushing, muscles stretching, he raced through halls of stone. Each beat of his heart taunted, and he knew every breath his daughter took might be her last. That thought was more potent than the Brimgrog burning through his veins. The Wild God ran towards the King's Walk.

A knot of soldiers stood in his path. He roared, scattering them like hens. Soldiers scrambled over each other to give him room as he barreled down the last corridor, and met a locked gate.

The god bellowed, driving his fist into the metal. The stone walls shook with his rage.

"Oenghus! By the Sylph, stop it." A woman stood beside him, doubled over, gulping in air.

More stone rained on his head. He did not care. The woman stepped in front of the gate as he brought his fist back. He paused, eyes burning into her.

"It's *sealed*. Is there another way?" The question sparked thought. And memory. He remembered who he was in this current life.

Oenghus blinked. He remembered who the woman was, too. Acacia. He lowered his fist. Battered soldiers stared at him with fear in their eyes. And the dead stared, too—strewn across a blood-smeared floor.

Oenghus stomped over to the closest Fey and took his frustration out on the corpse.

"There is another way," a voice interrupted. "If that idiot would calm down."

Oenghus glared at the source. "Thira."

Acacia drew her sword.

Thira raised her blood-covered hands. "I'm on your side. And by the gods, I never thought I'd say this, but I'm glad to see you."

This gave him pause.

"I'll vouch for her." A woman with a bow stepped forward. "And I'm glad to see you, too."

"Evie," Acacia breathed. "Where's Bram?"

The Valkyrie looked at the gate. "In there."

"You trust her?" Oenghus asked.

"I do."

That was good enough for him.

"Pyrderi Har'Feydd—" Thira began.

"Killed Tharios. Yes, we know," he growled. "The bastard is in the throne room with Isiilde."

Thira's lips formed a grim line. "He knew her name. He wanted her."

"What do you mean?" Oenghus demanded.

"Pyrderi ordered us to leave... except for Morigan. I think he meant to use her as bait. Morigan answered him with a spear."

"Where is she?" His voice was raw with emotion.

"There are gaps in the castle wards—one is in the King's Walk. We fought, but had to fall back. Morigan pushed me through and dropped the gates to keep the Fey from escaping."

His heart thundered in his ears. The King's Walk ran under the curtain wall. It was lined with one gate after another.

"I can't weave another transformation—"

There was no time. Oenghus growled, turned to Acacia, and hoisted her over his shoulder.

"Oenghus!"

Before Acacia could fight her way free, before Evie could loose the arrow she'd notched, he slapped his palm against a wall, and whispered to the earth. The stone welcomed the Wild God home.

THE STONE SPIT him out into a chamber of carnage. Blast marks scorched what remained of the walls, and the first gate had been rendered to shards. Bodies, both human and Fey, littered the rubble.

Oenghus set Acacia down. She swayed on her feet, trying to regain her bearings. The source of the blast was apparent. A barbed stave lay in the center of the wreckage. One end was splintered and ash lay at its top.

The remains of Soisskeli's Stave.

"Morigan!" he bellowed, searching the faces of the dead.

Acacia stopped beside the body of a gnome. Her throat clutched as she pressed her fingers to his neck.

Bram was dead.

"We need to help Isiilde and Marsais." Her voice was tight with grief.

Oenghus was shifting through the wreckage, tossing it aside. "Morigan!" His heart tore in two. But in the haze of rage, he felt an old stirring of familiarity. His palm itched. And then he heard a faint voice—a child's voice.

"Oenghus?"

Acacia looked at Oenghus, and as one, they bolted for the far wall. Oenghus heaved stones aside until he uncovered the source. A filthy, bloodied child hunched over the head of a warrior. The boy looked up with one eye.

"Zoshi..."

A dozen questions flashed through his mind, but they could wait. Oenghus gently lifted Zoshi in his arms. Tears and blood streaked the little boy's cheek, and he clung to Oenghus for a fierce moment.

Oenghus glanced down at the warrior he'd been protecting. Morigan. He passed the boy to Acacia, and pushed back the rubble, making room. She was half-buried; her legs pinned, her face covered in blood. With inhuman power, he tore at the stones and beams, tossing rocks and wreckage aside. When she was free, he felt for a pulse.

"No, Mori, please, no." He summoned the Lore, sending a burst of

Life into her broken bones. With trembling fingers, he unbuckled her armor, and slipped a hand beneath the chain. But rage and grief filled him, and he could not see past the red haze.

Another pair of hands joined him, and a warm silver glow wreathed Morigan's body. Acacia drew back with a gulp of air.

Morigan's chest rose, a single shaky breath. And then another. Oenghus willed her to take a third. She did. Tears cooled his rage, and he watched as her fingers curled, then fell limp.

Calmer now, Oenghus pressed his hands to Morigan, summoned the Lore, and plunged into her body. Her wounds took his breath away, and although he could not mend them all, he did enough. There was a rot inside of her—a darkness that he could not touch. When he withdrew, her breathing was weak but steady.

Oenghus cupped her face in his hands, pressing his lips to her forehead. "Ah, my girl," he whispered. "You're not finished yet. Keep fighting for me."

"I tried to move the rocks, but I couldn't. I tried to save her," Zoshi said.

Oenghus straightened, raking a palm over his eyes. "You did, lad. It's up to her now."

"There's some kind of taint in her. What was it?" Acacia asked.

"I don't bloody know."

"The... man, he stabbed her with... with a spear," Zoshi stuttered, and then the past weeks came pouring out in one long rush.

At the end of his tale, a sob tore from his throat. Zoshi began to cry. Acacia scooped the boy up and held his head to her breastplate as he wept. And Oenghus searched the face of his closest companion in this life.

Morigan had always urged him to think before acting, and even half-dead, she got through to him. He thought, but more importantly, he let himself remember.

Oenghus climbed to his feet, and stared at the palm of his hand. It was tingling. Yes, he remembered.

"*Slàtra*," he said.

The rubble shifted, a rock tumbled to the floor, and a war hammer flew through the air. The haft smacked into his palm. Runes flared to life, and energy crackled around the head, sizzling down his arm like a net. A deep growl rumbled from his chest.

Acacia held the boy protectively, eyeing the berserker with growing realization. "Another lost war hammer of yours?"

"Stay with her," he ordered.

"There's an army of Fey in the throne room."

"I'm not going there."

"Where are you going?"

"To finish what I started," he growled.

Pyrderi had not called him Ulfhidhin without reason. And it took everything she had not to cower from the wild god.

"I'm coming with you," she said.

"I need to know Morigan is safe."

The man before her had changed. He'd taken on a hard, feral edge, and he seemed to loom like a storm cloud. Even his voice had changed —there was power in that voice and a thick accent she couldn't place.

"These Fey won't stay dead," he said. "This is my only chance. Do you understand?"

Acacia hesitated for a moment, then glanced at the dead Fey in the chamber. "I do. But what about Isiilde and Marsais?"

"She's my daughter. She can take care of herself."

CHAPTER 60

IN THE CONFUSION, in the scene of death and insidious suggestion, no one noticed a small human boy slip through the twining gate. Elam slapped his palm against the panel behind the throne. The metal gate opened, sliding up into the ceiling.

Marsais limped into the throne room. The fight with the elemental had drained him, and he already had an air of defeat.

The Fey warriors closed in, but Pyrderi held up a hand. "I trust Marsais will be civil. He is one of us, after all." Pyrderi nodded to a Fey, who trotted off to close the gate. And Isiilde found herself standing between Marsais and Pyrderi. Both men stared over her head at one another.

One of us. Pyrderi's words registered, and her ears twitched.

"Oh, didn't you tell her?" Pyrderi arched a hairless brow. "All seers are touched by the Fey, and there is a tad more than a touch in that Lindale. But he is broken, whereas I am not." Pyrderi dragged a long finger across his own chest, mirroring the path of Marsais' scar.

"It doesn't matter what he is; only who," Isiilde said. "I won't let you kill my friends. And I won't slaughter humans because of what they are."

"I will not kill them. I'm going to drive every last human into the Bastardlands. And there they will remain, corralled like cattle. But do you know what the humans will do? They'll slaughter each other, as they have been trying to do since they first drew breath. That is why I wished to speak with you, Isiilde. I offer you a place in my kingdom, not one forged by ruthless men, but by faerie."

"You mean Fey."

"Fey is the name that humans gave me. To put a face on the monster they brought upon themselves. No, I mean what I say. Faerie. Wisps, nymphs—the few that remain of our scattered kind."

"And what shall I be? *Bound* to you?"

"Walk with me, please." Pyrderi raised his arm, beckoning her towards the obsidian throne.

She glanced at Marsais, but he betrayed nothing. He simply waited for her to make the next move. One end of the throne room seemed no different than the next, so she accepted Pyrderi's invitation.

Marsais limped behind her, and an escort of Fey fell in step beside him. As they walked, Isiilde furtively searched for Elam, but the throne room was vast and shrouded in mist. At least he had the sense to hide.

Pyrderi stopped in front of the throne. Memories washed over her of the day she'd stood on that very dais, in front of a sea of human eyes that gawked and stared. Even now, their whispers seemed to brush her ears.

"I would not ask anything of you, Isiilde. But I will offer."

"And what is your offer?"

"I offer you the throne," Pyrderi said.

His words struck more soundly than a sword. It cut to her marrow, stirring her blood. Time stretched, and in her mind's eye she saw all she could accomplish, all she could do to right the injustice against her kind.

Isiilde climbed the steps to the dais, and ran her fingers over the cold, unforgiving stone. "This throne?"

"Yes," Pyrderi said. "With no demands." He knelt, gazing up into her eyes. "I only ask that you let me serve as your general. Let me put the humans where they belong, and I assure you, our people will thrive."

Isiilde sat on the throne. It was, she found, more comfortable than she'd imagined, and the view from the dais was remarkable. Monolithic pillars stretched before her like soldiers in formation. The faces of the Voiceless called to her. *Command us*, they whispered.

Isiilde rubbed her hands along the armrests, considering the possibilities. The stone vibrated under her fingertips.

A world without humans. How tempting. That thought was like a small seed falling on fertile ground. Her mind grasped it, turned it over, and it blossomed into a beautiful idea. How simple, she thought. And then she looked at the Fey, their faces and joyless eyes, and she remembered another pair on a sunny beach, so long ago. Those eyes had shone with joy, and laughter, and everything warm. In the sea of faerie, she searched for those very same eyes.

"And what if I desire Marsais?"

"That is for him to decide, my Queen."

Pyrderi rose fluidly to his feet, and half turned, gesturing for his warriors to step aside. But Marsais did not immediately climb the steps. He stood still as a statue, his face unreadable, even to her.

Isiilde tucked her legs on the throne, and leaned back, making herself comfortable. She liked the view. "He is my druid. He will do as I say. Won't you, Marsais?"

Marsais inclined his head.

"I think he's right," she said. "Humans *are* a blight on this realm. I'm tired of their leers, sick of their butchery and lies. I know you are, too."

In answer, Marsais slowly climbed the steps, and knelt at her feet. "I am," he said, bowing his head.

The thing of it was, he spoke the truth.

Isiilde leant forward, grabbed Marsais' hair, and jerked back his head. He dropped to both knees.

"But why would I take this man when I can have you?" Isiilde looked to Pyrderi and saw a twisted pleasure in his pinprick eyes. "For my first act as Queen, I'd like to issue an order." She felt Marsais tense beneath her hand.

"As you wish." Pyrderi's eyes glinted with triumph.

"Kiss. My. Faerie. Arse!" She slapped her palm on the armrest, activating the teleportation rune. Marsais had been banned, but no one had bothered with a mere nymph.

The familiar pull of stone sucked her through, but at the last possible second, Marsais slipped from her hand.

Time stopped in that frantic moment. She saw his eyes: so calm, so sure, and full of love. And then the rune pulled her away.

CHAPTER 61

Pyrderi laughed, low and soft. The sound danced in the cavernous throne room. It might have been beautiful, if it had not chilled his bones. Marsais gripped the throne's armrest and climbed to his feet.

"I *like* that nymph," the Fey confided. "You were right to go to such lengths to keep her spirit intact. But she has nowhere to go. She's trapped herself, and you foolishly remained—to do what? You can't possibly hope to stand against me."

"I am not so boastful of my own meager skills."

"A pointless sacrifice, then."

Marsais shook his head. "I'm giving her time."

Pyrderi smiled, the look of a wolf about to devour its prey. "To do what? Hide?"

It was Marsais' turn to smile. He was the older, wiser wolf, and more than a little mad. "She's Isiilde. I'm certain she will find trouble in no time at all."

Pyrderi's humor faded. "She's young; still pliable. She's already taken her first steps with me. With time, I will mold her into a perfect queen. After all, she was never meant for you."

The words echoed his very own, and the visions he'd glimpsed over and again. "It was you."

Pyrderi gave a mocking bow. "The one and only."

"You manipulated my visions."

"You don't sound surprised."

"Time and distance bring clarity of thought."

Marsais had begun to question his visions after he absorbed the last fragments of the Orb. All this time, Pyrderi had been manipulating events from prison—delicately moving his pieces into play. And Marsais had been played for a fool.

"I seeped into your cracks," Pyrderi purred. "Your mind was so shattered you couldn't tell vision from lie. I learned much from Karbonek. The fiend manipulated and used me for his own gain. I had plenty of time to reflect on my mistakes, and I have little doubt you will, too."

Pyrderi drew a curved sword. It was elegant and deadly, and Marsais backed away, putting the throne between them.

"Don't worry, Marsais, you have until the Shadowed Dawn," Pyrderi mocked. He stepped off the dais with a twirl of his blade and the other Fey made room for a duel.

Another lie.

"You planted a seed in Tharios' mind and let it blossom," Marsais realized. "No matter what course he took, the tomb would be opened. You have no intention of releasing Karbonek."

This had all been an elaborate prison break.

"I won't make that mistake again," Pyrderi said. "I prefer to play the puppeteer. The power that lies in subtle suggestion is formidable."

"Subtlety is a lost art, I'm afraid." Resigned, Marsais limped down the steps to face his opponent.

"Butchery is the art of the day," Pyrderi agreed, circling him like a panther. But Marsais did not turn to watch the Fey's restless prowl; he was too busy thinking.

"What of the stave, then? What part did that play?" he asked. What was real; what was vision; and what was whispered suggestion?

Pyrderi stopped in front of him. "We were scattered, cut off from the ol'River, banished. I will bring my warriors back from the farthest realms."

"Noble of you, but where *is* the stave?" Marsais asked. "I doubt a prize like that would leave your hand."

"That does not concern you." The Fey's eyes blazed for a moment. Answer enough. "Your only concern is whether your spirit was cut from the ol'River as well. The Shattering affected you most curiously. I've long wondered about your scar. I think a part of you is drifting. After today, you'll be lost for eternity—a Fate worse than oblivion."

"I've long wondered, too," Marsais admitted. "But the question you should really be asking yourself is the one that Isiilde said matters most."

"And what is that?"

"*Who* am I, Pyrderi?"

The Fey cocked his head. And Marsais struck.

CHAPTER 62

Isiilde landed on the floor—alone and desperate. She blinked at her surroundings. The Archlord's study was nearly barren. Only a few artifacts remained. Her frost bear pelt was gone, leaving the stone floor naked.

It made her ache for Marsais. The thought of him brought up a well of oaths. She knew what the man was about. He intended to sacrifice himself—to give her a chance to run.

Isiilde had no intention of running away. She darted from the barren study, sped past doors, and skidded around a corner, flying into the alcove at the end of the hallway. There she stopped, hand poised over the teleportation rune that would take her back to his side.

What was she going to do against an army of Fey?

Isiilde hesitated, chewing on her lip. Her fire hadn't been enough for the Fomorri. And it certainly wouldn't be enough for the ice elemental.

Time pressed on her shoulders. Every wasted second felt like it would be Marsais' last. She'd not waste his sacrifice—a strategy was needed. With that realization, an idea sparked in her mind.

Isiilde hurried back down the hallway and stopped in front of the vault. The door was cracked. She peeked inside, and was dismayed to find it as barren as the rest of Marsais' study.

"Bloody Void," she muttered. What now? She started to turn, but stopped. It was not *entirely* empty. A crude circle had been drawn on the stone floor. It looked like chalk. And it filled her with hope.

Isiilde stepped to the center of the circle. "Witman *is* Wondrous," she said with feeling.

The stone underfoot turned to air. For a terrifying second, she fell. Then landed on a slippery mess.

Isiilde gagged at the rotting fish. She scrambled away, but didn't get far. The stinking room was small, and a single Everlight flickered in a rusty sconce, revealing walls of bristling spikes, every tip aimed at her.

A sound whipped her head upwards. Gears turned, chains moved, and a split second later a net plucked her and the fish off the floor.

Isiilde fought against the rope as the world spun. "Blast you, Witman. Marsais needs help!" she screamed.

Fire leapt to her hands.

"Not fire!" called a frantic voice.

The net released its hold and she fell, landing with a thud. The rotting, smoking fish plopped on top of her, burying her in stench. Her fire was smothered. A sound like a rummaging badger came to her, and large, stubby hands pulled her free.

"Oh, it's you," a gruff voice said.

Isiilde fell to her hands and knees, and retched. A pair of curled carpet slippers met her eye. She looked up, past the patched trousers, the lime green waistcoat with little yellow flowers, and into the face of the legendary enchanter.

Witman smoothed two strands of greying hair over his bald pate, and looked beyond her at the wall of spikes. "Where's the laddie?"

"Hiding in the fish," she snapped, climbing to her feet. "Marsais needs your help."

Witman retrieved a pair of half-moon spectacles from his waistcoat pocket and threaded the wire over his ears. He squinted at the fish, then pushed the spectacles down to the tip of his nose so he might get a better view. "I don't see him."

"He's in the throne room. Pyrderi Har'Feydd and the Fey are back."

"Oh, is that all? They never left, lass," Witman said with a shrug. "But don't you worry, the laddie can watch himself."

Witman turned and waved a hand. A segment of the spiky wall swung out, and the dwarf walked through.

"Not this time, Witman," she said, following on his heels. Her next words died on her tongue. Isiilde gawked at the space. She had walked from filth into an elegant sitting room. The gleam of rich woods, Xaionian rugs, and plush leather sitting chairs shone in the light of a cheerful fire.

Witman walked over to a decanter and poured himself an ample glass of some golden liquid. "I'm not sure the laddie would want you to 'ave this, but I won't tell."

Isiilde's ears twitched. "Witman," she said, taking a deep breath. "I *need* your help. Marsais could very well be dead already."

"I can't blood—" The dwarf cleared the curse from his throat. "Bring the lad back from the dead."

"No, but you can bloody well tell me where his treasure is." She advanced on the dwarf, and he backpedaled, retreating from the enraged nymph.

"It's mine," he defended. "As payment for services rendered."

"Payment for what?"

"I was hired to open his vault."

"You mean you *stole* his treasure," she corrected.

Witman smoothed his tattered waistcoat, and drew himself up. "I did not."

"That's what it's called when you open a vault that doesn't belong to you, then empty it into your hole."

"This is my workshop."

"You've been hiding here while people have been dying."

"I've been working, lass," he grunted. "People die, that's what they do. None of my concern."

"I'll tell the *Others*," she threatened.

Witman clutched his heart. "You cruel creature," he spluttered. "You wouldn't."

"I would," she said with relish.

The color drained from his face. "I'll need payment."

Isiilde wanted to strangle the enchanter. "You can have his treasure."

"I already have it."

"Because you stole it," she pointed out.

Before he could argue, she loosened the string of her pouch and pulled out the jagged sun. It crawled over her skin, and she dropped it on the carpet.

Witman set down his glass, not caring that the table was ten feet away, and stepped forward. He adjusted his spectacles and bent close. "I haven't seen this beauty in *ages*. Where did you find it?"

"It doesn't matter." She snatched a handkerchief from his pocket and used it to pick up the artifact. "I need to use it to bind the elemental in the throne room."

Witman scratched his head. "Why don't you just stick it on the stave and call it good?"

"I don't know where the stave is. Can I use it without the other pieces?"

Witman frowned at her. "Can you use a wagon without its wheels, lass?"

"If it's on snow and it has runners, then yes."

Witman chortled. "I like how you think. But that makes it a sleigh, and that's no good without snow. Using this artifact without the stave is like turning summer to winter."

"Can't we just stick it on another stave?"

Witman huffed. "Now you're asking for pigs to pull an ale wagon."

She sighed. "Can you make another stave?"

"Oh, now ye want me to put wings on the pigs."

"You are Witman the *Wondrous*."

"And I always require payment."

"If you help me help my friends, then you can keep the artifact."

Witman rubbed his beard. After a moment of consideration, he spit on his palm, and thrust it at her. Isiilde frowned at his hand. With a sigh, she spat on her own, and sealed the agreement.

"I'll need a bit o' your hair."

"What?"

"Your hair."

"Why?"

He squinted at her. "We have an agreement. It doesn't give you the right to question my methods."

Isiilde yanked out a few strands of her hair, and handed them over. Witman stuffed them in his waistcoat pocket, then held the artifact up to the light, studying it from all angles. She waited, but all he did was carry on a long mumbling conversation with himself.

The nymph grew impatient. "Witman, we have to go. Now. What are you going to do?"

"I'm going to help your friends, lass." He made a shooing gesture towards the door. "Get on with you. Even as lovely as you are, I can't work with you staring down my neck."

"I need the stave; I need it to work."

"Per our agreement," he agreed.

"How long will it take?"

"Soon." Witman flashed his teeth.

One moment she stood in his workshop, and the next she was lying on the stone floor in the vault. She hopped to her feet in the center of the circle. "Witman is Wondrous," she bit out. When nothing happened, she tried again. "Witman is a lying bastard!" Nothing.

Clenching her fists, she raced from the vault, hesitated in the hallway, then shot towards Marsais' old study. She didn't even have Rivan's sword. There had to be something in there she could use.

Desperate, Isiilde began rifling through objects and books. Recalling his cabinet of potions, she sped into his bedchambers.

The bed was gone, and so were all his potions, books, and clothes. The room looked empty, and it made her sad. Her gaze settled on the massive armoire in the corner, then slid right off to the floor. A small wine flask and a rune-etched flagon sat forgotten on the stone.

Isiilde cocked her head. She knew that flagon. She'd held it after breaking into Marsais' vault. At the time, there had been two. One contained Luccub. But she'd never got around to opening the other.

Marsais had known the imp's name and been able to command it. Would he be able to control whatever was in this second flagon?

Isiilde grabbed the flagon and stuffed it into her pouch. Feeling optimistic, she dumped the flask of Primrose wine in, too. At the very least, her plan would finally sate her curiosity.

CHAPTER 63

A SINGLE THREAD in a weave held together the weft, the very fabric of an enchantment. A Barrier was no different. Marsais plucked a thread from the weave, and his Barrier unraveled like a slingshot.

Light flared, blinding the Fey, and a split second after, a thunderous explosion rocked the throne room. It blew the warriors off their feet. But Pyrderi remained standing, his hand outstretched, deflecting the chaos of runes.

With deft strokes, Marsais sent a beam of white hot energy at the Fey. It blasted through Pyrderi's defenses, but he dropped, rolling under the charge. He came up with a slash of his sword and a wave of blue flame.

Marsais scattered the fire with a gesture, but the blade tore through his shirt, biting into flesh. He grunted, throwing a bind at Isiilde's discarded sword—the same that bore the mark of the ol'Father. It leapt to his hand and he brought it up, catching Pyrderi's attack. Steel rang, energy burst, and the two combatants were flung apart.

Marsais slid across the marble floor. The air around Pyrderi rippled like a mirage, his edges became indistinct. With swift silence, the Fey wavered, then reappeared—right behind him.

Marsais raised his sword, catching the descending blade and diverting its course. The blade bit into a Voiceless, slicing through the stone face. Marsais drove his foot into Pyrderi's knee. He staggered and skipped back, and his warriors closed in.

Marsais slapped the stone. At his command, Time stopped and the Fey were caught in a moment, but only for a breath. It was enough.

He rolled through the charging Fey, and came up on his feet, sword biting into the back of the first, and another, a third, and finally a fourth.

Time marched on.

Marsais slashed his own arm. Blood dripped onto the floor, and he directed Abyssal words into that crimson puddle. Darkness rose from the blood, sweeping over the throne room. And to his blood, he bound light.

The Fey were blind in the darkness. He was not.

Pyrderi called to the ice elemental in the ancient tongue. The old one stirred and shifted, and its creaking rocked the throne room. It passed through the shields and crashed through the twining gate.

Blue flame burst in the darkness. Pyrderi was haloed in its glow. With a shout, he charged, and Marsais met him with uncanny speed. The men moved across the dark throne room—one bathed in cool flame and the other possessed of unholy sight.

Blades and power clashed. Steel bit again and again, and blood flowed freely from both men. Pyrderi gripped his blade, and drove the hilt into Marsais' face, quick and brutal. Marsais staggered from the blow, tracing a final rune, unleashing his weave. White, hot light burst from his palm. It shattered the darkness.

Pyrderi brought up his sword, catching the pure energy, channeling it through the blade and sending it ricocheting back. The weave hit Marsais with a force that flung him off his feet. He landed with a grunt. The sword flew from his hand and he stared at the ceiling, so far away. Blood filled his mouth.

Pyrderi raised his sword for the killing blow, but he moved sluggishly, as if through sand. Marsais had all the time in the world. It flowed through his veins.

He saw each lick of flame outlining the Fey god; his sword, too far to reach; and the burnt corpse of Zianna and the forgotten spirit blade.

Marsais flung out his arm. Time sped up again. His fingers curled around the dagger, and he threw. The spirit blade sunk into Pyrderi's gut, but his sword still moved. It plunged through Marsais' armor weave, breaking the last of the threads, piercing flesh.

Marsais did not scream. He did not feel a thing, only a vague awareness of a blade protruding from his own chest.

Pyrderi abandoned his sword, and grabbed the dagger in his gut, wrenching it free. It fell from his limp fingers, and he followed. A mist rose from his body, his spirit trying to escape, but it was pulled back down; trapped for eternity.

The air was icy, and Marsais heard the creak and rasp of an approaching titan. Calmly, he grabbed the protruding blade and yanked the sword from his own body. He felt so very far away. Something heavy and solid pressed down on his chest. He found it hard to breathe.

Beside him, Pyrderi stirred. One breath, and then another. The Fey crawled forward, grabbing the spirit blade on his way.

Pyrderi's face swam into view, and Marsais stared helplessly into his cold eyes. "You didn't think it would be that easy, did you?"

Pyrderi sliced open his shirt. Marsais felt the cold caress of a blade over his scar, then the tip, poised over his heart. He grabbed weakly at Pyrderi's forearm.

"Are you sure you want to kill me?" Marsais choked on the blood bubbling from his lips.

Pyrderi froze at the question. His eyes narrowed to pinpoints, and he looked from Marsais' face to the scar slashing across his chest. In the intimacy of murderous intent, Pyrderi finally had an answer to the question of *Who*. He sucked in a breath. "You *are* mad."

Marsais started laughing, blood spraying with every wheeze. "So they say." And then he screamed a word of power; a lost word.

Pure, silver light flared across his scar and burst from his hands. The spirit blade turned to ash, and the Sylph's power slammed into Pyrderi, flinging him across the throne room.

When the Orb's light faded, Marsais tried to rise, but failed. He fell back on the stone. Helpless before the approaching elemental, he could only laugh.

The world was fading. But a streak of red caught his eye. It seemed a dream.

A lithe woman with hair like fire and an entirely too impish face came into view. "This is probably *very* unwise."

With a flourish, she uncorked a flagon.

CHAPTER 64

"Can you heal it?" Zoshi asked. There was hope in that question.

"I'm sorry. I can't put your eye back." Considering what he'd been through, Acacia was amazed he was alive.

The boy nodded, resigned. She gently packed a clean, herb-soaked cloth from her kit into the socket. When it was secure, she tied a bandage around his head. "We'll have to clean it better when we get out of here."

Acacia glanced at her other patient. Morigan was still breathing, but it was shallow and uneven. She'd found a cloak in the rubble and laid it over her, but there was nothing more she could do.

Acacia began sifting through the debris, searching for more survivors. The body of a spiky-haired gnome caught her eye. Eiji had stood with Tharios and poisoned Oenghus. That was months ago. Acacia nudged the gnome with her boot. Her throat had been slashed, and the body was already stiffening.

The bodies of human and Fey lay in the wreckage, but mist clung to the Fey like a spider's web. Acacia had fought Blighted and Voidspawn, and countless other creatures. She knew from harsh experience that things did not always stay dead in Fyrsta.

Acacia drew her sword to chop off a Fey's head, but another body caught her eye. A female Rahuatl. The woman's skin was more tarnished than copper, and she was deathly still.

Acacia had some experience with the race. The warriors entered a trance-like state to heal wounds. Only there were no obvious wounds on her body.

Isiilde had mentioned having a Rahuatl friend.

Acacia crouched beside the body. She put a hand over the woman's breast, and bent close, listening for a breath. A faint heartbeat pulsed against her palm. Surprise shook her to action. Acacia closed her eyes, silently praying to the Sylph. Silver light flared around the Rahuatl, seeping into her bones and burning away the poison in her blood.

The Rahuatl took a deep breath. Her color returned, and she slept, deep and peaceful. As Acacia dragged her towards Morigan, the earth began to tremble, and a panicked voice called to her.

The adjoining hallway was empty, save for a swirl of mist, but the boy was not looking at the sickly, reaching tendrils. He was pointing at a far wall. A white line of chalk appeared, steadily growing on the stone.

"Stay with Morigan," she ordered. Acacia unslung her shield and stepped over to the wall with a sword in hand.

The chalk curved in a wide circle; the end reaching towards the beginning. When the two tips touched, the stone rippled, and a dwarf stepped out. A sleek, arrow-like object hovered over his open palm. It turned like a compass needle, pointing directly at her. The dwarf looked from his hand to the paladin, and gave a start of surprise.

"Stay where you are," she ordered.

The dwarf threw up his free hand. "Now, now, don't be hasty."

"Who are you?"

"I'm passing through—that's all."

"Your name, Dwarf."

"If you say so."

Acacia pointed the tip of her sword at the man. "Are you a resident of the castle?"

"I'm out for a walk." The dwarf pushed his spectacles farther up his nose and squinted at a dead Fey by his feet. "This place has really gone downhill since I was last here. Never liked the last Archlord. Didn't have the laddie's flair."

"The laddie?"

His gaze strayed to the Sacred Sun around her neck, and he cleared his throat. "Not that I was close to him, mind you." He tucked the slim arrow into his waistcoat pocket.

Acacia glanced at the chalk circle and back to the disheveled man. "Are you a Wise One?"

The dwarf started chortling, a wheezing laugh that brought tears to his eyes. "Oh, aye, real wise I am. Don't need a fancy robe for that." He rubbed his hands together, and his eyes settled on the remains of Soisskeli's Stave. He edged two small steps in that direction.

Acacia quickly stepped in front of the artifact. "What do you want with the stave?"

He feigned surprise. "What do *you* want with it?"

"I'm asking the questions."

"That's not a question; that's a statement," the dwarf said.

"Are you a friend of Marsais?"

"That depends," he said slowly. "Are you with *Them*?"

"Them?"

"The *Others*," he whispered.

"I... no. Who are the others?"

"Exactly!"

Acacia's head hurt. Beyond a doubt, the man knew Marsais. She lowered her sword.

The dwarf whistled his way towards the stave, scooted around her, and picked it up, studying it carefully. His eyes darted to her.

The stave was splintered and cracked, and the Gateway enchantment had been turned to ash. Despite that, she watched him warily. When he pulled out an intact end piece, the very same they'd taken from Finnow's Spire, Acacia raised her sword to his neck. "*Where* did you get that?" she demanded.

"The lass gave it to me," he spluttered.

Acacia hesitated.

"The laddie's in danger."

"Who's the laddie?"

"Marsais."

Acacia would not use the term 'laddie' for the immortal. "*Who* are you?" she asked again.

The dwarf cleared his throat. "Witman the Wondrous. I've been hired for a bit o' work. So if you don't mind..." He put a finger to the tip of her sword, and nudged it aside.

"You're Witman the Wondrous? *The* Enchanter?"

"Unless the *Others* switched me when I was soused. I might not know. Now there's a thought. Would *They* do that to me?" He cleared his throat, and touched his nose. At first tentatively, and then with more force, squashing the bulbous appendage. "No, no, I am me."

He looked relieved.

Stories of the enchanter were legendary. Even the Guardians of Iilenshar did not cross Witman the Wondrous. Given the chalk circle and his unlikely entrance, she could not think of another explanation.

Acacia sheathed her sword.

Witman twisted the jagged sun onto the intact end of the staff. "There. Fixed. Maybe." He scratched his beard, shrugged, and handed the stave to Acacia. "The lass seemed to think this would be needed. There's trouble in the throne room."

At his words, the ground shook with more vigor and a crack split the stone wall. Witman was nearly thrown off his feet.

When the stone settled, Acacia studied the stave in her hand. It was foul, both cold and sticky all at once. She wanted to fling the thing across the room. "The boy and the two women here... Will you watch them for me?"

"Are they trouble?"

"No, they're injured."

"That's trouble."

"One of us needs to get this to Isiilde."

"That's why I gave it to you."

Acacia grit her teeth. "Don't leave them," she ordered, and took off running.

"That's my payment," Witman yelled at her back. "So don't try to run off with it. I'll find you."

It was not a threat, but a fact. No one, legend went, crossed Witman the Wondrous.

CHAPTER 65

Smoke billowed from the flagon like a chimney. Isiilde dropped the flagon, and kicked it towards the approaching ice elemental. The smoke was black and choking and all-consuming, and a moment later, a monstrous coal-black face poked out of the smoke: slitted eyes, large fangs, flesh scaled and thorny. A pair of leathery wings spread with a snap, and a tail lashed, felling columns with a sweep.

Isiilde's mouth fell open. It was a dragon.

The dragon sucked in a great breath that stirred her hair. Veins of molten heat flared over its body, and then it roared. A wave of flame shot towards the nymph, rushing into her arms like a child to its mother.

Isiilde gathered the fireball with a rising song, and for a moment, she stood in rapture, clothed in a rush of flame.

The dragon cocked its head. She gave it a secretive smile, and spun, hurling the fireball into a knot of Fey warriors. It seared the flesh from their bones. Weapons and charred bodies dropped to the ground, and the remaining Fey scattered in terror.

At the sound of creaking ice, the dragon spun, searching out the largest, most threatening foe like a brute in a tavern. The two titans clashed with a stone shattering crack.

Isiilde was thrown to the ground. As the earth shook, and stone rained all around her, she scrambled over to Marsais. With every wheezing breath, blood bubbled from his lips.

A column tipped, crashing into another. In the dust and fire and ice, Isiilde wove a quick armor weave, then shielded Marsais with her own body. When the crashing was over, she opened her eyes. A large chunk of stone had landed a foot from her.

Isiilde pressed a hand over a hole in his chest, trying to stem the blood seeping from the wound. "Marsais," she said desperately. "You can't leave."

His eyes were unfocused. And fading fast. She brushed the hair back from his face, and his eyes focused for a moment. He tried to rise, but barely got his head off the ground.

"Go," he wheezed.

"Not without you." She tried to pull him across the floor, but he was far too heavy for a nymph.

A Fey leapt over the rubble and came for her. Isiilde sent a blast of searing flame into the warrior, but he caught the burst on his shield and kept coming.

A stone pegged the Fey on the side of the head. It was a small distraction, but it was enough. With flashing fingers, she switched tune, throwing a grease enchantment at his feet. The Fey slipped and fell, and the fire clinging to his clothes mingled with the grease. He went up like a torch.

Isiilde snatched up Rivan's sword and charged with the point leveled like a lance, impaling him through the gut.

Elam hopped over a fallen stone. "Kiss my arse!" he yelled, loading another stone into his sling. She had forgotten all about the boy.

Isiilde wrenched the sword free and started to toss it aside, but thought better of it. With deft fingers, she traced a feather rune over Marsais, layered it with air and a spirit, and attached a sturdy bind. Marsais floated off the ground. His entire body convulsed with pain, and she quickly lowered him, switching focus, until he brushed the ground, cushioned by a mattress of air.

Not near as heavy, Isiilde grabbed his wrist and pulled him towards the shattered gate. Three Fey appeared, grinning like maniacal hounds.

"Take him!" she ordered Elam.

The boy grabbed Marsais by the arm and took off as she called to her fire. Flame leapt to her hands, rippling along the blade. The ol'Father's wolves glowed red on the steel.

A sword flashed from the smoke. Isiilde braced herself, but it wasn't a Fey. It was a paladin.

Acacia rushed into the fray, slamming her shield into the first and following with her sword. "Go!" she barked.

Isiilde ran towards Marsais and Elam, but another Fey leapt in her path. She swung her burning sword. Steel bit into flesh, and she wrenched it free. She did not stop; she did not look back, but grabbed Marsais' arm and dragged him through the shattered gate into a realm of ice. Only the realm was melting.

At the end of the great hall, ice and water dripped down the Storm Gates, and with every bellowing roar and lash of tail, a piece of the castle gave way.

The dragon rammed the elemental, but the creature of ice only turned to gas and reformed, swinging a massive fist at the scaled monstrosity. A tail crashed into another column and an entire section caved in. Isiilde and Elam started running.

Ten feet from the exit, a final slab of ice slipped off the gates, and the Storm Gates slammed shut with a flare of wards.

"Bollocks!" she screamed at the gates.

Acacia sprinted down the center of the great hall. Her shield was gone, and her arm hung bloody, but she had her sword. The dragon squeezed through the Nameless chamber and spread its wings in the expansive hall.

Elam dropped Marsais' arm, and turned, advancing on the dragon with a slow whirl of his sling. The boy took aim. With a rush, he put power into the swing, and the stone shot from its cradle. It soared through the air and bounced off the dragon's head. The beast bellowed.

Isiilde pulled Marsais behind the relative safety of a pillar, and hurried back to the gates. The wards glowed and pulsed. She had always wanted to unravel these gates. She raised a hand—

"Wait!" Acacia screamed.

Isiilde glanced over her shoulder. Acacia skidded to a stop and yanked a stave from her belt. It was topped with a familiar artifact.

Isiilde gaped in surprise. But there was no time to ask where she'd gotten it. Acacia raised the stave over her head. Barbs dug into her palm, drawing blood, and for a heartbeat, the jagged sun gleamed. And then it died.

The dragon kept charging.

Acacia dove to the side, and Isiilde and the boy followed. There was thunder, a roar, the song of fire, and a quaking that stole her breath.

Isiilde threw herself over Marsais. The air smelt like the aftermath of a forest fire—sharp and tingling and full of char.

As stones crumbled and columns crashed, a cool wind swept over her, bringing a flurry of snow. Isiilde cracked open an eye. Through the swirling wreckage, she watched the dragon take flight, soaring into a wintery sky.

Sky. Fresh air. The Storm Gates had been blown open, its wards broken.

Acacia dragged herself over. Wasting no time, she laid a hand on Marsais' chest and closed her eyes. Silver light flowed down her arm to his body. Acacia drew back with a gasp.

"What is it?" Isiilde asked. She pressed her fingertips under his jaw and was relieved to feel a pulse.

"I can't get all of it," Acacia said. "He's... difficult to heal." But he was breathing easier. "You both need to leave."

Acacia climbed to her feet. Determination was etched on her face as she looked back at what remained of the throne room.

"Where is Oen?" Isiilde asked.

"I think he went down... into the tomb."

"Where is that?"

"I'm not sure."

Acacia had every intention of finding out, but she never got the chance. The earth convulsed, and it did not stop.

CHAPTER 66

Bodies littered the hallways. Soldiers with red armbands, Isle Guards, Wise Ones, peasants—children. Some were still dying, but Oenghus did not stop. He raced down, and farther still, until he stood at the mouth of a gaping tunnel. A line of Fey blocked the way, silent, watchful, shrouded in fog. The warriors might as well have been formed from ice. They knew what he was after—their lifeline.

The ritual had never been severed. As long as that Chain remained, the Fey were tethered to this realm. He knew that as sure as he knew his name.

Oenghus glared at the warriors. He reached for his sacred flask, and drank deeply. Fire raced through his veins, muscles bulged, and his skin hardened. He shook the rock with his roar.

Slàtra flared to life. A crackling net of lightning spread over his skin as he beat his hammer against his shield in challenge. The wild god charged the line.

He hit the Fey like a storm. Red filled his vision and carnage sang to his ears. In that haze, down the long tunnel, the slaughterer of thousands added more blood to his hands. One pale face after another fell, and each cut and slice against his skin drove his fury, until he was drunk on it. Time fell away, leaving only the moment.

Instinct pulled him forward, through a maze of tunnels that his feet had walked in another life. This was his Fate, to die in the dark yet again. Only this time, he would not leave the thing half done.

When the last Fey's skull caved to his hammer, Oenghus stood panting. His chest heaved, and his senses were filled with blood—some of it his own.

Memories drifted in the haze. An ancient battle surged across the cavern, phantoms drifting in time. Pyrderi Har'Feydd and an army of Fey against Hengist and his loyal warriors. And the wild god was there, too.

A wave of disorientation washed over him. He had been here before. And died.

Oenghus shook the vision from his mind, and stepped into the tomb of fallen legends. In the light of his hammer, he saw the bones of companions long dead. And that Chain. It rasped against the stone, pulsing like a heartbeat. For millennia, it had tethered the fiendish nightmare to this realm.

The sight filled him with rage. He stalked towards that Chain, until his light illuminated Karbonek's prison—a void in the stone; a crack in the earth; a tear in the realm.

Terror beat from the dark portal on powerful wings, and fear crawled along the Chain like a living thing. Inky tentacles reached from the void, slithering from the edges, reaching through and curling around the stone walls.

A vision, a memory, or reality? Oenghus did not care. He approached with a roar, shaking stone and bones.

Rage was his shield.

The thick Chain slithered and rasped and he followed it to the void. There it rose, leaving the ground, wrapped around the fiendish god within.

Oenghus tossed aside his targe and gripped the Chain with his left hand. With a booming chant, he sent white furious energy crackling into the ancient metal. It heated and sizzled, and he pounded his hammer against the links like a smith at his anvil. Again and again, until his arm went numb with the ring of iron.

As he beat at the links, inky tendrils of shadow reached and grew, twining around the Chain like vines.

He did not let go.

Thunder bellowed with every crack. The Chain jerked and twisted, glowing red with heat. Shadowy tendrils writhed and reached, wrapping around his arm, binding him to the metal.

Oenghus ignored the pain, and gripped the tether with all his might, his hammer swinging, pounding, crushing the metal.

The Chain gave. But when it snapped back like a whipcord, it pulled him towards the void. The force of the tug wrenched his shoulder from its socket. With a bellow, he dug in his heels, fighting against a tremendous force.

Karbonek was dragging him inside.

Desperate, he beat at the shadowy tentacles, driving his hammer into the tethers, but the weapon passed through the shadows. Oenghus clenched his teeth, gathered his strength, and heaved, pulling the Chain an inch out of the portal.

An eye moved beyond the veil, watching, waiting. And realization came like a flash. The fiend wanted the god to tug and fight—to drag himself away. In saving himself, he would unleash the fiend.

Braced against the stone, Oenghus raised his hammer and hurled it into the void. Energy crackled and surged, and the eye swimming in the void jerked back. The Chain yanked Oenghus forward, but he stopped on the edge.

Shadowy tendrils twined around his forearm and with every passing second, they reached for more, binding his own Fate to the Chain.

"You bastard!" he roared, drawing a knife. "Kiss my arse!"

Oenghus sent a charge of energy into his blade, and when the metal heated with lightning, he drove the blade into the crook of his arm. He cut and sliced, and pried with savage strength. White hot fire burned along his nerves. His knees went weak.

With a last roar, he cracked the joint. Flesh gave way, and Oenghus fell to the ground. The Chain snapped back into the portal, taking his arm.

The portal collapsed in on itself. And the earth quaked, a great rumbling in its core. Bleeding and delirious, Oenghus dragged himself across the chamber, laughing along the way. The link was severed, but the tear in the realm was still there.

"Never again!" he bellowed, and added his own voice to the quake, bringing the mountain down on his head.

CHAPTER 67

Panic reigned. Soldiers and paladins fled the inner bailey, running across the quaking ground. Isiilde and Acacia joined the stream, dragging Marsais over the trampled snow.

A crack split the earth and sundered the Spine. Isiilde looked back in time to see the tower collapse. The ground shook, its thunder stealing her breath.

A cloud of earth and stone enveloped her. She coughed, fighting for breath as she blindly dragged Marsais through the ruin. A hand clamped around her arm and dragged her into the gateway tunnel.

As the world fell, she huddled over Marsais, choking and gasping for air. It seemed to last a lifetime. And when the earth finally settled, it came as a surprise. The silence was shocking.

White dust swirled in the air, tickling her nose. Isiilde sneezed, fire bursting from her ears with each jerk. "Sorry," she wheezed.

Acacia climbed to her feet. She was covered in white stone dust and streaks of dark blood. A smaller chalk figure uncurled to stare numbly at the ruins. Elam's eyes were wide with shock.

Isiilde looked down at her own body. The dragon had burnt her clothes to a crisp, but her pouch had survived and the dust clung like a second skin. She checked on Marsais. He looked like a corpse, but he was breathing—that's all that mattered.

Acacia offered her a handkerchief, which she pressed to her nose. The sneezing stopped, and the two women staggered out of the gatehouse, leaving Elam to protect Marsais.

The Spine was gone. All that remained was a great mountain of rubble, a crushed keep, and a single guardian statue. A shimmer of power still crackled from its massive stone sword. It was surreal—a dream—and Isiilde drifted unattached over the broken ground.

"By the gods," Acacia murmured.

"My father..." Despair spurred her towards the ruin. Numb to the cold and pain slicing the soles of her feet, she sprang over crevices and cracks and bodies, racing through the slush of snow and stone.

A chalk-caked man stood in front of the remaining guardian statue. The man was not her father. Thedus caught the nymph as she tried to run into the ruined keep.

"Let go!" she hissed. But he held fast.

Thedus looked into her eyes. His own were milky and half-blind, but she felt *seen*. The entirety of his focus settled on her, and he gave a shake of his head.

That slight gesture drained the last of her strength. Isiilde dropped to her knees in the soot and slush, and stared numbly at the ruins.

An armored hand rested on her shoulder. "The mist is rising," Acacia said. "Come away, Isiilde. We can't leave Marsais alone."

Isiilde let the paladin draw her back, but halfway across the bailey, a chant rose into the air. It was more a rasp from a damaged, little-used voice. Thedus croaked the Lore. He stood before the single guardian statue with his arms raised towards the grey sky.

A beam of sunlight cut through the clouds to touch the tip of the statue's sword. It flared for a blinding moment, then the castle shield crackled and gathered like a vortex, sucking the mist into its core.

Acacia shielded Isiilde with her own body. But there was no explosion, no burst of energy—only silence as the mist was sucked into the shield and a bright beam shot towards the sun.

Thedus lowered his arms. The clouds closed over the sun, and he fell over. Acacia rushed over to heal him, but when the flare of healing faded, she looked up with a shake of her head.

Isiilde felt hollow—a husk of flesh standing in ruin, unable to move or even fall over.

Other ghost-like forms drifted out into the open, and then one stalked across the wreckage towards the nymph.

"Isiilde." It was not a kind voice, but the sharp edge it usually possessed was absent. Thira was covered in blood and dust, and her shoulders were hunched. A dozen things seem to flicker across the woman's face at once. For a flash, emotion softened the flint in her eyes, but as fast as it appeared, it fled. "I suppose you had something to do with this."

Isiilde looked Thira straight in the eye. "I did. And I am not sorry in the least."

There was a gleam of pride in the woman's eyes. "Finally," she said. "You've grown a backbone."

"If this is how it feels, then you have my pity."

Isiilde turned on her heel and walked towards the gatehouse, back to Marsais. He was alive. She held onto that thought, and she held on to him, laying her ear over his heart, listening to each comforting beat.

At some point in that numb haze, a cloak was draped over her shoulders. Barking orders echoed in the bailey, and the humans moved with purpose.

A gentle hand gripped her shoulder. "They've set up a makeshift infirmary. They're going to carry Marsais there."

Acacia looked as worn as she felt. And it took a moment for the words to work through her emptiness. Two paladins of the Blessed Order stood behind their captain. A stretcher lay on the ground. But Isiilde barely glanced at the men; her gaze strayed beyond, over their shoulders.

A line of chalk appeared on the rough stone. Acacia followed her gaze.

"Witman," both women said together.

Isiilde watched as the circle grew. It stopped halfway, disappeared, and started over again. The next circle was larger.

The stone wavered and a dwarf stepped out of his workshop.

Witman hooked his thumbs under his waistcoat, surveying the mess. When he saw the vast space where the Spine had once stood, he gave a low whistle.

"As fine a destruction as I've ever seen. Who in the Void released that dragon?" Witman asked.

"Pyrderi did it," Isiilde said. Some habits died hard.

"Iilenshar's gonna piss its divine pants." Witman began chortling. When he finally stopped wheezing, he wiped the laughter from his eyes and looked at the two women frowning at him. "Oh, look there, the laddie's fine. I told you, didn't I?"

"He nearly died," Isiilde said. She wanted to turn the enchanter into a crispy shell. The thought sparked flame, and fire smoldered in her eyes.

"I uhm..." Witman took a nervous step away. "Have come for my payment there." He pointed at the stave thrust through Acacia's belt.

"It didn't work," Isiilde growled. "That was our agreement."

Witman's eyes widened. "It was not."

"It was too," she argued. "I hired you to fix the stave."

"No, you didn't."

Fire burst to life around her hands, and her cloak smoldered.

"Wait now, no fire, lass."

Witman hastily reached under his waistcoat and yanked out a battered scroll. He opened it with a flick, and held it out to her. Puzzled, Isiilde let the flame fall and bent to the read the scrawl.

It was a long contract, written in tiny print with a sloppy hand. Her own hand decorated the very bottom. Tired and impatient, she directed a burst of fire at the thing. But the parchment flared and snuffed her flame.

Her ears twitched. "I didn't sign anything."

"Your word bound the contract, lass. There's no escaping it." He held out a hand.

"Fine, all right." There was no use in arguing. It wouldn't bring her father back.

Acacia handed over the stave.

Pleased, Witman tucked the stave through his belt. "Next time, lass, be more specific."

"I was."

He jabbed a stubby finger at a paragraph. "See, right here, it says, and I quote, 'If you help me help my friends, then you can keep the artifact.'"

Satisfied, Witman rolled up the scroll and tucked it under his waistcoat. With a twinkle in his eye, he snapped his fingers. The stone wavered, and Witman the Wondrous delivered his end of the bargain.

CHAPTER 68

THE FIRST THING he felt was the brush of fingertips across his forehead. He swam in a haze, and that idle, caressing touch pulled him to the surface.

Oenghus cracked open an eye. A dark-haired woman sat by his bed. Her lips curved in a smile.

He wanted to hold her and kiss those lips; to caress the face of the woman he loved. And in his mind, he reached for her, but nothing moved. His arm hurt, and his fingers burned. He stirred and looked at what was left of that arm—a bloodied, bandaged stub above the elbow.

Oenghus gasped in shock. It was real. Past *and* present memory.

"You've still got your cock and bollocks," Morigan said.

"Aye... there is that," he croaked, looking around the cell-like room. "Isiilde?"

"She's fine," Morigan assured. "And Marsais is recovering, too. Isiilde has been running herself ragged, bouncing from your room to his, waiting for you both to snap out of a fever."

Oenghus tried to rise, but he felt like half a man. With his remaining hand, he pushed himself to a sitting position, then slumped against a stone wall.

"Where is she?" he asked.

"I convinced her that Marsais needed a bedwarmer."

"Gods, don't remind me," he groaned.

"I can't think of a better man for that nymph. And neither can you."

Morigan gave him a knowing look. But as she reached for a mug on a nearby table, he noticed she was trying to hide a spasm of pain.

Oenghus glanced down at her legs, but a blanket covered them. "Can you walk?" he asked softly.

"With effort," she said, handing him the mug. "Iilenshar opened a portal a few hours after Witman hauled us out of his workshop. The castle is swarming with Wraith Guards and Clerics—what's left of it, at any rate. I had good care. We all did."

He sniffed at the mug and wrinkled his nose. It was water.

"I've got your grog. And no, you can't have it."

Oenghus muttered something rude, and drank. His head cleared and Morigan's words finally settled in. He looked up, startled. "Witman?"

"*The* Wondrous." She poured him another helping from a pitcher. "Isiilde hired the enchanter to help her friends. He pulled you out of that hole."

"How?"

Morigan lifted a shoulder. "In a wondrous way?"

Oenghus snorted at the woman. He set his mug down and took her hand. She squeezed it back. Morigan was pale and there was a strain around her eyes that worried him.

"Blood and ashes, woman, you look no better than I feel. It's frigid out. Get over here."

"You haven't seen yourself."

"I need a bedwarmer."

"Says the man who has kicked off my blankets for more years than I'll admit to."

"A hundred and fifty."

"Not counting the time between." Morigan eyed the bed. "I don't think that bed will hold us."

"Wouldn't be the first bed we broke."

"You brute."

"Shrew," he shot back, baring his teeth.

Morigan put weight on her good leg. With clenched teeth, she shifted from chair to bed. The wood creaked, but held, and after she scooted over to his right side, Oenghus slid the hem of her nightgown up her leg, revealing angry bruises and a heavily bandaged thigh. He sniffed at the poultice. "What did those clerical bastards slather on you?"

"I don't know," she sighed.

"You're the most gifted herbalist in the realm—what do you mean, you don't know?"

"I haven't bothered checking."

Oenghus frowned. After a moment, he gave her knee a soft squeeze and tugged on the blanket until she was under it with him. They sat with their backs to the stone.

"Brinehilde's dead," she said at last. "She died on her feet."

"Piss and wind," Oenghus sighed. She told him everything then. All that had happened since he'd been chased from the Isle. When Morigan fell silent, he wrapped his good arm around her, and she leaned in close.

"I'm sorry, Mori. I should have been here," he whispered against her hair.

"You had your own problems. If it weren't for the Fey, we'd have stopped Tharios ourselves."

A pleased sort of rumble vibrated from his chest. "I'd take two Nuthaanian women into battle over twenty men any day." At this, he fell silent, thinking of Brinehilde. "Gods, I'll miss that woman. She had a fine pair of breasts."

Morigan snorted. "You can raise a mug to her and the twins soon enough. I'm sure she'd be pleased."

"May she piss in the ol' River," he agreed.

"Without a doubt."

"Do you remember that time the three of us got soused during the Feast of Fools?"

"Three? You're forgetting Breeman."

His brows knitted together in thought.

Morigan patted his broad chest. "I'll remember Breeman, and you can keep forgetting he was there."

"Was he really?"

"You were distracted, Oen."

"Oh... aye." Oenghus grinned, and then a swell of emotion clutched his heart. He held her head against his chest and pressed his lips to her hair. "Gods, my girl, I thought I'd lost you."

"I'm as stubborn as you."

Oenghus held on tighter, with his one good arm, aching to hold her with two.

"The Sylph asked me to watch over your hide. I couldn't very well go and die," she said.

"Aye, well, I hold her to her word, too. I may have told her to do the same for you."

Morigan pulled back, searching his eyes. "The Sylph did, and more. Yasimina's ritual would have done me in. Besides, without me, there'd be no one to patch you up after you do something stupid."

He shook his head. "You just like me in bed."

"You make a fine furnace," she agreed. Her eyes dropped to his throat, and she toyed absently with his beard. "If Pyrderi hadn't put that hot blade to my leg, I'd have bled to death."

"That Fey was a bastard, Mori."

"After what Isiilde told me, given the same cards in life, I think we'd all become him."

Oenghus touched her cheek. "Not you. You'd have stopped long before getting to where he did."

"And neither would you."

"That's because I have you to knock sense into me now."

"It's been a long road."

"Ulfhid—" Oenghus stopped, closing his eyes as a wash of ancient memories welled from another life. When he spoke again, it was of things never uttered. But it needed saying. "*I regret taking sides with humans. If I had stayed out of that war, he and his might never have taken such a dark path. But at the time I went where there was war; I was never one to much think on the end, or which side might be right.*"

"There's never a right side in a war. It all leads to the same end: misery, suffering, and hate." It was, he knew, precisely why she set her axe aside to walk the path of a healer.

"I do love you in armor, though. Gets me all hard."

"Everything gets you hard," she said, patting his leg. The touch proved her point. "Your cock is always a reliable health gauge. It's a sure sign you're feeling better. You gave the healers a scare, you know. They were about to shave off your beard."

Oenghus growled. "I'd have—"

"Slaughtered the lot of them and pissed on their graves," she interrupted. "Yes, I told them that's what you'd do. They wisely decided to let you die with it on your chin."

Oenghus grunted with satisfaction, and raised his hand to stroke his beard. Or tried to. The stub of an arm moved, and he looked at the ruin. "Void." He closed his eyes and let his head hit stone. In his mind, those fingers moved. They curled as if they were still there. "How will I—" The words stuck in his throat.

How will I heal?

Morigan brushed the hair from his brow. "I'm sorry, Oen."

He forced his lips to move. "I can't heal one-handed." The words thudded in the room like a hammer's blow.

"You'll manage."

But he shook his head.

"Can you plow one-handed?" she demanded.

"Not you—takes two hands and all my energy for that."

Morigan slapped his chest. "If you can plow, then you can heal."

He looked doubtful. "I don't heal with my cock."

She buried her fingers in the thick hair on his chest—mostly grey where years ago it had been black. "It's been my cure for many a night."

Oenghus did not rise to her bait. He was silent. And that worried her.

"All I'm saying," she said. "Is that if the will is there, you'll find a way. You're a berserker who can heal and weave. Have some faith in yourself. I *know* you, and there isn't a more blockheaded, stubborn skull than yours."

Mist filled his eyes, and he nodded, blinking it away.

Morigan stretched to kiss his lips. Some life returned to him, and he kissed her back, slow and savoring before pulling away to rest his forehead against hers. "What would I do without you?"

"Bleed to death." Morigan smiled as she settled in the crook of his arm. And she felt right, lying there, a part of the man he was now. They both had had lovers aplenty, and other Oathbounds besides, but it was each other's arms they sought after terror and strife. It was at her hearth where he laid his boots time and again.

"Take an Oath with me, Mori?"

She laughed at his rumbling proposal. "You're fever mad."

"I'm serious." His voice was grave.

"Oen, I… there's no reason to bind ourselves again. The Keening's took my womb. I'm no good for child-bearing. Find a lusty young lass and sire another clan."

"I don't want some mindless young thing. I want you."

"There's always been room for you in my bed, and your bed has always been open to me. That won't change. We come and go as we please. Besides, you asked me to take an Oath last time. It's my turn to ask."

"Then ask, Woman. Come home with me."

"What of Isiilde?"

"She's grown now. I have to let her go—as hard as that will be."

"What will we do?" she asked. "Grow old together? We've shared our lives, our beds, had our children. Why bind yourself to me?"

He gripped her shoulder. "Because when I'm with you, I am Oenghus, and no bloody other, especially not some blasted god."

"You are who you are, Oen. *All* of you. Ulfhidhin, bound to the Sylph; a berserker, slayer of countless; a healer of many and a lover of even more. And when you put your mind to it, a bloody fine father."

"You forgot one," he said, pulling her near.

"And what's that?"

"I'm yours."

Morigan paused at this. "And mine," she agreed softly.

CHAPTER 69

Isiilde opened her eyes to an empty bed. For a moment, she feared she'd dreamed the last days. That Marsais had not survived. Panic clutched her, and she hopped out of bed, searching the small room. There were signs of another occupant: bandages and poultices—none of which she needed.

How long had she slept? It felt like weeks.

Disoriented, Isiilde tugged on her clothes. She worried he'd died in his sleep and the clerics carted him off without telling her. She flew across the hallway and opened the door across.

Isiilde froze in the doorway. Oenghus still slept, and Morigan slept, too. Her head on his chest.

Careful not to disturb the pair, Isiilde backed out and softly closed the door. A smile warmed her heart. Witman had been true to his word. He'd saved her friends. And when Witman's enchanted constructs dragged them through the chalk portal, Isiilde had wept with joy.

She made her way through the barracks, which were serving as the infirmary. Aside from the curtain walls and outer ramparts, it was one of the few buildings that still stood. The cots were nearly empty now, but a few patients lingered. A white-robed Cleric of Chaim drifted near. He did not know where Marsais was.

"I'll call for a search. Be at ease and rest," he urged in hushed tones. But the nymph turned to dart outside.

The world was quiet with the grey before dawn. The camp was still asleep, and the few remaining fires smoldered in ash. As she wove through the tents that dotted the outer bailey, her teeth knocked together with cold.

Sentries watched the nymph's passing, but her eyes were on the horizon. It looked naked without the Spine reaching towards the sky. Only a mountain of stone remained, shrouded in freezing mist.

No one knew what to do about the lingering elemental. For now, the old one slumbered under the ruin, and no one dared disturb it. Not even the Wraith Guards.

Isiilde hoped it had found a new home.

With the wards and rot gone from the Isle, the Portals of Iilenshar could come and go at will. She'd watched a pair of the cowled and masked beings glide across the bailey. Mystery shrouded the Portals, along with everyone from the floating Isle.

Isiilde walked up to a grey-cloaked Wraith Guard. Two silver earrings adorned the woman's left ear. Acacia claimed the earrings signified rank. One earring marked an initiate, and two, a soldier. The more earrings, the higher the rank.

"Have you seen a white-haired man? Marsais the Seer?"

In answer, the guard pointed to the ramparts. Isiilde squinted at the looming walls in surprise. He was not supposed to leave his bed.

Isiilde darted across the bailey, and up the narrow stairs. Marsais stood on the rampart walkway with a white-robed cleric. Their heads were bent together, deep in conversation. But when she walked towards the pair, two guards blocked her path with crossed spears.

Her anger blazed. And so did her hands. "Excuse me," she said, fire licking up her sleeves.

Their eyes widened a fraction—the only betrayal of emotion on their impassive faces. But they did not stand aside.

Marsais looked up at the sound of her voice. "By the gods, let her through before she burns you to a crisp."

One guard looked to the cleric for permission. Isiilde thought that odd. The guard wore ten earrings in her pointed ears—one of the highest ranks. Why was she looking to a cleric for permission?

The cleric gave a barely perceptible dip of his head, and the guards stepped smartly to the side.

Isiilde sauntered past the guards. She walked up to Marsais and brushed his hand in greeting. His fingers closed around her own. There was strength in that grip.

"I didn't want to wake you," he murmured.

"You should have."

When his fever had burned at its hottest, the clerics had cut his long hair. Now it was an unruly mass of white, curling around his pointed ears. He wore a doublet and a shirt with billowing sleeves, and the combination made him look like some mischievous young faerie lord. His left arm was still tucked and bandaged to his chest.

"It's freezing out here, Marsais. You shouldn't be outside so soon."

"That is precisely what I told him," the cleric said. She turned to the man, but his cowl was as deep and low as his voice, and all she saw was a dark brown chin.

"I needed to stretch my legs."

"That's why they're so long," the cleric said, wryly. "You're always stretching."

"Apparently not long enough to escape the cleric who shaved off my goatee."

"It was scruff."

Marsais rubbed his chin. He looked like a freshly shorn sheep, smooth and bashful. Isiilde didn't even try to hide her grin.

"Isiilde, this is..." Marsais gestured at the healer.

"A cleric of Chaim," the man said. With his hands tucked in wide sleeves, he bowed low. "A pleasure. I'll leave you to him, my lady. I think you'll have better luck convincing him to lie back down."

As the cleric straightened, she saw a flash of silver from beneath the cowl. His eyes. The cleric turned and made for the rampart stairs, and she watched as the two high-ranking Wraith Guards fell in step behind him.

"Who was that?" she asked.

"A friend."

She narrowed her eyes, but Marsais turned from her suspicion and sat on the wall between crenellations. A cold wind blew a flurry of snow at them. Isiilde tugged her cloak up to her chin, and edged next to Marsais, using him as a windbreak.

He turned towards the rising sun. Isiilde studied his profile. A noble brow, sharp ears and nose, high cheekbones, and long lips. Pyrderi's words swam to the surface of her thoughts: *There is a tad more than a touch in that Lindale.*

He'd admitted he was elven—of the Lindale race, like the Guardians. *One of the last of my kind*, he'd told her once. But considering the forbidden knowledge he possessed, the power he wielded, and the company he kept—was he one of the Fey, too? Is that where his foresight stemmed from? Or was he something more?

"I wanted to see the sunrise," he said, interrupting her thoughts.

"You didn't think you'd ever see another."

"No," he admitted. "And by all accounts, I shouldn't be alive to see this one."

Marsais wrapped an arm around her waist, drawing her near. And she breathed in his scent: the sand and sea and everything warm.

"I'm glad you're alive."

"Plenty of chance for that to change. We still have a bit before the sun rises."

Isiilde smiled against his neck. "I don't have any plans to push you off the ramparts."

"Thank the gods for that," he murmured into her hair. "Have I ever told you how brilliant you are?"

She drew back, catching his eyes with her own. "Now and again."

"You're remarkable too."

A blush warmed her cheeks. And she idly toyed with his hair, running her fingers through the unruly mass. "Did you know Witman would be in your vault?"

"I wanted you to run."

"I would never leave you."

"That's what I fear."

"Marsais, I..." She hesitated.

I want you. I need you. Her heart ached for him. He was a part of her. But what did he want?

Marsais waited for her to find the words. His eyes were gentle and warm with love. And sadness, too.

"I'm already torn without you. Whether or not we're bonded, you're a part of me. And *if* you die, you will take a part of me with you, regardless. Do you understand?"

"I do," he said urgently. "I've bought myself time—nothing more."

"What did you do?"

Marsais pressed his lips together and looked to the horizon. He did not answer.

The sun cracked over the moody sea, bringing a dim, cold light. And in silence, they watched the sunrise. That silence stretched like a chasm between them. He felt distant—unreachable. And then he finally offered a hand by way of an answer.

"The coins," he said.

Isiilde glanced at him in startled confusion. It wasn't much of an answer, but she was used to his cryptic ways.

"When I disappeared for six months," he went on to explain. "It wasn't only to stretch my legs."

"Imagine that."

Marsais turned to face her. And Isiilde blinked in surprise. His eyes were like a myriad of stars shining from a clear night. They glowed silver.

"I went to the Bastardlands to investigate a ruin under Iilenshar—in the west chasm."

"It's bottomless," she blurted out.

"So legend claims," he agreed. "At one time, when the realm was whole, the citadel of the Guardians sat there. A section of it was salvaged, and now the isle floats over the chasm, but the ruins where Zahra and Dagenir battled are still at the bottom. I recovered three artifacts from the ruin. The ones I showed to Witman at the festival."

"You said they were trinkets from the Bastardlands."

"Strictly speaking, it was the truth."

"You're worse than me, Marsais."

"Hmm."

Isiilde crossed her arms. "You're going to make me ask, aren't you?"

"Aren't you curious?"

"What were the artifacts?"

"I'm sure you could work it out."

"Humor me," she said dryly.

"They were the last fragments of the shattered Orb."

It took a long moment for her brain to recover from this shocking revelation. "You had Witman disguise them?"

"Yes."

"Why?"

"I think you know the answer to that."

"Because a lot of powerful people would like to have the fragments?"

He inclined his head. "Gods of other realms, the Guardians of Morchaint, and even... Iilenshar."

"Why didn't you leave them at the bottom of the chasm?"

"A vision—which I now know is true—and not a seed of suggestion planted by a vengeful Fey. If Tharios had known about the fragments, he would have snatched them from me when he had the chance. And if Pyrderi had known, he wouldn't have faced me with such arrogance."

"Where are they now?"

Marsais pointed to his chest.

"In a pocket?"

"I am now bound to the fragments. They are a part of me."

Her gaze flickered to that scar beneath his doublet. The one that was no longer as raw as it had once been. Her mind reeled. "What does that mean?"

"That I've revealed myself. I used the Orb's power on Pyrderi."

"Can't you just cut them out?"

"It isn't the shards themselves."

"Then what is it?"

"It's *who* I am."

A memory tickled the back of her mind. It was something Marsais had once told her: Fyrsta was known as the Realm of Gods.

Marsais picked up a waterskin sitting on the wall. "What is this?"

"An empty waterskin."

"Ah, but it can hold wine or ale just as easily. Would you say a more literal answer is a cured pig's bladder?" Marsais traced a water rune on the leather. It flared and filled with moisture gathered from the air. "Now what is it?"

"A pig's bladder full of water."

"And now we can call it a waterskin. But what makes it that?"

"The water inside."

"Does it make the water?"

"No."

"Where did the water come from?"

"The air."

"Did the air make the water?" he asked.

"Water comes from the sky, the clouds, underground springs."

"Exactly." He carefully set the waterskin aside. "The Guardians are the skins that were filled with the essence of Life. The source is the Sylph. Whereas I am the skin that was filled with the essence of Time. The source is the ancient cycle of light and dark. Essentially, I'm a cracked pig's bladder about to burst."

"You're the ol'Father, aren't you?"

Marsais winced. "I detest that name."

Isiilde could have slapped herself. "Oen's been saying it all along... Is ol'bastard more apt?"

"It is." He flashed a grin. "Contrary to legend, my relationship with the Sylphs was not paternal. And I've never been a favorite of the remaining Sylph."

"It's true then—there were three Sylphs?"

Sadness swirled in that starry gaze. "There were," he whispered.

"Time loved Death most of all," she quoted softly.

A shudder swept through his body. "She was... my heart."

"You still love her."

"I do. Despite being reborn countless times, my spirit remains the same." He nodded to the waterskin. "The vessel may change, but the water is caught in an endless cycle. The same drop will fall to earth time and time again."

"Pyrderi was right, then. He knew. Oen *is* the wild god, Ulfhidhin."

"Spirits do not always stay in the ol'River," Marsais explained. "After a time, the veil thins between lives. Once, he was; now, he is not, and yet, he is. Like a diamond with many facets, it all depends from where the light is shining."

"It would be a dull diamond with only one facet."

He smiled. "Precisely."

"And what of me? Was I the first queen of Kambe in another life?"

"A few are born who have never lived before. Those spirits shine the brightest. You are many things, Isiilde. That's why I worry about your safety."

She brushed that subject away. "Why aren't the other Guardians in danger? Why will others seek you out?" She thought of Witman and his fear of the *Others*. Hearing the steel in Marsais' voice, she wondered if the dwarf might not be as crazed as he sounded.

"I know many things." His voice was worn and tired. "Secrets that would make a god weep with fear."

"When you can remember."

"There is that," he admitted. "There are gaps in my mind—hallways that lead nowhere; doors that do not open."

"So you're a maze?"

"I'm not sure I have an end, or a beginning. But yes, such is the tapestry of time."

"That's fine. I like puzzles." She considered his words for a moment. "You said you were wounded when the Orb shattered... That's when you got that scar."

He nodded.

"Your scar changed after the coins disappeared in the desert. It's nearly healed."

"Unexpectedly, the shards acted as a kind of patch to this cracking waterskin," he explained, gesturing at himself.

Clean and shaven as he was now, Isiilde had a hard time envisioning that comparison. She wanted to drag him to the closest bed and ride him until he forgot his name.

"I know it's a lot to take in," he said.

"Hmhmm."

Marsais gave her a knowing look. "You're distracted."

"I can ponder more than one thing at a time." She knocked her thoughts back on track. "So if the Orb held the Sylph's power and caused the Shattering when it broke, what happens when the vessel of Time is destroyed?"

"No one knows, myself included. When the Orb shattered, it tore down the veils between my lives, destroying the wards that I had woven around my spirit before being reborn. It's similar to the wards I weave into a transformation, only infinitely more complicated. I was both lost and changed in ways I don't fully understand, and my death could trigger another Shattering. Time itself may stop."

And she'd thought releasing an imp into the realm was bad.

"Or not." He lifted a shoulder. "But there are those who would risk such a destruction."

Isiilde stood, turning away to think. Confusion swirled in her mind like an endless weave. She began to pick out the threads, snipping, connecting, until she unraveled the knot. "Then why did you bind the shards to yourself? Why expose yourself?"

"It was a reckless whim. I'm broken already, and so is the Orb. What further harm could it cause?"

"You said it acted as a patch... What about your visions?"

"I haven't had a vision since I absorbed the Orb's power."

She cocked her head. "That sounds more like a plug than a patch. If you hold the essence of Time, then..." She trailed off as another thought took root. "Did the Orb's power interfere with your own in some way? Has it silenced your foresight altogether?"

"I don't know."

"That doesn't mean you don't have a theory."

"You've spent entirely too much time with me."

"Not near enough." She waited, and he obliged.

"Do you remember, years ago, when I took your fire rune during King's Folly, and you were so incensed that you tipped over the table?"

Isiilde cleared her throat. "Perhaps."

"I think I may have done the equivalent to this realm." He took a shaky breath. "Instead of adding more threads to the tapestry of time; the tapestry is unraveling."

She wrinkled her nose. "You know I abhor knitting metaphors."

"The board was cleared; the pieces haven't been replaced. Therefore, I haven't seen *any* future—everything is in chaos."

"I find that strangely comforting."

"I'm glad someone does," he said dryly.

"If everyone is in darkness, then no one has the advantage."

"I prefer to have the advantage."

"That's a dull way to live. You'll never be surprised."

"My heart can only take so many surprises."

"Did you know Pyrderi would be on the Isle?"

"Not in the flesh. The spirits of the Fey, certainly. They've always been here, but seeing him in the throne room was a shock," he admitted. "There was someone lurking in the shadows of my visions, but I assumed it was Karbonek whispering from his prison. An unforgivable oversight on my part."

"You must first ask forgiveness before you can call it unforgivable."

His lips quirked. "Wise words. Then I ask yours."

"For what?"

"Pyrderi manipulated some of my visions. Skillfully, I might add. He led me to believe that if we bonded, things would go badly."

"Oh."

A cascade of cause and effect spiraled in her mind, of all the little choices, the wrong turns, the spiral of events that had landed her in the washroom. And that small insidious voice that whispered, 'if only.' She crushed that voice. It was pointless.

"Why would he do that?"

"Regardless of what set him down his dark path, Pyrderi became the very monster he loathed. My confusion, my... suffering, and yours, gave him pleasure."

Her skin crawled with that thought. "Did you think I would accept his offer?"

Marsais did not answer immediately. "I did not know what you would do," he said at last. "You're faerie, just as Pyrderi once was, and you too have faced horrors. To be honest, his scheme was not without its appeal. Humans have caused this realm endless grief."

"Then why help them?"

"It's not my place to destroy hope. And that is precisely what Pyrderi would have done. He could not be trusted."

"I'd have been his puppet."

"Indeed. How did you see through his lies?"

She snorted. "He said *My* Queen; not Your Majesty. I'm not a fool, Marsais. The only one I will tolerate that from is you. I'm *your* dear, and no one else's."

"Hmm, by the way, how am I doing?"

"With what?"

"Not indulging you."

"I think I missed being indulged," she admitted.

"Only when you feel like it?"

"Exactly," she said cheerfully, and then sobered. "What happens next? Why are you telling me this? Is this some roundabout way of telling me we can't bond?"

"You have your fire," he said gently.

She crossed her arms. "I'm Nuthaanian. I can bloody bond with as many as I want."

Marsais barked out a laugh. "It would not surprise me," he said with a grin. "I am, after all, your druid, and nothing more. But to answer your question, I told you all of this because I'll not have secrets between us."

"You keep secrets from yourself, Marsais."

"Not on purpose," he defended.

"Then I'll accept the same."

He inclined his head.

"You need to know what you're getting into. There will come a time when I ask you to run. I expect you to do so."

"Is that an ultimatum?"

"Yes."

"You know I won't."

"I know," he sighed. His eyes dimmed to the color of a moody sea, and he turned his gaze back to the horizon.

Isiilde was at a loss. Not from his revelations—she had always suspected there was something more to the man—but by his ultimatum. How could he ask such a thing?

"That's fine," she said lightly. "As long as you do the same."

Marsais cocked his head.

"There will come a time when I ask you to run. I expect you to do so."

"You know I won't."

"Exactly." Her point was made.

An iron voice called his name, interrupting their conversation. Marsais winced. "Quick, push me off the ramparts."

Isiilde poked his shoulder. "Considering your ultimatum, I'm tempted."

He set his back solidly against the stone as they watched Thira stalk up the stairs. She looked lonely without her wretched familiar. Isiilde almost felt sorry for the woman.

Zoshi told them a bright light had hit the crow in the throne room. Apparently, it was Pyrderi's spirit possessing the creature. But Isiilde wouldn't put organizing a jailbreak past the wretched familiar. At any rate, Crumpet had been reduced to a burnt husk at the bottom of the pit.

Isiilde almost felt sorry for the woman.

As usual, Thira got right to the point. "What will you do about the state of this Order?" she demanded of Marsais.

"I'm not Archlord anymore."

"You were wrongly accused." Thira sounded like she was chewing on something unpleasant. "You are Archlord, but I still think you're a horrid one."

"I agree."

Her eyes narrowed. "You do?"

"I do." His lips twitched.

"This isn't a joke, Marsais. Our Order is on the verge of ruin. We need your guidance."

"I tire of fixing this realm, Thira." It might have sounded arrogant if not for the bone-weary exhaustion in his voice. "I'll use my right as the current Archlord to choose another."

"There are over nine Wise Ones left. Plenty for a vote."

"Can we be sure of their loyalties?"

"With Morigan, Oenghus, Rashk, you, myself, and Eldred—" she stopped short. That only made six. "No. That brings me to another issue. Do you have any idea where Isek Beirnuckle might have run to?"

Marsais gave a heavy sigh. The sting and regret of betrayal were clear. "No, I do not. But knowing Isek, when things became complicated, he cut his losses, and ducked back into the shadows."

"I thought as much."

"I doubt he'll surface anytime soon. Consider him removed from the Order."

"Noted." Thira inclined her head. "I suppose you've heard Iilenshar has offered our Order a home in Westhaven. However, I suspect it has more to do with spying on our activities."

"Spare me, please."

"If you hand over the seat to Oenghus—"

Marsais raised a hand. "I'm not *that* mad."

"Then who?"

"You."

The words stunned her. Thira froze, and Isiilde gaped. The thought of Thira as Archlord terrified her.

"Me?"

"Yes, you. I can think of no better person for the throne. Despite our differences, you have always acted in the best interests of this Order."

Thira's gaze flickered to Isiilde. Her lips formed a hard line, and she glanced away. "Not always."

"We *all* make mistakes, Thira."

The woman sniffed his understanding aside. "Some more than others."

"I'm sure you'll set my own blundering aright."

"I've done more than my share," Thira admitted. "That's it, then?"

"You are Archlord," he confirmed. "I apologize that you have neither the Spine nor the Runic Eye."

"I've always said this nymph would destroy our Order." Thira looked sharply at her. "And a good thing you did. Rot lay at its very core."

"A dubious foundation indeed," Marsais agreed.

Thira drew herself up. "We will rebuild."

"I have no doubt of that."

Thira focused on the nymph with a gleam in her eyes. And Isiilde braced for whatever was to come, her bond stirring in response, ready to defend.

"As Archlord of this Isle, I'll forgo the Trials—you've proven yourself a hundred times over, Isiilde. You're no longer an apprentice, but a Wise One with all the titles and responsibilities." Thira thrust out a hand. "If you like."

Isiilde tilted her head, searching for any sign of deception.

"If you haven't learned how to shake a hand, Nymph, then I'll retract my offer." It was said sharply, but there was a trace of humor in her eyes.

Isiilde shook her hand.

"Welcome to the Order."

Before Isiilde could open her mouth, Thira turned on her heel and stalked away.

"Well," Marsais said, sounding pleased. "*That* was certainly a surprise."

CHAPTER 70

Acacia Mael stood at parade rest, hands clasped behind her back. In front of her, the Sacred Sun hung on the wall. High Inquisitor Multist had commandeered a tailor's shop the moment he arrived, bringing all the golden trappings of the Blessed Order. She wondered where the tailor was now.

"There *is* another chair," a drawling voice interrupted her contemplation.

Her gaze slid to the man. Marsais slumped in a chair, one arm thrown over his sling, long legs stretching over the floor. He looked almost boyish with his hair clipped short and his shaven cheeks. It emphasized his high cheekbones and pointed ears, giving him an ethereal beauty.

Despite awaiting an interrogation, he looked utterly relaxed. She chalked it up to his apparent exhaustion. Multiple Healings took a toll on the body, and now, his own needed time to mend. His arm was still bandaged to his side to prevent the pectoral from tearing.

"I'm sorry, Marsais," she blurted out. "I didn't intend for you to be here, too."

"It was your duty to pen that report. You stated the facts, nothing more. I take great comfort in the fact that your Order generally strangles a criminal before sawing them into quarters."

She closed her eyes and blew out a long breath. What she would not give for the weight of armor resting on her shoulders. But the moment she'd handed over her report, Multist ordered her stripped of armor and weapons, and tossed in a makeshift jail. The implements of the Inquisitor's trade now waited on a table.

They had spared her chains. And for that small dignity, she was grateful.

"I left out your relationship with the fiend," she admitted.

His hand went to his heart. "You lied for me?"

"I said you were attacked." It wasn't a stretch. She'd seen the wounds on his body afterwards.

"Hmm, I'll likely be the first man in your Order's history to be drawn and quartered for being raped by a fiend and her cohorts."

Acacia paled at his candor. "Would you stop saying it's *my* Order."

"Isn't it?"

Acacia clenched her jaw. "It doesn't matter. You're still here, and you don't need to be."

"I thank you for throwing yourself on the sacrificial flame for my sake. We both did what was needed, Acacia. And you did not let the Law cloud your judgment. That's a rare thing."

"Not in the eyes of the Blessed Order."

"Ah, yes, loyalty blinded by divine light. There has never been a more insidious combination."

"Do you realize *everything* that comes out of your mouth is considered heresy by this Order?"

"Marsais the Heretic," he said with relish. "It has a better ring to it than seer."

"It won't help your inquiry," she pointed out.

But the gravity of the situation was lost on Marsais—he looked amused by the whole affair.

Acacia looked away from the thoughtful elf. Confident madmen were far from reassuring. Iilenshar was as rigid as the Blessed Order, and even the Guardians were held to their own laws. Or so it was said.

Acacia sighed at her last doubting thought. Marsais had gotten under her skin. She now questioned everything she'd been taught. The mere thought that the Guardians didn't actually abide by their own laws was heresy.

Nearly two hundred years ago, she'd joined the Order as a young woman. She'd lived and breathed the Laws, and now, without that structure, she felt adrift.

What would it mean to serve the Sylph? There were sacred shrines of oak and wilderness, tended by half-drunk priestesses who were fond of bedding men and women. No structure, no discipline, no martial training.

The Blessed Order was all Acacia knew. And the thought of leaving that structure terrified her.

The door opened, and two paladins walked into the room. Acacia snapped to attention. The two bore the sigil of Iilenshar: the Sacred Sun caught in a maze-like circle. Dread climbed up her throat. When Iilenshar was directly involved, their paladins outranked all others.

The High Inquisitor, dressed in his golden armor, followed on their heels. She detested the man. It was clear he was accepting bribes, but she hadn't uncovered sufficient evidence to prove his guilt. There had been no time.

A white-robed cleric entered last. That was odd. Clerics of Chaim were not usually present for an Inquiry, unless it was expected to turn violent. The cowled cleric stepped silently to the side.

"At ease," a grizzled Kilnish paladin said.

Acacia relaxed, but only a fraction. He was a commander of the First Order, and one did not stand easily in his presence. The man flicked a look of disapproval at the elf.

Marsais inclined his head. "Thank you, but I'm already at ease."

Despite herself, humor replaced dread. She nearly laughed. His madness was rubbing off on her—that, or her giddiness was simply a side-effect of stress.

The commander nodded to the High Inquisitor, and with a glint of glee, Multist stepped forward. "Hold out your hand, Acacia Mael." He stressed her name, a reminder that her rank had been stripped.

The request surprised her. She'd expected a long-winded speech followed by an intense interrogation.

Acacia held out her hand. With a ritual chant, and grand gestures that were wholly unnecessary, Multist teased the aura of her spirit into the air. A silver light flared to life.

Multist frowned. He crushed her hand with his own, snuffing the light. "Open it again."

"That won't be necessary," the Commander said. "I'd rather see your hand, High Inquisitor. Hold it out."

Multist turned red-faced. "I am not under scrutiny."

"You are," the Commander corrected. "And you have been for some time. Hold out your hand."

Multist's eyes danced between the paladins, clearly gauging his chances. But in the end, his shoulders slumped, and he did as ordered.

The Commander stepped forward to test the man. A dingy, murky mess of grey rippled in the air over Multist's palm. Not enough to execute, but certainly enough to oust him from the Blessed Order.

The Commander nodded to the second paladin, and he stepped forward to grip Multist's shoulder. His arguments thundered in the room long after he was marched out. Without a word, the commander followed, leaving Acacia with the elf and a cleric.

Marsais had not even been examined.

"That had to be the shortest Inquiry in the history of the Blessed Order," Marsais mused.

The cleric pushed back his cowl. "Trust me, I've tried to shorten them, but humans do love their rituals."

Acacia stood for a breathless second. She took in the cleric's curly white hair, rich brown skin, silver eyes, and aquiline nose. Years of training snapped her to action. She sank to one knee, bowed her head, and kept her eyes on the floor.

She heard a rustle of fabric, and a pair of fine boots stepped into her line of sight.

"Please, Captain Mael, don't kneel on formality."

The Guardian of Life reached down and took her hands in both of his. She stood to look into his eyes. They were reassuring, kind, and distant as stars.

"You have served Iilenshar well, but mostly…" His gaze slid to Marsais. "Anyone who can put up with him for as long as you did has my respect."

Acacia cleared her throat. "The journey certainly had its moments."

"All this flattery is making me blush," Marsais drawled. "If I can test your divine patience, Chaim, then I consider my day well spent."

Chaim released her hands, and stepped back. "Next time, I'm going to shave your head."

"I'll look like a dying vulture."

"An improvement." Chaim flashed his teeth at the man. And Acacia looked from one to the other. Although Marsais was a few shades lighter than the Guardian, they could nearly pass as brothers. She'd noticed the resemblance before, but now, with the two in the same room—the resemblance was striking. As it had been with the Fey.

"No, we are not related. Well, distantly," Chaim corrected.

"*Very* distantly," Marsais added.

"Please sit, if you like, Captain." Chaim gestured towards the single remaining chair. It was not an order, but a courtesy.

"I'll stand, thank you, Guardian."

"Call me Chaim."

Acacia opened her mouth. The world was spinning decidedly fast. With an abrupt change of mind, she walked over to the chair and sat.

"I never have that effect on people," Marsais sighed.

Chaim smirked. "When was the last time you told someone your name?"

"I did this morning."

"And?"

"She became annoyed with me and threatened to push me off the ramparts."

"Which is why the captain has my utmost respect."

"And mine." Marsais looked over at her. "I would have assured you that the Inquiry would end well, but I doubted you would believe me."

"No," she said, faintly. Acacia gripped the armrests so tightly that she feared they would break.

"Captain—"

"If I'm to use your name, then please show me the same courtesy."

Chaim inclined his head. "Marsais has nothing but praise for you. I've read your report and heard the full account of events. Not only did I want to thank you personally, but I have a request... an offer, really."

"An offer?" Her voice sounded distant in her own ears.

"I need your help," Chaim said. "I need warriors who will do the right thing—no matter the risk. But I warn you, if you accept, the things you learn of Iilenshar will shake the foundation of your beliefs."

"More so than Marsais already has?"

"He would shake anyone to their core."

"All madmen are heretics," Marsais muttered.

Acacia needed to be on her feet. She pushed herself out of the chair. "Would I serve as a cleric?"

Chaim shook his head. "A Knight of the Blessed Order, as you are serving now. I need people I can trust."

"To do what?"

"It's easy to lose sight of the ground when you live on a floating island. Zahra, my mother, is..." He hesitated. "My mother has lost sight of the ground and those who live on it. The state of her Order reflects that."

"Are you planning to overthrow Zahra?" Confusion filled her voice.

"No, nothing so drastic. But I have, for years now, been mitigating many of her actions."

"I can't imagine how I could help you."

"You already have." He gestured at Marsais. "If my mother had sent her Wraith Guards and Valkyries, Marsais might not be sitting here so casually. In her mind, there is no leniency, no mercy—only Law. You, however, see all sides of a situation. That is what I require. I need you to do what you've always done, Acacia. You have the Sylph's favor because you choose mercy over law, and what is right over what is easy."

"I..." She started to deny it, but she knew in her heart it was true. "Yes, I will. I would be honored to serve you."

"You won't be serving me, Acacia. You'll be serving those who need it most. And it will not be without danger."

"It can't be worse than spending a month in his company."

"You wound me," Marsais said.

"It may be slightly worse," Chaim mused. "There's a certain dragon that needs relocating."

Acacia's heart sank. "Will it involve portals?"

"I'm afraid so."

CHAPTER 71

Oenghus glared at the two paladins flanking the door. His fingers flexed and stretched, and his knuckles cracked. Eventually, he would have to test his prowess with one arm. The thought deflated him.

A war hammer hung on his belt, but it wasn't *Gurthang*, and it most certainly wasn't *Slàtra*. He didn't even have an arm to hold a shield.

Suddenly tired, Oenghus sat on a bench beside his daughter. Her leg bounced nervously. She was worried, too. Instead of reaching for his weapon, he wrestled out his pipe and stared at it. He only had one hand. How was he going to light his pipe?

With care, he set the pipe on his leg, and fished out a pinch of weed from his pouch. Bending forward, he braced the stub of his arm against the wood to steady it, then sprinkled the weed into the bowl. It would have to do.

Oenghus thrust the pipe stem between his lips, looking for the closest fire. A flame sprang to life under his eyes. It burned cheerfully on the tip of Isiilde's finger. She put the flame to the bowl, and he lightly puffed until the weed smoldered.

"Thanks," he muttered.

Isiilde hummed softly, watching the flame slither down her finger to dance on her palm. "Why did they march Multist out? What's happening in there?" The flameling wavered, mirroring her anxiety.

"I'm as clueless as you, Sprite."

"I won't let the Blessed Bloody Order draw and quarter either of them."

"Course we won't." An angry line of smoke seeped from his lips.

Isiilde glanced at his bandaged stub. "Does it hurt?"

"Feels like it's still there."

"I'm glad you cut it off, Father. I thought I'd lost you again."

"I'm a stubborn bastard." He did not tell her the truth—that he wished he'd died in that pit.

His daughter fell silent with thought, and the flame flickered and disappeared. A Wisp buzzed around his ear, and he carefully waved the fluttering faerie away. It zipped over to Isiilde, playing in her hair. She didn't seem to notice.

"Do you remember your other lives?" she finally asked.

"What has that ol'bastard been filling your head with?"

"Pyrderi said your name." She loosened the strings of her enchanted pouch and reached in for a strawberry.

"My name is Oenghus." He sucked on his pipe, and blew out a long line of smoke. "There's a saying in Nuthaan: leave the past where it belongs. And I agree. I don't like talking about it."

"Ignoring something won't make it go away," she pointed out. "It's like a cobweb in a corner; it only gets larger."

Oenghus grumbled.

"Did Ulfhidhin really abduct the Sylph?"

He shrugged. "Depends on who you ask."

"I'm asking you."

"It was for her own good. I had to hit her over the head and toss her over a shoulder."

Isiilde blinked at him. "That was very... forward of you."

"I'm a forward man."

Isiilde chewed thoughtfully on her strawberry, then reached for another. She offered him one. Oenghus took it, but he had his pipe in his mouth and only one hand.

With a curse, he plucked the pipe out and stuffed the berry in one-handed. It worked. Progress, he thought, and tried not to think of everything Morigan had helped him with that morning. She'd wrapped his kilt and tied his boots, all without him asking. But then that's what healers did for cripples.

"Was my mother a nymph?"

"What the Void did Marsais tell you?"

"Nothing. I do have a mind, Oen. And the *ol'bastard*, as you call him, left me with more questions than answers."

Oenghus grunted. "You mother told me she was a nymph."

"She told you."

"Aye."

Isiilde plucked another strawberry from the pouch, turning it towards the light. "I haven't added a single strawberry to my pouch since I packed in Mearcentia."

"Imagine that."

"Hmm."

He looked sharply at her. There was a glint in those emerald eyes.

"That answers that," she said.

"What?"

"A great many things." Isiilde popped the strawberry into her mouth. "Every single one of these strawberries is perfection. Imagine that."

"Aye."

Isiilde answered his wink with a grin, but then she sobered. "Marsais doesn't want me to bond with him again unless I agree to his terms."

"What are his terms?"

"That I abandon him to some horrible fate when he tells me to."

"Did he now?"

"What do you think of that?" she asked.

"I think he's a fool."

"Really?"

"What did you expect I'd say?" Oenghus asked.

"That's he's right to protect me."

Oenghus snorted. "You can take care of yourself, Isiilde. As much as any of us."

"You think so?"

"I'd want you at my back in a fight."

"Aren't you worried?"

"Course I am, but we all die eventually. Charging death is as dangerous as running from her." He lifted a shoulder, his left one, and instantly regretted it. The muscles were still weak from the dislocation. But it wasn't the pain that got to him, it was the reminder of loss. "If it helps any, the ol'bastard is always trying to protect those he loves. Myself included. There's a lot of hurt in that heart of his. A whole sea of pain. And each drop breaks a bit more of him."

Isiilde frowned. He would have severed his other arm to take the grief from her eyes. "I don't want to cause him more pain," she whispered.

"Now you're being the fool."

She cocked her head, waiting.

"You're both already hurting, Sprite. If I could get my arm back, even for a week, you think I'd say no, even knowing it'd be gone at the end?"

Her gaze drifted to his bandaged stump. "It will get better, Oen."

"I can't grow my arm back."

She slipped her arm through his good one, hugging it tightly. "You'll make do."

"I have you," he rumbled.

She sat for a time, and then stood, saying she'd burn the paladins if she waited any longer. He watched her leave, and knew she needed some time to think.

Two boys, one shorter than the other, raced across the bailey, weaving through wagons and bumping into soldiers, making a sword's edge towards him. They skidded to a stop. Elam started waving his hands and chatting in his tongue while Zoshi grinned from ear to ear.

"Calm down, the both of you. And Zoshi, watch it with that eye. Your sense of depth is all off."

The boy shrugged. "It's fine." He plucked at his new eyepatch, flashing the hollow socket. And Elam gave a thumbs-up gesture.

"Aye, it's healing good," Oenghus agreed.

"Morigan said I'm a pirate now," Zoshi said. "On account of all the treasure I found down in that mine. And the one eye."

"Zoshi One-Eye and Elam Fey-Slayer," Oenghus said around his pipe. "Sounds fearsome."

Elam proudly thumped his chest. Both boys were scrubbed from crown to toe, and dressed in fine clothes straight out of Iilenshar. The clerics had taken excellent care of the pair.

"But my mum says I can't actually plunder any ships. I'm not sure that makes me much of a pirate."

"You've got your treasure. Time to retire."

"Not sure about all that, sir. But Elam and I've polished it all good."

"You teaching him common?"

"Yes, sir, and he's teaching me Lome." Zoshi said something in the Lome language, a single trilling note that sent the older boy laughing. "I'm workin' on it."

"That's a start. Sorry about losing the war hammer you found."

Zoshi shook his head. "It wasn't mine."

Oenghus mussed the boy's hair. "How is your mum?"

"The Wraith Guards brought her from Drivel for me. She had a rough time in the fog, but the twins are fine."

"Glad to hear."

"A cleric. He had funny eyes, all silver, said we could go to Iilenshar to live if we liked."

"Did he now?" Oenghus looked thoughtfully at the door flanked by the paladins. "Both of you?" He pointed at Elam, and then to Zoshi, and the older boy nodded, throwing his arm over the smaller boy's shoulder.

"Brothers," Elam said proudly.

Oenghus smiled at the pair. His heart felt lighter. "Will you go?"

Zoshi shrugged. A shadow entered his joy, and he glanced nervously back at the frozen ruin. "I'm not sure I should."

"Why's that?"

"This whole mess is my fault," Zoshi whispered.

Oenghus felt a pang deep in his chest. "That's a lot of mess for someone so little. How'd you manage to bring down the Spine?"

"I didn't exactly, but I helped, didn't I? I took the spear out of the Fey."

Oenghus scratched at his beard. "Did you know Pyrderi would come alive?"

"Course not." Zoshi looked at his new boots and shifted. "That fellow, the cleric with silver eyes, he explained what happened. The Fey spirit possessed Crumpet in the throne room—that's what happened when I got slammed by the light. Then when I woke up, the bird's wing was healed. I should have known."

"I'm not sure I'd have known," Oenghus admitted. Some lies were worthwhile. This was one of them. "Strange things happen in these realms. Void, the bloody dog turned into a mammoth and a crow. How were you to know?"

"Maybe so, but it's still my fault."

Oenghus placed a heavy hand on the boy's shoulder. "You know what's your fault?"

"Everything?"

Oenghus shook his head. "Morigan being alive." He squeezed the bony shoulder. "Even if you tore that bloody tower down, stone by stone with your own bare hands, you saving her would erase all that. You saved the woman I love. I'm in your debt, Zoshi One-Eye."

Zoshi stood a little straighter. "You and her saved me plenty in the past."

"So what of it? Are you headed to Iilenshar?"

"The Isle is my home. But there are a lot of bad things here now. I don't much like thinking about it all." Zoshi glanced at the older boy. "And I think Elam feels the same."

"Me either," Oenghus admitted.

"Even as big as you are?"

Oenghus tapped the boy's head. "We have the same size brain. If you ask Morigan, she'd say you have the larger one, though."

The boy's smile returned.

"Just remember who's still standing. You. And when those shadows start creeping over your mind, turn your back on them, lift your kilt, and tell them to kiss your arse."

Zoshi looked dubious, but Elam snickered.

"It's a Nuthaanian thing," Oenghus explained.

The smaller boy wrinkled his nose. "I'll try it."

"That's the spirit."

The door to the makeshift temple opened, and Acacia stepped out.

She was dazed, and a little stunned. Oenghus climbed to his feet as she walked over.

Zoshi gave her a hug, and asked if she'd come meet his mum. After she agreed, both boys darted off, and the one-eyed lad promptly ran into the side of a tent, fell on his backside, and bounced right back up, continuing on undaunted. Elam burst with laughter, grabbing his hand and pulling him along.

If the boy could get used to one eye, then Oenghus decided he could live with one arm just fine.

"You still have all your arms and legs attached," Oenghus noted.

"I do."

"How'd the Scarecrow fair? Did you throw him under a wagon?"

Acacia arched a brow. "I tried."

Oenghus bared his teeth.

"He's talking with a erm... Cleric of Chaim."

"Oh, right, the Guardian."

Acacia blinked. "You knew?"

"About him and Chaim? Course I do. Never met the bastard, though."

She winced at his use of words.

"Chaim helped Marsais when he was in a bad way after the Shattering."

"That explains some of it." She glanced back at the door.

"Why do you look like you've seen a Forsaken?"

Acacia took a breath. "Truth is a hard potion to swallow."

Oenghus grunted in agreement. "There's a lot of lies in this realm."

"Yes, but necessary ones."

"Maybe."

"How's Morigan?"

"Same as me—limping around like a stubborn stump."

Acacia smiled. "Good."

"Thank you... for staying with her. And for helping Isiilde."

"I'd have wanted the same for someone I loved."

"Aye well, I wasn't quite myself."

Acacia eyed his beard and kilt. "I think you are precisely who you are. The stone... the hammer. Honestly, I'm relieved. When Pyrderi said your name, it answered a lot. You're like some page out of a legend that's larger than life."

"Most women say that about my cock."

Amusement lightened her eyes. "I'll take your word for it."

"You sure? Mori loves to shove me off on other women. Says it's the only time she gets a rest."

Acacia shook her head. "I will never understand Nuthaanian culture."

"We live each day like it's our last. That's all."

"My idea of living is a cup of tea, a good book, and a warm fire at the end of the day."

"You need to get out more."

"I do get out, far too often. That's why I dream of comfort," she said.

"Is that what you plan on doing now? Spending the rest of your years by a warm fire?"

She shook her head. "I'm headed to Iilenshar. Chaim has asked for my help."

Oenghus tugged on a braid. "You watch yourself."

"He's told me of the dangers."

"I mean on Iilenshar. I've never had much use for the Guardians."

"You're Nuthaanian, and... more." She shifted. "Speaking of which, do you have any idea how one goes about serving the Sylph?"

"I know how *I* serve her."

The suggestion in his voice brought color to her cheeks. "I haven't blushed in years."

"Like I said, you should get out more."

"Noted. What does the Sylph expect of me?"

"If you're expecting one of those bloody tomes of Law that the Blessed Order is fond of, you won't find it."

"Splendid."

"Listen, Acacia." Oenghus bent closer. "The Sylph needs help. She doesn't need another mindless devotee asking for direction at every turn. She needs a friend to watch her back like you watched mine. Someone to help her guard this realm. Understand?"

"I do."

Another revelation; another lie revealed: the gods were not all powerful. And he could see that hard truth dawn in her eyes.

Oenghus held out his hand. "You're not bad for a paladin."

"And you're not bad for a berserker." Acacia grabbed his forearm, and he gripped hers in the custom of warriors.

CHAPTER 72

Isiilde stared at the door. Her thoughts spun as she gripped a furry bundle under her arm. The feel of the pelt brought memories of a happier time. And of a dark one. She'd curled on this rug after Stievin attacked her.

That day darkened every day before and every one after. It tainted her memories. And she could not wash it from her mind. It was a part of her now. As were her own dark deeds. Blood stained her hands. She could not go back—only forward.

Isiilde raised her fist to the door, but it jerked open before she could knock. With a squeak of surprise, fire flared around her fist, surging towards the man in the doorway. He twisted to the side.

The nymph froze in alarm, then swiftly shook out her flame.

"Isiilde," he said.

"Marsais."

The two stood on either side of the threshold, both at a loss where to start.

Isiilde breached the silence first. "A guard found this stuffed into a storage room." She held out the frost bear pelt that used to be in his study. "I came to give it to you."

Marsais awkwardly took the bundle with one hand, then dropped it on the floor. "I was on my way to see you."

"In your small clothes?" she asked.

Marsais glanced down in surprise. "It would appear so," he said, clearing his throat.

Everything about the man spoke of determination, from the steel in his eyes to the set of his shoulders. She had seen that look before, in the days leading up to a prolonged absence, when he would leave to stretch his legs.

Isiilde didn't want to hear the words that he had for her—that he was leaving. She wanted time to stop, to stay in the present and not go forward or back.

"Would you care to walk with me?"

His manner was courtly, and for a moment she forgot he was half-naked. "It's snowing outside, Marsais."

"Yes, of course. One moment." He stepped inside his room, and she followed.

"I'd rather wait in here, unless you don't want to be alone with me, temptress that I am."

The edge of his mouth quirked. "I'll try to control myself."

"A pity."

Clothes had been flung around the small room, and a wet cloth and bandages lay on the floor by the washbasin. She could not decide if he was absentminded or restless.

"Have your visions started again?"

"No."

Isiilde frowned at the man. Water was dripping from his hair onto his bare chest. His left arm hung limp at his side. The sword wound was still raw and ringed with deep bruises. She doubted the healers would approve of his arm out of bandages.

"It's freezing outside," she said, handing him trousers. "We can talk in here. If you're going to leave, I'd at least like a final game of King's Folly."

Tears threatened at the last, and she quickly turned towards the discarded pelt. As clothes rustled, she shook out the pelt, laying it on his bed. Her heart felt like it was climbing out of her throat.

"I don't know what I'm going to do, Isiilde," he murmured. His voice was close, right behind her, and she turned to him, burying her face against his unlaced shirt. An arm came around her, fingers buried in her hair. He smelled of the sea, and a faint, lingering scent of herbs. She arched her neck, catching his eyes.

"Why are you insisting I leave you to your enemies?" she demanded.

He cupped the side of her face. "I will not put you in danger."

"It's because of my mother, isn't it?"

Surprise widened his eyes a fraction. She opened her mouth to say more, but he cut her off with a gesture and quickly traced an Orb of Silence.

"Is someone listening?"

"One never knows. Your bloodline must remain a secret."

His grave tone stole some of her anger. "Oen didn't exactly tell me, but it wasn't hard to put two and two together after I found out he was Ulfhidhin. You should have told me."

"I didn't know until after we bonded," he said. "Oenghus kept your lineage a secret, even from me."

"You didn't think to tell me afterwards?"

"When your bruises were still fresh? When we had only just bonded? Or should I have revealed your lineage moments before the duel?"

"We walked through Vaylin for nearly a month," she pointed out.

"It wasn't my place."

She sighed. "You're right—*Oen* should have told me."

"I'm sure he had his reasons, Isiilde. It was hard enough on you, being a nymph, let alone the daughter of the Sylph. Would knowing have made a difference?"

"It might have. I don't know. It's not as if I can go back and change anything."

"Such is time," he sighed. "It's why I'm so hesitant to rekindle our bond. If anyone of power were to discover you—"

She snorted, and took a step back. "I'm surprised you don't bond with me so you can order me about and lock me in some faraway tower for my own good."

"I would not do that."

"Not even for the good of the realm?" she asked.

"No, not even for that. But my presence *will* eventually draw attention to you."

"As if I won't manage that on my own."

Marsais shifted on his feet. "Point taken," he conceded. "All I'm asking is that you flee when the powers that be come hunting for me."

"That's not how love works, Marsais."

"If our situations were reversed, would you wish for me to stay and die with you?"

"I'd have a better chance of surviving with you at my side," she growled. "Why are you being so... stubborn about this?"

Marsais sat on the bed, ran a tired hand over his face, and hung his head. He did not raise his eyes. The answer came to her like a spark. Understanding melted her heart, and she hurried to his side.

"You're blind," she realized softly. "Have you ever been without your foresight?"

The muscles in his shoulders tensed. He shook his head. "When I finally get what I want, I fear the unknown."

The back of his neck looked so vulnerable without his long hair. She moved between his legs, hugging his head to her breast and idly toying with the soft curls that touched his nape. "A wise man once told me that fear makes us human," she whispered into his hair.

"That man is a fool." She could feel his breath against the fabric of her shirt, feel the sigh that traveled through his body.

"He's *my* fool."

Marsais drew slightly back and looked up, his grey eyes misty with emotion. She smiled down at him. "I have a proposition," she said.

"Hmm?"

"Since you are blind to the pathways of Time, we will play for our course."

His brows drew together. In answer to his confusion, she brought out her pouch of runestones and dropped them on the bed.

"If I win this game of King's Folly, then we will bond with no strings attached; if you win, I'll accept your ultimatum. When you tell me to run, I will run. For you."

He considered her for a long moment. Slowly, he dipped his head, and she held out a hand. With an amused tilt of his lips, he shook it.

While he arranged the runes, she shed her cloak, and removed her boots, sitting on the bed opposite him. "Would you like to rest first? Food, water, more sleep? I don't want you claiming a disadvantage because of injuries."

"My mind has not been this clear since the Shattering."

"Very well," she said, tucking her legs on the bed.

The game commenced; a blur of cycling runes and counter attacks; a swirl of destruction and strategy. Soon, she settled into the rhythm of the game, and decided that distraction was needed, but it did not manifest in its usual form. Rather, her thoughts took a more serious turn.

"Marsais?"

"Hmm?"

"Have you ever become used to taking a life?"

He paused, fingers poised over a death rune. After a moment, Marsais sat back, running a hand over his chin. "In war, or during a battle of any kind, I have no regrets. Kill or be killed. It's a simple matter of survival."

"You don't feel... tainted? As if there were blood on your hands?"

"I do, but only for the lives that were lost because of my failures: a trap that I failed to see; an error in judgment; troops sent to the slaughter for the sake of a victory; people I could not save, like my own daughter so long ago. That blood never comes off, and frankly, I would worry if it did."

He moved the death rune into his shadow rune, and death slipped through, emerging from another shadow into the inner cycle, obliterating her sun rune.

"I don't know what else I could have done with Zianna."

"You defended yourself."

"But then I killed her."

"A clean death is not a bad thing. Pyrderi would've let her suffer. You showed her mercy at great cost to yourself."

Isiilde frowned at the death rune. Something about the runes pricked her instincts. It felt like a trap, but she failed to spot a dire threat. She moved her water rune onto his stone. The runes flared, water seeping into stone. Unless he moved his sun rune over the combination in three rounds, it would crack his stone.

"I tried to save Rivan..." Her voice caught, but she forced herself to speak through the lump. "I think I would feel worse if I hadn't tried to heal him. The same goes for Zianna. Watching her die like that might have been worse than plunging my sword through her heart. But I'll never know."

"All my life, I've been able to glimpse every possible path taken, but seeing differs greatly from knowing. Foresight does not make me privy to emotional consequence. Regret is a persistent enemy of mine."

As she mulled over this revelation, Marsais moved an air rune, blowing her fire off course. The fire rune swept over two cycles, decimating his knight, heating an iron rune, and burning the life rune to a crisp. The backlash took out three of his own runes, and one of hers, but threw the air into the innermost cycle. Air and death surrounded her queen rune. Her fire and earth rune were within striking distance, but death was impervious to fire, and air might blow it in another direction entirely, or destroy her own queen.

There was the trap she'd failed to catch. Isiilde frowned. She could leave things up to chance, or plant her earth rune in front of the queen. Both options would put her on the run. The game no longer held her interest. Her thoughts turned towards the past month, and her heart filled with grief.

"You asked me why I denied Pyrderi, but I didn't tell you the whole truth. When I was on that throne, I was so very tempted to accept his offer, but then I remembered that day on the beach with you." She looked up, meeting his gaze. "The love in your eyes and the warmth in your voice was everything opposite of the Fey. I'm not sure I would have said no to Pyrderi otherwise."

Isiilde moved her hand towards the fire rune. It seemed fitting to leave their path up to chance. But when she started to nudge her fire towards his air rune, he reached out, gently grabbing her wrist.

Marsais looked into her eyes, and he lingered there, caught in a moment. Suddenly, without warning, he swept the runes off the bed.

Isiilde blinked with surprise. "Why did you do that?"

"You win," he said simply.

"But you were on the verge of winning."

"I surrender." And he kissed her. Gently at first, then with more passion. For a long minute, she was lost in that kiss. It was hard to breathe, hard to think.

He pulled away to search her eyes. His fingers were buried in her hair and his touch was pure fire. There was a question in his eyes: Are you sure?

"I won't run away," she whispered.

"I know."

"I could lie."

"It would make me feel better."

"I'll do *whatever* you say, Marsais."

"You're a horrible liar."

"Only with you."

Careful of his arm, she tugged off his shirt. His chest was mottled with bruises. She brushed her lips over a bruise, then another, and finally kissed his throat. His skin was warm and familiar.

Isiilde traced his ribs with her fingertips, following those delicious twin lines that dropped below his trousers.

His breath caught; his eyes lost focus.

Marsais kissed the pulse under her jaw, his breath hot against her flesh. He was tugging at her clothes; she was unlacing his trousers. His hand slid down her naked spine.

A gasp, a soft moan, and she lost all sense of time. Heat flooded her body, settling between her thighs. She ached for more.

Frantic moments followed where clothes were tugged and tossed to the far corners of the world. Cold air brushed her skin. He trailed fire between her breasts and down her stomach.

Isiilde buried her fingers in his hair as he pressed his lips to one stark hipbone, and then the other.

Marsais breathed in her scent. "In all of time, I have never tasted anything more exquisite than you."

His deep voice sent gentle vibrations through her body. It made her head swim, and her legs part. She was heavy and aching and so very ready. And when he touched her with a soft, teasing caress, every nerve in her body lit up with pleasure.

It was too much; it'd been too long. It was agonizing bliss. Her senses ignited, her body arched, her lips parted. She cried out. Fire surged from her skin.

Marsais threw himself off the bed. When the wash of pleasure released her body, she drifted, and her fire dimmed. Isiilde stretched with languid pleasure and looked over at him. Flames danced over her flesh in soft waves, and his eyes were wide, and full of desire.

"I'm not done with you yet," she moaned.

Marsais cleared his throat. "Perhaps a Weave of Silence is in order."

CHAPTER 73

Marsais drifted in a dream. Fiery-curls spilled over his skin and a sleek body twined with his own. Isiilde idly traced the mark on his chest. Not that dreadful scar, but another mark: her bond. The fiery dragon had its tail wrapped around his upper spine, while its body draped over his shoulder and crossed his collarbone. Its head, with emerald eyes that were ever watchful and protective, rested over his heart.

He ran his hand down a cascade of fire, brushing aside her hair to trace the ouroboros dragon on her back. It had not moved. The head still ate the tail in an endless cycle of flame. And he was glad for it. That he was no longer an intrusion, no longer a pillar on which she leaned.

Isiilde had changed since they'd first bonded in the Spine. Her spirit no longer flickered weakly; it burned so bright that it filled his heart, his mind, the very marrow of his bones. The strength of her spirit gave him hope.

A breeze slipped through a crack, and he felt it touch her back—felt a shiver zipping up her spine. Shifting, Marsais reached over the edge of the bed and dragged the blanket over her. She smiled against his shoulder.

"I've missed you," she moaned. "You still feel like the sun."

"So do you."

Isiilde half rose, staring down at him with a quizzical tilt to her ears. "I do?"

"Hmm," he said, caressing her cheek. "And everything wonderful."

She smiled, free and easy, and tasted his lips. Not with need, but a slow, savoring kiss. "You were right," she whispered.

"Aren't I always?"

Isiilde snorted and settled in the crook of his arm. "Nymphs *are* meant for gods."

"It's a good fit," he agreed.

Heat spread across her breasts. He rolled on his side, gently taking the edge of her ear between his teeth. A soft scrape sent a wave of sensation rippling through their bond. Her skin tingled with pleasure, amplified by his own, one feeding off the other.

"I don't think we'll ever leave this bed."

"I don't plan on it," he said, twining a strand of silken hair around his fingers. "I forgot to tell you something."

"Hmm?"

"I'm a pauper," he admitted. "A vagabond with no land, no home—not even a copper to my name. I can't even settle my debt to you from our wagers."

"That's all right, Marsais. I'll only charge you ten percent interest per month until you hand over the coin," she said generously.

He frowned at her. "Or what?"

The edge of her lip quirked. "You're imaginative. I think you'll find some way to work off your debt."

"You *think*?" He trailed his fingers between her breasts, painting soft swirls of heat over her skin.

"I know," she corrected. "For that matter, I'm a pauper, too. How does one make money?"

That gave him pause. His brows drew together in thought. "From what I recall, it takes work. Tedious, back-breaking, work."

She wrinkled her nose.

Marsais lifted his hand, looking at his palm. "I'll get callouses," he sighed.

"The horror," she said dryly, nudging his hand back down.

"Indeed."

"Oenghus says hard work builds character."

"My dear, I have over two thousand years of character, and then some. Do I really need any more?"

"I like you just the way you are. Any more and the realm wouldn't fit the both of us. But still, do we *really* need to work? I'm a horrible cook, and I can't make potions. I could work at the bellows, I suppose."

"You could."

"What will you do?"

He thought for a moment. "Juggle?"

"You could make water runes."

"There is always that," he said without relish.

"How did you make your fortune before?"

"You mean the one that Witman stole?"

"He did make a deal."

Marsais grunted.

Isiilde turned towards him, slipping a leg between his own. "Piracy?"

"Rogues are irresistible, but I'm not your pirate." He gripped her thigh, and pulled her closer. "I may, however, have plundered a tomb or two in my time."

Her eyes lit with wonder. "That sounds splendid." Isiilde pushed him on his back, rolling with him to straddle his hips. She was flush with excitement. "When do we start?"

"It's dangerous."

"Of course it is."

"It could be deadly," he pointed out.

"What's life without risk?"

"A long one."

"And boring."

"Hmm."

"Where will we go?" she asked.

"Wherever your whim takes us, my dear."

"I like that. I like that very much."

"I thought you would."

If you enjoyed *GOD OF ASH*, and would like to see more of Isiilde and Marsais, please consider leaving a review. Reviews help authors keep writing.

Keep up to date with the latest news, releases, and giveaways.
It's quick and easy and spam free.
Sign up at www.sabrinaflynn.com/news

Discover the story of Oenghus and the Sylph in the prequel: **Untold Tales**

ABOUT THE AUTHOR

Sabrina Flynn is the author of the ***Ravenwood Mysteries*** set in Victorian San Francisco. When she's not exploring the seedy alleyways of the Barbary Coast, she dabbles in fantasy and steampunk, and has a habit of throwing herself into wild oceans and gator-infested lakes.

Although she's currently lost in South Carolina, she's lived most of her life in perpetual fog and sunshine with a rock troll and two crazy imps. She spent her youth trailing after insanity, jumping off bridges, climbing towers, and riding down waterfalls in barrels. After spending fifteen years wrestling giant hounds and battling pint-sized tigers, she now travels everywhere via watery portals leading to anywhere.

You can connect with her at any of the social media platforms below or at www.sabrinaflynn.com

APPENDIX

Acacia Mael (ah · kay · shaa may · el) - Knight Captain of the Blessed Order on the Isle of the Wise Ones.

Afarim - Winged race of the Isle of Winds

Ardmoor - Void-worshipping barbarians in Vaylin.

Asmara - A Guardian of Iilenshar, or the Guardian of Love, also known as the Everchild. Asmara was six when the Orb shattered, and has not aged a day since. Daughter of Zahra, sister of Chaim.

Assumer - A race that can assume any shape.

Auroch - A massive bull-type creature found in Nuthaan and the Fell Wastes

Bastardlands - The continent that lies between the west and east. Separated by two chasms on either side, it's believed that the Keeper erected the Gates (chasms) to trap the Guardians of Morchaint.

Berserker's Rite - Some Nuthaanian warriors risk drinking Brimgrog on the eve of the Reddened Month. Most warriors die. The ones who survive have a reputation for being volatile and lethal.

Blessed Order - An Order that worships the Guardians of Iilenshar.

Blood Moon - A day and a night of light. All three moons are visible in the summer sky. The Dark One's moon is closest, playing havoc on coastal areas.

Brimgrog - Nuthaan's sacred brew. Few dare drink the burning brew, and of those few, most die. The rare Nuthaanians who survive the Rite are known (and feared) as Berserkers.

Brinehilde (brin·hillda) - A Nuthaanian Priestess of the Sylph who runs an orphanage in Drivel.

Carpinvale - A small fishing town in the south that exiled Oenghus.

Chaim (high·em) - A Guardian of Iilenshar, also known as the Guardian of Life and the River God. Son of Zahra, older brother to Asmara.

Circle of Nine - The ruling council of the Wise Ones.

Coven - A harbor town that sits directly beneath the stronghold of the Wise Ones.

Da'len - A barbarian tribe in Vaylin.

Dagenir (day·jen·near) - A Guardian of Morchaint, also known as the Dark One. He tried to steal the Orb, and battled with Zahra. The Orb shattered during their struggle.

Drivel - A large city on the Isle of Wise Ones.

Easthaven - The east side of the city of Haven, separated by the Gate and chasm.

Eiji (ee·Gee)- a gnome Wise One.

Ethervenom - An addicting drug made from harvested Plague Viper venom.

Everwar - The endless struggle between light and oblivion.

Fell Wastes - A harsh, mountainous region to the north of Nuthaan, populated by Wedamen.

Fey - Lindale (a race of elves) who rebelled against their nature and were twisted by their dark deeds.

Fomorri (fah·moor·ee) - A race created and twisted by the Fey's foul experiments.

Fyrsta (fears·tah) - The Sylph's favored realm.

Galvier Longstride - A legendary wanderer whose feet never stop moving.

Grawl - The Dark One's Own. Monstrous Voidspawn with void-like eyes.

Guardians of Iilenshar (ill·en·shar) - Six Guardians who survived the Shattering and were blessed with the Orb's power: Zahra, Chaim, Asmara, Zemoch, Oshimi, and Yvesa.

Guardians of Morchaint - Six Guardians who sided with the Void: Dagenir, Shade, Indrazor, Pazia, Mourn, and Silvanthe.

Gwaith - A Merchant kingdom along the Golden Road.

Haimon Goodfellow - Owner of the Glass Goblet.

Harsbane - A poisonous herb. The leaves contain an hallucinogen when smoked.

Hengist Heartfang - First Archlord of the Isle of Wise Ones.

Ielequithe (ill·ay·quith) - Lord General of the Isle of Wise Ones.

Iilenshar- Floating Isle of the Guardians. Coat of arms: the Sacred Sun caught in a maze-like circle.

Isiilde Jaal'Yasine (is·seal·dee jawl·yah·seen) - A combustible nymph with an affinity for fire.

Isek Beirnuckle - Spymaster to Marsais.

Isle of Blight - An island to the south of the Bastardlands that was ravaged when Ramashan, a druid, opened a Portal to the Nine Halls.

Isle of Winds - A grouping of islands off the Spotted Coast.

Isle of Wise Ones - An island off the Fell Coast where the Wise Ones Order is located.

Kambe (cam·bee) - A powerful kingdom ruled by Emperor Soataen Jaal III in the West.

Karbonek (car·bah·neck) - A Greater Fiend from the Nine Halls. A god revered by the Fomorri.

Keeper - A favored servant of the Sylph who was tasked with protecting Fyrsta.

Keening - The inhabitants of Fyrsta do not age like others. They only die of old age when the will to live fades. Someone who has lost the will to live is said to be in the Keening. As a result, many die in their twenties and thirties.

Kiln - A powerful kingdom to the East.

King's Folly - A game of runes that involves two hundred stones, and a cycle of ever-changing power.

Lindale - A race of elves (faerie) who were wiped out during the Shattering.

Lispen's Folly - A whirlpool of chaotic energy churning on the ceiling of the outer sanctum of the main hall, just outside of the Council Chambers of the Nine. Lispen was a Wise One who tried to open a Runic Portal, and disappeared.

Lome (low · meh) - A barbarian tribe in Vaylin.

Lucas Cutter - Paladin of the Blessed Order.

Luccub - An Imp with a tooth fetish.

Marsais (mar · say · es) - A sexy elf immortal.

Medwin - A barbarian tribe in Vaylin.

Miera Malzeen - A Wise One teacher who tried to link with Isiilde and was subsequently burned to a crisp.

Morigan Freyr (more · eh · gen fray · er) - Master Healer on the Isle of Wise Ones. Matriarch of the ruling Nuthaanian tribe. On and off Oathbound to Oenghus. Adopted mother of Isiilde. Savior of Nuthaan.

N'Jalss (nah · jaal · ss) - A Rahuatl Wise One.

Nereus (near · rose) - God of the seas.

Nine Halls - A realm that was overrun by the Void.

Oathbound - Inhabitants of Fyrsta take oaths, vowing to remain together as a couple for a specified amount of time determined by the couple.

Oenghus Saevaldr (oh · won · gus say · val · der) - A formidable Nuthaanian Berserker. Also known as: Wise One of the Isle, Bone Mender, Skull Crusher, the Bloody Berserker of Nuthaan and the Grimstorm of the Fell Wastes.

Oshimi (oh · shim · mee) - Guardian of Wisdom, also known as The Serene One.

Pip - A street urchin from the Dock Districts of Drivel. Brother to Zoshi and Tuck.

Pits o'Mourn - A deep chasm in Kiln. Criminals are lowered into the gorge and none ever emerge.

Pyrderi Har'Feydd (pie · deer · rhee haar · fade) - The first fey.

Rahuatl (raw · tule) - A race of humanoids who live in the Jungles of Rraal. Their culture is steeped in ritual and pain.

Rashk (rash · ka) - A Rahuatl Wise One who has a knack for enchanting.

Reapers - Voidspawn with a taste for fresh blood. Sometimes called Death's children.

Rivan (riv · en) - A young paladin of the Blessed Order.

Shattering - A powerful artifact that the Sylph imbued with her power to fight the Void. When Dagenir, its own guardian, attempted to steal the Orb for himself, Zahra tried to stop him. During their fight, the Orb was shattered, releasing a cataclysmic wave of power that nearly extinguished life on Fyrsta.

Shimei Al'eeth (shim · mee awl · eeth) - A Kilnish Wise One

Sidonie (sid · own · ee) - A Mearcentian Wise One

Soisskeli (soice · kill · ee) - The Chaos Lord who crafted a stave capable of opening Runic Gateways and binding any creature not of Fyrsta. Oshimi, the Serene One, defeated him in battle.

Somnial's Realm (salm · knee · el) - The Realm of Dreams, where all realms touch.

Spine - A tall, naturally formed spire that towers over the Wise Ones' stronghold.

Suevi (sweh · vee) - A barbarian tribe in Vaylin.

Sylph - The Goddess of All.

Tharios - A Wise One from Xaio.

Thedus - A sunburnt man who wanders around the Wise Ones' tower naked.

Thira Olander - Wise One of the Isle, Mistress of Novices, and High Alchemist.

Tuck - Urchin from the dock district in Drivel. Brothers: Pip and Zoshi.

Ulfhidhin (ulf · fid · hin) - The wild god who once abducted the Sylph and fought Karbonek.

Unspoken - or Disciples of Karbonek. A group of devout Bloodmagi who worship the Greater Fiend.

Void - Everything opposite of life.

Weeping Mark - A venomous spider.

Westhaven - The west side of the city of Haven, separated by the Gate and chasm.

Wisps - Tiny faeries who are often captured, put in jars, and used as a light source until they die.

Witchwood - A rare wood that has a natural resistance to enchantments.

Xiao (zow) - A merchant kingdom in the Bastardlands known for their pleasures.

Yvesa (yeh·veh·saa) - A Guardian of Iilenshar. A sprite who is revered by jesters and bards. She has a reputation for being a prankster.

Zahra (zah·rah) - A Guardian of Iilenshar, also known as the Radiant One, Goddess Of All That Was Just, Guardian of Good, and the Divine Savior. She battled with Dagenir when he tried to steal the Orb.

Zander - A Wise One who served Tharios, attacked Isiilde, and was burnt to a crisp.

Zianna (zee·anna) - A gifted Wise One's Apprentice.

Zoshi (zo·shee) - Urchin from Dock districts in Drivel. Brothers: Pip and Tuck.

CALENDAR OF FYRSTA

350 days in a year
10 Months in a year
35 days in a month

MONTHS
Wintertide
Thawing
Greentide
Sowing
Summertide
Faded
Harvest
Reddened
Carvers
Frostmarch

FESTIVALS

The Shadowed Dawn: 35th of Frostmarch to the 1st of Wintertide. Marks the new year with a night and a day of darkness, when all three moons align and the Dark One's own moon smothers the sun.

The Lightened Dusk: 17th-18th of Summertide. A day and a night of silver light when all three moons align and the Sylph's moon shines bright.

The Sylph's Fortnight: 10-24th Summertide. Fourteen days of Festivities dedicated to the Sylph.

Feast of Fools: 1-7th of Greentide. A week of costumed festivities that celebrate the end of winter.

www.ingramcontent.com/pod-product-compliance
Lightning Source LLC
Chambersburg PA
CBHW010838190726
48286CB00012BA/2900